WENDELL BERRY

The Collected Stories

Jayber Crow

The Memory of Old Jack

A Place on Earth

Three Novellas

Also by Wendell Berry

FICTION

The Discovery of Kentucky
Fidelity
Nathan Coulter
A Place on Earth
Remembering
Two More Stories of the Port William Membership
Watch with Me
The Wild Birds
A World Lost

POETRY

The Broken Ground
Clearing
Collected Poems: 1957–1982
The Country of Marriage
Entries
Farming: A Hand Book
Findings
Openings
A Part
Sabbaths
Sayings and Doings
The Selected Poems
A Timbered Choir
Traveling at Home (with prose)
The Wheel

ESSAYS

Another Turn of the Crank
A Continuous Harmony
The Gift of Good Land
Harlan Hubbard: Life and Work
The Hidden Wound
Home Economics
Recollected Essays: 1965–1980
Sex, Economy, Freedom & Community
Standing by Words
The Unforseen Wilderness
The Unsettling of America
What Are People For?

WENDELL BERRY

A Place on Earth

[revision]

COUNTERPOINT
BERKELEY

A Place on Earth was first published by Harcourt, Brace and World in 1967.
First Counterpoint paperback edition 2001.

This book is a work of fiction. Nothing is in it that has not been imagined.

Library of Congress Cataloging-in-Publication Data
Berry, Wendell, 1934–
A place on earth / Wendell Berry.—1st Counterpoint pbk. ed.
p. cm.

ISBN 13: 978-1-58243-124-6
ISBN 10: 1-58243-124-8
1. Port William (Ky. : Imaginary place) Fiction. 2. Aged men—
Kentucky Fiction. I. Title.
PS3552.E75M4 1999
813'.54—dc21 99–16086
CIP

Jacket and text design by David Bullen Design

Printed in the United States of America on acid-free paper that meets the American National Standards Institute Z39-48 Standard.

COUNTERPOINT
2560 Ninth Street, Suite 318
Berkeley, CA 94710
www.counterpointpress.com

Distributed by Publishers Group West

20 19 18 17 16 15

For Mary and Chuck
For Katie, Virginia, and Tanya
For Den and Billie
For Emily and Marshall

Contents

PART ONE

1

The Empty Store 5
Missing 8
The Card Game 12
A Dream of Absence 14
A Departure 16
Rain, Rain 17
I Can Do It by Myself 19
A Voice from the Distance 22
A Little Shift in the Wind 23

2

Port William 26
Company 27
Like a Bird 32
The Carpenter Shop 33
An Old Wound 34
A Pretty Good Boy 36
Feeding 37

3

The Last 40
The Hotel 48
The Grass May Grow a Mile 56
Images Like Seeds 59
Waiting 61

4

The Barber's Calling 63
Talk 67
A New Calling 73
Light and Warmth 79

5

Keeping Watch 87
The Sheep Barn 88

PART TWO

6

A Dark Morning 93
A Difference Made 94
A Comforter 95
The Sanctuary 101
A Knack for the Here 103

7

Born a Idiot, Educated a Fool 109
The Farm in the Valley 112
Flood 115
Where Are You? 120
Coming to Rest 125
A Vigil 126
The Keeping of the Place 128
Changed 131

8

Something Ain't Right 133
Never What It Was 144
Some Cleaning Up 147
A Pleasing Shadow 151
For Someone Who Will Come Later 153
A Spring Night 155
Green Coming Strong 157

PART THREE

9

Look a Yonder 163
The Bridge 165
A Guest at a Strange Table 170

10

The Wanting of What May Be Lost 176
Something in the World to Do 186
A Pleasant Place to Sit 193

11

Green Pasture 196
Caught 198
Daylight 200
A Birth 217

PART FOUR

12

Going Down 229
Dangerous Ground 230
He's Dead 235

13

Hard at It 237
A Widow Alone 239
Haunted 243

14

A Famous Escapade 244
The Presence of Grief 248
A Ramble 250
A Result 258
The Sense of Time Passing 259
What Is Left 260

15

That's Fine 263
Another Result 271

16

Six Feet 274
It's Over! 277
Redounding and Sublime 281
A Passing Dirge 301
Among the Dead 304

PART FIVE

Straightening Up 311
A Homecoming 315
Into the Woods 317

Author's Note

This book has had an editorial history sufficiently humbling to its author. I began it in January, 1960, and it was published by Harcourt, Brace and World in 1967. Dan Wickenden, then editor at Harcourt, helped me with patient intelligence to shorten and improve my unwieldy manuscript. But as I recognized after publication, the book was not satisfactory. Later, Jack Shoemaker of North Point Press offered me the opportunity of a new edition, to be published in 1983, for which I made many cuts, some large, and a lot of editorial changes. For this Counterpoint edition of 2001, thanks once more to Jack Shoemaker, I have made a good many further changes, both to improve the writing and to correct geographical and historical discrepancies between this and my other books about Port William.

A Place on Earth

Part One

1

The Empty Store

The seed bins are empty. The counters and rows of shelves along the walls, stripped of merchandise, contain only slanting shadows and the slanting rainy light from the front windows. The interior of the store has been reduced to a severe geometrical order over which the light breaks without force, colored but not brightened by the white of the walls, the pale green of the counters and shelves. Its swept surfaces outline precisely the dimension of its silence and emptiness, but the strict order and cleanness of the room make it a silence that seems actively expectant of sound, a carefully tended emptiness anticipating an arrival. In the back, near the entrance to a small screened-off area once used as an office, a black iron safe stands against the wall. When Frank Lathrop cleaned out the store after his son Jasper went into the Army at the beginning of the war, he left the door of the safe ajar for fear that if he closed it he would never be able to work the combination to open it again. He did not foresee that he would ever want to open it again, but at the time the precaution seemed necessary, consistent with the careful neatness in which he had left the place.

The four men who sit at the card game in the makeshift office feel the vacancy of the larger room as a condition of the smaller, which, like the seepage of wind through the back wall, subtly qualifies their presence there. All afternoon the sound of rain on the tin roof has pecked and swiveled through the hollow building, constantly changing in force and inflection, but never ceasing, until it seems to them the very presence and noise of emptiness. They have got used to the sound; consciousness, attentive to the details of the game, has overridden it, but at the back of their minds it persists. And the rain itself has persisted for days into the beginning of March, making the dawns sluggish, the evenings early and sudden, so that they have come to think of time as a succession of nights rather than days.

A large desk, its cover pulled down and locked, stands at the end of the room farthest from the door. On its top are several neatly marked boxes of accounts and receipts, and a radio playing so quietly that the music is no more than a series of stuttering accents like the far-off rattling of a snare drum. Between the desk and the heating stove at the opposite end of the room Jasper Lathrop's meat block has been placed to serve as a card table. The two windows in the back wall look out on a narrow lot covered with dead weed stalks, chicory and poke and burdock, and the lighter brown napping of foxtail and wild oat. In the center of the lot there is a disjointed heap of weather-blackened crates that Frank Lathrop once intended to burn; but on the day, a week or so after Jasper's departure, when he set the store in order and shut the building, he felt his duty to his son was more finished than he wanted to believe. The act of burning seemed too final, too suggestive of a conclusion he was unable to face. In the three years that have gone by since then, the crates have stayed there, and now in the steady rain they have the look of permanence, the stack of them monolithic and at ease, an indelible feature of the casual back view of the town. At the rear of the lot, built sidelong to the fence, is the small carpenter shop of Ernest Finley. Black coal smoke comes from its chimney, twisted off the bricks by the wind and driven to the ground, turning delicately amber as it thins. The carpenter's pickup truck is parked in front of the door, and through the afternoon the men at the card game have heard the measured sounds of his hammering and sawing. Beyond the shop a broad pasture swags down to a creek branch and tilts up again, gently, to the top of a long ridge. A flock of sheep, heads down against the rain, straggles toward the barn at the top of the ridge for the night feeding. Beyond the ridge is the opening of the river valley.

The light is still strong in the room. The card faces turned up on the hacked surface of the meat block are still white and exact. Outside the windows the gutter drips, also exact, as steady and half-heard as a clock ticking. The sounds of voices and automobile engines out on the street reach back to the room only occasionally and faintly. The smoke from Mat Feltner's cigar, which he has balanced fire-end out on the edge of the block, rises in a straight thin shaft a yard high, then scrolls out beneath the ceiling, clouding bluely down again into the light at the tops of the windows. Mat taps the fingers of his left hand against the seat of his chair, repeating the same rhythm half a dozen times, and then stops; the nervous rapidity of the sound seems to him to have communicated his uneasiness, and he glances at Frank Lathrop and then at Jayber Crow and Old Jack Beechum to see if they might have noticed. But they are occupied with their cards. He hooks his thumb into his belt.

He sits with his feet drawn back to the sides of his chair, his hat pushed back off his forehead. He is a fairly big man, and although his hair is white his body is still solidly composed, without excess or diminishment. The whiteness of his hair emphasizes the prominence of his features, the green of his clear eyes. Except for a slackening in the flesh of his cheeks his face has retained its angularity and firmness. It is a flexible, expressive face, deeply lined around the mouth and eyes, so that now in its apparent calm it seems near to both humor and sorrow. So far only his hand has betrayed him.

It is his turn to play. He draws from the deck and looks down to study his cards, his metal-rimmed reading glasses set a little low on his nose; he discards and leans back, taking up the cigar again.

Nobody else moves.

"Jayber, it's your play, ain't it?" Frank Lathrop says finally.

"Let a man think."

"Hell," Old Jack Beechum says, "a mule could've thought by now."

Jayber plays. They play out the hand, and Frank Lathrop gathers the cards and shuffles and deals. Mat arranges his cards and tilts his chair back against the desk. He and Frank and Jayber wait quietly, watching Old Jack.

The old man holds the cards clumsily in his huge hands, fumbling them from one semblance of order to another with the forceful deliberate movements of a man laying bricks—a man building a spindling unwieldy tower of bricks that constantly requires the addition of one more brick to balance it upright. The earflaps of his corduroy cap have come untied; they flail out at warped angles from the sides of his head, dangling their strings, like the wings of some disgruntled bird. He reaches out, turning his cards face down against the block, and looks aggressively at the others as though to answer an insult.

"Your turn, old mule," Jayber Crow says. He grins as he speaks, but speaks with a patience that amounts almost to gentleness.

Old Jack draws a card from the deck, stares at it, deciphers the message, and swats the meat block with it. He rolls his chew of tobacco over his tongue into the opposite jaw and clamps it there and turns away, aloof and silent; the movement abruptly repudiates his involvement in the game, dismisses his opponents and the game itself as finally as if he had gone out of the room.

They know that when his turn comes again they will have to call him back.

Missing

Mat looks out the window at the crates tumbled together in the lot; the leafless weedtops poke through them, jerking and wavering in the wind. The pile of them, like the vacancy of the store, is a fact of the war; it remains for the same reason that he and Frank together have allowed the store to remain empty; they've foreclosed no possibilities. But now the boxes cluttered together in the rain seem to Mat to insist upon his own disquiet. His anxiety has become, after the first violence of its onset, more a physical state than anything else, a remote vibrance of numbness clenching and unclenching in his body as acutely as pain. The feeling is intensified by a vague awareness that, if he examined it, it would declare itself to be an extreme and desperate fear; but he has resisted any acknowledgment. He feels simply that he is bracing himself to confront an actuality not yet apparent—which, in loyalty to his son and his son's life, he cannot allow himself to anticipate.

When he went to the post office shortly before noon to get the mail, there was no letter from Virgil. There had been none from Virgil for

Frank Lathrop, Mat Feltner, Jayber Crow, Jack Beechum

more than three weeks; but they had hoped, he and Margaret and Hannah, that there might be one on Monday. But he carried the mail home folded in the newspaper without looking at it, hastening then, in the presence of the fact, to qualify his hope, admit beforehand that he would be disappointed, to say that although he had hoped, he had expected nothing.

When he stood on the back porch a few minutes later, looking at the envelopes of what mail had come, he realized that he had failed to prepare himself; his precaution had spared him none of the force of his disappointment. It was not until he thumbed through the mail a second time that he noticed the government envelope addressed to Hannah, and felt change pass over his head like a chill. He picked the letter out from among the others, as though to dispose of it. And then he laid it down again, straight, with the others inside the newspaper, and he began an almost soundless whistling under his breath.

It is in his mind forever, that moment. For what seems a long time he stands as though deep in thought, though he is not thinking, the thin dry thread of his whistling crossing the edges of his teeth. His fingers tap nervously on the underside of the troughed newspaper. And then he thinks of Hannah and Margaret, and steps back into the angle between the wall of the house and the enclosure of the back stairway so he cannot be seen from the window. He leans against the stair door, looking out across the yard.

Rainwater has collected shallowly beneath the maple trees, making a large irregular pool stretching from the walk along the edge of the porch to the lilac bush beside the gate to the chicken yard. The rain is falling slowly in large drops so that the circles it makes striking the surface of the pool remain intact. For a moment at the center of each circle the black branches of the trees are mirrored perfectly, and then distorted and fragmented as the circles interlink and subside and renew. Across the fence in the chicken yard seven or eight hens stand together under the eave of the tool shed.

The chicken yard is bounded on one side by the wall of a large feed barn. The barn is painted white, and on its red roof there is a white red-roofed cupola with a spire and wind vane. Opposite the barn, beginning within the L-shape of the chicken yard and extending beyond it, is a large garden plot. To Mat's right, looking off the porch toward the side of the lawn, a fence overgrown with honeysuckle hides the town from him; he can see only the roofs of the store buildings, the bare treetops among them, the roof and tall octagonal steeple of the church.

For a moment these things occupy his attention without his naming or thinking about them, as though his mind has become simply the cool grey-lighted space containing them, into which the rain falls.

But now he hears the pounding of his brother-in-law's crutches coming up the walk beside the house. The familiarity of the sound is suddenly welcome to Mat. It fixes him steadily again in the day and place. Ernest is home for dinner. They will go into the house now.

Coming around the corner of the house, Ernest looks up, smiling at Mat. "Dinner ready?"

"I don't know. I just got here myself."

Ernest swings up onto the porch with a movement both cumbersome and strangely agile. He is ten years younger than Mat, his dark face finely modeled, strong-boned, the lips set firmly and evenly together in denial or concealment of the difficulty of his lameness. His faded work jacket fits him tightly across the shoulders. A flat yellow carpenter's pencil sticks out beneath the band of his cap.

He stands beside Mat, leaning on the crutches while he reaches inside his jacket for a cigarette. "Did you hear from Virgil?"

Mat shows him the envelope. The two men look at each other a moment. Ernest shakes his head and starts to the door.

Having put it off as long as he can, Mat turns to follow him.

Margaret and Hannah are sitting at the table, Margaret beating eggs in a bowl she holds in her lap, Hannah sewing, holding the piece of white material a little awkwardly above the bigness of her pregnancy. They look up as the two men come into the kitchen. The room is warm, the air heavy with the smells of cooking. Nettie Banion stands at the stove, a lifting rag in her left hand, which she rests against her hip.

"Here they are," Margaret says. "Put the biscuits in, Net."

Ernest goes out into the hall. Mat goes to the table and holds the letter out to Hannah. There comes over him a great need to do this gently. But he can only do it bluntly, with a kind of shame as though there might be a polite way to do it but he does not know what it is.

She reaches out for the letter and takes it. Mat knows she is looking at him, but he does not look at her. And he knows when she looks away from him. She tears open the envelope and reads the letter, and lays it slowly and flatly down on the table, indicating that Mat should read it. And Mat reads it, and then, as though the duty falls to him, he reads aloud: "Virgil Feltner . . . missing in action."

Nettie closes the oven door and turns around. She says "Oh" very quietly, her mouth holding the shape of the sound. "He ain't dead."

"No," Margaret says.

Mat hears Ernest going up the stairs to his room.

Hannah has not moved. She sits staring out the window, her hands lying quietly on the piece of white material folded in her lap. Mat picks up one of her hands and holds it, awkwardly because she doesn't respond. Her hand remains passive for a moment, and then she squeezes his and gently takes her hand away. She has not looked at him.

"It may not mean a thing," he says.

"No."

And Margaret reads the letter and puts it back on the table. She takes up the hem of her apron and wipes her eyes. Mat lays his hand on her shoulder.

"Wash up," she says. "It's nearly ready."

Mat washes, and goes and sits down by the front window in the living room. He opens the paper, but looks at it without reading.

As if obeying an instinct, he has done what he usually does. But his eyes only follow the print of the page without reading; the headlines are a black strict architecture; he cannot, somehow, bring himself to assent to a meaning in the words. He folds the paper and moves over to sit on the sofa. Out the window the rain strikes and splashes on the black road.

The sounds become more brisk and rapid in the kitchen. Mat can hear Hannah setting the table. Ernest is in his room at the back of the house above the kitchen; now and then his crutches thump across the floor. Presently Hannah comes in and sits on the sofa beside Mat. She holds up her sewing for him to see. It is a small white gown, delicately embroidered with white thread.

Mat touches it with his fingers. "It's going to be a mighty dressed-up baby."

"Oh, you're going to be proud of this baby."

"I am. I know it."

She folds the dress and turns and looks at Mat, smiling. "Tell me what you did this morning."

And he tells her, the calm of his voice uncertain at first, contradicted by his effort to keep it calm. He was busy all morning with the cattle, he tells her. The cows are calving.

Virgil would be pleased to hear about the calves. But he does not speak of Virgil.

The Card Game

"Uncle Jack," Mat says, "it's your play."

Old Jack draws an ace from the deck, and with a large avoidance of looking either at his hand or at the card slaps it into the discard pile; and Mat, who holds two aces in his hand, decides he will wait until his next turn to pick it up.

The four of them have been there since the early afternoon. The rain by now has dried out of their coats, which have been spread carefully over the back of a wooden bench under the windows. They have, as usual, a fire going in the stove; as usual, except for Old Jack's occasional fits of swearing, they have played pretty much without talking.

By now the card game in the empty store has become an institution, a kind of unnamed club that in the years since its beginning has acquired a fairly stable membership and meeting time. The habit of gathering there in the afternoons began in the late winter of 1941–42 with Mat Feltner and Frank Lathrop. The two of them had been neighbors and friends as long as either of them could remember. In the last thirty or forty years their friendship had led them in and out of perhaps a dozen business partnerships of one sort or another—the latest being the joint ownership of the old building in which, only a year before the war, Frank's son had opened a general store.

But in the early weeks of the war, after their sons had gone into the service, their friendship changed from a casual fact to a necessity. Their talk stayed offhand and easy, but it was conditioned now by the presence of the war, the uncertain nature of their involvement in it, their sense of helplessness before an immeasurable fact. The silences they had always allowed to occur comfortably and simply between them were complicated now by the recognition that there were concerns too grievous for talk. They came to speak to each other with a kind of gentle vigilance, surrounding their conversations with sensitive boundaries, but also with a deepening need to speak.

In those first weeks of the war, after the tobacco had been marketed and they had begun the long and relatively idle wait for spring, they had taken to walking down to the store in the afternoons. It comforted them to build a fire there in the back room and sit and talk.

For a while they went on the pretext of seeing what would have to be done to maintain the building during Jasper's absence, and what improvements ought to be made when he came back. "When and if he comes back," Frank said cautiously only once. And after that they left Jasper's name out of it. In spite of their avoidance of his name they both knew that he continued to be implicated in all they said. Any consideration of the future of the store became intricately a consideration of Jasper's future, of the future and outcome of the war, of what would be lost. Something would be lost, was in the process of being lost, and they dreaded to ponder what. Their talk had become an obscure dealing with fate. It made them nervous.

But by that time Jayber Crow, the town's barber, had begun coming to the store to sit and talk with them. Port William, Jayber said, provided a short supply of heads to barber, and an even shorter supply of heads that could make a satisfactory connection between a service rendered and a promise to pay, so he might just as well be talking.

"You might just as well," Frank told him.

"If you can abide the company," Mat said.

"I'll do you the kindness," Jayber said, "of not judging."

In the afternoons he fastened to the knob of his shop door a battered paper clock which, because of the looseness of the hands, announced perpetually that he would be back at six-thirty; in consideration of the obtuseness of Port William heads he felt obliged to make no further explanations. "Hair's my business. Let it grow."

Jayber's presence made the gathering permanent. There was an air of permanence in his idleness, his long body stretched in a straight line from the back of his tilted chair to the edge of the seat to where his shoe heels bracketed on the rim of the sandbox under the stove, his fingers laced behind his bald head. He would come and sit as long as they would stay, talking for the love of company and the love of talk. It was Jayber who brought the deck of cards.

So the rummy game is a creature of the war, shaped in the suspension of action, the suspension of all certain knowing, that the war has imposed on them. It came about almost by nature, they feel. They know it by its presence, which holds them there in the afternoons from the end of autumn to the beginning of spring, allowing them a dependable silence, masking and comforting them in the solitude of their fears. They are waiting—for the war to be over, for whatever resumption will take place at the end of it.

A Dream of Absence

When dinner was over Nettie set the table again for Joe Banion and herself. Ernest put on his jacket and lit a cigarette and went back to the shop.

Now Mat has come back into the living room. He takes his shoes off and lies down on the sofa. He lies on his side, facing the window, his left arm bent back and propped against the pillow beside his head, his right arm resting across his hip, the hand dangling. He no longer thinks of where he is. He looks out the window, near sleep. The stillness of his hands comforts him. Out the window he can see the yard fence blind with honeysuckle, and above it the roof and white steeple of the church. The branches of the trees in the yard thatch across the steeple, the green shutters of the belfry under it. At the top of the sash a single bead of water swells and drips; the bead grows heavier, touches the point of the steeple, breaks; the drops, blown one at a time against the window, streak down, twisting the steeple, holding its whiteness against the glass.

The rain falls harder, the wind blowing it in against the window. The water beads and streaks over the whole pane, the sound sheeted and vibrant there, the rain striking and flaring, blurring the light. The steeple crumbles, its white and green held, with the black of the trees, in shivering transparent smears in the square of the window.

The surface of the water stirs when the wind stirs, ripples barring the reflected blue of sky with the green of water. Several blue dragonflies hover and dart over the pond and in the cattails at the pond's edge, their transparent wings blurring the hard shine of the sun. The mud at the edge of the water is pocked with cow tracks, covered in places with a thin green skim of algae; in places it has begun to dry and only the earth in the cups of the tracks is wet. It is early afternoon. The sun is high. There are no clouds. The sky is hot and brittle, a vast sheet and splintering of blue light turning the eyes down. White and yellow and blue butterflies have lighted on the wet mud; their wings open and close slowly, mottling the light. The pond is at the center of a large field where Queen Anne's lace and daisies are in bloom. The air is heavy with the noises of insects, the hot pungent spices of weeds. The wings of the butterflies open and close over the dark mud.

Mat sees the whole field circling the shimmering round blink of the pond, dipping down to the wet banks. He is aware of the tense articulation of white translucent petals around the yellow eyes of the daisies, the green smooth grassblades under which the ants traffic in a frail crosshatching of shadows.

It is the middle of the afternoon. The shadows have lengthened and become intricate over the banks of the pond. The steeple of the church points whitely up over the horizon of the field. He expects Virgil shortly.

The yellow butterflies all fly up at once. They whirl and flurry in the air a moment and settle back onto the mud in a single movement like one small animal lying down.

The cattle come down to drink, wading out shoulder deep in the water. They drink leisurely, pausing to lift their heads and look at him. Flies swarm over their red backs. Mat can smell the water, the sharp cool mud-smell of it stirred up from the bottom. The cattle wade out again, slowly, muzzles and bellies dripping, hooves sucking out of the deep mud, and climb the bank. He watches them graze into the field. He can hear the grass tearing. It is late in the afternoon.

Virgil has not come. Mat suddenly is afraid. He calls, "Oh, Virgil!" but the sounds will not leave his mouth.

A Departure

He sits up, his throat tight with the unuttered sound of his voice. The suddenness of the movement makes him dizzy, and he sits motionless for a few minutes on the edge of the sofa, stiffened and weighted with sleep. He is still very near the dream, its colors and sounds continuing in his waking, his mind still caught in the abrupt fear that ended it. The house is quiet. He rubs his hands over his face, pushing his hair out of his eyes, and picks up his shoes and goes down the hall to the kitchen.

When he comes through the door Margaret looks around and touches her lips with her finger.

"Hannah still lying down?"

"Yes." Margaret turns back to her work. "This is going to be hard on her."

Mat walks over and stands beside Margaret, putting his arm around her. "On us too. But we can't help it."

"Yes."

They stand without speaking for a minute. Then, "What're you making?" Mat asks.

"Some chocolate pies. Bess and Wheeler and the boys are going to be here for supper."

Mat smiles at her. "Well, I'm glad they're coming for supper. And I'm glad we're having pie." He laughs. "And they'll be glad too, I expect."

"The boys will."

He pulls a chair away from the table and sits down to put on his shoes.

"You slept."

"A little."

Mat goes into the hall to get his hat and coat off the rack and comes into the kitchen again. "I'm going to town a while."

"All right."

He goes out and turns down the street towards the store. It is raining still, and he walks with his head bent.

He is already in front of Jasper Lathrop's store when he sees Nathan and Burley Coulter standing in the shelter of the little porch roof over the entrance to the drugstore. The soldier and his uncle stand there watching the rain fall onto the road. It will be some time yet before the bus comes, but they seem to have no intention of going into the drugstore to wait, as if now that Nathan's departure has begun they will do nothing to interrupt it. Nathan's brother Tom has been dead two years, killed in the war. As he looks at them, that death seems to Mat to be somehow implicit in their waiting.

Pausing, his hand on the doorlatch, Mat speaks to them.

They turn their heads. Burley raises his hand. "How are you, Mat?"

"Hello, Mr. Feltner," Nathan says.

"Well, are you leaving, Nathan?"

"Yes sir."

"I wish you luck," Mat says, and regrets the words, which seem to him to say both too much and not enough.

They thank him. He opens the door and goes in.

Rain, Rain

The rain slackens, falls loosely and waveringly for a moment, and stops, but after a few minutes begins again suddenly and more heavily than before. It is only after this renewal, when the familiar rattle on the roof has steadied again in their hearing, that they become aware that the drip from the gutter never stopped.

Jayber Crow looks up, frowning, at the top of one of the windows. "Why don't you all fix that gutter?"

"Did once," Frank Lathrop says. "She sprung again."

"Why in the hell don't *you* fix it?" Old Jack says.

"It's a weary old tune," Jayber says. He speaks to nobody, the tone of objection gone out of his voice, as though nothing was said before.

"If you ever owned a gutter it'd be leaking."

None of them replies. Old Jack's most casual observation is apt to take the form of a final judgment—which could be considered an insult if anybody wanted to take the trouble. They know better than to take the trouble. Though the old man is willing for his remark to be taken better than halfway as a joke, they know that he himself takes it more than half seriously. Jayber owns his barber shop, but it is a fact that he does not own a gutter. It is Old Jack's theory that a man who owns a roof ought to own a gutter, and a cistern to conserve the water, and livestock to drink at the cistern.

They hear the street door open, the slapping of rain against the wet pavement coming abruptly into the building, and then slam shut.

"Who's that?" Old Jack asks, speaking to Jayber again because he is still looking at him.

"Burley, I imagine."

They sit with their heads turned, listening to the approach of Burley's footsteps, the sounds distinct and clear in the hollowness of the larger room, as though he bears toward them his own portion of its emptiness.

He stops in the doorway, leaning his shoulder against the jamb. He grins at them. The brim of his misshapen felt hat, weighted by the rain, bends over his eyes.

"Gentlemen."

"Looks like rain," Frank Lathrop says.

Burley nods. "I look for it."

He shakes the water off his hat and leans there, creasing and smoothing the crown of it with his fingers, burlesquing his care. He watches their faces, prolonging his interruption of the game while he elaborates the joke of his concern for his hat.

"Looks like a man who could afford a ten-dollar hat for a ten-cent head," Jayber Crow says finally, "could afford an umbrella."

Burley stares at him, his face nearly expressionless, but with enough attention that it seems he shapes and completes the silence he allows to follow Jayber's remark, as delicately as he now holds the perfected shape of his hat.

"It looks like to me," he says then, "a two-bit barber with no hair ought to be more respectful of heads."

He puts his hat on, nudging it a little toward the back of his head with his thumb, a gesture that seems both to finish the quiet and detach him from it.

"Well, Burley," Old Jack says, "is the boy gone?"

"He's gone."

Burley unbuttons his jacket and comes into the room. He shakes the ashes out of the stove and puts in a lump of coal, and spreads his hands to the warmth. He shivers. When his hands are warm, he turns his back to the stove.

"Burley," Mat says, "you might as well play."

They make room and Burley pulls up a chair.

They play without talking—two more hands, and into a third. Mat pushes his glasses up on his forehead, rubbing his eyes, and turns to look out the window.

"Rain, rain."

"The river'll be out of its banks," Frank says.

"Is now," Burley says. "A little. It could get troublesome."

"Well, I've seen it rain," Mat says, "and I've seen it get troublesome."

"You've seen it worse than it is now," Old Jack says.

"Several times."

"And if you don't die you'll see it worse."

"I expect."

Jayber plays, and Frank, and Burley.

Old Jack draws and slaps down the ten of diamonds and rams his final card into the discard pile. He looks triumphantly from one of his opponents to another.

He has played his ten of diamonds on Jayber's seven, eight, and nine of hearts, but they choose not to notice his error, knowing what it would cost them to try to undo it. Once the old man has committed himself to a play, the rules, as far as he is concerned, no longer apply to it.

I Can Do It by Myself

Old Jack is difficult. When the mood strikes him he can be magnificently difficult.

For nine years after the death of his wife the old man stayed alone on his farm and kept house for himself. But then, because his health seemed to her to be failing, his daughter insisted that he come to Louisville to live with her. He refused. She insisted that he hire a housekeeper; a man his age ought not to be left alone, she said. He refused again, and this time put himself to pains to see that she retreated with her plans and opinions thoroughly dismantled.

Finally, though, there was a partial surrender on Old Jack's side. But it was none of her doing—he saw to that. It was Mat Feltner's son-in-law, Wheeler Catlett, who brought about the compromise: that Old Jack would come to live out the rest of his life in the hotel at Port William. Wheeler was Old Jack's lawyer and, when they agreed, his friend. And in this undertaking he had also the advantage of not being the daughter.

It was not that the old man had ceased to love his daughter. But her marriage to a prominent Louisville banker had long ago set her apart from his world and out of his reach. He saw that clearly at the time and admitted it unhesitatingly to himself, and so when she came to him with her invitation, well meant as he knew it was, he could see no reason to back off. And with perfect understanding of the consequences, for his daughter and for himself, he kept loyal to what he considered his own place in the world.

But Old Jack admires candor, and Wheeler Catlett stated the proposition to him with candor: "Uncle Jack, you're old. You could get sick. It won't be any pleasure to you to die out here by yourself."

"I can do it by myself," Old Jack said.

From the tone of his voice Wheeler judged he would do it to prove it if he had to, and after that he let him alone.

Old Jack held out another six months, to proclaim his independence and recover ownership of the decision, and then came to town. He arrived at the hotel toward the end of last October in Wheeler Catlett's automobile, his clothes and shaving equipment packed in two five-gallon buckets that Wheeler afterwards carried back and set down on the well top in front of Old Jack's barn.

Mrs. Hendrick's hotel, in the time of her departed husband, had subsisted on the patronage of a fellowship of traveling salesmen who came and went more or less regularly through the town. But by the time of Jack's arrival it was a kind of boardinghouse, inhabited for the most part by Mrs. Hendrick and two other, much older, widows who turned out to be extravagantly unsatisfactory companions for Old Jack. And he, by nature or by calculation, proved just as unsuited to the conversational purposes of the three ladies. Aside from the fact that the presence of a man under their roof seemed a breach of respectability, Old Jack's language assumed for them, in this unsteady social predicament, the nature of a direct assault on their virtue. His disregard makes a kind of bridge on which he tromps across the chasm of propriety that once supposedly protected them in the insular delicacy of their sex. He says very little that they can reply to without seeming to countenance a liberty as opprobrious as seduction. Their precautionary muteness in his presence has been further intensified by Mrs. Hendrick's discovery that he urinates in the back yard every night before he goes to bed and the first thing every morning—and by the knowledge, discreetly gossiped to them all, that the three of them are customarily referred to, by Jayber Crow and Burley Coulter among others, as "Old Jack's harem."

Mrs. Hendrick has a face like an auger, an imitation of the corkscrew twist of hair at the back of her head. She had accustomed herself to widowhood more readily than she ever had to marriage; the memory of Mr. Hendrick she had stashed away neatly in the phrase "My blessed husband, God rest his soul." And then Old Jack's coming put a sudden end to the satisfactions and conveniences of her widowhood. Between the two of them a kind of second marriage took place, enforced by circumstance, consummated by Old Jack's unreckoning invasions of her privacy. But in consideration of the advanced age of the offender and the dollars he pays her punctually on the first of every month, she has felt obliged to tolerate him, and does, with the comforting sense that her virtue somehow prevails.

Old Jack made the card game in Jasper Lathrop's vacant store his winter outpost. Except for the one afternoon a week when Wheeler Catlett drove him out to oversee the work on his farm, he sat by the fire in the little room, talking when he saw that the players' interest in the game had flagged and they would listen to him, and talking at times when he knew none of them listened.

That lasted until Jayber Crow got the idea to teach the old man the game.

"Take a hand, Jack. We'll show you how."

"Play," Old Jack said, gesturing refusal with the cane. "I don't know one from the other."

But they repeated the offer, and he finally agreed to let them try to teach him. "It'll be uphill," he told them.

It was, Jayber Crow said, like pushing a loaded wagon uphill with a piece of string. But once they got him into it the old man stuck. He stuck, not from any love of the game, but because he immediately hated it. He hates the impersonality of it, he hates it for the chance involved in it, he hates the implacable rules of it, he hates it because it is a game. He plays as if it is his obligation to wipe the game from the face of creation. That they have been able to teach him no more than half the rules has preserved his bafflement. His opponents are constantly trounced by his anger, for their persistence in playing against him, for being able to play without anger, for having caught him in the game in the first place. They accept his anger with equanimity, and usually with amusement. They oppose him as honestly and gently as they can, out of sympathy—realizing that the conflict has become necessary to him, one of the last staples of his life—and out of respect.

A Voice from the Distance

Jayber grins and pitches his cards onto the block. "He's won. Let's call it a day."

"You're laying it on us, Uncle Jack," Burley says.

The old man picks up his cane and wrenches his chair around to face the windows. "Yes sir, it's a wet time, Burley."

Frank Lathrop gathers the cards and shuffles them once, and places the deck in the center of the block. Mat relights his cigar.

Their gestures deliberately and a little gravely establish the game's conclusion.

Frank nods toward the radio. "The news, Mat."

Mat reaches behind him and turns up the radio. They make way for the voice of the announcer as for a procession, their gathering broken as each of them moves his eyes away from it, staring out the windows or at the floor. This solemn hearing of the news, after so long a time, has become a kind of ceremony with them. All afternoon, while the game goes on, the radio hums and murmurs in its niche among the boxes on the desk top, like an idol come to life above its altar, a crude cyclopean head erected and drowsily alert on the room's edge. Until one of them, noticing a new inflection in its voice, calls attention to it. And they hush for the precise voice of the announcer stating the facts of the war, continuing from the point at which it left off the hour before or the day before; the voice carefully objective, studiedly calm, a fact itself which remains whole and remote among the facts it utters. The words come to them unjudged, without lamentation or joy. Their quiet listening becomes an obedience, an homage. For a few minutes they let the war exist there in the room, calmly mouthing its deaths.

"That's that," Frank Lathrop says. He shuts the damper on the stove and they leave the room. Old Jack leads the way down the row of counters to the street door. He walks rapidly, his pants bagging a little over the tops of his leather leggings, the dangling earflaps waving above his coat collar as though he flies as well as walks.

A Little Shift in the Wind

When they step out on the sidewalk Frank Lathrop pulls the door to and locks it.

The sky is still clouded, but no longer darkly. The wind has shifted a little to the north, driving the clouds into the southeast. The wind is steady and deep; it seems to move the whole sky, holding the shapes of the clouds intact. The wind is colder now and they brace their shoulders against it, pulling their collars more snugly around their necks. Tomorrow, they hope, will be clear.

Under the clouds the air is already clear; the light is hard and precise on the wet surfaces of the buildings and the street, and on the bare upstroking branches of the trees. Northward, beyond the edge of town, is the broad opening of the river valley, seeming abruptly nearer with the rain gone. The farthest barns and houses appear nearly and solidly rectangular.

The road follows the river upstream and south from where it empties into the Ohio at Hargrave. For most of its distance it stays down in the floor of the valley, bending along the first steepenings of the hills, leaving the bottomlands intact between itself and the river. A couple of miles downstream from Port William it begins its one digression: it crosses a bridge at the mouth of a tributary valley, passes the sagging rusting coal tipple and shut store at the old town landing, turns away from the river, and climbs the bluff. It follows the backbones of ridges across the upland, goes through the town, and after another mile or so twists down the bluff into the valley again. From the sidewalk in front of the store they can see three-quarters of a mile of it—marked, for most of that distance, by brushy fencerows on either side: an irregularity of the landscape, like a scar or seam where two halves of the country have been divided or joined. In places they can see the asphalt surface of the roadbed; in places it goes out of sight between embankments or clumps of young locusts. It dips into a hollow, and turns toward the town, becoming visible again as it passes the graveyard and the first straggling row of houses on the outskirts.

They stand in front of the store, talking disjointedly on the verge of going home, leaning against the face of the building now to keep out of the wind. The departure of the rain seems to them to have altered the terms of their own departure, and they stay on—a little precariously, without definite reason, but deliberately nevertheless—to observe and speak of the difference.

"It'll turn cold," Frank Lathrop says.

"It's March now," Old Jack says. "You can't tell what it'll do."

"Well," Jayber says, "after it's stayed one way long enough you'll settle for nearly anything as long as it's different."

Burley nods out the road in the direction of the river. "Speaking of anything, here comes Whacker."

Even at that distance he is immense, his great paunch flaring his coat around him like a funnel. And at that distance it is already obvious he is drunk. They knew he would be before they turned to look at him. Drunkenness is no longer simply his habit; it has become, for them as much as for Whacker Spradlin himself, his natural state.

They watch him pass in front of the most distant of the houses and come slowly down the row of them toward town, his walk a little unsteady but neither awkward nor faltering; he never strays out of his direction. It is the gait of a man intricately skilled and practiced in being drunk. There is a ponderous grace about it like that of a trained elephant or a locomotive. He sways heavily back and forth across the line of his direction, like a man carrying a barrel across a tightrope, his progress a sequence of fine distinctions between standing up and falling down. His drunkenness has become precise. He walks with pomp, his knees lifting as though he is climbing a stairway. By the time he comes even with Mat Feltner's house they can see the smoke rising from his pipe.

He bears down on them, puffing his pipe, his overcoat held together at the neck by a safety pin and at the waist by a piece of twine. He wears a wide-brimmed straw hat, the crown full of raveling holes, which seems to them as much a part of his character as his drunkenness. They have never seen him without it. The hat sits on his head emphatically, bending his ears down. Behind him, in a child's red wagon, he hauls a rusty cream can, the establishment of the bootlegger's trade by which he subsists.

As Whacker goes past the front of the store, the five of them nod and speak to him. And Whacker nods to them without looking at them or altering his gait, moving implacably forward, the downhill momentum of his great body seeming to dominate and threaten the pavement in front of him. He goes on past the drugstore and the poolroom.

He goes on past Jayber Crow's barbershop at the bottom of the hill and starts up the next rise, looking straight ahead, his movements the same going uphill as going down, precarious and deliberate, as though he will go on through the town and beyond it in the same direction forever.

They watch him out of sight, and then start, separately, home.

2

Port William

It used to be asked, by strangers who would happen through, why a town named Port William should have been built so far from the river. And the townsmen would answer that when Port William was built they did not know where the river was going to run.

The truth is that Port William no longer remembers why it was built where it is, or when, or how. In its conversation the town has kept the memory of two or three generations haphazardly alive. Back of that memory the town was there for a long time—there are a few buildings still standing that are surely twice as old as anybody's certain knowledge of them. But the early history has to be conjectured and assumed.

It is as though in their crossing to this new place, the first-comers lost everything to the wilderness but their names. And for a considerable length of time after they arrived, the wilderness continued to make demands of them. It asked, among other things, too much of their attention and energy to leave time or strength for record keeping. That the town had been begun, and was there, was more important than explanations and motives and reasons and memories. That they half exhausted the country, in surprisingly few years, testifies convincingly enough to the intensity of their preoccupation. The black ground broke open to their plows like a pile of ashes. There was never anything like it—that black humus, built up under the forest for thousands of years. There it was, dark as shadows under the trees, abundant and deep, waiting to be opened. Surely no dirt was ever more responsive or more alive. You could believe, for once, that the earth might give back to a man more than it took from him. It welcomed him everywhere he put down his hand or his foot or his seed. It had advanced through millennia to break itself open on the coulter of his plow; he could not have helped but feel that jointure and breaking in every nerve.

In two or three generations the country was imponderably changed, its memories, explanations, justifications fallen away from it. The first-arrivers left it diminished and detached from its sources. It was like an island, the past washing up to it, in fact, as the force of its becoming, but not as knowledge. Past and future bore against it under cover of darkness. Whoever wanted to make a beginning, then, had to begin with something already half-finished. And scarcely known.

Company

Across the street from Jasper Lathrop's store the white steeple ascends and narrows to a point above the green-shuttered belfry, higher than the tallest trees in the town. As he looks up at it from the sidewalk in front of the store, and at the clouds moving steadily southeastward in the deep wind, it seems to Mat for a moment that the clouds are still and only the earth moves, drawing the point of the steeple in a curving stroke through the sky.

Up the street, divided from the church by a vacant lot that contains a single broken-branched old locust and a stone chimney with the ruin of a hearth and mantel, is Mat's house, its weather-boarded white walls visible through the branches of the maples in the yard. From the angle of the boundary in which his house stands, Mat's farm extends in a wide irregular triangle to the river. The west line of the boundary follows the road out of town; at the top of the first ridge it makes shape for the graveyard, and then follows the road again to the top of the farthest ridge and down the wooded bluff; at the foot of the grade it turns away from the road and crosses the bottomland to the river. The land has been shaped by water. It has kept something of the nature of water in the alterations of its shape and character as it moves away from the high ground Port William is built on, descending to the river.

At the top of the ridge above the river bluff is the cluster of farm buildings that has been known to the Feltners since Mat's father's time as "the far place." In the field below the barns white-faced Hereford cows graze with their new calves around the banks of a little pond.

The house and the land beyond it have become intimately the possessions of Mat's mind. Before he looked he knew the lay and the shape and color of the field, and knew where the cattle would be. Even their erratic distribution over the field seems familiar to him as though, turning his head, he did not begin but continued to look.

Looking back at the house now as the gathering breaks up in front of the store, he sees his grandson running toward him out of the corner of the yard.

Old Jack, who has already gone halfway to the post office, stops and turns around. "You've got company at your house, Mat."

"I see I have."

"That's a fine boy there," Old Jack says. "He'll grow up to be a shotgun of a lawyer like his daddy, you watch and see if he don't. Tell Wheeler I said so."

"I'll do it."

The boy waves. "Wait, Grandad."

Mat goes on across the street and waits on the sidewalk in front of the church.

"Hello, Grandad."

"Hello, Andy." Mat puts his hands on the boy's shoulders and hugs him. "When did you come?"

"After school. Daddy had to go down on Bird's Branch, and he brought us by."

"Who's us?"

"Mother and Henry and me. We're going to eat supper with you."

"You are? Well, you haven't asked me if you can."

Andy laughs. "Can we eat supper with you?"

"I reckon so."

"Granny's already told us we can."

"Well, you're all right then, if both of us say so."

"She said tell you to go down to Burgess's and get a box of salt, and stop and tell Uncle Ernest to come home. Supper's going to be ready as soon as Daddy gets back."

"All right."

And they go down the street, past the old stone building that houses the bank, toward Burgess's store.

Neither of them hears the plane approaching. It has come in low over the town, and appears suddenly; the four engines and wings and grey fuselage take shape abruptly among the tops of the trees. For an instant it seems to have risen vertically, out of the top of the rise beyond the store. The racket of the engines comes on them all at once, so near they not only hear it but feel the vibration of it in the air and in the ground under their feet. As it comes nearer they can see the blur of the propellers, the black gun-barrels spiking out of the glass blisters, the rivet-heads along the fuselage and wings.

It passes above their heads, shaking the ground.

"A big one," Andy says.

The plane goes on beyond the town, becoming toylike, familiar, as it gains distance and altitude, circling eastward over the river.

The overcast has thinned, become dappled. The light glares on the town. Going into the dim interior of the store, Mat shuts the door slowly, allowing his eyes time to adjust.

Milton Burgess, his striped sleeves rolled two neat turns above his wrists, sits on a tall stool behind the counter, his elbow propped against the cash register. He has been talking with the band of loafers congregated on the opposite side of the counter, two of whom have hefted themselves up to sit in front of the cash register, their backs to Milton. With the loafers Milton allows himself a choleric indulgence in whatever news or argument is current—the one prolonged conversation that he has grudgingly allowed to continue there for forty-five years.

The store is a sprawling frame building, the foundation of which bridges the small creek that runs down out of the pasture behind Jasper Lathrop's store and around Jayber Crow's barbershop and under the road, so that after the creek goes out of sight in the culvert below the barbershop it does not come into the light again for two hundred feet or so. Beneath them, in wet weather, in the lapses of speech, the talkers in the store can hear it running.

With the loafers Milton condescends to loaf, his condescension apparent enough that he seems not to join their gathering but to permit each of them separately to intrude on him, so that above his idle participation in their talk his proprietorship still reigns undiminished and austere.

Seeing Mat and the boy come through the door, he climbs down off the stool and stands erect, his sparrowlike face becoming alert. He poises there, his spread fingers delicately touching the countertop, ready to jump instantly right or left at the slightest command from his customer. The quick sparrow face poises above the counter, waiting as if time halted when the door opened and will start again from the beginning the moment the customer speaks his order. It always happens. Mat knows that if one of the loafers, in the midst of their talk, should glance at the tobacco case and reach into his pocket the thin fingers would immediately graze the surface of the counter, the eyes quicken. "What can I do for you today?" Here, in this dim big room containing nothing that isn't for sale, Milton Burgess has made his life. The husband of his ledger, he never married. Over the years, wringing every possible penny out of his business, spending nothing more than is necessary to keep him and his old mother alive, he has made what the town confidently believes to be a solid fortune, which he puts to no use. Nothing interests him unless it can be made to add up. Though he is growing old and has no children, his ambition is still to squeeze out every other merchant in ten miles. At present he is enjoying the absence of Jasper Lathrop.

"What can I do for you today?"

Mat gives his order, adding a box of cigars.

The plane comes over again. The store is caught up, lifted, shaken in the noise of the engines, the windowpanes rattling.

Andy runs to the door, too late, to see.

The men at the counter follow the sound of it with their eyes.

"What in the hell's going on?"

"That boy of Grover Gibbs's, I reckon. They made a pilot out of him."

"He come cutting didos over Grover's place that way a week ago. Said he about tore the roof off his daddy's barn."

They laugh.

"Said Grover's mules run off when he done it."

Milton looks up at Mat, inquiring. "Will that be all for you?"

"That's all."

Andy, who has come back to where he was standing in front of the candy counter, becomes conscious that Mat is watching him, and not wanting to appear to hint, he moves away and begins to look at a stack of tinware in the window. Mat takes a nickel out of his pocket and steps up behind him.

"What's that you've got in your ear?" He takes hold of the boy's ear and pretends to pull the nickel out of it.

"Oh," Andy says. He turns around, laughing, and takes the coin. "Thanks, Grandad."

The men at the counter laugh.

"Is that Wheeler's boy, Mat?"

"He's Wheeler's."

"He's a Catlett all right."

Milton Burgess's fingers are touching the glass top of the candy counter now, his eyes cocked at Andy, who has gone back to stand in front of it. "Something for you today, young man?"

Mat leans against the counter with the loafers now, waiting for the boy to be done.

"You all heard from Virgil, Mat?"

Mat starts to say what they have heard, but then, on the verge of speaking, hesitates. The truth, divided from his own love for his son, seems a betrayal. He does not want to expose himself to any drawing of conclusions, any offer of sympathy. Sympathy for what? For what?

"Not in a while."

"Well, when you write to him tell him I asked about him."

"I will. I appreciate it."

Mat turns to the storekeeper, handing him another nickel. "Give me one more of those, Milt."

Milton hands him another bar of candy and he puts it in his pocket.

"Call again," Milton Burgess says. The door swings shut behind them. Andy takes Mat's hand as they start across the road.

Like a Bird

When the plane made its first pass over the town, Burley Coulter and Jayber Crow, having walked that far together, had stopped again in front of Jayber's shop. Jayber stood with one foot on the step, his hand holding the doorknob turned, ready to go inside.

The sounds of the plane's engines dropped down onto the town roofs like rocks, crashing and tumbling into all the crannies of their hearing, and then seemed to fill up the air above the town like water pouring into a glass jar.

"What's that thing doing here?" Jayber said.

"Billy Gibbs, I imagine. He flies one of them."

"They'd better hurry up and send him to the war before he kills somebody."

"Or *gets* killed."

Jayber stepped through the door. "I'll see you, Burley."

"I expect you will."

Now Burley walks up the rise, heading home.

His mind freed, he has Nathan's departure to think about. He walks back into Nathan's absence. And with the sorrow that has come to belong to his life, into Tom's.

He has gone a good way up the slanted street when the plane comes back. He stops and watches it go over the town, low over the treetops.

When he comes to the top of the rise he sees Uncle Stanley Gibbs standing out on the edge of his front yard above the road cut. The old man is in his shirt sleeves, hatless, his hair blowing, waving his cane.

Uncle Stanley's life takes its shape, has taken its shape for years, around his Sundays. On Sunday mornings he goes across town to the church and rings the bell, long and loud, while the clapperstrokes penetrate luxuriously into his deafness. His little splintery body dangles ecstatically on the end of the pull rope, the bell lifting him. And then he goes out to sit on the step, while the congregation assembles and silence issues from the church door, waiting for the meeting to be over, to go in and straighten up.

"That boy of Grover's come over here in that airplane of hisn" he shouts, waving his cane. "Come right up out of that woods back of Grover's place."

"I saw him, Uncle Stanley."

"Says *which?*"

"I *saw* him!"

"You did!" The old man bends forward, looking down at Burley, startled and proud. "Like a God-durned *bird.*"

The Carpenter Shop

Ernest's shop is orderly and warm, filled with the odors of shellac and lacquer and wood resins, the sound of a strong fire licking in the stove, light from the single large window in the rear wall. The room is neat to perfection. There is only the one day's disarray of tools, the one day's litter of wood fragments and shavings and sawdust.

Hanging on hooks and pegs and resting on the floor against the wall opposite the window are the ladders and rope tackle and jacks necessary for the building of barns and houses. At the end of the room farthest from the stove, nearly stacked, sorted according to kind and quality and size, are the stores of fine woods he uses in his cabinetmaking. His hand tools, their handles worn to a polish, hang above the workbench from a row of pegs driven into the long sill of the window. On the wall to the left of the window there is a pencil holder into which are wedged a number of thick-leaded pencils of various lengths and colors, a ball of twine stained with the dust of blue chalk, a calendar with a picture of an idyllic farm in the small valley of a creek where flowers and fruit trees are in bloom. While Ernest is at work he does not use his crutches, but leaves them propped in the corner behind the stove. The interior of the shop has gradually conformed to an arrangement that requires the least amount of walking. By a kind of natural growth, everything here has come within his reach.

Mat and Andy come in and close the door. They cross the room to the stove, and Mat sits down on a nail keg in front of it. Andy wanders here and there in the shop, looking, but touching nothing; Ernest will not stand for meddling. After a minute or two Andy comes back and stands beside Mat at the stove. Ernest is working at the bench, carefully dressing the edge of a walnut board with a plane. He has not yet looked around at them. They watch him without talking, waiting for him to be done.

An Old Wound

In the early summer of 1919, when Ernest came home at last from the war, both his parents were dead and the house sold. Port William had got used to his absence, and he came back changed.

His wound had been difficult, complicated at the beginning by infection, and the healing was painful and slow. After his discharge he had to spend the better part of a year in the hospital. His foot was finally made as well as it would ever be; but this, the end of the healing, was the hardest for him to accept—that to be "cured" meant only that he would remain crippled. The fragmented bones and tendons were spliced back; the irreparable mutilation was made to heal and live. There would be no reason, they told him, why he should not live a normal life. Adjustments would have to be made, of course.

Still, as he prepared to leave the hospital, learning, as though it was some ultimately unsolvable problem of mechanics, to piece out his loss with the crutches, he was aware that he had suffered a defeat. And he knew that this defeat was real and final, allowing for no recovery or revenge, permitting no illusion to mitigate its permanence. And it was from this defeat, more than from any place he had been, that he came back to Port William.

He came back with his mouth shut, permanently, on these realizations. There were two things that he could neither speak of nor forget: his defeat, and the implausibility of the fact that something so vast as a war had picked out and defeated so small a thing as one man, himself. The difficulty was that this was an implausible *fact*. He was getting ready to leave the hospital; he was going back to Port William, to begin whatever would have to be begun, and now he realized that these thoughts belonged to him as permanently as his wound. He would go back to town, then, this much changed, and nothing could ever be as it was.

But Mat, who came on the train to bring him home, made it easier than he had imagined. When Mat walked into the hospital that morning, he raised his hand in greeting.

"I'm half contraption," Ernest said.

And Mat said, "Not hardly that much."

He smiled; they shook hands. Mat picked up Ernest's suitcase and led the way to the door. To Mat it seemed that they brought home, between them, the recovery of a time—an injury and vacancy in all their lives, healed over, like Ernest's wound, but with diminished pain.

They got off the train in the early morning. The town of Hargrave had not begun to stir, and the valley lay under a fog that seemed to weight the quiet and to separate the town and themselves immediately from the rattling departure of the train.

After an hour's driving over the rutted road, disappearing always a few yards ahead of them into the fog, they climbed out of the valley into the open daylight. From the top of the first ridge they could see Port William lying in the sun ahead of them, the white steeple of the church pointing up over the cluster of treetops and roofs. They drove along the ridge, the car chugging and jolting ahead of its plume of dust, dipping out of sight of the town, climbing the rise into it. The maples, in the perfect foliage of early June, dappled the road and the white house fronts with their shade. Flowers were in bloom in the yards and porch boxes. On an old millstone in a patch of sun a yellow cat sat licking itself. Behind them the fog, a white sunlit cloud, filled the valley to the brim.

The town had settled into the quiet of workday mornings. Mat turned the car into the driveway beside his house and stopped and shut the engine off. And the quiet came over them—a susurration of the wakefulness of the town, in which the noon meal was being prepared, the floors were being swept, time was unwinding in the kitchen clocks, the sun was climbing in the warm clear sky toward noon and solstice.

There were the smells of honeysuckle, of barns, of cooking, of hay curing, of horse dung warming and drying in the road. Mat, waking from death, would have known in an instant the place, the time of year, the time of day. Looking at the house, he saw Margaret walking toward them across the porch, smiling, though she saw and knew what he had brought.

In the fall of that year Ernest built his shop. He did most of the work alone, with help now and then from Mat and Joe Banion when they could spare the time. The shop became, in a way, a town project, not of work, but of interest and curiosity—and then surprise that Ernest could lift and carry and climb and, more alone than not, frame and wall up and roof a sizable building. But Ernest had quickly developed the judgment necessary to his lameness, which enabled him to estimate accurately what he could and could not do—and to do more, by a considerable sight, than most of the townspeople would have guessed before they saw him do it. In the town they renamed him Shamble. Though the thumping of the crutches went ahead of him, he held up his face, and there would be a direct straight look in his eyes.

It was understood from the first that Ernest would make his home with Mat and Margaret. He took the room over the kitchen in the back of the house, which had a separate entrance by the back stairs and the upper porch. After his carpenter's trade had been established, he seemed to withdraw into the established certainties and clear limits of it. He perfected his shop, making its work spaces neat and convenient. He perfected his silence.

A Pretty Good Boy

Ernest straightens up from his work and looks around.

"Hello, Mat. Who's that you've got with you?"

"I don't know who this fellow is. He just followed me in."

Ernest blows the shavings out of the plane and lays it down on the bench. He takes the board out of the vise. Holding to the end of it with one hand, he runs his thumb down the edge of it, and then, drawing it to his eye, sights along it.

"I believe he's a good boy, though. I think I'll keep him."

Ernest looks away from the board and, with the same squint in his eye, sights down at Andy.

"He looks like a pretty good boy."

Andy laughs. "Uncle Ernest, Granny said to tell you to come home for supper before long. She's made a pie for dessert."

"Ho," Mat says. "That's who he is."

Ernest nods his head. "I knew him as soon as I heard him say pie."

Feeding

When they go into the kitchen, supper is cooking. Margaret and Hannah and Bess Catlett are all sitting around the table, talking. Bess is holding her younger child, Henry, on her lap.

When he sees Mat coming to the door, Henry jumps down and runs across the kitchen to meet him.

"See what's in my ear, Grandad."

He cocks his head sideways, putting his ear into the proper position.

Mat slips the bar of candy out of his pocket, concealing it in his hand, and with a great show of effort fetches it out of the little boy's ear, and hands it to him. Henry takes it and looks at it, his eyes big.

They all laugh. Mat walks over to the table. Bess takes his hand, and he leans down to kiss her.

He stands there a minute to talk with them. None of them speak, as they usually do at these times, of Virgil, and they are all conscious of the avoidance. Over all they say there is a tension of awareness that the day has become strange. Mat has understood from the moment he came in that Bess knows of the letter—that, soon after she came, Margaret found a time, out of the hearing of Hannah and the children, to tell her. He can all but hear the sound of her voice, deliberately firm, discovering, by instinctive goodness, the least painful words.

When Wheeler comes, he knows, they will have to tell him. And so it has begun, and will go on. He buttons his coat around him again, and, getting the milk buckets from the pantry, goes out.

At the barn Joe Banion is already at work, watering the mules. The old Negro comes out of a stall, carrying a lead rein in his hand. The brim of his hat is turned down so that it nearly touches the turned-up collar of his mackinaw. The coat is too large for him, hanging nearly to his knees, the sleeves half covering his hands. His pant legs are stuffed into a pair of leather leggings, also a little large, which have been buckled and then tied top and bottom with pieces of twine. He is small and a little stooped, a little flinched against the chill. His face is that of a man who has learned long ago to do what is necessary: to work, to take pleasure as he finds it, to make do, to be quiet. His face does not show his age; his hands do. As early as Mat remembers anything he remembers Joe Banion.

Joe Banion shuts the stall door and slips the latch to. Turning then, and seeing Mat, he nods his head and smiles. He is thinking of the letter. He is thinking of Virgil, and is sorry.

For a moment, looking at Joe's face, touched by the kindness in it, Mat would like to tell what he has on his mind, say what he is afraid of. But he does not name his fear even to himself, and he says nothing.

"It sure ain't getting any warmer, Mr. Mat."

"It's not spring yet, Joe." Mat speaks without thinking, and hears, almost with surprise, the casual tone of his voice.

"It'll be before long," Joe Banion is saying. "We'll be sweating before long, I expect. Soon enough."

Mat hangs the milk buckets up inside the door, takes a larger bucket to the crib, and fills it with ears of corn. He goes from stall to stall, down one side of the long driveway and up the other, dropping into the feedboxes each mule's ration for the night.

He puts the bucket back when he has emptied it, and climbs the ladder into the loft. He moves above the rows of stalls, forking hay down into the mangers. Below him he can hear the mules feeding, rattling the corn in their troughs.

He goes out the back door of the barn, through the lot gate, and up the long slope of the pasture to the sheep barn at the top of the ridge. The sod gives under his feet like sponge. Behind him his tracks are filled with water.

The flock of ewes, most of them with lambs now, grazes along slowly in the direction of the barn, picking here and there at the short grass. Seeing Mat on his way to feed them, they raise their heads, and come along more quickly. In this sudden forward movement of the flock, lambs get separated from their mothers, and the commotion increases. Mat goes into the barn and pulls the doors to behind him. In the dim light that comes in between the boards of the walls, the troughs and mangers stand end to end in a long rank down the center of the driveway. He makes two trips from the feed bin with buckets of grain, spreading it evenly in the bottoms of the troughs, and forks hay into the mangers. And then he covers the wet bedding with a layer of fresh straw. He looks over his work, again with satisfaction: the feeding and the night prepared, perfected.

He pushes the doors open and calls the sheep, standing back out of the way as they come in and crowd to the troughs. He stays there a while, looking over the field, making sure that none has been left out. He feels growing in him now, in spite of all, a familiar and precious calm. The flock is in the barn, well fed, safe from dogs and the cold, warmly bedded. They will be there safe until morning. If not today, on most of the winter days of his life this completeness has filled his mind.

The sun, almost down, breaks out of the overcast, throwing a warm orange light over the town and the house and the ridge where Mat is standing. Against the brightness of the clouds in the west, the town has become a silhouette. The naked branches webbing over the tops of the houses stand out clearly. The wall of the sheep barn is an intense glowing white. Everywhere the colors are stronger. The light picks out the smallest beginnings of green in the pasture. The damp left by the rain shines. Mat stands in the change of light as he has been standing all along, but changed. He knows he will not think of it as winter again; spring has become imaginable. He feels an elation, and then, in the same thought, sorrow that the first change has come beyond what has happened to them. Now they move again toward what will happen.

❦

3

The Last

A little less than a mile from town Burley Coulter turns off the blacktop into the gravel lane that goes back through the fields to his house and Jarrat's. The lane runs somewhat windingly along the backbone of a ridge which points toward the opening of the river valley. To the sides of the ridge, though not so noticeably, lie the openings of the lesser valleys of Sand Ripple and Katy's Branch. From so high Burley can see a lot of the country, in which the only sounds audible to him now are his own footsteps. He walks along carefully between the two depressed and puddled wheel tracks.

Toward its outer end the lane forks, as does the ridge, the left fork going to Jarrat's house, the right to Burley's. Here the two farms are divided by a hollow that becomes a deep ravine where the easy slopes of the upland steepen to the wooded bluffs above the river valley.

Since the death of his wife more than twenty years ago, Jarrat has lived alone, leaving his two sons to grow up in the other house, in the care of their grandparents and Burley. The boys lived too far away to know Jarrat as a father, near enough to know him as a taskmaster and judge. Jarrat has remained a good deal apart from the family, cooking and keeping house for himself.

Jarrat and Burley were born in the other house, the log house begun by their great-grandfather, completed by their grandfather, and weatherboarded by their father. Except for a reluctant trip to France in 1918, Burley has never left, and now the deaths and departures of the other members of the family have left him alone there. His father, Dave, died in 1940. And both the boys went away—Tom before the old man's death, Nathan later—because of quarrels with Jarrat. It is not in Jarrat's nature to indulge a small disagreement, and so his quarrels with his sons were the only real ones he had ever had with them, and the last ones. It is a severe manhood that Jarrat has, that feeds on its loneliness, and will be governed by no head but his own. Each of the boys was able to make a reconciliation of sorts between himself and Jarrat, on the terms of a quiet and mostly one-sided friendship, but the separation, once accomplished, was permanent, and neither of them came back home to live. And now Tom is dead.

After old Dave's death and the departure of the two boys, Burley and his mother lived on there together, oppressed sometimes by the emptiness of the big house, but managing, as Burley said, to peg along.

"We'll peg along, old girl," he would say to her.

She would sniff, and then laugh, at his impudence.

The old woman lived on in bewilderment, divided from the lives that had been her care and duty. She went through times of deep loneliness; sometimes at night, after Burley had gone to bed, he would hear her wandering among the empty rooms of the house, whispering to herself.

During those last few of her years, Burley made the first honest attempt of his life to please her. He tried—always fumblingly, often with extravagant miscalculation—to be the kind of son he figured she had wanted him to be. He left off, as nearly as he could bear it, what she thought his most wayward habits, and when he was not at work or in town on some errand he mostly stayed at home with her. They would sit in the living room at night, and talk; or, more often, he would listen and she would talk, her old voice wandering at random among her memories. The past had come near to her, and she would talk on and on, remembering idly and easily, but also obsessively and endlessly. She would exhaust his ability to pay attention to her, and he would sit there, his mind drifting, nodding his head. She repeated the same stories time and again, reminded of them by new memories, until finally he was able to tell what story she was on just by the sound of it.

Occasionally in these ramblings of hers she would stumble, by accident, onto one of his misdemeanors. She would be taken by surprise; the recollection would come to her as forcibly as if it had just then happened. She would look up at him suddenly, crossly, over her glasses, and point her finger at him.

"And you, Burley Coulter, were drunk."

She would shake her head, surprised and grieved that a son of hers could ever have been drunk.

"Yes, Ma'am," Burley would say. "I expect." And he would get up quietly and go out of the house, leaving her to whisper and gesture her way through her old anger.

Her early memories came back to her in swarms, but her ability to keep the immediate past in mind grew weaker. She could remember what happened fifty or twenty-five or ten years ago with lucidity and clarity of detail that were surprising even to her. She would have sudden recollections of things that she was no longer aware of having forgot. But she would be unable to remember what came in the mail the day before. She would hunt sometimes for half a day, having forgot where she had put down her glasses or her thimble. Her lifelong habit of putting things away was transformed, by this failure of her memory, into the interminable and wearisome process of hiding things from herself and finding them again, always by accident and with great pleasure, sometimes months later. A few things that she regarded as keepsakes or valuables she put away carefully and never found again.

One Christmas she put away a box of candy—thinking that she would ration it out carefully and it would last a month or two—and never came upon it again until the week after Easter. By then the candy was hard as gravel, and she had forgot how long it had been since she put it away. Burley, to please her, ate nearly the whole box—in two nights, to get it over with—talking the whole time about how tickled he was that she had saved it. And she nibbled along at it herself, looking inquiringly over her glasses, uncertain whether to believe him or not.

Finally she said, "I'll declare, Burley, these false teeth of mine seem to have got out of whack."

When he had time he helped her in the kitchen, and helped her keep house, sparing her as much of the work and worry as he could. In good weather he would sometimes persuade her to let him do the washing, and set up the tubs and wringer in the back yard to avoid cluttering the kitchen, and do in an hour what would have been a half day's work for her. When he finished, the clothes he had on would be as wet as the ones he had washed.

"Burley Coulter," she would say, "you're worse than any kid." And then she would laugh.

Seeing that his recklessness and awkwardness amused her, he plunged and rubbed over the scrubbing board more furiously than ever, making the water splash and spout higher than his head. Performing these elaborate exaggerations of his incompetence, he could make her laugh like a girl.

She made, finally, a kind of household pet of him, made a child of him, and he submitted painstakingly. She fixed special treats and desserts for him. In the years between Dave's death and her own she crocheted a set of doilies for his room.

He remembers the heavy day, after her death, that he spent burning the leftover odds and ends of her life that she had carefully preserved in the closets and the bureau drawers: postcards and letters from people whose names he had forgot and hastened to forget again, photographs of people dead before he was born, whose names he never knew. Though he wanted none of it, though he lightened himself by getting rid of it, there was an awesome finality in the burning of those things, dear to her for reasons that would never be known again in the world.

Since his father's death and the boys' departure, and even more since the death of his mother, Burley has devoted himself to Jarrat—not because Jarrat ever has required devotion of him, but because he is touched by Jarrat's loneliness, and in the absence of so many is lonely himself.

Jarrat lives for work. He has grown nearly silent. If Burley wants to talk, he has to wait for a chance to go elsewhere. But he and Jarrat have continued to work together, and there has been a great deal to be done and always more to do. During the past two years, in addition to farming their own places, they have sharecropped on Mat Feltner's. Jarrat took this new work. Burley knew, simply because the acreage became available—and because he is, within the limits of his strength, unable to let the opportunity of a crop go by.

Burley has made himself Jarrat's friend. Though Jarrat will never acknowledge any dependence on him, Burley has made himself dependable. He has been, as he never was earlier in his life, faithful to their work, not for his own sake, but for Jarrat's. In these years of their loneliness devotion has become Burley's habit. He has become more gentle as Jarrat has become more hard.

Now, as he comes up to the yard, Jarrat is waiting for him, standing on the stone walk between the back porch and the cellar house. He is past fifty now, and looks older—all leather and bone and lean meat, taller and leaner than Burley, a little bent in the shoulders. His face, beginning to hollow in the cheeks and temples and around the eyes, is covered with a week's growth of nearly white beard. His mouth is cleanly shaped, firm, and tightly, deliberately, closed. His eyebrows are coarse, heavy, completely black; below them his eyes are set deep and have a peculiar fixity of gaze.

He is wearing an old hunting coat, soiled and stained and frayed. His large hands hang down at his sides, the knobbed heavy bones of his wrists showing beneath the coat cuffs. His hands are scarred and hardened, weathered to the color of an old saddle. Jarrat's face invites no sympathy; to Burley, all the humanness and vulnerability of him are in his hands, and he is always touched by the sight of them. For three or four years, Burley knows, Jarrat has been unable to sign a check. His hand has become incapable of performing the small movements of his name, can scarcely grasp and hold steady so small an object as a pencil. It is the peculiar adaptation of his strength that he can do small work only clumsily or not at all, but manages the roughest and heaviest labor with grace and seemingly without strain.

He stands midway of the walk, awkwardly waiting. He asks, "Did he catch the bus?"

"Yes."

"You got him there all right. And saw him off."

"Yes."

Jarrat is looking down at his feet. He nods. And then, as though he had been not waiting but passing on some errand, he goes out the gate and starts home.

Burley walks up the steps and onto the porch. He wipes his feet on the piece of old carpet beside the door and goes into the kitchen.

He lays a fire in the cooking range and lights it. Once the blaze has caught, he goes to the living room to build up the fire there, and then goes out along the path to the barn to do his feeding.

When he leaves the barn, the sun, just before setting, shines out of a breach in the clouds, and below him the valley is suddenly filled with a transparent mist of rich light. He stops to look. A window in a house he cannot see, on a ridgetop three or four miles away on the other side of the river, catches the sun. His clothes are still damp from the rain; his feet are wet and cold. He stands there, watching the light, thinking suddenly of spring.

Back in the house, he gets out a pair of dry shoes and a change of clothes. He stands in front of the stove in the living room, taking off his wet clothes and putting the dry ones on. He waits there, holding his hands over the top of the stove, until he is warm.

The house has become dark. He goes through the cold hall to the kitchen and turns on the light and begins preparing his supper. He goes about his work in about the same way as his mother would have gone about it.

Usually his housekeeping seems to him to be too painstaking, even wasteful, for one man living alone. At times he has thought it would be better to move his bed down to the kitchen and live in the one room with the one fire, as Jarrat has always done, and close up the rest of the house. But he has never been able to bring himself to the change. He follows the old habits of the household, keeping at least the three rooms alive. And he keeps Nathan's room clean and waiting, refusing to accept loneliness as the culmination of anything. He knows better than to hope outright for the return of anybody, but he is careful to leave the possibilities open.

When his meal is done with and the kitchen is set to rights, he goes back to the living room and sits and smokes in his chair beside the stove.

The room is furnished sparely and to Burley, despite his own presence in it, it feels deserted. There is a checkered linoleum on the floor, a small carpet in the center of it in front of the stove. Besides Burley's rocking chair, there are four straight-backed chairs, a sofa, and a table under the front window. On the mantel behind the stove a stopped clock stands between two glass vases. Between the clock and the vases are pictures of Tom and Nathan in their uniforms, and an enlarged photograph of the family taken by Jarrat's wife in the year before her death. They are standing in a row in the yard in front of the house. It is Sunday, or else they have dressed up especially for the picture—he cannot remember. The two little boys, at either end of the row, are grinning, looking into the camera. Jarrat and Burley, almost unrecognizably younger, stand with the boys beside them and the old people between them; they have their hands behind them, their feet apart, their eyes squinched against the sun; Jarrat, self-consciously, is smiling. The grandmother stands with her hands clasped in front of her, her feet placed together at a prim angle, in what was considered graceful posture in the time of her girlhood. Beside her, peculiarly apart from her, and from all the rest of them, old Dave is leaning forward over his cane. He might be there alone for all the deference he pays to the presence of the others. He is as tall as Jarrat, and as lean, his white hair uncombed. He is wearing a white shirt and tie and a dress coat of an old-fashioned cut which fits him too tightly across the shoulders, but his pants are work pants, without creases. The set of his face is stubborn. He has submitted only grudgingly—only, finally, at the insistence of his pretty daughter-in-law—to the taking of the picture. He stares straight ahead.

They look into the room: the living faces of the dead, the different younger faces of the living, more perishable than the paper of the photograph. Jarrat's young wife was the first to die, leaving Jarrat and the two boys to become what they would not have become if she had lived, changing all the possibilities. And old Dave held on to his life as if nothing was less obvious and less certain than death—until a simple sleep, like a child's, pried his fingers loose. And the old woman died, among the gathering of her memories, as though she died into a death she had already lived in for years.

And Tom is dead. And Nathan is gone again, bound to them now only by the thin strand of departure.

Burley leans forward, opening the door of the stove, and throws in the butt of his cigarette and empties the ashes out of his hand.

He picks up a newspaper and looks at it a moment. But it is yesterday's paper—he forgot to get the mail when he came in. He puts the paper down and turns on the radio, and then, anticipating with a kind of fear the breaking of the silence, turns it off again.

He gets up and walks to the window and, shielding his eyes from the light in the room, looks out. There are no stars. The wind has quieted and the overcast, he imagines, is thickening again. He stirs the fire and sits back down.

For a long time there is only the sound of the fire burning, the occasional shifting of the coals. Occasionally, marking the silence into long spans, he hears the cracking of the floors and walls as the house contracts and settles into the night cold. He is thinking of Tom.

Tom had been a bulldozer operator with a battalion of engineers, following the invasion into Italy. One morning they were sent up into the mountains where a battle had been fought the night before. The field was strewn with the dead of both armies, and Tom's outfit had orders to bury them. The area was still under threat of counterattack, and they were to do their work in a hurry. The ground was stony and thin and frozen, covered with a layer of snow. With considerable difficulty, Tom scooped out a long shallow grave. The bodies were laid in quickly, side by side in the naked grave, and he began covering them. He replaced the dirt he had moved, and to make the burial as deep as possible he began scraping up dirt from the area around the grave to mound over it. It was desperate work. Twice he became confused about the dimensions of the grave and dug out the bodies he was trying to cover. The forward movement of the heavy machine rolled them out of the pit before he could stop.

Now, grown still in the chair, the warmth of the stove around him, Burley doesn't know if he is awake or asleep. Cold in his mind, he digs in the skimpy dirt, moving back and forth on the narrow shelf of the mountain. Beneath him he can feel the shove and pitch of the machine, the sound of the engine alternately straining and idling. Looking down as if from a height, he sees the unfinished long mound of a grave. Under the mound are the dead, lying side by side in their torn uniforms, a single long rank of them, facing up into the raw dirt. He scrapes at the frozen ground, loosening only handfuls at a time, and pushes it onto the grave—to make the dead safe there, to be done with them, to hide them forever. He is in a terrible hurry, and there is not enough dirt.

He uncovers a face. Tom's. The boy lies on his side, his right arm crooked beneath his head. His eyes are shut, the dirt against his cheek like a blanket.

He wakes up. The house and the fire tick on into the silence. He sits still, trying to recover his presence there in the familiar room. It is time he was going to bed. But he puts on his hat and coat, and picking up his lantern at the kitchen door, starts back along the road to town.

The Hotel

The lobby of Mrs. Hendrick's hotel, considering its public intention, is a cramped small room. The ceiling is too high for the length and breadth of it. Light from the one-eyed ramshackle fixture in the ceiling thins and dims, reaching down into it. In a steep diagonal across the back wall of the room a stairway goes up to the second floor.

Beneath the stairway, divided from the rest of the room by a short counter, there is a small triangular alcove, which was the office of the establishment in its more or less flourishing days. The alcove contains a double row of empty pigeonholes. The counter bears a frayed ink-marked green blotter, a crusted inkstand and pen, a small nickel-plated bell. None of this has been in use for years. Now all the business of the place can be transacted well enough in and out of Mrs. Hendrick's snapping change purse, but she has maintained the little office as an appearance or reminder of her better days. The lobby is furnished with three wicker chairs and a wicker settee. They sit there empty, in conversational arrangement, offering hospitality in the empty room.

The dining room is a little better than twice as long and half again as wide as the lobby. Four ample tables stand in a row down the center of the floor. Light fixtures hang by cords from the ceiling at either end of the room, but only the most distant one is lighted. At the far end of the room a door opens into the kitchen, showing beyond it a large black cooking range. The table nearest the kitchen is the only one with a cloth on it.

At this last table Old Jack and the two lady boarders are seated. The old man sits at the end of the table toward the front of the building. At the opposite end is Mrs. Hendrick's empty chair. The old ladies sit, facing each other across the table, on either side of the landlady's place. The plates of the three women make a small close triangle, leaving as much of the table's length as possible between them and Old Jack. The old ladies have woolen shawls drawn around their shoulders, and Jack still has on his coat and cap. The meal is nearly finished. The old ladies have stopped eating, and are leaning toward each other, talking almost in whispers. Now and then they glance down the table at Old Jack, but covertly, so as not to violate their pretense that they are unaware of his presence. As their glances at him show, their exchange of womanly confidences is a little thrilled at its surreptitious occurrence in the presence of the old man.

Old Jack is still eating. He has heaped his plate full for the second time, and has no more than half finished it. He eats with the forthright assistance of his left thumb, with a great wielding of his elbows. Whatever the old ladies say to each other at mealtimes, it always has a tacit reference to the old man's table manners. At the moment there is a trickle of gravy on its way down his chin; sooner or later, they know, ignoring his napkin, he will wipe it off on his sleeve.

Mrs. Hendrick is standing just out of reach of his left elbow. She is holding out, vaguely in his direction, a nearly empty meat platter. She has been standing there for a full minute, waiting for him to notice her, her face set in a twist of impatience. Jack continues to eat, concentrating on the space between his plate and his mouth.

She pokes the plate at him. "Do you want any more of this meat, Mr. Beechum?"

"Naw'm," Jack says. "You can take that away, Suzy. I'm done with it."

Mrs. Hendrick's name is not Suzy. None of the three women is named Suzy. But Old Jack simplifies matters by calling them all Suzy.

One of the old ladies giggles in confidential outrage at the other.

Mrs. Hendrick makes hard rapid tracks to the kitchen with the meat platter. She comes back and scrapes up the old ladies' dishes and her own, and carries them to the kitchen. Her steps peck brittlely back and forth over the floor. She brings in the coffee pot and fills the triangle of cups at the ladies' end of the table and sits down again. She passes the sugar and cream to her lady boarders.

Old Jack finishes eating and pushes back his plate. Mrs. Hendrick gets up and hustles around the table, her heels again picking out the thin hard code of her martyrdom. Sometimes she gets furious at Mr. Hendrick for having died and left her alone, and poor, and dependent on these distresses. She brushes Old Jack's crumbs into his plate and takes it out to the kitchen. She pours his coffee and sets the cream and sugar by him, and goes back to her place.

The old man scoops in three heaping spoonfuls of sugar and pours in cream until his cup fills to the brim. He stirs, slopping the coffee out into the saucer. Holding cup and saucer unsteadily in his big hands, he pours the saucer full, and blows on it and drinks. He finishes the coffee in five saucerings, rapidly, with a loud mixture of breathing and blowing and guzzling, and gets up, scraping his chair backwards, scrubbing his mouth on his coat sleeve. He unhooks his cane from the corner of the table.

He looks at Mrs. Hendrick and gives her a large smile. There is a blunt obtrusive kindness in his expression, utterly unaware of the displeasure that she has been at such pains to make obvious.

"I thank you, Suzy. And good night to you."

He turns and goes, walking heavily the length of the dining room and out the door, leaving his chair pushed back at an angle from the table.

Jack's departure, as far as the two old ladies are concerned, is as disturbing as his presence. His leave-taking is absolute. The turning of his back completely dismisses the entire circumstance of the meal and its company—themselves. He bears away from the table a filled belly, but beyond that not a thought. The set of his head and shoulders, the momentous stomping and hobbling of his gait, suggest that he has never looked behind him in his life. He seems to participate unequivocally in the continuing deaths and completions of things. His knowledge is as forthright as his hunger. He speaks of the approach of his own death as much as a matter of fact as he speaks of the approach of Tuesday. He accomplishes everything as if he is both aware and willing that every breath he draws will be the last of its kind. To the old ladies there is something obscene in it. They exchange a series of self-conscious glances—as after a near stroke of lightning.

From where they sit they hear his cane and his footsteps thumping slowly up the stairs.

At each end of the hall a bulb the size of a walnut gives a thin weak light shadowing the offsets of the doorways. Into the half-dark of the hall the rooms exhale the cold musk of emptiness. Jack goes into his room, leaving the door open so that a little light drains in from the hall. He feels his way to the light switch, and turns it on. The room contains only an iron bed, a tall bare-topped chiffonier with a peeling oval mirror, a large rocking chair. That the bed is made up is the only sign that the room is lived in. Old Jack's coming has changed nothing.

He shoves the rocking chair over to the window and hooks his cane over the arm of it and sits down. He leans back.

The room contains his sleep. It is there, waiting for him, folded in the iron bed. But he has to prepare for it. He has to get his mind ready for it beforehand. In the last few years, since he has become too old to work, he has slept a light short sleep. A sleep too easy to wake up from—his mind is always just barely submerged under it, as though he is looking up at light through an obscuring thin film of water. Unless he is careful he will wake up in the night and think of his fears.

Most of all he is afraid that before he dies he will be sick and unable to attend to himself. Death does not worry him so much. He has no time for the solemnity usually attributed to it, but it is a fact, at least, and can be considered and dealt with. He thinks of dying as a kind of job that will have to be done, and, as he tells Wheeler Catlett, he can do it. But the thought of sickness makes him afraid. He fears living on past sickness into dependence on other people. He dislikes the uncertainty of these thoughts. He has lived all his life loving solid objects, things he could hook onto with his hands and pull. He has loved to feel in his hands the thrown-back weight of his body.

Other times he will wake up thinking of the imperfections of his life. He will lie there, remembering his mistakes and stupidities and errors of judgment, furious at himself, furious and sickened at the impossibility of correcting the past. These recollections return to him like old pains. And once they start they come at him one after another. They are worse than nightmares; he cannot wake up from them, and he cannot go back to sleep.

And so he sits up by his window each night, waiting to need to sleep. He waits to go to bed until he feels he can trust his sleep to last until morning.

He goes to bed a good deal later now than he used to. But he has kept his old habit of getting up early. Long before dawn these winter mornings he will be out of bed and wide awake. After he puts on his clothes he draws the covers back over the bed. And then he turns out the light and feels his way to the rocking chair and sits down. When daylight comes he will be there at the window, waiting for it.

A single set of footsteps goes along the walk in front of the hotel, and farther down the street somebody is talking loudly in front of one of the stores. A door slams somewhere off in the town. Below him in the kitchen Mrs. Hendrick is rattling the supper dishes.

Up the street he can see lights in Mat Feltner's house. Wheeler Catlett is there for supper, he remembers. For a few minutes he considers going over to Mat's to pay a visit and talk to Wheeler. He thinks a lot of Wheeler—admires him, in fact, a good deal more than he aims to let him know. He imagines going in and sitting down and talking a while with Wheeler and Mat. They are fine men, and have good heads on them. And he would like to see Wheeler's little boys. Wheeler has taught his sons to call the old man "Uncle Jack."

"Uncle Jack," the littlest one said, "you've got tobacco juice on your shirt." That tickled Jack. And Wheeler's embarrassment tickled him even more. That littlest boy of Wheeler's would walk right up and tell Franklin D. Roosevelt he had tobacco juice on his shirt. Old Jack's face creases into the shape of a large laugh, and he snorts. He thinks a lot of those boys of Wheeler's. Every Christmas he buys a little something to give them. Wheeler appreciates that.

He would like to hear Wheeler say something about the war. Jack stays troubled about the war. There is too much dying. Too many young men dying. He mistrusts what he reads in the papers. The war is more serious, it seems to him, than the papers make it out to be.

It may be necessary to use up the lives of young men; Jack will agree to that. He has no liking for defeat. But after a choice has had to be made between terrible sacrifice and terrible defeat, it is a time of mourning.

The newspapers add up the deaths of young men as if they were some kind of loan, an investment in something.

What is dead is gone.

He reaches into the bib pocket of his overalls and takes out a small notebook in which there is a carefully folded newspaper picture of the President. He opens the picture and looks at it. The President sits there behind his great desk. His eyes look direct and straight out of the picture so that they seem to focus on Old Jack.

The President's face is sober and tired, sorrowful. The strain of the war shows in it, the burden of knowing of so many deaths. It would take a lot of strength to know so much.

A great man, with a powerful head on his shoulders.

Jack thinks how it would be to sit in Mat Feltner's living room, and talk with Mat and Wheeler and Franklin Roosevelt. It would be brilliant.

"Mr. President," Wheeler says, "how much longer do you think it'll last?"

"I don't know." The President looks straight at Wheeler. "It's a hard proposition. We'll have to fight them until they quit."

That's a responsible answer, Jack thinks. He has to say so. "That's right," he says. "Go to it. By God, we're for you, sir."

"Thank you, my friend," the President says.

It is too late, now, to go over to Mat's. They would not be expecting him. He will see Wheeler later in the week, anyhow.

Saturday afternoon, or maybe Friday, the two of them will drive out to spend a couple of hours or so seeing to things on Old Jack's farm. And then maybe they will go on over to Wheeler's daddy's place, as they do sometimes, and visit a while there. Or go somewhere to look at a farm that Wheeler will be thinking of buying—and spend a while pointing out and describing to each other what could be done by way of improvement. Or maybe—it could be any day—Wheeler will have a case to try in one of the counties upriver, and will stop by and pick up Old Jack and take him along. They usually ride all the way to the courthouse without talking much, Wheeler's briefcase and maybe a law book or two on the seat between them. There's too much going on inside of Wheeler then. It is as if, while they are on the way to the trial, Wheeler's mind and his nerves are drawing down like the spring of a steel trap. And with Wheeler—who, in Old Jack's opinion, has a mind like a steel trap—that is a mighty formidable thing to see happening. Because once he stands up in one of those courtrooms, with the judge and the jury and the opposing lawyer and the plaintiff and the defendant and the crowd of courthouse regulars and loafers and idle farmers and the framed portraits of four or five generations of judges all looking at him, Wheeler's intelligence shines. Whether he wins or loses, Wheeler shines, Old Jack can see that. Every point Wheeler makes has the clean sound to it of a good axe chopping into a locust stump. And Old Jack, in his seat in the back of the room, says "Ah!" On the way home, after Wheeler has got limbered up and relaxed a little, Old Jack will slap him on the knee and tell him: "You're all right, son. You've got a powerful head, and that's fine. *Mighty* fine."

He folds up the President's picture and puts it back. He thumbs through the notebook until he finds a clean page; and then he takes a short pencil out of his pocket, and begins to write down a column of figures.

That pocket in the bib of his overalls is Old Jack's place of business. That is where he keeps his old silver pocket watch and his notebook and pencil; he tells Wheeler he uses the pocket to hold what he has got left of his mind. He and Wheeler both know that he's still got a shrewd head on his shoulders, but they let on as if he would have no mind at all if he had no pocket to put it in.

It is true enough that the old man no longer has any memory for figures. And all his accounts and receipts are kept in a file in Wheeler Catlett's office in Hargrave. He does his figuring in the notebook by guess, estimating and imagining what he cannot remember or never knew, and coming up invariably with a monstrous error in the result. But he has the habit of figuring, and so he figures, night after night, sitting by himself in his room, chewing furiously at his cud of tobacco, his imagination freewheeling among wishes and guesses, going up one side and down the other of what he presumes to be his farm accounts.

This is his farming, the remnant of habit and fascination from his life's work, which he claims he has died out of now, all except his mind. He relishes his ciphering. The figures come into his mind smelling of barns and grain bins and tobacco and livestock. His figures grunt and bleat and bray and bawl. This is the passion that has worn him out, and made him old, and is still a passion. As he labors over it, the notebook becomes as substantial in his hands as a loaded shovel.

Scratching and stabbing with the pencil, he makes a column of figures representing his guesses as to what his earnings have been since the first of the year, and his predictions of what he will have earned by the year's end. Beside that column he makes another, guessing and predicting his expenses. He adds both columns, and subtracts expenses from earnings. If the margin of profit strikes him as too small he begins again, and repeats the operation, increasing the earnings and economizing on the expenses, until he comes up with a figure that suits him. The next night he does the same thing, disregarding all the figures he has already made. And then, while they make their weekly drive out to the farm, he reads off his latest figures to Wheeler.

"No, Jack," Wheeler says. "You can't make that much."

And then they have an argument. Old Jack argues. And then Wheeler argues. And when Wheeler stops the car in front of the barn they both figure in the notebook.

"Lord no!" Wheeler says.

It is an argument that neither of them ever wins. Jack never admits that he has lost, but he can never bring himself to think that Wheeler has lost, either—not for a minute. What he does believe, what he keeps very firm in his mind, is that between him and Wheeler it does not matter who wins, which is to say that between them the idea of winning is not a very important idea. As a matter of fact, nothing would trouble him more than to beat Wheeler in an argument.

"Well, then, Wheeler," he says to mend their dispute, "I reckon we're going broke then."

Wheeler laughs. "No we're not, Jack. We're going to do fine. Don't you worry."

Old Jack slaps his hand down onto Wheeler's knee. "You're all right, son."

To tell the truth, Old Jack loves Wheeler as much as he would have loved his own son if he had ever had one—maybe more. Loves him stubbornly and strictly by his own rules, but devotedly and generously nevertheless. He has been seen more than once sitting on the back bench of a courtroom, grinning and crying shamelessly as a child while Wheeler makes his closing speech to the jury.

"Listen to that boy," he says. "He's a shotgun. Lordy lord."

The Grass May Grow a Mile

The room was Virgil's. It was hers and Virgil's. Now it is hers.

But not hers. And this house is not hers.

When she and Virgil married they came here to live—a short time, they thought, until their own house would be built. They had made their plans.

And then, soon, Virgil was called into the war. Both her parents were dead. She stayed on, to wait.

"They want you to stay here," Virgil told her. "And I do."

"You're welcome here. You know you are," Margaret and Mat told her.

She knew she was. She could not have refused them if she had wanted to.

Margaret and Mat made her welcome. They did all that was possible to make it easy for her to be there. She stayed, feeling that she belonged because Virgil belonged.

In the still room, Virgil's and hers, not hers, she lies in bed, looking up into the dark. She is not sleepy yet. With the bigness of her pregnancy she is uncomfortable any way she lies. It will be difficult to sleep.

Below her own window she can see the elongated shape of the living-room window printed in yellow light on the yard. Mat is still down there. At this time on most nights they would all still be there in the living room, still talking. Now, divided in separate rooms, they have made themselves lonely—to think alone, as now they must.

Virgil was gone more than a year and a half, and then, in the last summer, he came home for two weeks. He had to leave again. For her, that short time of his presence was nearly as painful as his absence. It began nothing, ended nothing—a brief touching, an interruption of his absence, in which there seemed little to be said, nothing to be planned—a troubled bearing of the nearness of his departure. She loved him; she would be with him a few days; she would live beyond them, as she would have to, remembering them. A certain amount of happiness was possible for a little while; she would see to it that he knew nothing but her happiness. After that she would wait again. It was simple enough. She would do what she had to do. Wait. She had learned to do that.

"I'm getting better at it every day," she told Virgil. "I'm a champion waiter."

"You're a champion waitress," Virgil said.

She never wasted a chance to smile. And it seemed to her that there was a finer reality in her bogus happiness than in her sorrow. It was a gift to Virgil—what she could give him; she kept him from knowing what it cost her. And, curiously, this bogus happiness became the source of a real happiness—fugitive and small, but triumphant in a way, and precious to her.

One afternoon, two days before he had to go, they filled a picnic basket and walked out across the ridges in the direction of the river. They stopped on the point of the farthest ridge. At the end of a long gentle slope, the ground tilted upward again and made a small grass-covered knoll over the woods on the bluff. From there they could see the bottoms in the long bend of the river, and for miles on either side of them the valley lay open and broad.

They stood together at the top of the knoll, looking.

"This would be a fine place for a house," Virgil said. "What do you think?"

"Yes. The loveliest place."

"Then right here is where I'm going to build you a house."

"Build *us* a house."

"I'll build you a house. And then you can give me back half of it. If you want to."

She laughed. She still remembers the sound of her laughter. "Yes. I want to. I'll give you all of it. And you can give me all of it."

"And that's the way it'll be. We'll give this house to each other. We'll pass it back and forth, like a kiss."

"After the war?"

"After the war. And now too."

He picked up a flat rock and laid it down on the center of the knoll. "There's the front doorstep."

He found more stones, and, pacing out the dimensions, marked the boundaries of an ample house, its rooms and doors.

Watching him as he moved back and forth in the imagined courses of walls, she was happy. She was happier than she remembered being. Beyond his absence, it began. She could see it.

He finished his design, and stood in the middle of it, smiling, looking at her.

"Come in."

She came in.

They gathered wood and built a fire. A little later they spread their picnic and ate. Afterward, while the fire burned, they sat on in the light of it, talking. At dark a soft wind had got up; it made sound now in the woods below them.

When Virgil was a child, he told her, Mat took him and Bess out to where he was having a new barn built; they had wanted to watch the carpenters, and pestered Mat until he let them come along. The framing of the barn had been completed, but the roof and the siding still had to be put on. They stayed through the afternoon, playing with wood scraps and watching the carpenters. And then, shortly before quitting time, it began to rain. Mat came hunting them and, taking their hands, hurried them inside the barn.

"Let's get in out of the wet."

And he brought them in, and stood there, his face extravagantly serious, while the rain poured down on them between the open rafters.

"Daddy, we're getting wet," Bess kept saying. She would look up at him, her eyes begging, pointing down at the wetness of her dress.

Mat looked down at her. His hat brim had filled with water, and when he tilted his head it poured down like a veil in front of his face. "It's lucky we got this barn built in time," he told her. "We'd have drowned if it hadn't been here."

And then they had to give in to his joke and laugh. They stood there in the warm rain, holding hands, laughing, until the shower went by.

Now, as by some return of that free joyfulness, he had made this house that was no house, and had given it to her. It was no house that was their house. Strangely, it had made them glad. After what had been their estrangement—in the seeming futility of talking or hoping, in the nearness of Virgil's departure—their desiring of this house was like a bet made, making the thought of winning possible. In this house that was the hope of house they gambled toward what might be.

Hannah was happy. Her sadness that he would leave again was still in her, and was not changed. But also she was happy, and now her happiness seemed to her to exist apart from her sadness, and to be as great.

As the fire burned out the dark grew. Hannah gave herself into the possession of this house of theirs. There, in the dark, away from the other house where she had spent her waiting, its walls were nearly real. It made a new belonging imaginable. The fire had opened a space of light which was the space of a house—which remained, though the fire had not. Her house was as near her as his hands touching her, the weight of him.

In his absence their child grew in her. She no longer felt herself to be waiting, sorrowful and mute, on the edge of Virgil's absence. Her body seemed to turn around a new center. The thought of Virgil's coming back enclosed her and she enclosed his child. Everything leaned inward around the child, the beginning, in her, of both their lives.

But now she is afraid.

How long?

The grass may grow a mile in the imagined boundaries of their house.

Images Like Seeds

Company gone, Mat stayed on in the living room, smoking and reading the paper. He heard Margaret and Hannah first talking in the kitchen and then stirring around, preparing for bed. Now the house is quiet. He folds the newspaper, moves over to his desk, and turns on the lamp. He takes a sheet of white letter paper out of one of the drawers, and searches among the pigeonholes until he finds a packet of photographs.

The last letter from Virgil asked for pictures of Port William and the house and the farm. He was forgetting what they looked like.

On the Sunday after Virgil's letter came, Mat and Hannah spent the afternoon taking the pictures. They made an excursion of it, driving and walking here and there in the town and on the farm, deciding what Virgil would want to see, pleased to be doing what he had asked.

Mat takes the photographs out of the envelope and lays them separately on the desk, making an orderly arrangement of them.

The first was taken from the walk in front of the house, looking down the street into the town. To the right of the picture Old Jack is on his way up the street to the hotel.

"Stand still, Mr. Beechum," Hannah called. "We want to take a picture for Virgil."

"Good God," Old Jack said. "He don't want to look at me." But he stood still and let them take the picture.

Looking backward from the same place on the walk, there is a picture of the house, the maple branches and their shadows brittle and clear against the white front.

By the time Hannah had taken this second picture and wound the camera, Old Jack had crossed the street. He walked up to Hannah and laid his hand on her shoulder and patted her.

"You get in it yourself, honey, and let Mat work the machine. What he wants to see is you." Old Jack waited to make sure she had understood. And then he smiled. "You're a pretty thing. If I was way off over yonder I'd want to see you."

And so Mat took the camera and Hannah stood on the porch steps and smiled for Virgil and Old Jack, and they took the picture again with her in it.

There are the photographs, arranged now on the desk, making a departure from the town and a return to it. Out of his remembering and knowing Virgil would be able to give them colors, movements, sounds, odors, histories. In his mind these small images would grow like planted seeds, become heavy in their dimensional depths, sizes, brightnesses.

Missing. From among these things.

Mat gathers the photographs and puts them back in their envelope. The sheet of paper lies on the blotter, filled with bright light. He picks up his pen. He writes the date. He writes "Dear Virgil." But then he lays the pen down and leans back.

My dear boy, today we have had grievous news.

For several minutes this sentence shapes and reshapes itself in his mind—the compulsion and limit of what he is able to think. The words form, particularizing his fear and grief as on a point, and then dissolve into the whiteness of the page.

My boy. We have had grievous news.

He puts the photographs and writing things away. He gets his hat and coat from the rack in the hall, and turns out the lights.

He leaves the house and starts down into town. A light is on in Old Jack's room at the hotel, the only one he can see still burning. While Mat is looking, the old man walks out into the center of the room, undressed except for his cap and underwear. He stops and stands still a minute, facing the window, leaning on his cane, scratching the back of his head. And then he moves out of the frame of the window and turns off the light.

Now all that part of the street is dark. No stars are out. It is clouding up again.

Waiting

Margaret sits by her window in the dark.

She has unpinned her hair, and is brushing it with slow long strokes. Her hair falls dark over the shoulders of her gown.

Mat has gone out. The house is quiet and dark.

She brushes her hair, gathers it, and, drawing it over her shoulder, braids it in a heavy braid.

With the day's last possible task finished, she sits quietly, overhearing, as if deep in her body, the sounds of outcry and of weeping. She expected this. She knows it has gone on through all the afternoon and evening, and only now she has become still enough to hear.

The house fills and brims with its quiet.

The brush lies in her lap. She rocks slowly in the chair. The rockers make a quiet creaking and tapping on the floor.

Her eyes have become used to the dark. Her gown, the white pillows on the bed, the white closed fronts of the buildings down along the street draw a little light now and are pale.

In the quiet of the house she waits, as though, divided from Virgil by half the world, she might hear him breathe.

Her waiting seems not so strange to her. She waited, after his birth, to hear him cry. She has waited, even in her sleep, to hear him wake. Here, in this house, she has waited for him to come back from a thousand departures.

He was born out of her body into this absence.

She will hear every footstep, the opening of every door.

4

The Barber's Calling

Jayber Crow mostly grew up and went through high school in a church orphanage called The Good Shepherd.

It was there, as the school barber's flunky and understudy, that he learned barbering, although at that time he had no thought of making his living by it; it was simply a duty, assigned him by the superintendent, to permit him to earn a part of his keep. He was, to the frustration and annoyance of his teachers at The Good Shepherd, both bright and utterly careless as a student. After he learned to read he would customarily read his textbooks, or read all that interested him in them, within two or three weeks after they were given to him, and after that he refused to open them again. He read everything he could lay his hands on; by the time he left The Good Shepherd he had read and reread the meager supply of readable books to be had there. He managed, by the random force of his curiosity, to learn a good deal, and most of the time there was enough coincidence between what he learned and what he was expected to learn to allow him to make passing grades.

He was vastly more inclined to learn than to be taught; that made him the natural enemy of his teachers, and he suffered for it. He came away from The Good Shepherd, he said, bearing more marks of scholarly discipline on his tail, by a considerable margin, than his teachers had ever been able to imprint on his mind.

In his last year of high school he decided to become a minister of the church that had raised him. Whether this was because of some feeling of obligation, or some vague wish to do good, or what, he no longer is sure. After the later failure of his motive, he was unable to be certain what it had been.

He was given a scholarship to a small college run by the church, and spent nearly three years there, waiting tables in the women's dining hall, and continuing to be a recklessly bright and unsatisfactory student. But the college had a better library than the orphanage, and he made good use of that. In his third year, by a sort of boiling over of his intelligence, he began to question the theological assumptions of his professors, and then his own. In the spring of his third year he resigned his scholarship, and said he was sorry.

He thought then that he might make a teacher of himself. He worked in a barbershop to pay his way through a year and a half of classes at the state university. After the religious confinements of the orphanage and the college and his pastoral ambition, his freedom in the university town excited him, and he began a careful exploitation of it. He divided his free time between the library of the university and the bars and brothels of the town—not anymore by his old recklessness, but by a strict husbanding of his time and money. By carefulness, he discovered, he could do pretty much as he pleased, and among other things he pleased to do more studying than was required of him. He became, for the first time, systematic and competent as a student. His grades improved. During that time he was quiet and deliberate; his extravagances were as methodical as his cautions; most of the time he was alone. For a while it seemed to him that he was satisfied with himself. He was managing to save a little money.

But he failed again, as if the failure of his first ambition infected his second. It was the same failure of certainty and of purpose. He was utterly free. It was, he believed more and more, the freedom of being on his way from nowhere to nowhere. It was often a depressing and lonely freedom. His leaving the church college had cancelled all but his earliest beginnings. His year and a half at the university had failed to offer an imaginable future. Sometimes he half believed that, having been born by nobody's intention, and brought up as a mistake by public duty, he had come finally into his fated inheritance, the failure of all purpose. He had made no friends. He owed nothing to anybody. He became more and more depressed under the burden of his freedom.

He left, less because he wanted to leave than because he no longer wanted to stay. He packed his clothes and books into a box, paid his rent, and put the rest of his savings into the lining of his jacket and his shoe. The simplicity of it startled him. In ten minutes he had cancelled out a year and a half. When he ate breakfast he was on his way out of town.

Three mornings later, having walked the better part of the way, wandering the backroads to circumvent the waters of the great flood of 1937, he arrived in Port William, near which he had been born and had lived his earliest years. The town's most recent barber had left. Using his savings as a down payment, Jayber bought the shop. He slept that first night in the barber chair, half freezing, his head drawn like a terrapin's into the collar of his voluminous raincoat. In two days he was in business. The question if this was the fortune he had come in search of passed out of his mind; barbering suited him well enough, and would support him—if enough hair would grow in Port William, and when he looked over the prospects he figured enough might. His given name was Jonah; he signed himself J. Crow; the town christened him Jaybird, and then Jayber.

His barbershop, which is both his place of business and his home, is a tiny frame building in the swale of the branch. The shop has two stories, a single small room in each. The downstairs room is the shop, walled with white-painted bare boards, the floor polished by the tramping underfoot of the shorn hair of generations; it smells of hair, hair tonic, shaving lotion, mug soap, and tobacco smoke. In the center of the floor there is a rusty stove, which serves in winter as a source of heat and a spittoon, and in summer as a spittoon and a foot-prop. The barber chair is placed near the door in front of a long mirror; beneath the mirror a board shelf bears an assortment of bottles of tonic and lotion, a whetstone, a large ornamented shaving mug and brush, an array of scissors and razors and combs, a cigar box containing the cash proceeds of the day. On a table at the end of the shelf a metal water container with a faucet perches on a two-burner coal-oil stove. In the open spaces along the walls are maybe a dozen ill-matching chairs. Jayber rarely has so many customers as he has chairs, but the shop is also a loafing and talking place, a sort of living room, for the townsmen, and for Jayber himself. In any assemblage at any time there will be more of what Jayber calls "members" than there will be customers. Around the walls are a number of calendars of various years, none turned past its respective January. And hanging here and there from nails driven in at random, there are Indian relics, hornets' nests, extra big stalks of tobacco or ears of corn that the farmers have brought in. Anything found or plowed up in the town or the neighborhood that might be classed as odd or interesting, and that conceivably could serve as a subject of conversation, is apt sooner or later to wind up hanging from a nail in Jayber's shop—and will be duly examined and talked about and forgot and left hanging. Over the years the shop has become a kind of museum in which the town has put down what it thought about.

The upstairs room, reached by a stairway up the side of the building, is as private as the lower one is public. Jayber has managed to cram all the essentials of his life into it: bed, books, table, chair, dresser, kitchen cabinet, cookstove. Few in Port William have ever been there, and those only rarely—not that Jayber makes any particular attempt at privacy, but there is seldom an occasion or reason for anyone to come there. The shop is his living room and guest room, to which most of the men of the town consider they have a standing invitation. To eat or sleep or read he goes upstairs and is alone. To work, or for company, he goes down and opens the shop. He keeps no regular hours. His shop may be closed for three days at a stretch, or open any hour of the night.

He has continued to be a student of sorts, as far as short funds and few books and erratic habits have permitted. He is likely to know something, if not a good deal, about anything—and likely to have to be asked before he will tell what he knows. He has come to a few friendships, all of them made and kept in the public atmosphere and easy talking of the shop. At one time or another, in one way or another, he has befriended nearly everybody he knows. There is an offhand goodness in him that has made him welcome among the men of the town. They know him for good company and a good talker. They take for granted that talking is as much his business as hair-cutting—at any rate, none of them ever feels obliged to get his hair cut to justify his presence in the shop. When Jayber finishes with a customer and asks "Who's next?" he is as likely as not to find that nobody is, and then he will climb into the chair himself, and, if no new customer comes in, talk half a day. He practices—sometimes willingly, sometimes by the sufferance of impositions on his good nature—a kind of poor man's philanthropy. He lends considerably more money than he ever has the heart to collect, and is apt at Christmas to play Santa Claus, secretly, to the children of the ones who owe him most. His shop is occasionally used as a roost by husbands and sons too drunk to go home. Now and then he puts in a weekend drinking and wenching down in Hargrave, and he makes no apologies. He is seldom invited into the domestic life of Port William; he knows it by its manhood and boyhood passing in and out the door of his shop.

Talk

After he ate supper Jayber had a smoke, and then unloaded his table and washed his dishes and put them away. He took his time. Working or loafing, his life is mostly public. Privacy is his luxury—his chance to be quiet, to pay a little attention to what may be going on inside his head. He did not come back downstairs until he remembered that the fire would be getting low.

When he opened the shop nobody was waiting for him. He sat down in the barber chair and leaned it back and crossed his ankles over the foot rest. And then remembered the fire again, and got up and fixed it, and sat back down. He came into the shop while most of the town was still at supper, and now he hears things beginning to stir again: doors slam here and there, a car engine starts and goes out of hearing over the rise—footsteps, two single sets and then a pair, come down the street, past the door—two or three doors up the street a boy's voice calls *"Here, Mike!"* The boy waits and whistles and calls again. It has been dark nearly an hour.

Jayber sits up and takes another smoke, wishing somebody would come in. Three times a day, morning and noon and after supper, the town starts up out of a silence and begins again. These are the times he finds it most difficult to be alone. There is an impulse in him, these times, to close the shop and go out and talk a while with anybody he may meet, take up with anybody who may be coming by, and go with him wherever he may be going. His absences from the town always begin with this impulse.

But now Uncle Stanley Gibbs comes through the door. This is the third time since morning that Uncle Stanley has been in. As a general rule the old man does not come to the shop except to get a haircut, but he got one just three or four days ago, and so Jayber supposes he must have something in particular on his mind. On his two previous trips the shop was crowded, and he seemed satisfied and even a little relieved just to sit down and pretend to be listening while the others talked. Both times he got uncomfortable after a few minutes and, muttering industriously to himself, throwing out the pretense that he was having an awfully busy day, hustled up the street toward the church.

He has pushed the door open, but is still standing out on the sidewalk. In his old age he has grown into the habit of doing only one thing at a time. He would not talk and scratch or look and walk at the same time to save his soul. Now that he has opened the door, he glimpses in, peeping up at Jayber and then around at all the empty chairs and then back at Jayber. His collapsed bristly old face is set in its normal expression of outrage that the world does not make enough noise. When he walks from his house over to the church—footing the white line down the middle of the road—he is always seeing shoot out in front of him automobiles and trucks and buses he never heard coming. He knows, he says himself, that he could burn up in his house any night while his neighbors all stand at the door yelling "Fire." And hard to tell how many times he has been insulted right to his face and not known it. Hour after hour the world pours itself into his deafness like a high waterfall that turns to mist before it can strike and make a sound. His face, by habit, wears his furiousness—not in response to anything in particular, but just in case something or somebody may be taking advantage of him.

Uncle Stanley stayed young a long time. He was wild as a bear, he claims, and stout as a mule and bad around the women. He has remembered himself a good deal worse than he ever was, but this "memory" of his wildness is a comfort to him.

In his prime he had a sort of local fame as a curser. The economy of his vocabulary, and the dexterity and versatility of his use of it, were remarkable. He could talk for thirty minutes without saying a word fit for the hearing of a woman or a child. They called him Stanley Ay-God By-God Gibbs.

His first vice, his professed badness with the women, was cured by time. He wore it out and discarded it—or was worn out and discarded by it; and lived beyond it, and kept the overhauled memory of it for stock in trade during his retirement.

And his vocabulary was completely renovated in collaboration with Brother Preston soon after he was hired by the church to be janitor and grave digger. Since then the only thing that has broken him loose from righteousness and sent him climbing back up into the upper ranges of his old eloquence was the news that his grandson Billy, Grover's boy, had become the pilot of a four-engined airplane. And he has continued to need all the words he knows to express his appreciation of *that* glory.

He pushes the door wider open with the point of his cane, and then grabs the doorjamb with his free hand and climbs into the shop.

"What do you know, Uncle Stanley?"

Uncle Stanley cannot possibly have heard, but according to his theory of social procedure, this is the time for a greeting to be offered and accepted. He bites into the air four or five times as though pumping himself up. And then he yells back, at the top of his voice, and as pathetically and sickly as possible at that volume:

"Fair to middling, Jayber, by golly. But, by dab, *ain't* it been a awful winter?"

Jayber's first inclination is to kick the chair around and help himself to the comfort of a private grin. But remembering that the mirror is behind him, he wipes his own face straight with the back of his hand, and waits. The old man has said exactly what Jayber and nearly everybody else in Port William could have predicted last week that he would say, for the second article of his theory holds that all greetings surely must take the form of a question about his health. But the townsmen, who know his theory, take pains to avoid the question, knowing he will answer it anyhow. With the exception of Brother Preston and two or three helplessly well-intentioned female members of the church, it has been ten years since anybody asked Uncle Stanley how he feels.

Now that the greeting is done with, he removes his grin and sits down. He looks up at Jayber out of the bristling of his whiskers and eyebrows, and bites off some more air.

"*Yes*sir, by golly, it's been a hard winter. It's been *hard* on the old bugger, by golly. I was just telling the madam here the other night, by dab, I believe it's weakened me. I believe it's aged me."

Jayber lets himself laugh now, and says loudly, "It's not the cold that's getting you down, Uncle Stanley. You've just been too active at night for an old buck."

That's flattery. Uncle Stanley grins. His mouth draws open like a rubber band; you could loop the corners of it over his ears.

"Aw-aw now, Jayber, that time's done gone." But he shakes his head, and then nods. "I've seen the time, though. I call back forty, fifty years, I could work all day, by juckers, and wench like a tomcat *all* night." He laughs in sincere admiration. "With the best of them. By grab, I didn't know what a night's sleep was. When I heard the roosters crow I just come home and et breakfast and went to work. But not anymore. It's done gone by."

"I can't believe that, Uncle Stan. Some of them told me they hear you romp and stomp and bellow like a bull all hours of the night."

"Naw. Too late for that, Jayber. If I *was* still able to bother any women it wouldn't be the madam. When Grover was born that about fixed it between me and her. Said all that foolishness might be a pleasure to me, but wasn't nothing but suffering and trouble to her. Said, by grab, I could just sleep in the back room. By juckers, I've put up with her all these years for her conversation. And can't hear what she says a third of the time. *Hard* on a man! By dab by grab."

Mrs. Gibbs is a stout member of the Port William church and sings in the front row of the choir. She was the only one of the congregation who voted outright against hiring Uncle Stanley to be janitor. For maybe forty years nobody has seen the two of them together in public. If Uncle Stanley is sitting out on the front porch, Miss Pauline will be sitting on the back porch. She keeps house for him and cooks his meals and sits down at the table with him, but only because it's her "duty as a Christian," not because she wants to. Otherwise they live like strangers who happen to have rooms in the same hotel. She has forced Uncle Stanley to live behind her back, and he probably forced her to force him, and she probably forced him to force her to force him, and so on and so on; it's just as well to accuse time and the world and Port William, which are also, and just as uncertainly, to blame. Since the first few years of it, the marriage of Uncle Stanley and Miss Pauline has been an armistice, likely to break into hostilities any minute. Neither of them makes any bones about it. Whenever the question of increasing Uncle Stanley's wages or of giving him a little "token" at Christmas is put to a vote before the congregation, Miss Pauline votes against it. And Uncle Stanley is apt to publicize, in the normal course of his conversation, at the top of his voice, anything from the trouble Miss Pauline is having with her bowels to the events of their wedding night.

Once the old man gets started there is no telling when or where he will stop. As long as he is doing all the talking he is certain, for a change, what the conversation is about, and he aims to make it worth his trouble. Jayber listens to him, usually, with a growing sense of guilt and alarm. If there was anybody else in the shop it would be mostly funny, but always when he is the only one in the audience Jayber feels himself helplessly implicated in what the old man is saying. He never intends to get him started. He will be carrying on what seems a harmless conversation, with the best intentions in the world, and then all of a sudden Uncle Stanley will have taken off into some outrageous confession—not just spoken, published. And Jayber feels like somebody who intended to light a cigarette and set the town on fire. The old man has no secrets, no concern for privacy, no wish for dignity, no notion of responsibility that might stop him or make him lower his voice. It is not that Jayber fails to be amused and even tickled at what he says, and not that any particular thing he says is not in one way or another more amusing than disturbing; but running along with the amusement is the nearly terrifying certainty that there is no limit to what he might say, or would say if he knew how. Once that awful mouth of his loosens up and starts running, anything is possible. Nothing has any value except conversational. Nothing is worth anything except as it maintains the sound of his own voice bubbling up into the silence of the world. Listening to him, Jayber sometimes thinks that the words don't come out of his mouth, but disappear into it. That mouth is an abyss that the whole world and the planets and stars might be sucked into and vanish forever. He can be heard distinctly, in calm weather, fifty or seventy-five yards in all directions, advertising at a shout the failure of everything to mean anything.

In the face of Uncle Stanley's devouring garrulousness, as confirmed and free a bachelor as he is, Jayber always finds himself taking up the defense of marriage. Not so much the defense of any particular marriage—not, by a long shot, of Uncle Stanley's—but of marriage itself, of what has come to be, for him, a kind of last-ditch holy of holies: the possibility that two people might care for each other and know each other better than enemies, and better than strangers happening to be alive at the same time in the same town; and that, with a man and a woman, this caring and knowing might be made by intention, and in the consciousness of all it is, and of all it might be, and of all that threatens it. At these times it seems to Jayber that, of all the men in Port William, he's the most married—not in marriage, but to this ideal of marriage. He is bound in this way, as he is bound, beyond his friendships and his friends, to an ideal of friendship.

These are the last remainders of Jayber's ideals. He holds to them against the possibility that life will mean nothing and be worth nothing. He is a despairing believer in these things, knowing that everything fails. The ideal rides ahead of the real, renewing beyond it, perishing in it—unreachable, surely, but made new over and over again just by hope and by the passage of time; what has not yet failed remains possible. And the ideal, remaining undiminished and perfect, out of reach, makes possible a judgment of failure, and a just grief and sympathy.

In Port William, or beyond it or above it, Jayber imagines a kind of Heavenly City, in which each house would be built in a marriage and around it, and all the houses would be bound together in friendships, and friendliness would move and join among them like an open street. His living in Port William has been a bearing of the descent of the town from that ideal—as though at the end of each night, out of his mind and his desire, he gives painful birth to the new real morning and the real town—as though he watches the descent of all things from Heaven, like a snowfall, into the aimless gap of Uncle Stanley's mouth. But he is also the adulterer of his marriage, the servant of opposite houses, faithful to both and unfaithful to both—slipping away from his Heavenly City, to which he has sworn his devotion, to become the lover of all the perishing lights and substances of Port William and of the weather over it and of the water under it. After so long, it seems to him that he is the native and occupant of both places, and passes freely between them, and in serving either serves both.

A New Calling

Tonight Jayber has ceased to listen to Uncle Stanley. He sits looking out into the dark street and at the light in Milton Burgess's store, letting his mind run. Out of kindness, he pretends to be listening, nodding his head now and then in a movement he intends to be ambiguous, but which he knows Uncle Stanley will take for encouragement.

The old man runs down finally, and Jayber lets him be quiet a few seconds to make sure. Then, with his voice carefully noncommittal, he says:

"Well."

"Says, which?"

"Well!"

"Yessir!" Uncle Stanley says.

He's quiet for nearly a minute, and Jayber sees that he is getting down to his business, whatever it is. He looks out the window, slowly opening and shutting his mouth, thinking over what he has to say. When he turns back, he prods Jayber's shin with the point of the cane and says, "I've got a proposition for you, Jayber. I've been trying to get a chance to talk to you all day."

"What's on your mind, Uncle Stanley?"

"Well, I got a job to offer you. Keeping care of the graveyard. Preacher told me to find somebody to do it."

"You mean dig the graves?"

"Well, that's part of it."

"About all of it, ain't it?"

"Well, some of the time. But in the summer you've got to cut the grass. And ain't so many dies in the summertime. In the winter just about all of it's digging the graves. Mud, or ground froze hard as a bull's horn, by grab, and every kind of weather, and ain't hardly enough pay to make it worth the trouble. But it's a job, and there's a little money to it, and every little bit helps if you want to look at it that way. I quit looking at it that way. And, by grab, I quit, I did."

"How come you've quit?"

"How's that?"

"What did you *quit* for?"

"*Why* now, by gob, preacher and that undertaker come up day before yesterday wanting me to go out there by myself in that rain and dig two graves in one day. I says, 'By grab, I won't do it. I'm too old. I *can't* do it. All I can do to dig *one* grave in a day.' 'Well now,' preacher says, 'Mr. Gibbs, perhaps you ought to try.' 'Try nothing,' I says, I did. 'You look at that ground out there. That ground's so wet you could dig a grave with a bucket as quick as you could dig one with a shovel. That's a job of work. I reckon you don't know a job of work. But I do. Because I've *done* several.' 'Well,' preacher says, 'what are we going to do?' '*Do?*' I says. 'We're going to get somebody to help me dig them graves or they ain't going to get dug, and you can just keep them corpses until I get around to 'em, that's what we're going to do.' 'Mr. Gibbs,' he says, 'you was *hired* to dig them graves.' Made me mad, he did. I says, 'Now look a here, they've set around here for six weeks in a row and ain't a one of them died, and now here two of them ups and dies in one day. It ain't right, and I quit.'"

"Did you dig the graves?"

"Well, I dug one of them two. Preacher got them big old boys of Siler Smith's to dig the other one. By grab, you ought to seen it. Them big old idiots wallowing and tromping around in that mud. They'd dig out a little hole and it'd cave in on them; and they'd throw out a shovelful of mud and a shovelful would run back in. And them a fighting it like killing snakes and cussing till you'd a thought they'd a woke up everybody there. Even I could hear them. I got mine dug and went home about the middle of the afternoon, and they'd just got theirs down about waist deep. Some of them said the preacher and that undertaker finally had to come in to help them, and they was all out there with a lantern still digging when midnight come."

Uncle Stanley has to stop and laugh.

"Well, they dug a pond, shaped sort of like a funnel. I know just how it happened because I made the same mistake myself when I was new at the work. When you dig one of them holes in the mud, if you don't be careful about tramping around the edges of it, and don't watch what you're doing when you cut down the sides, to do it just so, well it'll widen out at the top quicker than you can deepen it at the bottom. When the preacher and the undertaker and them boys got done gaum-ing around in it and tramping around it and falling into it and climbing out of it, that grave must have been eight foot wide. And tracked and tramped and muddied around the edges till it looked like where a sow'd had pigs. They throwed the dirt out on the downhill side because it was easier, and it rained a hard one before daylight, and there wasn't nothing to keep half the hillside from draining right into the hole, and she filled plumb to the brim. That undertaker was there half the morning unrol-ling that imitation grass of hisn, trying to make a kind of shore to it, so the family and friends of Mrs. Brewster wouldn't notice they was attend-ing one of them naval burials. He let on he didn't see me coming, on account of the words I'd had with him and the preacher the morning before, but I walked right up like the sun was shining and we was the only friends each other had. 'Well,' I says, 'the Jordan's running a little muddy this morning, ain't she?' He went right on about his work like he never heard me. I says, 'Is this going to be a baptizing or a funeral?' He tried not to say anything, but I see it coming up in him, and finally he had to let it out. 'You'd look a damn sight better with your mouth shut,' he says. 'I'm just here waiting for the boat,' I says. And then I let up on him and give him a hand. We bailed out the hole, but the rain wouldn't quit, and it was filling up again.

"Well, Grover come down by the house after the funeral, and he said in spite of all the talk and flowers and artificial grass it still looked more like a boat launching than a burial. 'You've heard of crossing to Jordan's other shore,' I says. 'Well,' he says, 'if that's how it's done, Mrs. Brew-ster's on her way. Go look.' I put on my coat and went up. That under-taker had just bundled all his muddy grass and trappings into the hearse and gone back, and nobody was left in the graveyard but the preacher. He was standing there in the rain with his hands in his pockets watching Mrs. Brewster's coffin. It was floating just as dandy as you ever seen. He was as glad to see me as if we was both preachers. It showed all over his face. He thought I'd just walk up and pull out a plug or something, and everything would be fine. But I knew it wasn't no simple matter, and I wanted him to know it, so I just happened up to the edge of the grave like a casual bystander and took a long look. I says, 'Well, well, well, you've got a right smart little problem here.' I says *you*. He looked across at me like I was an angel fresh out of Heaven. '*What*'re we going to do, Mr. Gibbs?' he says. He says *we*, so I taken it up. 'Well,' I says, 'we could catch her and tie her up until the water goes down. Or,' I says, 'if it don't go down, we could load her with rocks and try to sink her.' And right there's when the wobbling shaft jumped off of the bobbling pin. It come a little closer to him than I meant it to, to tell you the truth. He'd got his mind all made up to hire me back, I seen that. But I'd done ruined it and made him mad, and I swear to you, Jayber, I done it more or less by accident. But there wasn't no undoing it, and I just had to stand there and watch him swell up. He was mad enough to drown me and bury me right in the same water hole with Mrs. Brewster, but he didn't want to be ill-mannerly. I thought he'd bust. I says to myself, 'Now you're going to hear it.' Because if I ever seen a thirty-minute cuss piling up in a man I seen it then. But finally he says, just as even and quiet: 'Mr. Gibbs, after you get done filling these here two graves, perhaps you can find someone else to take your job.'

"It wasn't that I hated to lose the work and the little dab of pay I was drawing out of it, but I did hate to end on hard feelings. So I said very friendly: 'Well now, Preacher, it won't be easy, because you don't find a man that can dig a grave just anywhere you look. There's sleights to every trade, Preacher,' I says, 'by grab, and there's sleights to this one. You and that undertaker, now you all thought poor old Uncle Stanley didn't have no more brains than it took to bend his back, and that he'd been doing this work all these years without learning anything about it. But now you all can see from this here mess that it takes considerable know-how to do the job the way it ought to be done. Now it's a job that ain't going to be easy to fill, but I'll look around, Preacher, and I'll find you a good man. And no hard feelings.'

"But he never softened. 'Thank you very much, Mr. Gibbs,' he says, 'by grab, I'll appreciate it if you'll find someone right away.' I says, 'Now Preacher, there'll be some things he won't understand how to do right off, but I'll stay around with him and oversee his work and learn him how to do a good job for you. And no hard feelings, by grab,' I says.

"'That'll be perfectly fine, Mr. Gibbs,' he says. 'Well,' I says, 'do you want him to keep care of the church too, or just the graveyard?' 'Just the graveyard, for now, will be all right,' he says.

"So I've been studying about it, Jayber, and I figured you was the only one with enough brains and time that could use the money. The work's hard, but it ain't what you'd call steady. Sometimes *every*body'll be alive for three or four months in a row."

"What did you do about Mrs. Brewster?" Jayber asks.

"Aw, me and them old boys of Siler Smith's, we bailed the water out again and rolled in a few mudballs.

"Well, what about it, Jayber? You want to take this job? I've got to find somebody. You was the first one I thought of and I thought you might appreciate it."

"Are you sure the preacher won't hire you back, Uncle Stanley? Don't you reckon he'll change his mind if you go and ask?"

"Aw now, Jayber. *He* won't. I done tested him out. Well, to tell you the truth, I *did* go ask him, by grab. I went to his house last night, and I asked him. I even told him the madam wanted me to have the job again. But he said he'd just stick to the understanding we'd worked out.

"Anyhow, Jayber, I'm too old to do it much longer. It's just getting more than I can do."

"Why, Uncle Stanley, you just said you dug a grave by yourself in half the time it took the Smith boys and the preacher and the undertaker to dig one."

"Aw, I can still dig them all right, Jayber, ain't no worry about that. But I'm getting so derned old that when I get one dug I can't hardly get out of it."

The old man falls quiet, and confusion crosses his face like a shadow.

"Let me think," Jayber says.

"Says *which?*"

"Let me *think!*"

Uncle Stanley perks up and keeps watch while Jayber thinks.

The idea of extra money is foreign to Jayber's way of life. For a minute he doesn't know what in the world he would do with it. But he knows that in the back of his mind there has been, not exactly troubling him, but asking for his attention, the question of what he'll do with his old age. He has been a little uneasily on the lookout for an ending to his life. Until now he has silenced the question with the reply that he will just barber right on through to the end. But now, for the first time, here is another possibility.

Jayber would like to fish. He would like to become a fisherman. Suddenly and surprisingly the whole vision blooms before him. It becomes imaginable and desirable and even possible in a single stroke. Put a little money aside every week, and before too many years he could build a small house on the river bank. The land would not cost much, would be practically worthless except for such a use as he would have for it, and he would build the house himself out of used lumber. He would stay there and fish and be quiet until the end of his days. He would cease being a public man and become a private man. He would fish in the river as though that was the highest calling that had ever come to a man. And he would fish in his mind. He would have a boat—he could see it, painted green, floating lightly as a leaf among the willows at the foot of the bank.

"I'll tell you what, Uncle Stanley. I'll take the job. And then I want to hire you to stay on as supervisor. I'll do the work and you can furnish the know-how, and we'll split the money."

"And now," he says to himself, "you've started something."

He has, he realizes, changed his life. He has, from the moment just past, begun to live like a man possessed by an idea and a plan—a man who suddenly knows what he will do for years ahead if he is able—a man possessing not only a life, but a death. He has changed beyond anything he could have imagined a minute ago. But also, for the first time since he made up his mind to leave the university, he is uncertain that he wanted to do what he has done.

But there is no uncertainty in Uncle Stanley. He is delighted. This is a realization of his highest ideal: a position of authority with half-pay and no work. He would not ask more of Heaven.

"Well, Jayber, I was going to offer to stay along with you and learn you the sleights of it, and see to it that you don't get into any problems."

He saws his cane across Jayber's shin.

"But that proposition you just made, now, by grab, that was mighty kind. It was *white*, by grab."

Jayber starts to say something, but he does not have a chance. Uncle Stanley is going to do all the talking. They are partners now. They are a team, and Uncle Stanley is the leader. Now that he has said yes, Jayber is to have nothing more to say.

"Next one dies, now, that's our start," Uncle Stanley's saying. "Preacher'll let you know and you let me know, and we'll start in. Maybe tomorrow you ought to come and let me show you where I keep the tools and give you a key to the shed."

Every new idea is better than the last. Uncle Stanley never realized what great authority he had until he lost it, and now he has had it given back to him. It is a resurrection. He thought he was a goner, but now his life is twice as abundant as before.

He goes into a discourse on the sleights and subtleties of grave-digging, a discourse on method: how to dig a grave in the rain, in the snow, in mud, in clay, in rock, in hard ground, in soft ground, on sloping ground, on flat ground, on top of a rise, along the edge of a drain, in frozen ground, in hot weather, in cold; how to dig them big, how to dig them small; what to do with the dirt; how to fill, how to mound, how to sod, how to set a tombstone; what to do with wilted flowers. His erudition and eloquence surprise him. He knows things he did not know he knew. Gravedigging becomes the science and art that explains the world.

Still pretending to listen, Jayber gets up and sweeps the floor and sets the place to rights and begins stropping his razors. He is a fisherman, thinking of the river, biding his time.

Light and Warmth

A car pulls off the road in front of the shop. The door slams. The shop door opens and Big Ellis comes in. He stands inside the door nodding and smiling at Jayber and Uncle Stanley. It has been several weeks since Big Ellis has been to town, and Jayber is surprised to see him.

"Who dug you up?"

Big Ellis laughs as freely as a child.

"The woman run me out. Said not to come back until I got some of this hair and beard cut off. Said it was like living with a horse."

"Paying customer?"

"She let me have a little money."

"You mean I'm really going to collect? Let me see your money."

Big Ellis pulls a handful of coins out of his pocket and holds them out.

"Welcome, sir."

Jayber brushes off the barber chair. Uncle Stanley is still talking. When Big Ellis came in the old man just waved his arm at him as though he was passing by, and went on with his lecture.

"What's he talking about?"

"He's giving me a lesson."

"Oh," Big Ellis says. He begins unbuttoning his overcoat. His hair has grown out over his collar, and he has at least a week's growth of whiskers.

"I'll have to charge you twice for cutting all that off."

"Well, it's the woman's cream money. Go ahead."

The thing about it is that Big Ellis means it, the woman's cream money or not. His face, the smile widening on it to show Jayber that anything he wants to do will be all right, is the most pleasant and agreeable single object in the neighborhood of Port William. Smiles and laughs have wrinkled and creased it like an old leather glove. Big Ellis wants to please. He wants everybody around him to be pleased. That is his weakness and his nature and his passion. If he offers you a cigarette he means for you to take the whole pack. If you happen to be at his house when mealtime comes, you eat, and while you are reaching to the meat platter Big Ellis will spoon you out another helping of beans and his wife will refill your glass.

He gets into the chair and Jayber pins the cloth around his neck.

"What kind of lessons is he giving you?"

"Gravedigging lessons."

Big Ellis gets tickled and Jayber has to wait.

"Have you gone into that business?"

"I've just contracted to take over Uncle Stanley's job. The graveyard part of it."

Uncle Stanley has just finished saying that if you strike bedrock you've got to blast. And now he is telling how to set the charges. A few years back, after he got so deaf, he remembers, he let off a blast on one side of the hill while they were holding a burial on the other side. You got to be careful about that.

Burley Coulter comes in.

"Look who's back," Jayber says. "What do you know, Burley?"

"Not much. What do you fellows know? How's everything over at your house, Big Ellis? You haven't been out much lately."

"Pretty good," Big Ellis says. "Well, a fellow just as well stay home, hadn't he? Weather no good. No money. No place to go. Jarrat ain't working you too hard?"

"Not much he can do."

"You find any sand and plaster up there in my head, Jayber, don't be surprised," Big Ellis says.

"All right, I've got over being surprised at what I find in people's heads. What're you doing with sand and plaster in yours?"

"The ceiling fell in over home the other night. If it hadn't hit me in the back of the head, it would've hit the woman right square in the face."

Burley hangs up his hat and sits down.

"We're going to have some more rain, ain't we?"

"Looks like it. I'd have thought it would've cleared and frosted maybe."

"This keeps up there's going to be water in the bottoms."

"Well, everything happens for the best," Big Ellis says.

Usually such a remark would either end the conversation or change the subject. But this time, to Jayber's surprise, Burley takes it up, and in a tone that does not leave room for argument:

"It don't do any such of a damned thing."

"What I mean, the Lord knows best, don't He?"

"Well," Jayber says, "He'll have the final say, anyhow. So if there's a flood you all just as well go down and fish in it."

"Hanh?" Uncle Stanley says.

"Burley," Big Ellis says, "we've got a new graveyard man in Port William."

Jayber takes a bow.

"You?"

"Who else in this town has both brains enough and time enough?"

Burley laughs, and they can tell from the sound of it that he is sorry for his shortness with Big Ellis.

"You've gone into business. Port William's a corpse factory, and now you're the foreman."

"No, Uncle Stanley's still in charge. I'm just his second-in-command. I'm going to be the shovel specialist."

"How come the old man to give up his job?"

"Well, he says he's getting too old for it. Says he can't hardly get out of them graves once he gets them dug."

They laugh.

"Uncle Stanley hasn't wintered too well," Big Ellis says.

"He says he won't be around many more winters."

"Did he say that?"

"He said he can't stand many more like this last one."

Burley turns to Uncle Stanley and raises his voice:

"I expect the old boy'll be around a long time yet. Bothering the women. How about it, Uncle Stan, can you still take up on the bit?"

"Aw, ain't no good at all, Burley. Them days are *gone.*"

Jayber tilts the chair back, and begins lathering Big Ellis's face.

Now that he has regained his audience, Uncle Stanley goes into a long reminiscence of his younger days—his dog days, he calls them. And winds up:

"Oh lordy lordy lordy lordy. But not anymore."

"That's not what I heard, Uncle Stanley," Big Ellis says. "Some of them was telling me about you." He laughs and looks over his stomach at Burley. "Said they seen a bunch of young girls walk past Uncle Stanley's house a Saturday or two ago, and there was Uncle Stanley marching up and down the top of that road bank, nickering like a stud horse, and that cane just whirling."

He looks up over his stomach at Uncle Stanley, who is pleased out of his mind, and then drops his head back and laughs, splattering white flecks of lather up into the air over his face.

"You'd better be still," Jayber tells him, "unless you want your throat cut."

But Big Ellis is so tickled now at the picture he has made of Uncle Stanley that Jayber, laughing too in spite of himself, has to wait again.

As soon as Big Ellis finishes laughing he is immediately sorry to have made fun of the old man. And so now he will try to make up for it: "I saw Billy when he came over today, Uncle Stan."

Uncle Stanley wants to hear that again, clear. He leans over and puts his hand behind his ear.

"Says which?"

"I saw *Billy* when he came over in his airplane. He came right over my barn and then on over to Grover's place."

That's all it takes. That's the word. Billy! If Billy ever so much as hinted that he would like to bomb his grandfather's house, Uncle Stanley would get right up and walk out, and stand on the other side of the road with his hat over his heart and watch him do it. It seems to him that he and Grover and all their forebears back to Adam have lived only for these minutes when their Billy comes roaring over the town in his bomber. He dreams of this brilliant young man leaning his head and elbow out the window of his huge flying machine, swooping like a hen hawk over all the little towns of the world—majestic and glorious as a railroad engineer and the Archangel Michael rolled into one.

"*Yes sir!* By dab, by grab, God durn, I seen him *myself*."

He goes out the door on the crest of his wave.

And they resume.

"That old boy of Grover's didn't have brains enough to hold his ears apart, did he?"

"Aw, they've educated him since he got to flying."

"They may have trained him. They haven't educated him."

They laugh, and then Big Ellis, his voice so gentle and generous as to allow even Billy Gibbs a place on earth and in Port William, says: "Well, a fellow ought to think the best he can of a fellow oughtn't he? Old Billy, he was a little chuckleheaded and wild, but that's just a boy, ain't it?"

Suddenly—whether because Big Ellis said "was," or because his words recovered Billy Gibbs himself, their neighbor and fellow man—suddenly the war is around them again, as though it has come up in the dark to crowd the walls of the little room. They become silent. And a thought runs among them like a path, and joins them and divides them: What if he dies? What if he is sent away tomorrow and never comes back?

And now they feel the raw night leaning against the lighted small room, and they know with a terrible certainty that one will not explain the other. In this dimly lighted place they sit divided, filled with thoughts of struggle and of darkness. They contemplate the death of Billy Gibbs, as though it already exists and awaits him.

Mat Feltner comes in blinking from the dark street, and stands at the stove. They greet him, and he replies. He unbuttons his coat and pushes his hat back off his forehead.

"Nathan gone back, Burley?" Big Ellis asks.

"This afternoon."

"He was over to see Annie May and me the other day. We appreciated it. They're going to send him back across the water, ain't they?"

"He thought they might. He didn't know."

"That's a long way from home. Fellow like me wouldn't know what to do there, even if there wasn't a war. But I reckon a young man like Nathan, he'll do all right, won't he? Told me he was even learning to talk like them."

"Yeah. I guess in a way it's giving him a lot of chances."

"Take a fellow like me and put him across the river, and I'm lost. Ain't you?"

Jayber finishes shaving Big Ellis and sets up the chair, and turns it so Big Ellis can see himself in the mirror.

"How's that?"

"I wish I'd been born rich in place of pretty. What I owe you, Jayber?"

"Sixty cents."

"Is that double?"

"That's half-price."

"I'll match you for it."

"You match me. All right."

Each of them flips a coin and slaps it down onto an arm of the barber chair.

"Heads."

"Heads it is. Keep your money."

"Naw, I'm going to pay you anyhow."

"Why, I'm not going to take your money. You won."

"That don't matter. I want you to take the money. Come on, Jayber. I just done that for a joke."

Big Ellis's world is turning slowly upside down. For the sake of friendliness and fun, he is persistently in and out of trifling wagers on the fall of a coin or the length of something or the weight of something. "A fellow has to have a little sport, don't he? A little fun?" But he never means to win.

Big Ellis tramps along with the coins held out in his open hand, backing Jayber around the barber chair.

"Take your money and go on."

"Ain't going to do it."

And then Big Ellis, who would be a match for two like Jayber, picks him up by the waist and holds him and puts the money in his pocket. He takes his coat and hat, and goes out the door putting them on.

"Good night to you fellows. Thank you, Jayber."

And they hear him start his car and gun the engine, and the car lurch out onto the road.

Jayber climbs back into the chair.

They're silent a few minutes. As soon as they cease to talk they are surprised at how deep the silence is. Except for them the town is asleep. The light has gone out in Burgess's store. The silence in the little shop is also the silence of the town and of the whole dark countryside. In it the only living thing might be the fire stirring and breathing in the stove.

Though his hands are warm, Mat holds them out into the heat over the stove.

Jayber stretches and yawns, a long-drawn O with a grunt at the end.

Burley asks, "What have you heard from Virgil, Mat?"

It was coming. It was bound to come. He might be speaking out of a well, his voice sounds so strange to him: "He's missing. We had the notice today."

He feels as though he has run to the edge of something and jumped.

Burley and Jayber say nothing for a moment. But their silence turns toward him, and is an admission of the difficulty and insufficiency of what they will say.

And then they say that they are sorry. Their concern touches him and, as though still falling, he feels himself caught in what they are saying, and hears the sound of his own voice speaking among their voices, becoming familiar again.

He mentions what room he believes there still is for hope. He hopes.

The others agree. So long as a man doesn't surely know, he has to hope. And that is more difficult than to know the worst surely.

Burley knows that. It has been hard for him to free Tom's death from the hopeless hope that he may still be alive. So far away as he died, it is hard to quit hoping that it may be only a long confusion and a mistake.

Jayber sits quietly in his chair, keeping the shop open for them, their talk his gift. Finally, as the subject changes, he takes part again.

The light has been out two hours in Milton Burgess's store. Mat and Burley hate to leave the lighted warm room and start home by themselves.

Finally they have to.

5

Keeping Watch

From the first week of January, when his lambs begin coming, until the end of bad weather, Mat keeps watch on the barns, seeing to the lambing of ewes and the calving of cows. Whatever is born will be born into his wakefulness and his care. He makes his first round in the dark of the mornings, his last at midnight. He is out of the house at night nearly as much as in the daytime. The smell of the barns stays in his clothes. In the dead of winter, in the time of the long sleeping of most things, he becomes more wakeful than ever.

It is a weary time. The days will string together for weeks in a row, never divided by enough sleep. There are freezing nights when his feet break through a crust of ice into the mud on his first round after supper, and on his last round the tracked mud and manure at the barn door are frozen hard. There are thawing nights of heavy rain when he walks ankle-deep in mud, and nights of snow when the tracks he made going to the barn will be filled by the time he starts back. And there are nights sometimes when there will be a difficult birth, and he has to wake Joe Banion to help him, and the two of them work on into the second half of the night, their hands chilled and numbed by the birth-wet, their feet stinging in their shoes.

In the winter the country sleeps, withdrawn from summer. And Mat, in his growing weariness, will be aware of that rest. Sometimes his head will fall forward and for a few minutes he will sleep an oblivious sleep, at the table after a meal, or sitting in his chair in the living room.

From nightfall until midnight his weariness seems to grow less, and he sits with the family in the living room and talks until the others go to bed. And then he has the quiet to himself, and he sits by the fire, reading or figuring or planning, passing the time between his rounds. This is the easiest and pleasantest time of his day, and the most precious to him. Going his night rounds, walking among the barns and the animals in the light of the lantern, the weather and the moon working their changes, he hungers for the births and lives of his animals, as though the life of his place must be held up by him, like something newborn, until the warm long days will come again and the pastures begin to grow.

In spite of the difficulty and weariness, be goes about his work with greater interest and excitement than at any other time of the year. This is the crisis of increase—what he was born to, and what he chose. When he has made sure of the life of whatever is newborn—when he has done, at any rate, all that can be done—he is at peace with himself. His labor has been his necessity and his desire.

The Sheep Barn

Mat goes up the hill, walking in the room of light the lantern makes. The ground appears to dip and waver under the swinging light, and every track is filled with shadow. Beyond the light of the lantern he can see nothing. He goes now as by the inward pattern and usage of his life.

He comes to the fan of tracked mud in front of the barn and, raising the lantern, picks his way to the doors, and slides them open a little to let himself in. The sheep raise their heads and get up, but they are used to his coming and only step slowly out of his way as he moves among them. Shadows leap up around his light. As he moves the barn seems to sway and rise within itself. The ewes' breath smokes above their heads.

In one of the back corners of the barn he finds an old ewe stretched on the bedding, her breath coming in grunts. She lifts her head to look at him, but makes no effort to get up. A newborn dead lamb is lying near her, not completely free of the birth sack. Mat knows that this second labor prevented her attending properly to the lamb she had already got born. He should have been here earlier. In spite of the circumstances of the day, he thinks with guilt of his failure. His mind has fallen short of its subject.

But now the consequence requires his mind of him. Taking a piece of twine from his pocket, he ties the lantern to a tier rail above his head, and then brings a small hinged gate and pens the ewe into the corner where she is lying. He takes the dead lamb out of the pen and puts it by the doors so he will remember to carry it out. He beds the pen with fresh straw, making himself a clean work place. Already it begins to simplify. It is an act already complete in his mind that he goes about. There is no hesitation and no hurry in his movements. Where nature and instinct fail, he begins with his knowing. He desires the life of what is living. He requires the life of the body suffering to give birth and the life of the body suffering to be born. Nothing else is on his mind now.

Moving gently and slowly, he straightens the lamb's head and forelegs, and delivers it, wet as a fish, into the air. He holds it up a moment—a limp, dangling thing—to make sure its nose is clear, and then touches it to the ground. It begins to struggle and to breathe. It comes tense and alive in his hand, wobbling its head, reaching down with its legs. It struggles against its weight, and breathes in the cold dung-smelling air.

Mat feels a kind of magician's triumph. His trick is the trick of the life of a thing, almost as liable to fail as to succeed. His labor is a labor of joy whose joyfulness depends on this precarious result.

He takes hold of the ewe and lifts her to her feet, and she remains upright, head hanging and dazed, loins caved. He carries the lamb to her flank and works the tit into its mouth. As soon as it takes hold and begins to suck he scratches its wet rump with his finger, in imitation of the way the ewe would normally lick and nudge. It becomes more eager, shaking its tail and butting weakly at the udder.

Satisfaction comes into Mat, pressing up into his throat like laughter. Once the trick is set working, the longer it works the better it works. Its own strength and purpose come into it now, and he becomes less necessary to it.

When he puts the lamb down the ewe turns to it and begins licking it, snuffling and bleating quietly and anxiously as she tends to it. Mat takes the lantern and a bucket and brings water from the well, and brings an armload of hay.

He hangs the lantern overhead again, and sits down to watch. He is far from sleep now. He does not think of going back to the house. He holds himself and his thoughts near to these things that his work and care have made familiar again. He sits there on a bucket, his elbows resting on his knees, his hands clasped together, conscious only of the nearness of this place: the ewe and lamb in the lighted pen, the flock sleeping and stirring in the dark behind him, the cold night air on his face and hands.

Part Two

6

A Dark Morning

He wakes in the dark, unsure how long he has been asleep. He wakes without movement except for the opening of his eyes. For the moment he thinks of nothing. And then from the kitchen on the other side of the house he hears a footstep light and hard on the linoleum. He realizes with relief that he has slept all the way through the night. He reaches across the bed and feels the warmth where Margaret lay asleep minutes ago. The footstep in the kitchen is followed by the sound of the coffee pot scraping on the top of the stove, and by voices—Margaret's and Nettie Banion's. For a little while longer he lets himself lie quiet. As if by some movement of his mind during the night, the uneasiness of the day before has left him. It is as if without his will his mind has turned and opened toward the new day. There is, deep in him, an acceptance of time as persistent as time. He wakes on the rising of the morning. The future bears down, and as in hard times before he feels in himself the determination to let it come.

He turns the covers back and gets up.

A fuzzy paleness drifts into the room from the lighted doorway at the other end of the hall. He opens the shutters to close heavy darkness and the sound of rain coming down hard and steady onto the yard and the walk along the side of the house. It has been raining for some time; the sound is that of water striking water. He shivers at the sound and at his apprehension of the wetness of the day. Under such a rain, he knows, the surface of the whole countryside will be a sheet of water moving down onto the loaded streams. He thinks with a kind of panic of how briskly, in a more seasonable year, he would have things moving by now, with the spring coming and the crops to get ready for. This season he will be beginning late, in loss. It rains into Virgil's absence. The sense of loss has carried his mind out of the house into the wind and rain over the soaked fields.

A Difference Made

By noon on Tuesday Virgil has disappeared from the knowledge of the whole town. The news has gone its rounds among the gathering places, and has quietly set the young man's life into the past tense of the town's consciousness. The town has begun to speak and think of him by the act of memory alone. To speak of him in the present tense becomes the private observance of his family—the enactment of their hope.

Wherever Mat goes among the gatherings of his neighbors he feels himself surrounded by an embarrassment, which both he and they are powerless to relieve. Though he is troubled by this at first, it becomes understandable to him. Virgil's absence, which was once only an absence from the place, has become a vacancy in their minds. They are suddenly barred from the usual forms of politeness; they can no longer ask him about Virgil or offer him their greetings to be passed on. And so, except for the casual give and take of crop talk and weather talk, they have nothing to offer Mat but silence. He accepts this, and as time goes on he will accept it more and more gratefully.

He is most sharply aware of this estrangement in his meetings with Frank Lathrop. In their long bearing of the absence of their sons, and their waiting, Mat has finally gone beyond what either of them had dared admit was possible. He has become the proof of what they most feared. The anticipation of loss that once bound them has been replaced by a reality of loss that divides them. In himself, Frank Lathrop is divided between a kind of shame at this inequality of fortune and a gratitude for it—neither of which he can acknowledge to himself, let alone to Mat.

Now it is only with Burley Coulter that Mat feels at ease. Telling his news that night in the barbershop, he felt it was to speak to Burley that he had come. Common knowledge went between them as a bond. During the following days, in casual meetings on the street and at the card game, they seldom speak of those absences that are most in their thoughts, but they accompany each other into their talk with trust.

A Comforter

Early Wednesday afternoon Brother Preston leaves the parsonage and walks across town to the Feltner house. He walks quickly and attentively, sidestepping the puddles. The town is shut against the weather, and quiet except for the sounds everywhere of water dripping and running. He meets no one along the road. There is no sign of life at the Feltners' either.

Stepping up onto the porch, he closes his umbrella and props it beside the door. Leaning against the wall, he removes his rubbers and places them side by side next to the umbrella. He draws a small black leather Testament out of his coat pocket, faces the door, and knocks. His knock is itself an act of ministerial discretion; the sound is perfectly modulated, both quiet and loud enough. As he waits he continues to face the door, standing erect, lifting himself slightly forward now and then onto the balls of his feet, patting the little Testament with a sort of correct casualness against the palm of his hand.

Footsteps approach from the back of the house, and Margaret Feltner opens the door. Her apron is caught up in one hand, and he knows she has been at work in the kitchen. In a movement of understanding, his imagination sees her wiping her hands on the apron as she hurries along the hall toward the door. He takes off his hat.

"I'm sorry to break in on your work."

"That's all right. We were just finishing up the dishes."

She smiles, greets him, moves aside from the entrance in welcome. The openness of her welcome is a little disconcerting; she is putting him at *his* ease—which is not why he has come. He senses that she has anticipated him, foreseen his coming and his purpose, but greets him now on her terms, not his.

She takes his coat and hat, hangs them up on the hall tree, and leads him into the sitting room.

He goes to the chair she offers him.

"Make yourself at home a minute. I'll go take this apron off."

"Mrs. Feltner," he says, and she stops. "I hoped I'd find all of you at home is why I've come so soon after dinner. Is Mr. Feltner here?"

"He's out at the barn, I think. We'll call him. There's not much he can be doing."

Again he feels headed off. Her offer seems again an act of her own generosity, in no way a concession to his reason for coming.

He sits down as she leaves. Her footsteps go back along the hall. Again in his imagination he sees her: her hands reaching behind her as she goes, untying the apron. He sits erect in the chair, holding the Testament in his lap. The attitude of his body seems to isolate him from the room, to hold out to it a formality alien to it. Some part of his presence is withheld from it; he might be sitting in the tall-backed chair behind his pulpit.

Margaret's footsteps enter the bustling noises of the kitchen, which he now realizes to have been continuous since he came in.

"Net," he hears her say, "would you call Mat? Tell him we've got company."

Out of the sound of her voice—not speaking to him now, remote from him—and out of the look and atmosphere of the room where he sits, there comes to him the sense of the completeness of this household, the belonging together of Mat and Margaret Feltner, the generosity of these people, in which there is maybe no need for him. He feels himself alone here. He is alone in his mission which, whole in itself, surrounds him with its demands, and isolates him. Uneasiness coming over him, a swift tremor, he thinks of the burden of his duty. And then, as though under the pressure of his own hand, he knows his old submission to the mastering of this duty, and knows he will do it.

He stands as the footsteps approach the room. Hannah is with Margaret now. Greetings are exchanged again, and they sit down, he in his chair, Margaret and Hannah together on the sofa, facing him. They talk with a determined pleasantness about trifles—all of them conscious that they are delaying, waiting for Mat to come, that they digress from their feelings and from the purpose of the visit.

Nettie is on the back porch, calling Mat. She has difficulty making him hear, and calls several times before she comes back into the kitchen, slamming the door.

His mind only half-occupied by the conversation, the preacher watches Hannah. She is wearing a clean white smock, the sleeves turned back from her wrists. Her heavy hair is drawn neatly back from her face. She is a beautiful girl; he has thought so often before. And he thinks so now, as always a little startled to find that he does so emphatically think so. He watches her face, alert for some sign of what she must be feeling, but he discovers nothing. Her face is composed and quiet. He both wishes and fears to know her thoughts.

And he watches Margaret. He believes that he sees in her face the marks of her grief for her son—but no sign that she expects to be comforted, or asks to be. To the preacher she also seems to be a beautiful woman. But hers has long ago ceased to be the given beauty of a girl; it is beauty that she has kept, or earned, through all that has troubled her and aged her. In all she says there is an implication of Mat's presence in her life, an assenting to it. To Brother Preston, it is as if something in her leans in waiting, not for him to begin the business of his visit, but for Mat.

They hear him come into the kitchen. He stops at the sink to wash his hands, and then comes on through the house.

"Don't get up," he says, entering the room and stepping over to the preacher's chair.

Brother Preston, leaning forward, takes the hand that is held out to him. The hand is hard, weather-roughened, communicating the chill of the outside air. The brief tightening grip of it is an announcement of welcome, which doesn't, today, put the preacher at ease.

"I'm sorry to take you away from your work."

"You needn't be. There's not much we can do you'd call work."

And so they begin again, speaking now of the weather, the delay of work, the rising river. The preacher feels himself drawn again, helplessly, into the stream of pastime conversation, which moves by no force of its own but by a determination in all of them against silence. He speaks and listens with an increasingly uncomfortable sense of his own hesitation, feeling at every turn and shift of the talk that he is failing again the duty that brought him.

Mat's coming has added something implicitly formidable to the uncertain pleasantness of the gathering. Now, in the faces of all three of the Feltners, there seems to Brother Preston to be a secrecy preserved against him. They have, none of them, made any acknowledgment of what they must know to be his reason for coming. It is as though their very grief is an affirmation of something that they refuse to yield to him.

At last, taking advantage of a break in the conversation, he begins, straightening in his chair and leaning forward a little, his eyes moving to the eyes of each of them:

"My friends, I've come because I know of your trouble."

He is surprised by what seems to him to have been the forcefulness of his voice. It is as if some barely perceptible stirring has moved among them, as at the first rising of a wind among tree leaves.

Now Margaret Feltner lifts her hand out of her lap and touches the tips of her fingers lightly to the side of her face.

But he has begun and he goes on, hastened, like a man walking before a strong wind, moved no longer by his intention but by the force of what he is saying. His eyes have become detached from his hearers; he might be speaking down from his pulpit now, looking at all, seeing none. But beneath the building edifice of his meaning, he is aware of something failing between them. It is as though in the very offering of comfort to them he departs from them. And now he is hastened also by an urgency of haste. He feels that the force of his voice is turning back toward himself, that he is fleeing into the safe coherence of his own words, away from those faces shut between him and their pain. He speaks into their silence like a man carrying a map in a strange country in the dark.

At the beginning Mat only half listens. He sits, staring out the window, like a boy in church. But knowing what must be the difficulty of the situation for Margaret and Hannah, his attention is drawn to them, and his separateness from the voice of the preacher is destroyed. He watches the two women, sorry for them, determined to bear with them, as dumbly as he has to, what must be borne. It is of the loss, accomplished or to come, of Virgil Feltner that the preacher is speaking. And Mat's fear, which he has kept silenced until now, begins to take its words. It is the fear of the loss of his boy, his good and only son—the preacher's voice seems to search it out. The preacher's voice, rising, rides above all chances of mortal and worldly hope, hastening to rest in the hope of Heaven.

In the preacher's words the Heavenly City has risen up, surmounting their lives, the house, the town—the final hope, in which all the riddles and ends of the world are gathered, illuminated, and bound. This is the preacher's hope, and he has moved to it alone, outside the claims of time and sorrow, by the motion of desire which he calls faith. In it, having invoked it and raised it up, he is free of the world.

But in this hope—this last simplifying rest-giving movement of the mind—Mat realizes that he is not free, and never has been. He is doomed to hope in the world, in the bonds of his own love. He is doomed to take every chance and desperate hope of hope between him and death, Virgil's, Margaret's, his. His hope of Heaven must be the hope of a man bound to the world that his life is not ultimately futile or ultimately meaningless, a hope more burdening than despair.

It is from this possibility of meaninglessness that the preacher has retreated. So that the earth will not be plunged into the darkness, he has lifted up the Heavenly City and hastened to refuge in its gates. And Mat, in the very act of leaning toward that restfulness, turns away from it to take back his pain. His mind seems to steady and move out again to its surfaces. He watches Hannah and Margaret, anxious for them, sorry for their sorrow. He is conscious again of the room, the window, the wet street opening into the town. The buds on the maple trees leaning over the road have grown big. He notices this as he always notices it for the first time in the spring, with an involuntary pleasure, saying to himself that he is surprised to see it happen so early.

The preacher sits with his head tilted so that the lenses of his glasses reflect the window. In his rapt intent face the opaque discs of light look exultant and blind.

Mat and Margaret seem to look at him now with a peculiar kindness, nodding their heads, not so much attentively as indulgently. He feels that he has become again the object of their generosity, that they are offering to *him,* out of some kind of hospitality, the safe abstraction of his belief. They are releasing him from the particularity of the time and place, and of the life he is talking about.

Concluding, preparing to leave them, he looks again at Hannah. She sits at the end of the sofa, beyond the light of either of the windows, looking down at her hand which lies beside her on the cushion. She reminds him of some white-petaled delicate bloom. "Surely," he thinks, "the people is grass."

He stands up abruptly.

"I must go."

Mat helps him into his coat and walks out onto the porch with him. They make the small sentences of leave-taking while the preacher puts on his rubbers and opens his umbrella. They shake hands.

"Come back," Mat says. "Thank you."

He stands on the edge of the porch while Brother Preston goes down the steps and starts out toward the street.

Coming into the house again, he thinks: "Well, that's done. That's over."

The living room, as he goes back into it, holds the quiet of a Sunday, as though the voice of the preacher is still present in it. Margaret has got up and is moving about in the room, halfheartedly and needlessly straightening the furniture and the papers on Mat's desk. Hannah is sitting as before. He goes over to her and reaches down to pat her shoulder.

"All right?"

"I'm all right." She nods, smiles.

And then as though suddenly jarred, she cries aloud like a hurt child: "No! I'm *not* all right! I'm *not!*"

Margaret comes to her and holds her while she cries. Against Hannah's hair Margaret's face is turned to Mat. Their eyes hold them there a moment, admitting their sorrow for the girl and for each other and for themselves.

And then Mat turns and goes. In his life he has made this movement time and again, this turning away from himself or his loved ones, leaving them to bear what they must. With his children, time after time, he has come to this turning away.

His mouth set, thinking "If it has to happen, it'll have to happen," not daring to think what he means, he goes out of the house and turns down the street toward Jasper Lathrop's store.

Passing under a low maple branch, he breaks off a twig. He feels the softening bud at the tip of it, tastes the cold, bitter taste of the sap. And then, hating to waste it now that he has broken it off, he sticks it into the band of his hat.

The Sanctuary

Swollen by the wet weather, the door binds against the sill. Brother Preston shoves hard to open it, and the sound of its breaking loose falls like a long plank into the empty church. But entering, shutting the door behind him, he does not make a sound. He stands just inside the vestibule a moment, letting the quiet of the place come to him. To his right, within reach of his hand, the heavy bellrope hangs down, the lower foot and a half of it polished and darkened by Uncle Stanley's hands. It drops straight into the vestibule from the arm of the bell up in the steeple, the hole drilled for its passage through the ceiling worn whopsided by the rope's sawing through it, and the rope at that place fretted to half its original thickness. At the end there is a big club of a knot which Uncle Stanley can just reach, and which is just out of reach, it is hoped, of the members of the Intermediate Boys' Sunday School Class.

On either side of the vestibule a door opens into a high narrow room, stark in its proportions and furnishings. Uncle Stanley has been in to clean up in preparation for the Wednesday-night prayer meeting, and everything is in a state of neatness and order which now, in the quiet, seems to deny its dependence on the likes of Uncle Stan. Unviolated now by any presence but his own, the old church seems to Brother Preston to stand erect and coherent, enclosing him.

As though the racket he made opening the door signaled a division between the church and the town, the sanctuary is now filled with quiet. He might be moving across the bottom of a deep pool. Tiptoeing, not making a sound, he comes on down the aisle and sits on a bench near the pulpit and directly in front of it.

He came away from the Feltner house grieved by the imperfection of his visit. It was not, as he had hoped it would be, a conversation. It was a sermon. This is the history of his life in Port William. The Word, in his speaking it, fails to be made flesh. It is a failure particularized for him in the palm of every work-stiffened hand held out to him at the church door every Sunday morning—the hard dark hand taking his pale unworn one in a gesture of politeness without understanding. He belongs to the governance of those he ministers to without belonging to their knowledge, the bringer of the Word preserved from flesh. But now, sitting on the hard bench in the chilled odors of stale perfume and of vacancy, he feels that he has come again within the reach of peace. On the back of the bench in front of him, like some cryptic text placed there for his contemplation, are the initials B.C. in deeply cut block letters four inches high. Leaning forward, his finger absently tracing the grooves of the initials, he bows in careful silence while his mind seems to stand in the pulpit above him, praying as always: "Our gracious and loving Heavenly Father, we are come into Thy Presence today with our burdens, our troubles, our sorrows."

The afternoon goes on, and he continues to sit there, his mind coming slowly to rest. He leans back, his hands folded and idle in his lap. Showers come and pass over without his hearing them.

The outside door clatters and slams, and footsteps tramp in. The vestibule door is bumped open, and Uncle Stanley appears at the head of the aisle. In one arm he carries a load of kindling, in the other hand a gallon bucket of corncobs soaking in coal oil. Loaded as he is, Uncle Stanley manages a whole chorus of gestures which greet and exclaim and apologize. Peeping over his load, waving the bucket of cobs, he shuffles down the aisle, his walking cane, hooked into his hip pocket, trailing on the floor behind him like a tail.

"Go right on, Preacher," he yells. "Go right ahead. Don't mind me. Keep right on a talking to Him. I know you got it to do. By juckers, if you can squeeze it in anywhere, you can tell Him about me."

He drops the wood with a racking crash down against a leg of the stove. He opens the fire door and lays in cobs and kindling, and douses in coal oil from the bucket. He tosses in a lighted match, the fire ignites, and the crackling of the flames is immediate and steady. In all this he makes a large avoidance of looking at Brother Preston or speaking to him, leaving him to his prayers.

He goes out, and returns carrying two buckets of coal which he places beside the stove. He adds more kindling to the fire, throws in a few lumps of coal, and goes to the nearest bench and sits down, still wearing his hat. He has gone about his work, and now sits and rests, with utter familiarity toward the place. His attitude intimates that he is a fire builder by profession, the best in the trade, and that his skill and responsibility require a certain indifference to all other considerations. A large chew of tobacco is actively at work in his jaw.

Not wanting to appear unfriendly, Brother Preston comes back and sits near the old man—trusting that, by keeping a distance of four or five feet between them, he can hold the conversation to an exchange of formalities and then leave in a few minutes. But he is exactly as much mistaken as he was afraid he would be. Uncle Stanley gets up and spits into the stove, and then sits down next to him and claps a hand down onto his knee.

"Yessir! By grab, last thing I'd want to do is break in on a fellow's praying. I reckon there's plenty of need for it around here. I reckon I ought to know that. But I had to get that fire to going for the prayer meeting tonight. Take the damp outen this air." He laughs knowingly, slapping the preacher's knee again. "Take their mind off of their old bones while you say your say to 'em. We all got our calling. You got yours and I got mine. And we go about 'em and get along. Ain't that right, Preacher?"

"That is so, Mr. Gibbs," Brother Preston says.

A Knack for the Here

March 9, 1945

Dear Nathan,

I've laid off to write to you every day for the last four, but it has been hard to get around to. I've been hoping for some good news to tell you. But none has happened.

I was in the barbershop the night you left, and Mat Feltner was there and told us that Virgil is missing in action. I've been studying the last four days whether I ought to tell you about it or not. I know you'll be sorry to hear it, but my guess is you would want to know it anyhow. He was a good boy.

I talk like he's dead for certain, which there ain't any reason to believe yet. But in town I notice it's coming mighty easy to most to talk about Virgil as if missing means dead. You don't hear Virgil is. You hear Virgil was. It's understandable. It's simpler to go ahead and think the worst and get it over with, and hard for most people to hold out much for people they're no kin to. But Mat and them are holding out. I hand it to Mat. He's just himself, the way he always has been, as far as he's letting anybody see. He come up to this a man. And I reckon will go through it a man.

I never been what you would call close to Mat. In spite of knowing him right onto fifty year. He hasn't been the kind you would need to worry about, for his sake or yours either. He has minded his business and stayed at his work. Has known his place, as they say. But the last four days he has been on my mind. I have the feeling that I'm holding out for him. In my mind I stick with him and hope his boy is alive. That's sympathy, I reckon. And we've come to it a hell of a way. By what has happened to us we're set apart kind of, and made to know each other.

Wednesday afternoon, after the news had pretty well got around, I seen Brother Piston going in up there at Mat's. And I says to Jayber, "I know the speech he's going to make." And so would all of us. He come and said all that to me after we knew Tom was dead. And none of it quite fit. You could say that he didn't have too good of an idea who he was talking to. While he was having his say I sat there and thought my thoughts. Here in a way he'd come to say the last words over Tom. And what claim did he have to do it? He never done a day's work with us in his life, nor could have. He never did stand up in his ache and sweat and go down the row with us. He never tasted any of our sweat in the water jug. And I was thinking: Preacher, who are you to speak of Tom to me, who knew him, and knew the very smell of him?

And there he sat in your grandaddy's chair, with his consolations and his old speech. Just putting our names in the blanks. And I thought: Preacher, he's dead, he's not here, and you'll never know what it is that's gone.

The last words ought to say what it is that has died. The last words for Tom ain't in the letter from the government, and they won't be said by the preacher. They'll be said by you and me and the rest of us when we talk about our old times and laugh about the good happenings. They won't all be said as long as we live. I say that a man has got to *deserve* to speak of the life of another man and of the death of him.

The difference between people is what has got to be taken notice of. There's the preacher who has what I reckon you would call a knack for the Hereafter. He's not much mixed with this world. As far as he's concerned there is no difference, or not much, between Tom Coulter and Virgil Feltner. Their names fit into the riddle he thinks he knows the answer to. I wouldn't try to say he ain't right. I do say that some people's knack is for the Here. Anyhow, that's the talent I'm stuck with. For us it's important to keep in mind who Tom was. And for Mat and them I judge it's important to know who is meant when they speak of Virgil. We don't forget them after somebody who never knew them has said "Dead in the service of his country" and "Rest in peace." That's not the way these accounts are kept. We don't rest in peace. The life of a good man who has died belongs to the people who cared about him, and ought to, and maybe itself is as much comfort as ought to be asked or offered. And surely the talk of a reunion in Heaven is thin comfort to people who need each other here as much as we do.

I ain't saying I don't believe there's a Heaven. I surely do hope there is. That surely would pay off a lot of mortgages. But I do say it ain't easy to believe. And even while I hope for it, I've got to admit I'd rather go to Port William.

As Jayber says, when we seen Brother Piston go in up at Mat's, the worst thing about preachers is they think they've got to say something whether anything can be said or not.

Well, it's been raining right along since you left. The ground, you know, was soaked while you was here. So every drop that has fell has gone in the river. The river has got way up. It's into most of the bottoms. And the creeks are still running out big. And the radio says more to come.

Night before last Anvil Brant sent word up here by his son-in-law that he had a sow and nine pigs he wanted to sell to me and your daddy. So yesterday morning we got in the pickup truck and went down. When we got there Anvil's wife said he was out to the barn. And we could see why. There Mrs. Anvil was with her children, and there was her and Anvil's oldest girl with *her* children, children and grandchildren looked like all running about the same age, and looked like four or five in each set, and all of them been fastened up there together since the rain commenced. And there was Mrs. Anvil, with her hair sticking out right stiff in several directions like a frozen floor mop, and one child sucking and one hanging onto her arm and one standing under her dress so you couldn't see nothing but its legs, standing there in pee smell strong enough to make your eyes water, slapping here and there and yelling at them all to be quiet, taking three or four minutes to tell us Anvil was down to the barn, anyhow she reckoned he was, she hadn't seen him since breakfast.

We walked out that little rise the house and buildings are on, and found Anvil sitting in the back door of the barn. One of the older boys was there with him, and his dogs, and we could see right off that things weren't much more comforting at the barn than they were at the house. The river was up into the bottom there in back of the barn, and between there and the trees on the river bank was nothing but about three hundred yards of muddy water, with here and there a willow or a few dead horseweeds or a cornstalk sticking up out of it. And you just knew, as soon as you saw how things were, that Anvil had been coming out there to the barn every morning for the last three or four to watch it rain and watch it rise, and know he was doing nothing because there was nothing he could do. We went in the upper doors and walked down the driveway and spoke. I says, "How's it coming, Anvil?" "Up, by God," he says. I says, "How're *you* coming?" "Drownded out, by God," he says. "Britchies legs rotted off plumb to the knees." We sat there with him and the boy until nearly dinnertime and talked, none of us having anything better to do. And we wound up buying the sow and pigs. For more than they was worth. To your daddy's way of thinking, you don't what you would call trade with a man who is hurting. I know it has got hard for you to know your daddy, but he has that kind of rightness about him. He's very straight in his dealings.

Anvil didn't figure the river would get into his house, but I expect it surely was in his barn by this morning. They say the Ohio has got into a few of the houses down at Hargrave. And the rain falling right on.

March 10

Still raining. Off and on all night, and pretty hard and steady since before day. When the rain lets up you can hear water running anywhere you stand. The mud is a foot deep around the barns here, and the barns are as wet inside as out. We put down a little dry bedding every night, but it gets tramped out of sight in a few minutes.

Anyhow, it's raining and I've got nothing to do for a while but sit here and write to you. Which I aim to do, because once the weather fairs up it won't be easy to find the time. I'm writing at the table by the front window in the living room. The rain coming down steady outside, and a good fire going in here. When I look back I don't see many wet weather mornings in my life when I've been sitting inside and doing something quiet. And in a way I wish there had been. I notice that every now and then I do something I wish I'd done more of, that I've lost a lot of chances for.

I've quit minding to write as much as I did at first. When you boys was first in the army it give me some trouble. I don't reckon I'd wrote much more than my name for thirty years, and I did have an awful time trying to keep what I had to say inside of what I could spell. But finally it got so it come tolerably easy. I've got the habit of it now, and when I'm working or walking to town and soon, I think of a letter to you that says what's taking place. It's company for me.

The weather is throwing us behind in our work. Every day we lose, the loss gets a little more on our minds. We've got plant beds to burn and ground to break and the barns to clean and so on and so on. When the weather does fair up things are going to break loose around here in a mighty hurry. I was thinking about it while I was eating breakfast, and kind of dreading it. You know how your daddy will come untied the first day the sun shines. He'll be just like a fox. One minute he'll be laying quiet, and the next minute in a dead run, and you'll have to look mighty quick to see the difference.

There hasn't been many times this morning when you could see from here to the yard fence, but the rain has nearly quit now. A good deal more water in sight today than yesterday, so it must of rose considerably during the night. The bottoms are all under water as far as I can see in both directions. There's water from the foot of the hills on this side to the foot of the hills on the far side. Looks from here like the water is up to the window sills of the old Traveler house in the big bottom on the far side, and there's a car sitting in the front yard with just the roof and windows showing.

Awful as it is, I have to say that a flood can be about as interesting to me as anything ever I run into. As soon as I see the backwater get into the bottoms I want to be out on it in a boat. You remember. And I finally did get around to it yesterday afternoon. I was in the barbershop toward the end of the morning, after I got done writing to you, and just happened to mention to Jayber that all morning it had been awfully easy for me to imagine that you could have some luck if you was to go fishing. And for some reason Jayber jumps right up and says "Let's go"—which he never did want to do before in his life. He turned around that old paper clock of his that says "Back at 6:30," and locked up, and we got a pound of cheese and a box of crackers from Milton Burgess, and went over the hill. I had my boat chained up on the porch of the old cabin, and the water was nearly up to the joists, so all we had to do was just roll her over and slide her into the river. About fifty foot from the porch we caught her in a long eddy and went just shooting up through the trees along the bank. We went over the road at the creek bridge, and across the backwater, and right on up into the big woods in the creek bottom. We tied the boat, and sat up there inside the woods and fished in the rain all afternoon. We are cheese and crackers and smoked and talked and caught fish.

We carried what we caught back to town and fried them up at Jayber's little living place over the barbershop. It's not but a little bit of a room, and he's got everything he needs fitted into it just perfect. And you never seen the like of books he's got up there. I've known Jayber mighty well for a long time, and I never knew he read books. But he tells me he's read some of them books as many as several times. Some of the authors was ones I'd heard of. You've got to hand it to Jayber for the way he's held his learning and not let it go to his head. When he seen I was interested, Jayber told me that books has meant a lot to him, and there's some of them he puts a great deal of stock in.

I thought about you all along while the good times lasted, and wished you was here. Afterwards, while I was walking home, I was thinking about you, and our old times fishing and keeping batch down on the river. I can remember whole conversations that we had back in those old times. Them was good times, I says to myself, and one of these days we'll have them again.

Well, according to what they say I ought not to write you anything but cheerful news, and I see I've wrote little enough of that. There ain't but mighty little to be had around here right now, so it's hard to write much of it. Unless I lie. And I think I ought to save lying for when we need it worse. And I don't aim to ever start lying to you. If I lied to you who would I have for company then?

I think a lot about you, and a lot of you.

Your uncle,
Burley

7

Born a Idiot, Educated a Fool

In the latter two-thirds of his life Mat Feltner's cousin Roger Merchant has memorialized his father as a cultivated and enlightened gentleman farmer—which Mat knows the old man never was, never thought of being, and would have refused to be if he had thought of it.

The truth about old man Griffith Merchant is that he lived on his land like a blight, troubled only by the slowness with which it could be converted into cash, unable to see or care beyond his line fences. If Armageddon had blazed to those boundaries and stopped, he would have noticed it only to think that be had been rightly spared. But Roger—"born a idiot," as his father once took occasion to remark, "and educated a fool"—has believed otherwise. By luck, defect, or determination, he has thought himself the descendent of gentleman farmers and one himself.

He has lived by himself for forty years in the slowly collapsing house built by his grandfather, half log and half stone, on a point overlooking a wide creek valley to the south of Port William. The foundation under the log forepart of the house has been caved and splayed by groundhogs tunneling under it, and by dogs digging after the groundhogs. The yard-thick walls of the stone L are buttressed by locust poles wedged at uneven angles against them. The house and outbuildings haven't been painted in half a century. Bees hive in the cornices. Maple seeds sprout knee-high in the gutters. A rambler rose has completely overgrown the steps and posts of the front porch, live runners threading heavy meshes of dead growth. In the garden, briars grow as high as the fence posts. The wall of an outbuilding near the garden fence has burst, spilling an avalanche of tin cans and bottles down the slope. The barn provides shelter, but no longer confinement, only for an old team of mules, kept to validate Roger's assertion that he has in his "latter years" restricted himself to "a little light fawming"—though there is not a complete set of harness for either of them on the place.

In the last decade Roger has made a slow retreat from the opening cracks and leaks and bucking floors of the front rooms, and now lives entirely in the stone kitchen. That room is large and tall, in summer cool as a cellar and dim from the heavy shade of the maples in the yard. In the back of the room there used to be an enormous fireplace, now walled up and plastered, replaced by a tall, black cooking range. In a corner is an old kitchen cabinet whose doors customarily stand open, showing a supply of store-bought canned goods, mostly soups of various sorts, pork-and-beans and Vienna sausages and sardines, boxes of crackers and cookies. A broad table, at which a numerous family or a crew of field hands might be fed, stands in the center of the room. The room is filled—all its horizontal surfaces littered and heaped—with plunder that Roger has salvaged from the front rooms as he has needed it: a walnut fourposter bed of excellent make, an outsize rocking chair, a half-dozen or so split-bottom chairs, a chamber pot, a grindstone, a hand-cranked Victrola, a five-shovel tobacco plow. Hanging from nails around the walls are various articles of clothing, a hat or two, a pair of fairly new half-swinny mule collars, a double-barreled shotgun, and a minnow seine. Against the chimney there is a pile of ear corn for the Dominecker hens that roost on the back porch.

Surrounding this center, taking in ridge and bluff and creek valley, lie seven hundred acres of land, plundered by old Griffith Merchant in his lifetime, ignored by Roger in his. All the farming done on it now is done by tenants, who vary in number from two to four, and whom Roger may see three or four times a year. His only dealing with any of them is through an old lawyer in Hargrave, who arranges for their coming and going, and collects from them Roger's half of the proceeds from the sale of their crops. And the tenants, in turn, pester the lawyer in order to secure minimum supplies and to keep their houses and barns standing. Each of them raises a few acres of tobacco and corn, and is allowed to keep a few hogs or cows. Except for their shrinking islands of cropland, the place is overgrown with bushes and trees. Some of it Roger has never seen; much of it he has not seen since his boyhood; most of it, if taken to it, he would not recognize. In all his life he has built nothing, added nothing, repaired nothing. For twelve years Whacker Spradlin has kept him supplied with whiskey, making the seven-mile round-trip from his place to Roger's in all weather, as faithfully as the prophet's raven.

When Roger drinks his aim is prostration. His fits of drunkenness extend to remarkable lengths. He has been known to go for months without getting out of bed except to answer what he calls "the physiological summons." He has been known to lie dormant through the coming and going of a whole summer.

His trips to Port William are becoming less and less frequent. When he goes he drives a 1927 Ford, which since 1927 he has driven something less than three thousand miles, mostly back and forth over the same three and a half miles of road. Spangled with sparrow dung and rusted, the car wears as a hood ornament a cow's bleached skull with a four-foot spread of horns, the anonymous gift of some generation of Port William boys. Roger has never driven the car out of low gear. So far as he knows, that is the only gear it has. When he is asked—as he has regularly been asked for eighteen years by the boys of Port William—how he likes his car, Roger replies: "It is slow, sir, but powerful."

It's a taxing kinship that Mat has with Roger Merchant. It has been, if not one of the difficulties, at least one of the perplexities of his life, both obligation and nuisance. With something like regularity, over the years, Roger has presumed both to need Mat and to find him useless. When Roger's summons goes out to Mat and the old lawyer, they go. Usually Mat gets there first. And usually he waits, stopping his car at the roadside below the house, until the lawyer arrives. And then they walk together up the slope and around the house where Roger will be waiting for them—on the porch in good weather, in the cluttered kitchen in bad.

Roger greets them ceremoniously and solemnly, shakes their hands, offers them chairs, stands until they are seated, and seats himself. The order of business never changes.

At the beginning Roger defines and analyzes his problem in his prim, deliberate voice, in language so excessively grammatical and discriminating that Mat and the lawyer sometimes leave after two or three hours without any certain idea what is the matter. The problems vary from urgent to trivial without producing any change at all in the length of his deliberation or the tone of his voice. Once he wanted them to ponder "carefully, gentlemen, if you will be so kind, the perfectly alarming proliferation of mice in the corncrib." Once he was wondering "if the wild honey could not be extracted from the cornices of the house to some profit."

After he has stated the problem, Roger asks Mat what he would advise. And Mat, knowing that it can come to nothing, explains what he would do if he were Roger. And then Roger turns to the lawyer and asks him what *he* would do, and the lawyer invariably agrees with Mat.

Roger listens to each of them, attentive, nodding, polite. And then he leans back and, touching the tips of his fingers together, delivers a long discourse on what he, himself, Roger Merchant personally, considers to be "good fawming in the present case." This can go on for the better part of an hour, supported by no practical sense, no knowledge, no experience. At the end of this spiel it is normally discovered that the lawyer has footed quietly across from Mat's plan to Roger's. Mat is outvoted; Roger is delighted by the reception of his idea; the old lawyer is pulling his ear and looking at his eyebrows.

The Farm in the Valley

From Roger's front porch the view down into the creek valley takes in a tract of his land that is in itself a little farm. The house and its clutch of outbuildings stand on a low shelf of the hill on the far side of the valley. A little down the creek from the house, and a good deal nearer the floor of the valley, stand a large barn and corncrib and stripping room. Even from that distance, the buildings and the fields look better kept than any of the rest of the Merchant land.

And if you were to step off Roger's porch and walk down the hill to the front of the tobacco barn where Gideon Crop is standing now, you would see that the apparent good order of the valley farm is no illusion of distance. On closer look you would see that the extent of this orderliness, though it is real, is not large; the hillside that rises behind the buildings was worn out and given up long ago, and now is covered with thicket; the place is poorly fenced where it is fenced at all, and the buildings are old and rundown. You will guess that the place must have declined unimaginably from what it was when Griffith Merchant was a young man.

But what is left of it has been well cared for. The fields in the bottoms along both sides of the creek show the signs of having been regularly mowed and sensibly cultivated. Here and there on the old buildings a loose board has been nailed back in place with new nails. Hinges and latches are in good shape. In the sheds and outbuildings things are put away neatly on their shelves and hooks. In the barn the farming tools have been properly greased and stored for the winter; the dirt of the floor is swept clean. A sizable area to one side of the driveway has been partitioned off, whitewashed on the inside, and stanchioned for five milk cows. At opposite sides of the upper doorway there are stalls for a team of mules. On up the inclining path along the face of the slope, standing under an enormous white oak, there is a small building that has apparently at some time been rescued from collapse, pulled back, straightened, rebraced, and made into a toolshed. There is evidence everywhere—around the other buildings, the house, the garden—of the presence of a strong, frugal intelligence, the sort of mind that can make do, not meagerly but skillfully and adequately, with scraps.

To Gideon Crop, standing in front of the barn in weather that has been wet for days, the clouds so low now that they snag and unravel against the wooded bluffs on each side of the valley, it seems that he is still just barely ahead of his circumstances. He is thirty-seven years old, and in the years of his manhood he has held tight, and come out finally a little ahead of where he was when he began. Not much, but a noticeable little. That is how he is able to see it in his good moods. In the bad weather of his mind it can seem to him just as undeniable that the settled account of these years shows him falling behind. There is the money in the bank, all right, more by some few hundred dollars than there was when his father died. But what about the years? He has seen more good years and days than he will see again. His time of limitless energy and limitless hope is gone, and there is nothing yet to show beyond that hopeful column of figures in the bankbook and in his mind, growing, he is afraid, too slowly. His life seems to him to have become a kind of race to see whether those figures will grow to their power before he has exhausted his own.

From his father Gideon Crop inherited three things: a little bank account in the name of "John Crop and Son," an ambition to own the farm they have lived on, and Roger Merchant.

"Gideon," John Crop would say, "don't let *any*body tell you it ain't hell to do good work for another man who don't care if you do it or not. Who, by God, don't *know* if you do it or not.

"But, boy," he would go on, "have good ways about you. First thing, don't leave anything behind you that you wouldn't claim. Second thing, we don't want to buy a place we've ruint ourselves."

After the tobacco was sold in the winter Gideon was seventeen, John Crop made his only attempt to buy the farm from Roger. He had managed to save more money than he was ever to have at one time again. The morning after he had sold his tobacco he wrote his bank balance on a piece of paper and put it in his pocket and walked up the hill.

John Crop's savings would barely have made a down payment, if that. From his encounter with Roger that day he learned that if he'd had the full value in cash he still would not have had enough. Roger looked on the place as an heirloom. He would not sell. Beyond a half-dozen perfunctory courtesies, he would not talk.

Gideon, standing at the woodpile where he had been sent to work when they finished breakfast, saw his father turn out of the creek road and start back along the lane across the bottom, and stopped and watched him, leaning on the handle of the axe. John Crop came picking his way carefully over the thawing mud, and passed in front of the house and on down the incline toward the barn. When he went by Gideon he smiled and kept walking.

"Honey," he said, "that axe handle ain't made to lean on."

Flood

At ground-breaking time, the spring of 1932, John Crop was dead and buried, the Depression was on, and Gideon Crop's name was signed to the new contract in the office of Roger's lawyer.

Gideon had not forgot, and never has yet forgot, the silence his father kept when once or twice a year Roger and the lawyer would drive down to the valley farm. It would usually be in the middle of the day—as Gideon remembers it, it is the noon of a fair day in the summer; they have finished their dinner and are resting on the front porch—and Roger and the lawyer would drive in and stop in the road below the house and blow the horn. And John Crop would walk down to the car and stoop to the window. He nodded and spoke in answer to their questions, saying no more than necessary, volunteering nothing. Gideon, watching from the porch, knew that his father spoke out of the silence a man must keep when all abundance and order in his sight are to his credit but not in his possession.

In John Crop's pride and silence Gideon continued. He had the gifts of quiet endurance, of tolerance of rough work and poor tools, of makeshift, of neatness in patched clothes, of thrift.

He has seen the last year's tobacco crop through the market at a good earning, and is ready to begin preparations for the next, waiting only for the weather to break and the ground to dry. Today he has made the rounds of the buildings, cleaning and straightening and putting away. Since noon he has given a fresh coat of whitewash to the milking stall, and the afternoon is only half gone. The wet weather, the rising backwater, the delay of ground-breaking are worries, but the knowledge that for the time he has done all that is possible to do is deeply pleasant to him. It is a rare time in any year when he can permit himself to say that he is caught up.

He goes to the little toolshed under the oak tree, brings out a five-gallon bucket, which he upends against the face of the building, and sits down. From there he can see perhaps half a mile of the little valley, from the big woods in the slue hollows above the mouth of the creek to where the creek bottom narrows at the upper end and turns out of sight. Up the creek, among the trunks of leafless sycamores, he can see his and

Ida's little girl Annie sitting midway of the swinging footbridge, wearing a red coat. A brown and white feist named Speck is lying on the foot-plank beside her. She appears to be talking to it—playing something, he supposes, but who can tell about a child? Since the rain quit shortly after noon she has been outside with the dog, keeping to the good footing along the road and the stepping-stones of the paths as Ida warned her to do. Gideon has watched her, amused by her simple companionship with the dog, pleased to see her out of the house after being so much shut in. And for the last half hour he has watched the building up of a heavy rainstorm over Port William and the upland to the north and west.

But for days now he has been used to rain, even used to the reflection that he and the whole countryside are losing by it, and so the storm up there does not break his peace. He is looking at the fields in the bottoms in front of him. Empty of the last year's growth, awaiting the new season's crops, they seem to him to have the same serenity that he feels in himself, the same poised free rest between one time and another. Above the edge of the woods that cuts off his view downstream he can see where the flood has broken over the creek banks, and the brown flat of the backwater has begun to fan out a little over the bottom.

He takes off his boots and straightens his socks and pant legs and puts the boots back on. And then he stands and, unbuttoning his work jacket and loosening his pants, carefully straightens and tucks in the tail of his shirt. He sits down again and makes and lights a cigarette. Behind him, up on the hillside, his milk cows have started down through the thickets toward the barn; he can hear the faint ringing of their bells. And from half a dozen places comes the sound of water running through the rock-choked notches of the slopes.

And then he hears another sound, way off, like the hard whispering of the approach of a strong wind. By the time he has thought what it is, he can hear the bushes breaking under the weight and force of the water. He is on his feet now, running along the slope in front of the house toward the bridge. As he runs his mind knots in accusation against himself for not knowing sooner what he knows now.

"Annie! Come up here!"

He sees the girl look at him, turn and look back up the creek, and with what seems to him a weighted slowness stand and take two steps toward the near end of the bridge. Strangely—he will think of this a thousand times before he dies—she does not cry out. She just gets up and starts toward him with the slowness of the sun moving.

The wall of water bursts into sight among the trees, the full sound of it opening on Gideon like an unexpected explosion, though he knew it was coming. And he stops running and stands still. As if in those few running steps he left behind all that was comprehensible, Gideon stands there useless, stripped of all but vision—the unbelievable taking place before his eyes without bothering to become believable.

It hits the bridge. The cables and footboard tear loose at the near end, flinging the girl and the dog up and outward and then down.

And now Gideon is standing at the edge of a turbulent swift river as wide as the floor of the valley, the fields he was looking at a few seconds ago no longer there. The muddy water sucking around his boots, he is still looking up at the grove of trees, though he is already failing to know exactly how the bridge looked.

He stands there another minute, the water drawing nearly to the tops of his boots, hunting with his eyes over the wide surface of the water, the miracle he is looking for instantly clear in his mind. That red coat bright against the water. And then his mind bears up the remembrance of the two of them as they were moments ago, absorbed in their pleasure, balanced in the path of doom, and still free of it. He should have known.

Running again, he goes back up the slant of the ground toward the toolshed. As he goes he notices that the shoreline now strikes almost exactly midway of the length of the barn, the lower end of which has been slapped clean off its foundation as if its timbers had been so many straws. The water slides over his cropland, silent, muddy, a quarter of a mile wide, keeping pace with him as he runs beside it; its flowing seems already established, beyond thought of beginning or end. Even a serenity seems to be in it now, and to brood over the face of it.

At the toolshed he throws open the doors and goes in. Resting upside down on a pair of carpenter's trestles in the center of the floor is a small johnboat. He takes hold of the length of chain fastened to a ring on the bow-end and drags the boat forward off the trestles and out the door. Lifting the boat at the middle, his hands under the gunwale and then the bottom, he turns it over and over, rolling it down toward the edge of the water. He works in great haste. He is not deterred by his instinctive knowledge of the futility of what he is about to do. He works, maybe, simply in obedience to a determination that he must not stay still—as if to act now, even though it is too late, is the just consequence of his failure to act in time.

Leaving the boat balanced on the shoreline, he runs back to the shop and brings a set of oars, shoving the boat out and leaping into it. As he straightens up he sees Ida, bareheaded and bare-armed, running down toward him from the house, calling out to him: "Gideon, where is she? Where's Annie?" the weeping breaking suddenly up into the sound of her voice; she knows as well as he does where Annie is. Looking at her, moving away from her, he feels torn from her as he feels torn from Annie. More than that, with all the force of self-hate, he feels ashamed before her. He does not answer.

Before he can balance himself and turn and sit down and set the oars into the locks, he is already a good way past the barn; the house and Ida are out of sight. Thinking to combat somehow the power that has bereft him, he sees now, he has only abandoned himself to it. There grows in Gideon an awareness of the size of the thing that has taken him, the hurtling muddy current, carrying the trash of slope and woods, riding over his known place. He can smell it. He has failed again to consider what he has known all his life. The hope or the sham of saving his child is now replaced by the attempt to save himself.

The current is sweeping him rapidly down toward the woods. By the time he has straightened the boat he has already covered half the distance, and is caught in a strong current at about the middle of the valley. The boat is heavy and squarecut, dangerously clumsy in such water. Seeing that he cannot make shore this side of the woods, he turns the boat around, so that he is facing the direction of the current, pushing the oars rather than pulling. And now, working the boat as well as he can toward the right-hand shore, he gives his main effort to guiding.

Holding the boat straight with the current, he plunges forward into the woods, his speed appearing suddenly to quicken as the treetops heighten and come over him. He crashes through the thicket growth at the margin and breaks in among the big trees, the current hurling and sucking among the trunks. Problems, obstacles, dangers go out of sight before he can move in answer to them. He notices only that he seems to be carried ahead unobstructed for a remarkable length of time. And then one of the forward corners of the boat strikes a tree. He sees it happening, braces himself, takes the jar, and more feels than sees the boat hesitate, and turn, and continue turning as the current reclaims it and carries it forward again. Now Gideon thinks only of getting the oars out of the locks and into the bottom of the boat. Trunks and branches bear down, turn, go by. And then a limb strikes him and sprawls him backwards. He lies perfectly still, his eyes open, the calves of his legs resting across the seat. He does not move—because he cannot or because he does not want to, he does not know which. He expects that at any second the boat will strike crossways of a tree and be broken or rolled under. But he knows these things strangely now, without caring.

More quickly than he would have imagined, the sky clears of branches and the forward motion of the boat seems to be subsiding. He feels building in him the unearned exhilaration of a man alive by luck, who has gone by one of his deaths. Instantly he is on the seat and rowing again, straining for the shore. Having failed in fighting for his life while it was in danger, he will now fight for it when there is no need to. And suddenly he seems to have reached some apex of absurdity. He sees all that has happened to him stripped of reason or cause. He has been beaten by a power larger than he can imagine, much less understand, and now he comes out alive, not even by his own will, much less his own power. He rows strongly across an eddy at the creek mouth, and drives the bow-end of the boat onto the shore.

He steps out onto the mud and instinctively draws the chain out after him and stoops to tie the boat to a tree. He built the boat himself, and his pride clings to it. But this thought of his own doing immediately drives into him the memory of Annie's two steps along the bridge; and in repugnance and pain he flings the chain back into the boat, shoves it off the shore with his foot, and leaves it for the current to take.

He has come undone. The reality of what has happened begins to seem doubtful to him. He cannot be certain even of where he is in the joining of the two valleys, which are changed beyond recognition. He turns and begins running heavily through the sodden mud of a cornfield, which dips out of sight under the water at his right hand.

Where Are You?

It takes him a good hour and a half, in spite of his hurry, to get back, circling the in-reachings of the backwater.

Not long before dusk he steps around the upper corner of the barn, past his cows waiting to be milked—seeing them, regretting his neglect of them, forgetting them almost in the same thought—and stops below the oak tree where he started. His own tracks there seem to him unbelievably fresh. He stands, looking down at them. The darkening water flows high and quiet through the grove where the bridge used to swing.

He turns and starts up toward the toolshed. His direction and even his hurry are the same as when he went up to get the oars. His sense of this similarity is so powerful that for a moment he feels caught and confused, as if the first time was a dream, or he is dreaming now. But this time he turns toward the house. He goes through the gate and up the slope of the yard and around to the back porch.

Hearing his footsteps on the porch, Ida comes out of the kitchen. She has thrown around her shoulders an old jacket of his that she wears to do her chores.

"She's dead, ain't she, Gideon? She's drowned."

Her voice breaks on the last words. But she remains dry-eyed and erect, and continues to face him.

His own voice is even and steady, but he hears himself speak as though he is another person standing a few feet away.

"Hush now, Ida. You go on back in the house now."

It is the gently commanding tone of a parent speaking to a child, and to his surprise she minds him.

But when he has taken the lantern down and filled it at the coal-oil barrel behind the smokehouse, Ida comes back out, not wearing the coat this time, her bare arms folded against the chill.

"Gideon, don't you want to eat? I'll have supper ready before long."

Her voice seems to him now to have the stillness and solemnity of voices in the presence of death. He sees, through the door she has left standing half open behind her, that the meal is on the stove, and he is touched. But he cannot eat now. Again when he speaks he does not know what his voice will sound like, and again, almost without any attempt on his part to control it, it reveals no feeling except kindness.

"No, Ida. No, I don't want anything right now, sweet."

He runs down the slope of the yard, the lantern swinging and rattling in his hand. He has not heard the kitchen door close. He believes that Ida is still standing in the open door as he left her, unable for the moment to turn and face the meal that nobody will eat. But he cannot go back. He does not stop.

The rain has started again. He does not know when it began. The water is beading on his hat brim. It is raining steadily on all the darkening countryside.

Before long it is dark. For a while there is a grey mirage of twilight, which shifts and tilts over the surface of the water. And then that goes. The surface of the water becomes soft, absorbent, drawing the darkness into it, fusing with the air at some indeterminable distance from the shore.

He does not light the lantern, unable to bear the confinement of his vision. And he gives up the attempt to hurry. In daylight his compulsion was to run, as though if Annie were still alive, she would most likely be somewhere ahead of him. But in the dark his impulse is to go slowly and quietly, listening, afraid now that she is alive within his hearing and that he will go by without hearing her. He will save the lantern for when he needs it.

Before he has walked an hour he is wet to the waist, his matches sodden and useless in his pocket. The lantern swings in his hand, lifeless.

The difficulty of the going is enormous, the ground sloping, slick, and uneven. Feeling his way ahead, tensed against the darkness and his failure by now to have any idea where he is, he falls repeatedly. A number of times he slips down feet first into the water, clawing the mud with his free hand, and then has to crawl up the slope on all fours and take off his boots to pour the water out.

But difficulty and misery do not stop him. Again he knows with a furious concentration what he wants, what he is waiting for. In the dark the thought of the sound of Annie's voice is clear to him. Now and then he believes he hears her, and he stops and answers:

"Annie, where are you, honey? Holler *loud!*"

And then the valley is silent. His own silence seems to grow large around him, and he hears the rain falling.

He has lost all sense of time and distance. He walks in a dimensionless landscape of which the only characteristic is that each successive footstep proves it solid—of which the only landmarks are the sounds of water flowing, of rain falling.

His mind seems to have broken in two. His judgment tells him, as it has been telling him all along, that Annie is dead, that there is almost no chance that he will even find her body. But with another less controllable, more urgent part of his mind, which seems not to understand or even to hear the voice of his judgment, he fixes on the thought of the sound of Annie's voice calling to him over the water. And though he can hardly bear the smallness and loneliness of his voice he does not stop calling to her—at times calling in answer only to the silence, only because silence may mean anything.

He flounders through the fringe of briars and sumac at the lower edge of the woods and steps out into a cornfield. His boots are immediately clubbed with mud, but he feels lightened and goes more erect now that he is free of the woods. He goes on until the rain slackens and he sees house lights along the top of a ridge way off to his left, and he knows that he has turned out of the creek valley and come upstream along the river maybe half a mile. He turns, cursing the water and the darkness and himself, and starts back.

But now he makes no attempt at all to follow the edge of the water. Guessing at everything, with the fury of a man who has nothing to lose but time and is losing that, he turns away from the river at an angle that he estimates will take him back to the creekwater below the edge of the woods. He is running now, plunging through the darkness with as much abandon as if it were daylight, running into corn shocks and bushes and fences, cursing the darkness and everything in it, telling it to do its God-damnedest and be God-damned.

Sooner than he expected and without even the forethought of stopping, he cleaves like a diver into the briars at the rim of the woods, tangling his feet and throwing him forward—and like a diver he turns at the bottom of his fall, and makes his way out into the open again. He stands still, listening. Not hearing the water, he runs again, and before he has gone a hundred steps plunges in shoulder-deep, feeling, as his forward momentum decreases, the current begin to take him. He lunges, grabs to his left, and finds branches.

He goes up onto the mud and sits down and drains his boots.

He is shaking hard now from head to foot, though, blunted with fatigue as he is, he cannot determine the location of his misery, does not know if it is in his mind or in his body. Sitting on the mud, he can hear himself moaning at the end of every breath, and an old knowledge out of childhood tells him that he is trying not to cry. His clothes feel so heavy he cannot imagine that he will get up again.

But even while his mind frets at their weight, he is already getting up and starting into the woods. For a good many steps he cannot be sure whether he is still sitting down, dreaming of going, or going, dreaming of sitting down. With surprise he finds that the lantern is still hanging in the crook of his elbow.

He gropes and stumbles among the trees, no longer finding his way by conscious effort, repeatedly surprised, when his mind strays back to him, to find the water's edge still beside him. But now his body begins to quit on him—to balk, flinching from the punishment he is putting it to—and it takes him several seconds or several minutes, he does not know how long, to get it moving again.

During one of these involuntary pauses, while he waits for his body to move on, the outward nightmare of that regionless darkness begins to be accompanied by another that is inward. He becomes aware of the bearing down of a question that must have been pursuing him all night. Without a boat or a light, what could he do to save Annie if she should, by whatever miracle it might be, answer him? And he damns himself, with a willingness that startles him, for turning the boat loose, for having taken no precautions to keep the matches dry.

Taking the matches out of his pocket, he finds that the heads are either already gone, or that they crumble as soon as he touches them to see if they are there. But he continues to take the dead sticks out of his pocket one at a time and to stand them upright inside the sweatband of his hat. It is as though his mind, which like his body has begun to work apart from his will, is gambling that absurdity will be more bearable than reasonableness. He corrects the alignment of the matchsticks, making it a good job, and puts his hat back on. Off his head, the hat has become cold. His legs wait to walk forward until it has grown warm and familiar-feeling again.

Now all his stops are tortured by imaginings, the actuality of which he can neither prove nor disprove until his body lurches forward again into the unchanged darkness. He seems to hear Annie calling to him, and he stops and sits down and calls back to her, assuring and encouraging, through the night, afraid that if he goes out of the sound of her voice for help he will never find her again. And when morning comes she is not there; there is no longer any answer to his calling.

Hearing her, he swims out to her, to help her hold on until morning. But the current is too strong. He feels himself carried away from her, her voice becoming fainter and fainter behind him.

He risks leaving her to find a boat. He goes, telling her to hold on and trust him, for he will surely come back and he will bring a boat. And he goes, his mind plunging like a man running to all the places he might find a boat. He finds one and comes back—to discover, in the daylight, that he has no idea where *he* was when he heard her calling, much less where she was.

"Annie! Oh, Annie! Holler loud, sweet baby!"

Now the sound of his voice calling her name makes him cry.

His grief is no longer that of a grown man, but that of a child lost in the dark. And in his abjection and misery his desire still knows the sound of her voice answering him:

"Here I am!"

To his longing for it, her voice has become stronger, superior to his own, assuring and calm.

"Here I am!"

As if at those words the flood of darkness and water would be cleft by a light like the sun shining on snow, new heaven and earth.

Coming to Rest

He does not know how long he has been standing still when he becomes aware of a heavy grey light in the sky. He is divided from the open, he sees, only by a thin scarf of the woods. The rain has stopped, and there is no wind. The silence has grown perfect around him. Through the screen of bare branches, divided from him still by several hundred yards of water, he begins to make out the lurching outlines of the big barn. He feels growing in him, as simply as the growth of daylight, the intention to go home and sleep.

But his body's weight seems too great to move. He falls back into his stupor, oblivious as a tree among trees.

He is aware next of a flock of mallards feeding on the open water ahead of him. He believes that their flying down must have alerted him, and that his attention has been coming toward them slowly for some time, for they are settled now and calmly feeding, remote from the flurry of their arrival, scattered—forty or fifty of them—over the water. He is so close to them that in the grey, slowly strengthening light he can see not just the bold coloring of the drakes, but also the subtler patterning on the backs and wings of the nearer hen birds. He feels let into the depth of intimacy—the peacefulness of wild things among themselves. Their peacefulness stretches among them, holding them at rest on the shining surface of the water.

And so another knowledge seems to have reached him after a long approach: the water is standing still. The sound and movement of it have stopped—he wonders how long ago. A good way out a light, steady wind has begun to riffle the surface. And that is all. The debris of its violence has come to rest on it. The valley floor is covered no longer by a river but by a lake. The rise of the creek has been met by a rise in the river that has backed it and held it still.

The day, again, is heavily overcast, the clouds dragging low over the rim of the little valley. He reaches home, he judges, by sunup or a little after. All the way he has been hurried by the thought of his bed. But now as he comes abreast of the toolshed he turns out of the path, as if he understands, and has all along, that on this day he can bear anything better than comfort. He closes the door behind him and hangs up the lantern. He finds matches, shavings, kindling, and builds a fire in the forge, cranking the bellows until the brittle flame stands still and high, raking bits of coke into it as it burns stronger. As the room warms he sheds his wet clothes, and spreads them to dry. Hanging bundled from the rafters are several hundred-foot lengths of the light canvas used to cover the beds of tobacco plants in the spring. Now, having cleared a place on the workbench to lie down, he takes down one of these lengths of canvas, wraps himself in it, and sleeps.

A Vigil

When he wakes he sees that a meal has been set out for him, kept warming on the coals. His wet clothes are gone, except for the hat and boots, and folded on the bench near him there is a change of dry ones. It must have been Ida who awakened him, shutting the door as she went out. Through the windows above the bench he can see the milk cows straying up away from the barn through the bushes on the hillside, and the two sows feeding busily at their trough. So she has done the morning chores. He knows that she did them last night too, after he was gone. He puts on the dry clothes, and eats hurriedly, standing at the bench before the windows. It has begun to rain again, though now it is hardly a rain at all but a steady drizzle; the sound of it striking the tin roof is only a whisper. Under it the surface of the water has turned softly opaque. He can no longer see the far shore. There is no trace of a doubt in him about what he is going to do, though at the same time there is no trace of a conviction of the usefulness of doing anything. He puts on his jacket and hat. The hat is still wet, heavy, stiff-feeling, and cold. The feel of it recalls to him his last night's toil, the quick-grown familiarity of his ordeal. His vigil mends over the short interval of his sleep; it is as though he has never stopped. This time before going out he takes a burlap sack and capes it over his shoulders, pinning it at his throat with a nail. He opens the door to the sound of water dripping off the eaves and the branches of the oak—and to the sound, faint and sharp through the drizzle, of the church bell ringing at Port William.

In the step that carries him into the weather there is already established the pace that in three-quarters of an hour brings him out of the woods on the hillside above the house of a fisherman, his nearest neighbor on the upriver side of the creek mouth. Once he is clear of the trees he stops for the first time in his walk and studies his whereabouts, measuring in every direction the difference the flood has made. Here the slant of the hill drops from the lower edge of the woods to the top of the river bank, unbroken except for a tapering shelf of bottom just wide enough to provide a bed for the road, now under water. From the front porch of the house a row of stepping-stones goes down the slope and disappears into the flood. At the edge of the water below the house he can see two boats, the smaller one of which he recognizes as belonging to a doctor in Hargrave who uses it in the winter for duck hunting.

When he starts forward again, he goes toward the boats, letting the slant of the hill lengthen and hasten his stride. He has no thought of going to the house to ask for help. Help to do what? How would he bear to tell what it is that he no longer needs help for?

As he steps over into the doctor's boat, he sees from the litter of sticks and dead leaves along the shore that the river is still rising. And then pushing hard on the oars, he feels the boat free itself. He pulls strongly, threading his way among the treetops, breaking out then into the open river. And now, finally, he looks back at the house. No one is in sight.

He sets the boat into the current, staying just outside the channel to keep his oars clear of the drift. His old anxiety of haste has come on him again and he continues to row hard, the blades of his oars driving him on ahead of the current. Approaching the creek mouth, he eases over into the dead water, and then enters the narrower valley, crossing the road a little upstream of the bridge.

All day he can see no more than a hundred yards in any direction. He rides on the detached floe of his vision, which has for edge now the brushy or muddy rim of one shore and now that of the other—which contains, besides himself and the boat, now and again the top of a bush or a tree drifting aimlessly out of the mist and back into it. And in all that day he does not call once; in all the hours of his moving over the face of the water he does not hear himself speak.

The flood crests toward the middle of the week. The rain slacks and stops. The weather clears. As he continues his watching over it, the water slowly gives way beneath him, yielding the land back to the light.

And on the seventh morning—Saturday again, though he has lost all track of the days—when he wakens and looks out the window of the toolshed, he sees that the flood has withdrawn below the edge of the woods. Behind it the valley lies free of it, the mud streaked with the red sunlight of the early morning.

And he goes. He goes, it seems to him, through the opening at the end of his life as it was. To stay, now that the end has come, would be to plant and reap in the very earth of his ruin.

It seems to him that he has already been on his way for days, so that when he does step through the shed door, leaving it open behind him, he has not even the feeling of departure.

The Keeping of the Place

When the water came down Ida did not hear it. She was sitting beside the window in the kitchen with a pile of mending on her lap and pies for Sunday dinner in the oven. And she had the radio on. That Saturday, and the day before too, she had kept the radio on most of the day, waiting for the weather reports that were coming out of Louisville every half hour or so.

When the rain stopped after dinner, she got Annie into her wraps and sent her out to play, warning her to keep her feet dry and stay out of the mud, and then snapped the radio on again before settling into her afternoon's work. She left it going, paying little mind to it except when the businesslike voices of the news or the weather came over it, while she washed and put away the dishes, went to the cellar for jars of berries to put into the pies, made the pies and put them into the oven, went around the house to see about Annie, and saw her sitting with Speck on the swinging bridge—and then at last sat down to her mending.

When the radio stopped in midword a few minutes later, she got up and tried the light switch. She sat down again and took up her work, saying to herself that a tree surely must have blown down on the wire. That sometimes happened, she knew, though it never had happened since the line had come to them. But it occurred to her suddenly that there had been no wind. The thought frightened her, she did not know why. She sat forward in the chair for a moment, her hands still, listening. She got up and started to the front of the house. She was thinking "Uh-oh, uh-oh." She would remember that.

Before she got to the window, of course, it had already happened.

She stood at the window for a good many seconds, as if waiting to see what she would do next, not able to look a second time at the bare grove where the bridge had been. And then she ran to the telephone, put the receiver to her ear, found it dead, and hurried on into the kitchen.

Wondering at herself, she seemed to watch as she went to the stove and opened the oven and saw that the pies were cooking well and shut the oven. And then, running, she went out the back door and across the porch and around the house and down the path toward the toolshed, below which Gideon had just stepped into the boat.

"Gideon! Where is she?"

But she knew.

"Where's Annie?"

But Gideon did not answer. He stood in the boat, as the current caught it and began to turn it slowly, looking back at her, and then turning away as the boat turned.

She watched him go away on the current—trusting him to it, as she had trusted him to other absences, believing that he would bear the worst that could happen to him and come back. Maybe she even hoped he would bring the child back—though she knew what they were up against, she had seen, and the dirge in her mind never stopped.

She turned and started back up the slope toward the house. She went slowly, conscious of the weight of her body lifted stride after stride. In the kitchen she sat down in her chair, moving her sewing basket out of the seat onto the floor. She sat without moving, only looking now and again at the clock.

When the time came she got up and took the pies out of the oven. She seemed to regain something then, and she did not stop. She built up the fire in the stove and began to prepare supper. After that one lapse when it seemed that she kept living only because she could not easily break the habit, she began again her daily ordering and keeping of the place.

When Gideon came back at dusk, she had the supper ready except for the biscuits, which she had waited to put into the oven until he came, as she always did. But he would not eat, and she stood in the door and watched him go back around the corner of the house. When he was gone, seeing that it was getting dark, she went up the back stairs to the room over the kitchen, and brought down an oil lamp. She took it out to the barrel and filled it, carried it into the kitchen and wiped it clean, rubbing the inside of the chimney with a page of newspaper, and lighted it. And then, moving the food off the fire onto the other end of the stove where it would stay warm, she put on the jacket again and started to the barn, carrying the lamp in one hand and the milk bucket in the other. Though knocked off its footing at the lower end and half flooded, the barn, she thought, would stand. The pens and stalls at the upper end were dry. She would not worry about it yet. She milked the cows, fed and cared for the stock, and shut the barn.

When she returned to the kitchen she set a place at the table and made herself eat a little of everything she had cooked, and washed the dishes and put them away. She sat down in the chair again, with the lamp on the edge of the table beside her, and took up her sewing. Gideon would be back before long, she thought, and she would have to keep the light on until he came.

He did not come. She got up now and then and went around the house on the chance that she would see his lantern or hear him, but the darkness was unbroken all around, and it was quiet except for the water running and the rain falling. And she went back and took up her work. She seemed somehow to have gained an extraordinary control over her mind. When she went out into the yard to watch for Gideon, she seemed to know to the second how long she could stand it, to know to the second when to turn, as if away from the sound of her own crying, and come back into the lighted kitchen, where she would force her attention back to the sewing. It was Gideon's absence that occupied her. She thought about it, speaking to herself about it, as though it was the same as his other absences and this night the same as other nights: "He'll be along. He won't want to be *too* late." And then she would say to herself: "Yes, he's probably on his way. He may be coming up by the barn right now." And there was also a limit to how much she could stand of that, and she would have to get up and draw the coat around her and go out again.

And that other absence seemed still to lie somewhere ahead of her, a place she had not yet come to.

Later, with the light still burning beside her, she fell asleep.

Changed

She woke up cold. The lamp flame was pale in the full daylight. The fire in the stove had gone out. Waking she said, "Gideon?" From the sound of her voice in the unwakened room, not answered, she knew, with the same cunning she had had the night before, that her next utterance, if she kept sitting there, would not be so articulate as a word. She got up and put on the old coat and built a fire and, taking the milk bucket, started to the barn.

She saw the fire-heat rising out of the chimney of the toolshed. She walked around and looked through the window at Gideon's face. He lay there, wound in the soiled canvas, his arm under his head. She would have held him then. But glad of his sleep, she left him to it. She hurried through the work at the barn, giving it, she said to herself, "a lick and a promise." Back at the house, she made a breakfast for Gideon, wrapped the change of clothes in a newspaper, carried those things down to him, and, gathering up his wet clothes, slipped out again, hoping he would wake up presently and eat and go back to sleep.

When she went down to the woodpile an hour later, he was gone. After she filled the woodbox, she went to the toolshed again, and carried the empty dishes up to the house and washed them. She got through that day as she had got through the night before, and as she would get through the next five. She washed Gideon's muddied clothes and ironed them, kept the house, prepared the meals and had them ready at the usual times; made work for herself, made herself tired; slept, gratefully, when she had become tired enough.

Like Gideon, she did not, during that week, go back to their bed to sleep, but kept to the rocking chair in the kitchen, bringing down a quilt from a trunk in the back room to wrap around her.

As Gideon went back and forth in his watching, she watched him, aware of his trouble more clearly then, perhaps, than she was aware of her own. He was, it seemed to her, straining to survive the death of their child, as she had once strained to survive the birth. And so she did not approach him, except to meet him at the edge of the water with food.

When she woke on the Saturday morning at the end of the flood, a brilliant pool of sunshine lay across the kitchen floor. She sat still for a while, wrapped in the old quilt in the rocking chair, and looked at the light. It changed her. Before she moved at all, she understood that she was no longer the same. The weather and the place, changing, had changed her.

She got up and folded the quilt and made the fire and prepared to go to the barn. When she stepped out the door a steady drying wind blew against her, coming from the same direction as the light. Around her on the open slopes, above the line of the flood, she could see the faint green of new grass. Below the end of the barn, tilted at what last night had been the shoreline, was the boat. Around it the fields lay free of the flood and empty.

And now, looking over into the bottom on the far side of the creek, she sees Gideon's tracks going away.

She sets her buckets down and goes back to the kitchen. She takes off the coat and hangs it over the back of a chair. She goes through the hall door and down the hall and through the other door into the sitting room. She opens the stair door and starts up. She walks in great haste, hurrying ahead of the oncoming of her pain. She reaches the top of the stairs and goes through the door into Annie's room. Closing the door, she stands just inside it a moment, looking around her. It is a wide low room, the ceiling taking the slant of the roof. There are windows in three of the walls, and now the strong morning light floods into it. The floor is littered with playthings. She walks over to a chair near the bed and, holding to the back of it, lets herself down onto her knees beside it. Her outcry begins deep in her, and rises, and breaks out.

At last the sound of her weeping leaves her more easily, and then it quits. She grows quiet, letting her head rest on the seat of the chair. And then, lightened, able again, she gets up, and straightens the room, and leaves it.

8

Something Ain't Right

Mat hears the knocking before he is awake. The sound is repeated at regular intervals, politely quiet, but insistent. And then Margaret touches his shoulder.

"Mat, there's somebody at the back door."

He gets up, pulls his pants on over his nightshirt, and goes through the hall to the kitchen without turning on the light.

Burley Coulter is standing on the porch, wearing a pair of earmuffs under his old felt hat, his work jacket opened below the two top buttons and his hands shoved for warmth under the bib of his overalls. Back of him, the east has begun to brighten with the premonition of sunup. A steady east wind blows into the doorway, sharp with the night chill.

"Mat, I'm sorry to wake you up."

"That's all right, Burley. Come in. Come on in here where it's warm."

Burley begins pulling off his boots, using the doorstep as a bootjack.

"Don't worry about that."

He pulls them off anyway, and steps into the kitchen in his socks. "But I figured you'd be getting up pretty soon, anyhow."

"Yes. The night's about over."

Mat goes to the switch beside the hall door and turns on the light.

"What's the trouble, Burley?" And it was not until he heard himself speak those words that it dawned on him that something must be wrong.

"Well, Mat, what I've come about really ain't any of my business. I think it probably ain't any of yours either, really. But the reason I come is that if it ain't our business then it probably won't be anybody's."

Mat is clear awake and listening, but he raises his hand to stop Burley, and beckons him to a chair. They move over to the table and pull out chairs, and Burley goes on:

"Well, about the middle of yesterday afternoon, it was beginning to look like the weather was going to dry out finally, and I went over to Jarrat's, thinking maybe he'd want to plan a little work. We hadn't much more than got set down to talk when this horn started blowing down on the river road. I thought at first somebody must have had a wreck and stuck the horn. But then, after a good while it stopped and then started in again. We didn't know what to think. But since nobody lives close to the road along that stretch, and nobody has been passing over it during the high water, we figured it was sort of up to us.

"So we dropped down through the woods on the hillside pretty straight to where the sound was coming from, and a good while before we got down to it we could hear a motor running full-throttle underneath the sound of the horn. And then when we got down in sight of the road we could see this bright red Ford sort of leaning over the edge of the road into the ditch, all covered with radio aerials and foxtails and mudflaps and one thing and another until it looked like a carnival booth. Whoever was driving it had it running as hard as it would go, the rubber stinking and the blue smoke blowing and the mud spraying twenty feet behind the left hind wheel. And there was an old woman the size of a cow standing above it on the top of the road bank, with her fists doubled up on her hips, just looking at it.

"It wasn't the sort of situation you'd just walk into. And we stopped in the bushes at the edge of the road to see if we knew who it was, and to try to understand if we could what in the world was going on. The commotion was just a little hard to see through. We wasn't hoping to see through it to anything reasonable, but did hope for something recognizable.

"I'm telling you this from the beginning because I want you to know how I come to be meddling in it."

"Go on," Mat says. "Tell it all to me."

"Well, I didn't have any trouble recognizing the woman. She was a sister to Gideon Crop's wife's mother. Lizzie Kate Skinner. Used to be married to old man Albert Skinner in town here. You know the one I mean, the one they used to call Meathouse to her back. Big rough brass-mouthed woman. Spent half her life trompling Albert into his grave, and then married an old fellow by the name of Greatlow down on the other side of Hargrave. Well, that's who it was was driving. I knew him along back before he married her. He was a pretty tolerable decent sort of fellow, as big as a bull himself, but awfully quiet and shy, and not too well stocked with brains. A bachelor all his life, for sixty or sixty-five years, and had a little farm, a good one, which is how come her to fall in love with him.

"What had happened, as near as we could see, was they'd come down the hill from here and hit that layer of wet mud that the high water put down on the road, and of course after that couldn't either guide the car or stop it. And had gone scooting over into the ditch. And there they were. And the old man hadn't quit driving yet. The old woman had got out and up onto high ground, to save her life, I reckon. And the old man, I reckon, afraid she'd kill him if he ever once admitted he was stuck, was keeping on doing his level damnedest.

"Me and Jarrat waded across the mud to the other side of the road. We just sort of nodded and tipped our hats to the old woman, and eased on around the front end of the car, and then along the slope of the bank to the door on old man Greatlow's side. He was still driving right on, blowing the horn in great long bleats. The car was just shaking and bouncing, but aside from that wasn't moving. The window was streaked with two or three slashes of tobacco juice, where he'd got confused and tried to spit out it while it was shut. I had to lean close to get much of a look at him. And there he sat, both hands gripped onto the wheel, staring straight out the windshield, pouring the gas to her like Casey Jones. He had the door locked.

"I leaned down to the glass and hollered: 'Whoa there, Mr. Greatlow! Hello!' And then I knocked on the door.

"He never let up or turned his head, or gave any other sign.

"Finally I leaned over the windshield and waved and hollered, and directly he saw me. 'Whoa!' I said. And I went to his window again and tried to signal to him to stop the racket. He rolled the window down, and spit over my shoulder and hollered 'What?' and kept that old car bucking right on.

"I hollered to him: 'Shut that engine off. We're going to try to help you a little!'

"He seemed glad enough to do that, and he shut the racket down and scooted across the seat and got out. The door on his side was leaning too far over against the bank to open enough. And once he was out he didn't pay any more attention to me or Jarrat. The only one he was thinking about was the woman. He sort of backed out into the middle of the road, looking toward her but not at her, with his hand up. 'It's all right now, Lizzie. I'll get it out. Just let me alone, and give me a little time. And I'll get the son of a bitch out of there. The God-damned road department.'

"And Aunt Meathouse stood there on the top of the bank, sort of clouding up over him, like she was still waiting after six years for him to do or say something sensible.

"Well, I seen that wouldn't do, so I walked up the bank and raised my hat, and said, 'Where was it you all was aiming to get to, ma'am?'"

The sky has whitened. The first stain of the coming sunrise lies on the horizon. While Burley has been talking the two of them have turned to the window.

"It's going to be clear again," Burley says.

"Yes. Another good one," Mat says. "Well, go on. You asked where she was trying to go."

Burley pushes his hat off his forehead, and settles it, and puts his hand back in his pocket. "That's right. Sort of by way of polite conversation I asked her where they were going.

"Well, I found out. That is, I sort of gathered it in from among a good many strong statements about what old man Greatlow wasn't much good at, driving and so on. What it come down to is that it had been something better than a week since she'd talked to Ida Crop on the telephone, which she says she usually does every day or so because, with Ida's mother and daddy dead, she feels called on to take some interest. It's a worry to her and all, but she does it. Well, last Saturday, she said, she tried to get Ida and couldn't—it wouldn't ring. She called the operator, and the operator told her the line was out. She said she knew there wasn't much chance of getting into that creek bottom on account of the high water. So she called the phone company and told them the whole story, and told them they'd have to get down there and fix that line, and I can't remember all the strong statements she did make to them about it. Well, of course the phone company couldn't get in there any better than she could. And so the line stayed dead, and so on and so on. And she spent the week worrying about Ida.

"And so when the river began to fall, she didn't waste any time getting the old man into that beautiful automobile that her son had fixed up, looked like, to haul movie actresses in, and then left with them when he went to the Navy. And they'd been on the way since sometime in the morning. The old man surely hadn't driven anything since a Model A, and he poked along, fumbling at it, scared to death—and that old woman, I know, mouthing at him every foot of the way. They had to give up the river road about a mile out of Hargrave, and double back and come by the hill roads and the ridges. And, finally, when they got here in town they somehow thought they'd made it—and went rolling into the mess we'd found them in.

"I felt sorry for them, even her. She was sort of licked, for once, and it improved her. Or, anyhow, I got the feeling—which I never had before about her—that she was letting me live because she wanted me to.

"While she was talking he'd been standing down in the road, making a show of studying the situation. And when I stepped down off the bank I said, 'Well, Mr. Greatlow, what do you think about it?'

"And he said, 'A man build a thing like this, this day and time, and call it a road. It's a shame.'

"I'd seen about all I needed to see, and knew Jarrat had. So I said, 'Well, hold on, old chap. We'll have to go get a team to pull you out.'

"We started back up the hill toward Jarrat's house, and then Jarrat said, 'Second thought, you'd better go get your team too.' So I branched off to my barn. We got the teams geared up, and threw the singletrees and doubletrees and log chains and some digging tools onto Jarrat's sled. And when we got back they were still standing there just like we'd left them. As we stopped the teams, just as cheerful as I could I said: 'Well, now, folks, just settle back, just be at ease. We'll have you on your way in about five minutes.'

"It took forty-five. It was a hard enough pull, no more purchase than the mules could get on that mud. But to make it worse, it took Jarrat and me both to handle the teams, and we didn't have any choice but to let old man Greatlow handle the car.

"Jarrat fastened the log chains to the back bumper and hitched the teams one ahead of the other, and I dug behind the buried wheel so as to give it a way out. We got the old man back into the car and got it started, and Jarrat told him how, when we gave him the word, to give it just a little gas and let it pull along with us. We let the mules ease up over that slick footing into the slack of the chain. And then we called on them, and they tightened, and we called on old man Greatlow, and he jerked the clutch out and poured on the gas, and went to drilling away in low gear just like he'd done before. Pulling against us! And throwing mud all over us.

"We got the mules stopped, and got old man Greatlow stopped, and Jarrat put the gearshift into reverse for him, and told him not to give it too much gas, just let it pull easy. And we tried it again, and he mashed the gas pedal down to the floor again as if anything would save him that would.

"'Whoa! Jarrat said. And then he said to me: 'He's going to run clean over us if we do pull him loose.'

"So we stopped him again and told him we thought it'd be best if he just sat there and held the wheel the way we showed him, and let the mules do all the pulling. We called on the mules again, and in four or five tries finally pulled him out of the ditch and up onto the road.

"We unhooked the chain and drove the teams out of the way, and Jarrat told him: 'Go back easy, now. You're still on mud. Go slow.'

"And the old man started her up, and shoved her into second instead of reverse, and slipped her right back into the same hole, just like shutting a drawer.

"Well sir, I thought that old woman would die. Thought she'd fly all to pieces like a dropped clock. You could see that he'd done just exactly what she had thought he'd do, and she felt justified—but still it made her mad.

"So I sung out to him, like I'd never looked at a better job of driving,

'*That's* the time, old chap! *Now* you talking! Now you got her in shape so we can get her out!' For some reason or another that headed her off. It looked like, then, she turned him over to us. She stuck her chin up and turned her back.

"The second time we didn't take any chances. We made him hold the wheel straight, and drug him past the mud, and got him out, and Jarrat got in and turned the car around, and we loaded them both back in and told them to start on home so they'd get there before dark and told them the shorter way to go."

Margaret comes into the kitchen, and Burley hushes and stands and takes off his hat.

"Good morning, Mrs. Feltner."

"Why, hello, Burley. I didn't know it was you. You're out early."

"Yes ma'am, I know it's a mighty bad time of day to come knocking on your door."

"Oh, don't mind that. Any other time, we'd already be up. The wet weather made us lazy."

"Ain't it everybody?" Burley says.

And then Nettie Banion opens the back door and comes in. Everybody says good morning again, and what a fine one; and after that the women begin preparing breakfast. Burley moves to another chair to be less in their way.

"Well, Mat, I never gave another thought to what the old woman had said about not hearing from the Crops until I'd left Jarrat and had gone home. And then, while I was doing my night work at the barn, it got to worrying *me*. And I said, well, I'd go back over the hill as quick as I got a chance and see for myself how they'd made out. And then I'd see if I could get word to old Mrs. Greatlow, since I'd seen that she sure enough *was* worried. And, to tell the truth, I was sort of touched to think of Ida Crop's not having anybody outside their little valley to worry about her except that drastic old aunt. But by the time I'd finished my work it was getting on toward night, and I said I'd go first thing in the morning. I put the thought aside then, and fixed a little supper and ate and radioed until I got sleepy and went to bed.

"And, it must have been two-thirty or three o'clock this morning, I commenced to hear that horn again. And I says to myself, 'Well, Burley, your dreams are getting too loud to sleep with.' I rolled over and tried it again and it didn't stop, and it come to me then that I was *hearing* it. And I says, 'Well, durned if the luck ain't picked *you* out.' After I'd listened a while, I could tell it was stuck sure enough this time, wasn't anybody blowing it *that* way on purpose. I had the suspicion from the first that it was the same horn. But I somehow hated to admit it.

"I was out of bed by that time and had the light on and was climbing into my clothes, and hurrying. I went down and snatched up the lantern and lit it and started out. And hadn't more than made it to the yard gate before I realized I didn't have any idea at all which direction I ought to be going. That horn seemed to be bawling from every direction at once, the air just ringing with it. My head was full of it, and it seemed to be piling up around me, getting louder all the time.

"Figuring any direction was more likely than none, I took off running down the hill, because it was easier, I reckon, and into the woods. And then the sound began to fade out. 'Well,' I said, 'I've found out something.' And I turned around and started back up the hill. As I broke out of the woods I seen a light at Jarrat's, and then his lantern coming across the field toward my house. I swung my lantern and he answered with his, and we met and went on together. When we climbed over into the lane at the top of the ridge we struck a fresh car track.

"Well, you know that old lane used to go on out the ridge and down the branch, and struck the creek road there opposite Gideon Crop's house. But I don't reckon anybody's used it beyond my gate for twenty-five or thirty years. And that's where the car had gone. It had a sort of running start by the time it hit the unused part of the road, and it went down the slope of the ridge, spinning and slipping, riding down the weeds and bushes as it went, and then picked up speed where the road turned down into the first hollow, and went over the bank and wedged itself finally into a kind of jungle of undergrowth and grapevines and briars at the bottom of the slant. By the time we'd tracked it into that hollow, we could hear the engine running again just the way we had before. But even after that it took us a while to find it, buried in all that brush, and us with no better lights than we had. We finally caught the shine of one of the taillights and sort of dug our way in to it. And there they were.

"Only this time they were both still in the car. They were just sitting there, looking straight ahead, sort of hopeless and forlorn. And the old man was pouring the gas to it again, like it was that or else. Where the difference was, was with her. Instead of being sort of outside the situation, and mad about it, this time she seemed to be in it as deep as he was, just as puzzled and beat.

"We had to holler and whoop and beat on the roof for it seemed like five minutes before we could get them to see us and unlock the doors and let us help them get out. Which took some doing, the car was so wedged in among the bushes and vines, and at that we couldn't open but one door. We got them out and got the engine shut off, and then opened the hood to see if we could stop the horn.

"It was like the old man hadn't heard the horn, or paid any attention to it, until we did that. All of a sudden it just made him nervous all over. He hadn't listened to it a second before he'd had every bit of it he could take. And he reached in where the motor is and began pulling the wires loose. You never saw anything like it. A man as big and stout as he is, all of a sudden tormented and mad as he could be, pulling that wiring up with his hands like it was grass, and the sparks and blue fire shooting all over the place, and the horn blowing right on like it was coming down out of the sky. There wasn't a thing for Jarrat and me to do but hold the lanterns up and stand back. Well, he tore out every wire he could lay his hands to, and some of the other pieces besides, and the horn still kept on. And then he caught hold of one of the battery cables and picked the battery up and went to shaking it like a dog would shake a rat—the blue sparks still flashing and snapping—and finally jerked the fastening loose. That stopped the horn, and stopped him too. He quieted right down, then, and just stood there. And so did the rest of us, while the songbirds and mosquitoes and things flew out of our ears and off into the woods. It was so quiet you could hear yourself breathe.

"'Well, Mr. Greatlow,' I said, 'this may not be where you was going, but you've done got here.'

"'*Hanh?*' he said.

"And then he looked back at what the lantern showed of the sort of tunnel he'd bored coming down. 'The God-damned government,' he said. 'Build a thing like this, this day and time, and call it a road.'

"And for a while after that we just kept on standing there in the quiet, like maybe if we waited around it would finally begin making sense to somebody. And it *was* a right remarkable scene—all of us standing there, listening to the racket flying away, everybody standing sort of alone, all about the same distance apart, all facing the automobile but not looking exactly at it—like it was one of them things you ain't supposed to admit you know as long as there's a lady present. And the old woman was standing just where we'd helped her to, her mouth all puckered out like Whistler's mother. And I said to myself, 'She's going to kill him or she's going to cry.' Well sir, directly she began to cry.

"About the time she started that, and maybe because of it, it hit me what a comical scene it was, and I began to get tickled. And at the same time I knew that that old woman standing off there by herself, crying, was about the saddest thing ever I seen. She wasn't asking for any comfort because she never had and didn't know how, and probably suspicioned that she might not deserve any. And her old husband so hard rode that he couldn't have gone to her even if he'd wanted to.

"I went to her then, and consoled her the best I could—told her we'd get them home all right, and everything would be fine, and so on. And then I says, 'Ma'am, how in the world come you all to be trying this road? Mistook your directions, I reckon.'

"But that wasn't what they'd done. She calmed down before long and told me.

"After we got them unstuck in the afternoon, they went on back to Hargrave by the way we told them to go, and got there about dark. They stopped at the little store this side of the bridge to get some groceries, and the storekeeper tells them, first thing, that Gideon Crop had been in there about the middle of the afternoon. Said he had about a week's growth of beard and looked like he'd been dug up out of the mud. And acted to the storekeeper like he never saw him before. Just bought some cheese and crackers, and cashed a check for four dollars, and carried his eats out in a paper sack.

"Well, the old woman said she knew then that something wasn't right. That's the way she kept putting it: 'There's something ain't right. Lord, I know it.' So she didn't do a thing but get back in the car and make the old man turn around and head back up here. They went to Roger

Merchant's first. But Mr. Merchant, he"—and here Burley hesitates, and looks at Margaret—"wasn't in no shape to receive company."

"Drunk," Mat says.

Burley nods. "So when the Greatlows knocked and hollered at the back door, nobody came. The light was on inside and they could hear Roger talking—to himself, I reckon—but they couldn't raise him. They gave up there finally, and went on over the hill as far as they could go in the car, and then tried to get over to the Crops' house on foot. Of course there wasn't any chance of that. They had nearly a mile to go in the mud and the creek to cross, and it still running deep, and they never even had a light. They sort of felt their way along for a while, and finally admitted it was hopeless, and turned back. And then they see that they ought to have left the car lights on because it took them a good while, creeping along the way they had to in the dark, to find the car. They got to it, finally, and got it turned around and started back up the hill—and were just ready to give up and go home again when the old woman remembered the road that used to go down from our place. She figured that if they could get to the foot of the hill there she would at least be in calling distance of the house. So she decided to try it. She hadn't been down that road since she was young, but she thought that in all that time it surely was bound to have got better, not worse."

"Burley," Margaret says, "we're fixing breakfast for you. You'll eat with us, won't you?"

"Why, yes ma'am, Mrs. Feltner. Now that you've asked me, I reckon I will."

"Go on," Mat says.

"So, anyhow, we decided that Jarrat would take the old people home in the truck, and we'd let them know how Ida was as soon as we could find out. Jarrat started off ahead to get the truck, and I stayed back with the Greatlows, sort of helping the old woman up the climb. Jarrat had the truck waiting at my gate when we got there, and I helped them in.

"I'd already promised myself to go right on down to the Crops'. I hadn't said so, but seemed to me I had to agree with the old woman—something ain't right down there.

"Well, the more I thought about it, the more sure I got that they're in some kind of trouble, and the more I sort of hung back from the thought of walking into it by myself, to tell you the truth. And then I thought of you, Mat, and decided I'd ask you. I know it's Sunday and all, but would you mind?"

Never What It Was

At the bottom of the hill, just above the high-water line, Mat pulls the truck to the side of the road, and they get out. Before them in the sediment of the flood is the scrawl of the Greatlows' first catastrophe and rescue. Where it is broken by the clutter of tracks, the mud has begun to dry.

To avoid the mud as long as possible, they walk along the face of the hill just above what was the shoreline a few days ago. At their feet, the spring has made its small beginnings: narrow grassblades spiking out of their dead sheaths, spring beauties, a few white flowers of bloodroot. The sunlight again becomes a dwelling place. The life of the ground has begun its rise. And Mat walks, thinking, a kind of singing and crying pressing in his throat: "Yes. It has come again."

They walk as quietly as hunters over the soft ground along the slope as it turns from the river valley into the valley of the creek. The sun is well up now, the warmth of it pressing their heads and shoulders. On the hillside around them there is still that stain of green. In town Uncle Stanley Gibbs is ringing the church bell.

The brush thickens on the slope ahead of them, and to avoid it they turn down the hillside to the creek road. Their feet now weighted with mud, they go more slowly, laboring to walk. Before they have gone many steps, they come to the tracks of a man going out. The tracks turn out of the road just ahead of them, go up the bank, and disappear among the bushes on the hillside.

"They must be Gideon's," Burley says. "He went out the same way we've come in."

"And he hasn't come back. At least not by the same way."

They are coming toward the upper end of the woods in the bottom, the road going along the edge of the valley floor. They seem to have come, not back into the winter, but beyond any season. Around them everything has been flowed over, coated with mud. A few days ago the water stood higher than their heads where they are walking now, and they do not forget it.

They come out of the woods and Burley stops suddenly and points to the careening barn.

But the barn isn't all. Fences have been pushed over and weighted with drift. A great fan of rocks and gravel has been thrown out onto the cropland. Along the banks of the creek are several notches where big trees were torn out by the roots.

"Lord, she was rolling when she hit here."

"Awful," Burley says. "Awful. Look at them fences. Look at them rocks. It'll never be what it was."

The road crosses a rise of the ground, and from the top they can see the long curve of tracks swinging up past the house to the ford of the creek and back down to the road. Deep, brimming with shadow, they are the only marks.

"They're Gideon's all right," Burley says.

"He couldn't come out by the bridge," Mat says. "It's gone. Look yonder." He points to where the bridge hangs snarled in the tree branches.

"And we can't get in by it, either, come to think of it. We can cross at the ford, I reckon, the way he did."

They leave the road, walking beside the old tracks, around the openings of which a dry crust has begun to form. The going becomes harder now. They sink to their ankles at each step, and then, as they heave the other foot out of the mud, sink deeper. Every step requires a combination of main strength and delicate balance.

But they don't stop again until they come to the ford. There where the high banks have been tapered back to let the road across, they stand a moment looking at the water still running strong, and then they look at each other and laugh.

"Nosir," Burley says, "we ain't going to wade *that* in boots."

Each dreads it more than he wants to admit, and they stand there another minute, a little fidgety, looking up and down the creek, wishing for a bridge. And then they pull off their boots and socks and britches, and wade the thigh-deep icy stream.

When they knock at the back door, nobody answers. They knock and wait, and knock and wait.

They have just turned to start off the porch when Ida comes around the corner of the house, carrying a load of stovewood and an axe.

She says, "Hello, Mr. Feltner. Hello, Mr. Coulter. How're you all?" And steps up onto the porch, leaning the axe against one of the posts.

"Fine, thank you," Burley says. "Better weather, ain't it?"

Mat says, "We thought we'd stop by to see how you made it through the flood. Gideon ain't here, is he?"

"No sir, he ain't." And, when they seem to wait for her to say something more: "He went off. I ain't expecting him before supper."

"Well," Burley says, "that old creek surely did come out romping and stomping."

"Yes," she says, nodding, "it did."

Mat says, "I usually see Annie before I see you, Ida. Where's she?"

She hesitates, seems to brace herself between the porch floor and the load of wood; her eyes brim with tears. But her voice, when it comes, is steady and quiet:

"It drownded her. You seen the bridge. Well, she was on it when it tore out."

For a few seconds they stand, all three of them, as if startled by a sudden loud sound in the distance. And then Ida turns and looks directly at them and smiles, her eyes still blurred by the unfallen tears.

"Lord," she says, "I'm letting you stand out here like I haven't got any manners at all. Come in and sit down. I know you're tired. I know you must have had to walk nearly the whole way. And through that mud."

She opens the door and goes ahead of them into the kitchen. As she builds the fire, she begins her story: "I was sewing. In that rocking chair right there by you, Mr. Feltner. And all of a sudden the radio up and quit." And before long she interrupts herself: "I know you all would like some coffee." And without waiting to let them answer, she fills the coffee pot and sets it on the stove. And then she resumes, interrupting again, when the coffee is made, to fill their cups. She does not sit down with them, but stands, facing them, sideways to the stove, her right hand now and then, absently, reaching for the handle of the coffee pot, which she takes up twice again to refill first Burley's cup and then Mat's. She never once falters in her telling. Nor by her tone does she seem to expect help or consolation, as though she simply takes for granted that the time has long gone when she could have been either helped or consoled.

When she has finished, Mat says, "Ida, you oughtn't to be down here by yourself. Why don't you come up and stay with us—for a few days anyhow? It wouldn't put us to a bit of trouble."

She shakes her head. "I'm much obliged to you, Mr. Feltner. But I got this stock here to look after, and these chickens, and them old cows to milk."

Mat does not insist. "Well, if you get to wanting to come, you come. We'd be glad. Margaret would be." He hesitates. "Do you reckon it could be a *good* while before Gideon gets back?"

"Mr. Feltner," she says, "he'll be back. I know if a man's going to make a crop he ought to be here getting ready. But I'll see to things."

But her next words are borne on a pride that divides her from them:

"Of course, that's up to Mr. Merchant. It's his place."

"No," Mat says, "That's one thing I wouldn't worry about."

She nods, and then smiles. By another change of voice, she again makes them her guests: "You all have another cup of coffee."

But Mat gets up. "We'll have to get on. We want to go down and look at the barn before we leave."

They all go out together to the barn. They go from one upright to another, studying the sprung framing, now and again pointing to a burst mortise or a loosened brace.

"Well," Burley says finally, "she looks like she's sort of got herself propped up. She might stand up in this shape for a long time."

"Yes," Mat says, "but, still, I wouldn't trust her too long to a hard wind. She'll either have to be straightened back, or torn the rest of the way down."

They go out. At the house Ida thanks them and leaves them.

They wade the creek again, and start toward the river road.

Some Cleaning Up

It is past the middle of the morning by the time they get to the truck and start back up the hill. As they approach the entrance to the Coulter lane,

Mat says, "I'm going out to Roger's. But there's no use in your going, unless you want to."

"Well, I ain't got anything better to do."

At Roger's, as they expected, there is no one in sight. The only sound, after Mat shuts the motor off, is a loose sheet of tin on the barn roof grating in the wind. As they come up the slope of the yard a groundhog, sitting erect on his dirt mound at the corner of the front porch, tumbles into his hole.

As they turn the corner of the house and come in sight of the back porch, Roger's half-dozen old Dominecker hens come running toward them.

"Hungry," Mat says.

They go on to the back door. They shoo the hens out of the way, and the ragged old birds trot out to the limits of their fear and then come back like so many yo-yos.

Mat knocks, and they listen, and he knocks again, louder.

"Roger!"

No answer. They stand there a moment, the hens watching them, the flap of loose tin grating on the eave of the barn.

Mat turns the knob and gives the door a shove, expecting it to be locked; but it flies open, banging against a chair. The hens rush in and begin pecking at the corn piled against the chimney.

Roger is lying in the big four-poster bed, wearing shirt and tie and coat and hat, generously covered with quilts, his head propped against the bare headboard—sound asleep, his bottle propped beside him, a large briar pipe lying extinguished on his chest. That he has escaped burning himself up is owed, according to some, only to the Lord's noted solicitude for drunkards and fools.

Mat and Burley stand outside the door, looking in, a little startled by the sight of what they had expected to see. And then, as if by a sudden exhalation of the old room, they are hit by the stench of it.

"Pew!" Burley says, "Good God!"

"I reckon you can see now where you made your mistake," Mat tells him. "You'd have found things smelling a good deal better at your place."

"I will admit," Burley says, "them old hens have got a good deal better stomach than I do."

Breathing as little as they can, they go into the cluttered room. They plunge through the wrangle of furniture and tools to the windows—which come open with considerable difficulty, and once opened won't stay. Through all the rattling and banging Roger sleeps with the composure of a funeral effigy, emitting a series of remarkably lively snores. Having breathed the corrupted air as long as possible, they hurry back outside. Searching the yard, they pick up sticks to prop the sashes and plunge in again.

They come out this time ahead of the wind, which comes pouring through the opened windows behind them, and they stand in the yard to let it work.

"Let her blow. Let her breathe."

They stand a while and let her breathe, and then Mat says, "Well, do you want to see if we can wake him up?"

They drive the chickens out and toss several ears of corn into the yard to keep them busy, and go over to the bed. Mat leans and taps the old man on the shoulder.

"Roger."

Not a stir.

"Wake up, Roger!" He shakes him. "Oh Roger!" He shakes him hard, and the old man's eyes open.

"Roger, wake up! You've fouled yourself like a baby. Are you sick?"

"There's none here, sir," Roger says in a weak thin voice, raising a hand. "None here. In the bank, in the bank. There's not any here. It's in the bank."

"Roger, it's Mat and Burley. You've stunk the place up till a normal man can't breathe in here."

"Cousin Mat, I've lost control of my unavoidables."

Roger, remembering the bottle then, feels along the headboard for it, and slips it under the covers.

"What we want to know, Roger—are you sick?"

"I've—ah—been slightly under the weather. You might say. Yes."

"Or are you just drunk?"

"No, Cousin Mat. Indeed not."

"You've been here all night without a fire, Roger. How long has it been since you got up out of that bed?"

Roger's voice chirps with righteous sarcasm. "*Why,* I would imagine, not since about Washington's birthday."

Mat walks away. When he speaks again he speaks to Burley. "Let's build a fire."

They soon have the little stove roaring and crackling with as much fire as it will hold. They find a washtub and fill it and set it on the stove. While they wait for it to heat they set the room to rights. They carry out and pile up and rearrange and sweep until it is possible to cross the room in a fairly straight line without climbing. While they work Roger lies as they found him—asleep or awake, they cannot tell.

When the water is warm they set the tub on the floor in front of the stove.

They find a piece of soap, a scrap of a rag, an old towel, and put them on a chair beside the tub.

Mat goes back to the bed.

"We want you to take a bath, Roger. Can you get up?"

"If you please, Cousin Mat, I wish to sleep. Your visit, and Mr. Coulter's too, is appreciated, I want you to know. But now, perhaps, you will be so kind as to leave."

Mat jerks the quilts back and takes a handful of Roger's shirt.

"Get up! Stand up!"

And he brings him up, and stands him upright on the floor beside the bed.

Roger stands there in hat and coat and shirt and soiled underwear, sagging a little, but standing up, surprised—for once, silenced—by Mat's anger.

The two cousins stand face-to-face. They seem to balance a moment across Mat's pointing forefinger, which then buries itself up to the first knuckle in Roger's coatfront.

"Roger, I want you to clean yourself *up.* I want you to wash yourself. And when you get those clothes off, put them in the stove, you hear?"

And Roger turns, obedient as a child, and gets started on his buttons.

"Have you got other clothes to put on, Roger?"

"I should think so, cousin."

"Clean?"

After looking in the wardrobe, Mat takes the cleanest of the quilts from the bed and folds it and puts it down beside the washtub. "You just wrap up in that, Roger, when you get clean. And keep close to the fire." And to Burley: "Let's just carry that mattress and the bedclothes out and burn them."

And they do, each of them taking two corners of the mattress and doubling it, lugging it off the springs and out into the yard. They pile the debris of their earlier cleaning on top of it, soak the whole mess with coal oil, and set a match to it. A big fire stands almost instantly over the pile, the flame-end cracking like a whip.

"There's nothing here fit for a human to wear or sleep on or eat," Mat says. "If you don't mind staying with Roger, I'll go to town and see what I can find. We'll need to eat before long. And I'll have to stay here, I reckon, until I can get Roger straightened out."

"You go ahead. If Mr. Merchant lives through that bath, I'll see to him."

A Pleasing Shadow

Margaret has taken off her hat, and put on an apron over the clothes she wore to church. She looks around at Mat and smiles as he comes into the kitchen, and turns back to the stove. She is wearing her grey dress that so becomes her—a pretty woman. He takes that in. He comes into her presence as he would come into the pleasing shadow of a tree—drawn to her, comforted by her as he has been, usually, all his life. And in spite of all that he has to do, he pulls a chair out from the table and sits down.

"Widow woman, you look mighty nice."

"I was wondering when you'd be back. Did you all get down to the Crops'?"

He nods. "They lost their little girl, Margaret. Annie. She drowned in the flood. And Gideon's gone."

"Ah!" Margaret turns toward him, and though he does not look up he feels her looking at him while he tells her.

"We saw Ida," he says, finishing, "and she seems to be doing as well as you could expect. Better." He utters a kind of laugh, a sound of amazement and pity. "She's farming that old place like there never was anybody there but her."

"Mat, she oughtn't to be there by herself."

"I know. And I told her to come up here, but she wouldn't hear of it. 'I got this stock here to look after, and these chickens, and them old cows to milk.'"

"Well, I must go down there."

"Yes. You must. The next time I go. But now I've got to do a family duty."

She looks at him.

"Roger. He's been down drunk, and got in awful shape. I suppose we're going to have to arrange to take care of him, whether he wants it arranged or not. I'm going to call Wheeler and see what can be done."

"What are you going to do now? Today, I mean?"

"Well, Burley's out there with him. And I guess I'll have to stay a night or two until he's straightened up, and by that time maybe we can find somebody to live with him. First thing, though, we've got to have something to eat, and Roger's got to have something fit to wear. And since Burley and I burned up his old mattress and his bedclothes, I'd better get some bedding out of the attic.

"So"—he goes to the door, stops, and looks back—"why don't you see what you can scrape us up in the way of vittles? And I'll get the bedding."

"Lord, Mat, things are happening here, aren't they?"

"Yes. They are—and have and will." He comes back and kisses her. "Maybe you can find one of my old suits for Roger. He's particular what he wears, you know."

Half an hour or so later Mat finds Roger sitting by the stove in his hat, wrapped in the quilt. And Burley, having further simplified the order of the room, is finishing a second sweeping of the floor. The room smells of burning locust wood and the fresh wind.

Mat sets his load down on the table. "Well, did he get washed?"

"All but his hat, I think."

Mat hangs the fresh clothes over a chair beside Roger. "How're you feeling, Roger?"

"Somewhat refreshed, thank you, cousin."

"Good. Put these clothes on, then. And we'll fix a bite to eat."

He and Burley finish unloading the truck, and make up Roger's bed and a cot for Mat, and prepare a meal.

Roger sits across from them at the table, as bodiless-looking as a coat-hanger in Mat's suit, his frail old face and hands sticking unaccountably out of the collar and sleeves. There is a certain exaggerated delicacy in his handling of the knife and fork—a certain tilt to the face, as if he is balancing an invisible straw on the bridge of his nose. He looks, Burley thinks, like a cross between King Louie the Fourteenth and a turtle. When he finishes eating he leans his head against the chair back and goes to sleep.

For Someone Who Will Come Later

That night, after dark has fallen and the supper dishes have been put away, Mat sits in the small light of a lamp in a corner of Roger's kitchen, reading the Sunday paper that he brought back from town when he went in the late afternoon to do his feeding. In the bed on the opposite side of the room Roger lies asleep.

Mat is more than a little lonely, more than a little depressed at having to be away from home at such a time. Once or twice he has had to fight off the temptation to get in the truck, along with this fruitless dying branch of the family, and go back to Margaret and his own house. But he has plenty of reasons not to do that—not to be fetching in the worst to be served by the best. But still his own house tugs at his mind.

In this alien house, troubled only by its slow weathering and going down, Mat is aware of other houses: Gideon Crop's, the Coulters', his own—and others, at all distances, in all times of day and night, troubled by deaths and absences.

He sits alone with the brutal history of his time, reading bad news and bad good news, as if there is nothing else to read, believing that probably there is not. Once, in Port William, they might not hear of a death in Hargrave until after the burial. Now they know the outcome of a battle on the other side of the world before the dying are dead.

He sits, making his mind be led by the words, under the fall of light from the lamp. The narrowly opened window above the table breathes the freshening of the year, the moist night, the shrilling of frogs. And across the room continue the audible entrances and exits of Roger's breath.

In the left-hand pocket of his shirt since the middle of the afternoon has been his copy of a contract—drafted by Roger's lawyer in longhand on yellow paper, signed by Roger and by Mat—by which Mat is employed as overseer of Roger's property at an annual wage of something less than he imagines will pay for his trouble. That afternoon's meeting between Mat and Roger and the lawyer bore no resemblance at all to their earlier ones. Mat controlled it deliberately from the beginning, deferring neither to Roger's wish to speak nor to his own consideration, which once constrained him, of Roger's right of say-so. They sat at the kitchen table and made the agreement to Mat's specifications, the old lawyer writing on his pad below Mat's pointed forefinger. For Mat was angry enough, and he had told himself: "If anybody besides him is responsible, it's me, and I've sat and watched as long as I'm ready to." Before it was over, while the lawyer was still there, he said to Roger: "There'll be a man coming here, as soon as I can get hold of one, to live with you, and look after you, and keep this old house. You can't go on living here by yourself. Do you understand?"

And Roger said he did.

Mat takes no pride in that—it is only patchwork—but he is glad, relieved. And he has made some plans. Coming and going in the latter part of the afternoon, he has looked newly at Roger's land. Some of it, the steep ground of the hillsides, is worn out; it will have to be owned by its thickets longer than Mat will live. That part of it he has put to rest in his mind, turning to what can be kept and used and made better. While he was at home in the afternoon he hired Ernest Finley to work on the barn at Gideon Crop's.

Although he has increased his worries, he has no regret, no feeling that he has done less or more than he had to do. But a few days ago, if he had considered expending time and bother on this land, he would have considered also the possibility that he might later be able to buy it. But now Virgil is missing, and Mat needs no more land for himself. He is too old now to need it—if he ever did. This new work must be done for the sake of the land itself—and for the sake of no one he can foresee, someone who will come later, who will depend then on what is done now.

A Spring Night

Tuesday and Wednesday it turned cold again. The wind blustered all day both days. But sometime Wednesday night the weather quieted, and Thursday morning the spring seemed to have gained back all it had lost, and more.

On Tuesday morning Wheeler Catlett phoned and left word for Mat that he had found a man who might do to stay with Roger, and that the two of them would drive up to look at the place and talk wages that afternoon.

An arrangement was made, and the man—a hearty, loud-talking fellow named Bailey—promised to gather his belongings and return on Friday. Now, Thursday night, supper finished and Roger gone sober to bed for the fourth night in a row, Mat is sitting alone on the well top behind the house, smoking a cigar. Just the pale last minutes of the twilight are left. The sun's heat rises out of the ground, and the air is still and warm—summer air. During the day, taking Roger with him here and there in the truck, he has made the beginnings of his spring work, and he is tired with a familiar tiredness that now, near rest, comforts him. In spite of the bothering with Roger, it has been a good day, and the night is good. Tomorrow night he will be at home.

Behind him, in the old kitchen, he hears Roger cough and stir. And he becomes aware of a sadness, too, that he has been feeling, staying there those nights. Roger is old with his wasting of himself and with age—coming down to the end of the line, for him, and for the line too. Mat has been thinking of that. Roger is the last remnant of a history of which he is the only admirer. After him, there will be no sign that the Merchants ever existed, except for a diminishment of the earth and of human possibility. They have gone, and are going, leaving nothing behind but thicket growing back over the slopes they destroyed, and a remnant of usable soil on the ridges and in the bottoms that they would have destroyed if they had lived long enough.

Around Mat, the country throbs with the singing of frogs. Too high in the dusk to be seen, a flock of wild geese passes, a kind of conversation muttering among them. They will go talking and talking that way all night, flying into new daylight far off. That they do not think of him, that they go on, comforts Mat. He thinks of those wild things feeding along weedy lake edges way to the north with a stockman's pleasure in the feeding of anything, and with something more.

And now Burley Coulter steps over the sagged yard fence without breaking stride and comes on down the slope of the yard through the dead weeds, carrying an unlit lantern in his hand. He comes over to the well and sits down beside Mat and lights a cigarette. They sit smoking for a while.

Finally Burley says: "Spring night sure enough, ain't it? Frogs singing."

"Yes."

"And I heard a flock of geese go over just before I got here."

"I heard them."

There is another silence, and again Burley is the one who breaks it: "Well, Mat, since I saw you—when *was* it I saw you? Day before yesterday evening?"

"I think so."

"Well, after we talked I went and talked to Jarrat, and we did some telephoning to various ones about Ida's troubles. If everybody does like he says, we ought to be able to give her all the help she'll need. We went down this afternoon and broke some plant-bed ground on top of the ridge. Some of the others are going down tomorrow to haul wood to burn on the beds when we get them ready. And I reckon that's about the way it's going to go."

They talk on, considering possibilities, looking ahead through spring and summer and fall, thinking of what will have to be done and how they will manage to do it.

"Ida says all we need to see to is the heavy work—the plowing and so on," Burley says. "She'll do the rest."

"Do you think we ought to depend on her to do that?"

"She'll do it anyhow," Burley says. "So we might as well depend on her."

Green Coming Strong

March 25, 1945

Dear Nathan,

I laid off to write you last Sunday, but never got around to it, and reckoned you would be on your way across the water anyhow. I expect, if that's so, you'll get this one about as quick as you'd have got the one I didn't write last week. I hope so.

The flood is over now. It was a bad one, and come at a bad time, and done damage, and has throwed everybody way behind. We got awfully tired of looking at water.

The worst of it—which we didn't even know about until it was over—was that Gideon and Ida Crop's little girl, Annie, got drowned on the 10th. Gideon, according to what Ida says, watched over the backwater until it went down. And then he went. And hasn't been found either. Mat Feltner has been trying to find him, calling the police and such in different places, but hasn't heard a word of him. It seems a man is about as easy to lose in this world as a pocketknife. I wouldn't have thought it. But there's a lot I never would have thought that has turned out to be so.

Virgil Feltner, by the way, hasn't been heard from either. Nothing to say about that, I reckon, until Mat says something. Except it's bad.

I hate to write down these sad troubles. But I can't think of any argument why I oughtn't to tell you. They happened. And I'm in a way obliged to speak of them because they did happen and I know it. Seems to me that when you start home you'll want to know what's here and what's not. And if anybody's going to write it to you, looks like it'll have to be me. I said to your daddy the other day, "Why don't you write to Nathan?" And he said, "God Amighty, Burley, he knows what I'm doing."

Making tracks is what he's doing. Making that team of black mules realize what he fed them through the winter for. Which I imagine you do know.

Well, spring is here, finally. And we've had some days of fine weather. This is one, clear and quiet, hardly any air stirring at all, just warm enough to be comfortable in the sun, and the country turning greener all the time. I'm happy today, in spite of everything, glad to see it all come back.

The old spring comes up in me just like it comes up in everything, and I'm gladder to be alive today than three weeks ago I imagined I'd ever be. The night, say, of the day you left.

Speaking of time, I was fifty years old on March 12, and clean forgot it. Jarrat was the one finally thought of it. Day before yesterday he says, "Burley, you're fifty. You've been fifty for two weeks." It scared me. And then it made me mad. Which made him laugh, which don't happen every day. And we counted up and fifty's what I am. Half a hundred years I've been alive. And it's a mystery where they've gone. I used to think that when I got to be a man I'd do what I pleased. And what I aimed to please to do was hunt and fish, and breed as far and wide as a tomcat. But there's a great many pretty girls that I've gone by, and a lot of good hunting nights, and a lot of fishing weather. It has happened that that wasn't so much what I was called to as I thought. What it has been, I reckon you would say, is love, for Jarrat and you boys. I realize now that if my calling hasn't been that, I haven't had one. When I die there won't be much around here that anybody can point to and say "Burley Coulter done that." There's not any wheeling and dealing of mine that anybody'll remember. But for *me,* when I think of my life I have to think of it with Jarrat's and yours and Tom's. And even if there is a lot I've let go by, I don't say I ain't blessed.

Don't pay any attention to what I write, unless you want to. My mind just gets to going. Jarrat and I are so quiet, looks like I don't know what *is* on my mind until I go to writing to you.

When the ground dried off enough to let us get on it with the teams, which was last Tuesday morning, Jarrat went at it just like I told you he would. And I've been my usual hundred feet behind him ever since. We're both soft from the winter and from being idle so much during the wet weather, and pretty old too for such a pace, but I expect we've left as many tracks behind us in the last week as we ever did in our lives. The sun has been getting up mighty fast and going down mighty slow.

We've got ourselves behind an awful pile of work—farming on both of these places, and at Mat's. Plus we're trying to help Ida carry on until Gideon turns up, if he does. Plus there's no chance we can see of hiring much help. There's sort of nobody here but children and women and old men. I imagine I'm going to get mighty tired of looking at your daddy's back before October.

All week we've been burning and sowing plant beds—at Mat's, and then down at Gideon's, and since Friday afternoon up here. Fact is, that's what we're doing right now. Last night when we quit I said to Jarrat, "Let's get a little rest tomorrow." And Jarrat said all right. And we passed it back and forth awhile, saying we'd lay around today and get over some of our soreness and hit it hard again Monday morning. And then this morning early we got to looking over all we've got to do, and piddled around and greased the wheels on Jarrat's wagon and sharpened our axes. And first thing you know we're out here on the ridge, working like it's the last good day. And every time we get a little break I come over here to the wagon and write some on this letter.

It's on in the afternoon now, and we're just sitting here, resting and watching the last of it burn. I do like this work. There's something about this fire going before the new crop that's cleaning. The *thought* of it is good. All last year's old mongrel chances burnt out of the ground. And first thing you know we'll have them little tobacco plants speckling up through the ashes.

Everybody seems to be as behind in his work as we are, going early and late. From the house at night I can see the plant beds burning for miles, and smell them too. And you know people are awake and busy around them. It sort of brings the country together in a way it never is any other time.

Down in the bottoms they're still waterlogged, just sitting and looking at mud and waiting. Anvil Brant says if it wasn't for fishing he'd try to get in the Army.

Old Ike just come up and laid down under the wagon. I've heard him treed way down in the hollow nearly all day. And he's finally dug out whatever it was, and eat it. So I reckon I'll have to be the one to eat the leftovers tonight. He wants to know what's the matter with me, I haven't been hunting with him for so long. And I don't know what to tell him. I've been thinking that if you stay around this part of the country after the war, maybe we'll get hold of a good bitch and raise a litter of pups, and start over.

That's one of my thoughts. Amazing how I've got so I depend on my thoughts. I can take one I like and just about wear the hair off of it between supper and bedtime. I can remember a time when my head wasn't exactly the part of me that I was most interested in. And now there's actually some thoughts that I kind of look forward to getting a chance to think. I've got a pretty good pocketknife and a pretty good dog and three or four good thoughts.

And a good country to live in, I will have to say. This is about as pretty a time right this minute as you'd ever want to see. Still and clear, and little smokes here and yonder from the plant beds, and that green coming strong. And I'm tired enough that I don't mind to see the sun going down. I wish *you* was here.

Lord bless you, old boy, I think about you all the time.

Your uncle,
Burley

Part Three

9

Look a Yonder

From the top of the ladder, among the branches of the apple tree, Mat's horizon is enlarged. Along the crest of the eastward ridge he can see the line of white canvases covering the plant beds that Burley and Jarrat Coulter sowed five days ago. They make a single stroke of whiteness, drawn exactly along the horizon between the blue of the sky and the ridge, which, in the same five days, has become green. Down the gentle fall of the ground behind him is the town, which he turns toward and turns away from again and again as he goes about his work. The roofs are still visible, their angles sharp, among the treetops stippled with buds. Northward he can see the opening of the river valley, the folds of the upland on the far side, woods and fields clear in the sun. Feeling the limb on which the ladder is propped spring against his weight as he moves, Mat prunes the tree. He likes this work—the look of his hands moving and choosing, correcting, among the tangle of the branches. The orchard is one of the works of his life.

On the ground under the tree Joe Banion is gathering up the cut twigs and branches as Mat lets them fall, loading them onto the wagon. The black clear shadows of the branches tangle over him like a net as he moves. On the edge of the wagon bed, his sheepskin coat buttoned a foot off-center, Old Jack sits watching them, keeping them company. They weren't at work there a quarter of an hour before Joe said, "Well, we going to have help, Mr. Mat. Here come the old boss." Sure enough, there he came up along the row ends of the garden and into the orchard. And until now he has sat there holding the team, driving the few feet to the next tree when Mat and Joe move.

It's a little past the middle of the morning; the early chill has gone out of the air. The town has become quiet. The children are shut in the school, the men gone to the stores or the fields, the women to the kitchens. The voices of cackling hens in Mat's henhouse and barn come brassy and loud into the quiet, and from beyond the turn of the hill comes the bleating of sheep. From the wagon Old Jack's voice follows the turnings of his mind—sounding both comforted and comfortable, one of the sounds of the place come back into the open.

The garden gate opens and shuts, and this time it is Hannah they see coming up along the row ends toward the orchard. She walks heavily over the uneven ground, leaning backward a little against the weight of the child. The wind blows her skirt and her hair as she walks.

She does not come near them, but goes into one of the upper corners of the orchard where late yesterday afternoon Mat pruned a peach tree and left the branches lying. She waves as she goes by, and they wave back. They watch her as she moves through the clutter of branches, gathering the budded shoots. By an awkward stooping and bending she picks them up one at a time, holds them up to look at them, their graceful slendering weighted and knobbed with buds, and lays them into the crook of her arm.

Old Jack sits studying her. "She's a mighty fine girl."

"She is," Mat says.

Old Jack shakes his head. "Ay, Lord!"

They hear the sound of an engine in the air and, looking up, find a small army plane coming fairly low over the town.

"Look a yonder!" Old Jack says. "Yonder's one of them flying machines." A second follows, the look and the sound identical to the first. "God Amighty, there's another'n!"

One after another they come, spaced evenly, a considerable distance apart, their sounds building and fading in steady rhythm. The three men stand looking up, Old Jack braced on his cane like a tripod in the middle of the wagon bed, Joe by the mule's heads where he went to quiet them, Mat on the ladder in the top of the tree. They count. Four, five, six. Thirteen, fourteen, fifteen. Twenty-three, twenty-four, twenty-five, twenty-six. And when the twenty-sixth one carries its sound away, and none follows, they watch them out of sight.

The morning goes on. Mat's mind has been drawn away from his work into the uneasiness of the sky, empty of all sound now. He thinks of the young men enclosed in that deathly metal, their fates made one with interlocking parts and men and events. He feels a cry toward them grown in him, unreleased. It is a long time before his mind will content itself again to take back the tree and his own hands busy in it. Below he can hear Joe Banion:

"How'd you like to fly one of them things, Mr. Jack?"

"Ay, Lord! I wouldn't do it."

"You and *me,* boss man. You and me."

The Bridge

As he always does when the first outside work begins in the spring, Ernest felt a little reluctant to give up the orderly enclosure of the shop. And so he was glad enough to spend most of the morning getting ready—lugging his ladders and rope tackle and jacks and tool boxes out of the shop and loading them on the truck; setting the shop to rights, sweeping it out, putting tools away, feeling the place settle around him and grow still.

When he came up opposite the Crops' house, a few minutes before noon, he eased the truck out across the bottom to what, two weeks and two days ago, had been the outside end of the footbridge. He turned the truck around and killed the engine, and ate the sandwiches he had brought.

During the fifteen or twenty minutes he spent doing that, and the five minutes he spent smoking a cigarette afterwards, the place began to make its claim on him. It took him only a few seconds to foresee in some detail how he would have to go about the rebuilding of the bridge; after that his mind was free to take in the look of the place. Except for the singing of birds and the steady rippling of the creek, the little valley was quiet. There were no human noises anywhere. For a while he remained half alert for the sound of a voice or a door or an engine—one of the habits of his winter work in town. But he grew used to the peacefulness of the place. He quit expecting anything but the natural sounds. The silted bottoms, he saw, were beginning to show a faint scaling of green, and along the banks of the creek, running clear now over the rocks, the muddied limbs of the willows were putting out new leaves.

Almost without his realizing it, his thoughts going ahead of him, he has begun his work. The butt of the cigarette still burning in the corner of his mouth, he fishes a pair of rubber boots out from behind the seat. He sits down on the running board and puts them on. He places the crutches under his arms and, moving around the truck, takes a coil of half-inch rope out of one of the tool boxes, and starts up along the creek.

He makes his way with some difficulty into the swift water of the ford. The water comes nearly to the tops of his boots, caving them in coldly against his feet and legs. He is aware, almost as soon as he begins to move against the push of the current, of the absurdity of wading swift water on crutches. His gratitude that nobody is there to see him, and then his fear that somebody may come, make him ridiculous to himself. He crosses the creek, feeling his way over the uneven stones of the riffle with the crutch ends, and goes down the shallows along the far edge until he comes to where the bridge dangles in the trees. When he has fastened the rope to the loose end of one of the cables and weighted the free end of the rope with a rock and thrown it over to the other bank, he wades back across.

Using a block and tackle, he pulls the bridge out of the trees and across the steam and into place. He locks the pulleys and walks to the top of the high bank and stands there for three or four minutes, studying the job now that he has it out where he can look at it. The snarled skein of wood and cable and wire that he has hauled tense between the banks has not even begun to resemble a bridge. The footboards have been broken and split, some of the crosspieces knocked out or broken, the handwires wound and tangled through the mess of the rest—and the whole thing, crusted with silt, bearded and swatched with drift, twisted two full turns. But the beginning is there, made. While he watches, a kingfisher lights on one of the strands of the tangle, perches a moment, sees him, startles, flies off down the creek. "I'll finish her by sundown," he says to himself. And he goes back to the truck for his tools.

Until after sundown, until the bridge is a bridge again, and looks like one, curving its perfect curve between its fastenings, he does not stop. He untwists and splices the broken cables, binds them back around the trunks of the two trees from which they were torn loose, rebuilds the steps up to where the end of the footboard will be laid. He goes into it then, building his way across, wedging his way into the mess of it, leaving it made and straight behind him. Fixing as he goes, crawling back and forth for materials over what he has finished, he attaches the crosspieces and lays on and nails down the footplanks. And over his bent back the day moves toward the end of its own curve. He hurries at his work, excited by his high balancing out on the thing he has made, feeling the echo of every hammer stroke rock back under him along the taut cables—and excited by knowing that a bridge is what it is. There comes to be something deeply pleasing to him in the idea of a bridge—not, maybe, the first mark a man makes on the earth, but surely one of the first marks made by a neighborhood—and he hastens toward its completion. Long before he is done, he already knows how it is going to be, and he is driven on by an appetite for the finished look of it.

The sunlight goes out of the valley, rising up along the sides of the hills on the eastern side. The ground begins to cool. His mind begins to take leave of his work. He gathers his tools from the ground around the finished steps and goes back to the side he began on, walking without the crutches and having to move slowly with his load to keep balanced. At the other end he puts the tools down, and takes up his crutches. For a moment he stands there, looking at the bridge and the water under it. Finished, he is let down now into his tiredness. He lights a cigarette, smokes it a moment with deliberate pleasure, and turns and begins loading tools and rope and usable scraps back into the truck.

Hearing something, a footstep maybe, he looks across the bridge at Ida standing on the top step at the other end of it. She is wearing a plain faded cotton dress, and a sweater that he knows at once belongs or did belong to Gideon. She is smiling in reserved greeting to him, in expectation of what from him he does not know. She steps up onto the end of the bridge, and he feels the inwashing sense of the presence of her body, kept waiting inside that coarse, worn sweater of Gideon's.

"Can I come across now?"

"Yes. Come on across."

She comes out onto the bridge, giving her weight to the flexible strength of it, following down into the curve of it. And then, for the first time all day, he thinks of this woman's drowned child, and his remembrance flinches inside him. He is suddenly nerved tightly as one watching a tightrope walker. And he sees that a hesitance grows in her as she comes on toward the place where she knows Annie was sitting during the last half hour she lived. To Ernest she seems to force herself up to that place, and then past it. And once past it, she is all right. She comes on, the footboard rocking slightly under her.

He is standing beside the steps, and as she comes to the end of the bridge he reaches his hand up. He would not ordinarily have done so opening a thing—not, especially, hold out his hand to a woman nearly a stranger to him. But she takes it. And sensing the strength in that arm levering over the bar of the crutch, she looks at him. It is a look that he knew to anticipate—a look of surprise and of a sort of dismay, as if the only thing more odd than a cripple is a cripple of great and capable strength who smells and sweats and works and wears out pretty much the way everybody does. But Ida does not withdraw. She gives her weight to his hand, and steps down.

"Thank you."

And again she looks at him, this time with such immediate and open candor, such accepting of him as he is, that he feels himself made natural, made as if whole, by her look. It is as though she has reached into him with her hand. He turns and starts back to the truck.

"Lord, you sure did get it done fast. I thought, the mess it was in, it would take a week."

"Well, it wasn't too much trouble. Once you get started into a thing like that it'll usually turn out very well."

"I declare, it's nice to have it up again. I ain't been on this side of the creek in I don't know how long."

She is walking along beside him now, a little ahead of him—a woman not yet thirty, strongly and a little thickly made. Her face still keeps some of the prettiness of her girlhood, her hair pulled back out of the way and gathered and pinned. She walks with the naturalness of a woman who has gone a great deal on foot, and without the self-consciousness of one who has ever tried deliberately for grace—so calmly a woman of her own kind and place and way that she seems hardly aware of herself, and so quietly belonging to Gideon that the idea of him seems as near her, as much touching her, as his old sweater. Ernest is aware that she has given no thought to how she may look to him. His hand keeps the memory of the feel of her hand, nearly as hard as his own.

He throws the last armload of scraps into the truck bed with a satisfying completing slam. "Well, I reckon I'll call it a day." Looking up at the house now, he sees that she has already finished her work at the barn for the night—the rinsed milk buckets, which were not in sight earlier, are turned up to dry on a bench beside the cellar house.

"Mr. Finley—you're going to town, ain't you?"

"I'm aiming to."

"Well, could I ride out as far as the mailbox?"

"All right. Get in. I'm just ready to go." He hastens ahead of her, opens the door, and makes a place for her, shoving aside the tools, gloves, chains, water jug, pieces of rope that have collected on the seat and the floorboard. "It's a mess. Maybe that'll be room enough for you."

"It'll be fine."

He gets in, starts the truck, and they leave, jolting and rattling over the violent surface of the road.

"Gideon has to fix this piece of road every spring—all the way from our house out to the pike. The county's supposed to, but it don't much."

Ernest cannot think what to reply, surprised at the ease with which she speaks of Gideon. She mentions him casually, as confident of his presence somewhere she does not know as she could be if he had gone to Port William.

She stays silent for several minutes, holding to the door handle with one hand and bracing against the dashboard with the other to steady herself, looking out at the evening which is very slowly dimming toward twilight.

"You going to fix that barn?" she asks.

"Aiming to."

"Mr. Feltner said you was aiming to tear down that lower end of it."

He nods.

"Well, I reckon there'll still be room left for Gideon's tools and things, won't there?"

"I believe there will. I don't believe you need to worry about Mat mistreating you all."

"Gideon's always thought a lot of Mr. Feltner. So do I. Though I never had many dealings with him until here lately." She watches the road approach and pass under, shaking the truck. "You going to do all that work by yourself?"

"I imagine so."

She gives him another speculating look, her eyes as direct and unapologetic as if she is studying the back of somebody's head.

"Well, I imagine that'll be right smart of a job for one man."

"I imagine so."

He stops at the mouth of the lane, and she opens the door and gets out. Standing there looking back at him, holding the door ready to shut, she says, "I'm much obliged to you."

"Do you want me to take you back in? Save you the walk."

"No, I don't mind." She smiles for the first time since he looked and saw her standing on the bridge. "That's a better road for walking than it is for riding, anyhow."

She starts across the road to where the mailbox perches on its careening post, doorless, wide-open mouth tilted upward, like the hungry young of some big bird.

Ernest turns into the road and goes, but slowly, watching her in the rearview mirror. He sees her walk over to the box, look in, and turn back empty-handed into the lane.

A Guest at a Strange Table

He was on the roof the next morning before the dew went off. He set his ladders up against the eave, flung a long rope over the barn, tied it at both ends to give himself a kind of banister, and propping his crutches against the foot of the ladder, went up and began.

And he has been surrounded by his own noise now for nearly three hours—his hammer-claws driving in under the nailheads, the nails screeching out through the tin, the released sheets sliding down over the sheets still fixed and striking the ground. The sun is getting high, and the metal roof has begun to give back the warmth of it. From time to time he goes down and stacks the sheets he has torn off, and drinks, and goes back up. Aside from that, he has hardly raised his eyes from his work. After each interruption the sounds of his work have enclosed him again, and carried him on. And each time he settles back into himself and into the work, his habitual commenting to himself in his thoughts begins again. Finding he has worked beyond reach of his rope, he thinks, "Uh-oh!" Nerves aching with the smooth hard slant of the metal as he crawls after the rope, he thinks of falling, and his thought shudders and whistles. "Shoo! Watch that! *That* won't do!"

He hears Mat saying—having put him and Virgil to painting the roof of the feed barn, Virgil with a boy's bravery walking upright on the slant—"Be careful up there, boys. We haven't got time now for a funeral." And then, his voice lifting and hardening: "Virgil, damn it, when you move on that roof take hold of the *rope.* A man's work asks you to be a man. Don't play!" And again, his voice suddenly admitting what he feels: "Sweet boy, *don't* get hurt."

The rope in his hand, Ernest feels the dread of falling loosen from him. "Good enough. *All right.*" Taking up his hammer and laying the rope down beside him in reach of his left hand, he goes back to work. "Virgil," he thinks.

"Uncle," Virgil says, "why in the hell does he have to be after me all the time to be careful?"

"Well, if he didn't think a lot of you he *wouldn't* do it. That's one thing. And, another thing, being careful doesn't come natural to you yet, and he knows it."

"Well, if you know it too why aren't you after me all the time the way he is?"

"Because you listen to me better than you do to him."

Virgil laughs. "Why?"

"Because he's your daddy and I'm not. That's the way it always is, and he knows that too. That's the reason he sends you to work with me as often as he does."

For a moment he can see Virgil, paint bucket in one hand, brush in the other, sitting on the comb of the roof, looking down at him and grinning with a boy's perfect confidence in the superiority of youth to anything. The hot sky stands open above him.

"Mr. Finley."

He looks down and sees Ida on the ladder, holding up a half-gallon glass jar full of water.

"You want a fresh drink?"

He does. Though he has, as usual, his own jug of water in the truck, he hands himself down along the rope to the edge of the roof, and drinks and replaces the top and hands the jug back and thanks her. Pulling himself along the rope in a clambering, lopsided two-step, knowing that behind him she is still on the ladder, watching, he goes back up the roof.

"How did you hurt your foot?"

"In the war."

"Not this one."

"No. The other one."

"Well, you sure don't have any trouble getting around."

He nods. He takes it the way it is meant, a compliment, but his mind fumbles around it, not able to manage a reply. And then he says: "It slows me down some."

"Well, I reckon we've all got our troubles." But as if she did not intend to admit that, she smiles and steps down a rung. "I'll have dinner ready about half past eleven. You can come anytime around then."

"Well, I've got my dinner there in the truck. I reckon I'll just eat that. That's what I usually do."

"Oh, Gideon wouldn't stand for that, Mr. Finley. He says anybody that works here eats here. So you come."

Her head disappears below the eave, and he sits still and listens to her going down. She calls up to him from the ground, still out of sight at the foot of the ladder: "I'll just set this jug here by the wall."

"All right," he says.

He is not comfortable with the thought of going to the house to eat. For one thing, he never enjoys eating at a strange table, and he is particularly uneasy about eating at this one in Gideon's absence. For another thing, he takes pleasure in the quiet noon meals he eats alone between the noisy halves of his days. But the generosity of her invitation is familiar to him, and he knows he cannot refuse it kindly.

He is high on the roof and, looking over the comb of it, he sees her come around the end of the barn and walk up the incline of the road toward the house. He sits there not moving, the hammer dead in his hand, until he sees her go into the kitchen and hears the door slam. And then he slides the claws of his hammer under the next nailhead. The noise of his work stands up around him again. He goes back into it. He works steadily over the metal slope, letting the sunlight drop, after its long absence, through the dark meshing of the barn's framework to the ground.

When the time comes he goes down, hangs his hammer on one of the ladder rungs, and stacks the scattered sheets. He takes up his crutches, drinks, pours out what water he doesn't drink, and, carrying the jug, goes up to the house.

The kitchen door is open, and Ida calls him to come in before he has had a chance to knock. She is busy at the stove. On the opposite side of the room he can see an ironing board set up, and a pile of freshly pressed clothes on the seat of a chair. He comes in, ready to do without question whatever she tells him, sets the jug down against the door facing, puts his hat on the floor beside it.

She takes the teakettle off the stove and comes over to the washtable just inside the door, and pours two inches of hot water into the pan.

He dips from the bucket, diluting the hot water, leans his crutches against the wall, and washes.

"When you get washed you can sit down. It's ready."

There is only one chair at the table and he pulls it out and sits down, putting the crutches on the floor beside him. And she sets the food on—an abundant simple meal.

While he eats she does not sit down. She goes on about her work. As long as he is at the table she makes no attempt at conversation, seeming to take for granted that he has come only to eat, requiring nothing of him except that he fill himself.

He grows amazed at her, at the dignity of her quietness in which he knows she is lonely and grieving. What else he might have expected he does not know, or no longer knows.

When he has emptied his plate, she comes and picks up the meat platter and offers it to him again. "You help yourself, now."

And he does.

Finished, he picks up the crutches and stands and replaces the chair. "That was mighty fine. I thank you."

"Well. You fill that water jug at the pump and take it with you."

He has been stopped twenty-five minutes for dinner. He decides to give himself another twenty. Because he is slowed by his lameness, he usually works by the job rather than by the day. Still, though he never works by the clock, he always rests by it—because, as he has explained it to Mat, it is harder to stop resting than to stop working.

Having given himself those minutes, he becomes saving of them, and hurries back down to the barn so as to waste as few of them as possible. He brings out a feed bucket, turns it upside down against the wall, and sits down in the sun. The only sounds now are a few sparrows chirping back in the driveway of the barn and, continuous and more quiet in the distance, the running of the creek. He sits for a moment without moving, letting these sounds and the little valley and the sunlight and the white-clouded sky take their places in his mind, and then gets out a cigarette and lights it. He smokes slowly, carefully attentive to the pleasure of it. He flips the butt out away from him onto the ground, and leans back, his eyes closed, aware of being at rest in that place, feeling the sun draw the skin of his face and hands, feeling the air stir coolly over him, the light filling his shut eyes with red.

After a while he sits up and looks at his watch. He still has three minutes of his time. He yawns and rubs his eyes, and rather than sit there and watch the time run out, hating to see it go, he gets up. Groggy with sunlight and sleepiness and his full belly, he fights off the dread of movement. Moves. Takes up the crutches and goes around to the foot of the ladder. He drinks, picks up his hammer, and climbs to the roof.

The day and the work are established around him again. He goes on, deeper in, with a kind of excitement growing in him, a kind of hunger for what it is possible to do before night. It becomes easier to go on than to stop.

After about an hour he sees Ida come out of the house. She comes down to the woodpile, splits a day's supply of stovewood, carries an armload up to the house. The next time he sees her she is out in the bottom, mending and pulling up and straightening one of the fences broken down by the flood. Ernest does not stop to watch her. When he looks up as he shifts from one place to another, he sees her, farther along than she was before. Twice he forgets her completely for the biggest part of an hour, and when he looks for her again she has moved on but is still at work, the fence standing up behind her, makeshift and staggering, but stout enough to keep the milk cows out of the crops.

Later, when he looks up, she is gone. And then in one of his pauses he hears her beneath him in the barn. He sees that the team of mules and the cows have come down off the hill and are waiting at the upper doors. And they are not there when he turns in that direction again; she has taken them in, fastened them in their places for the night, fed them. He sees her on her way to the house with the milk buckets, and again pouring the skimmed milk in for the hogs.

When he winds it up, satisfied, the last sheet of roofing torn off and stacked on the ground, and turns in the chill of the evening to go, she is standing beside the truck, wearing the old sweater again.

"Would you care if I rode out to the mailbox?"

Getting out at the river road, she tells him she is much obliged, as before, and turns to her errand. And again, watching in the mirror, he sees that nothing has come.

10

The Wanting of What May Be Lost

When Hannah lay down for a nap early Sunday afternoon, Mat had not come in to dinner, but an hour or so later, when she wakes up and goes into the living room, he is there, obviously waiting for her, sitting with his feet propped on the desk, hat and jacket still on. He grins at her.

"How're you feeling?"

"Fine."

"Well, Margaret's gone to visit Mrs. Burgess a while. I reckon she's in for two or three hours' talking about rheumatism." He gets up. "I thought we might farm a little this afternoon, you and me, since you're feeling fine."

"All right," she says, "Good." She cannot, somehow, make her voice sound as glad as she is. But when he has helped her on with her coat and they are starting out the door, she puts her hand into his.

"Now you're talking," he says.

It is clear to her that this excursion has been on his mind since morning and that he has been looking forward to it. And she is grateful. It is good to be going farming with him, getting out of the house. A wind, high up, carries the overcast swiftly across the sky. The sun comes through. They stop while a bright patch of sunlight passes over and beyond them, and they watch it sweep rapidly on over the ridgetops.

While they get into the truck and go along the road toward the barns on the far place, there are a few minutes of silence between them, a little awkward.

But once they are through the gate, starting back the gravel road along the backbone of the ridge, they are among Mat's reference points. And he begins to talk, pointing out jobs of work that he has done lately or is doing or planning to do. One thing reminds him of another.

"This barn here," he says, "my daddy built it when I was a boy. I remember walking over here from town to watch the carpenters. An old fellow by the name of Walter Stovall built it. He had three or four grown sons and they all worked together. They were good carpenters, all of them. It was poplar lumber they had to build with then."

He gets out and helps Hannah out. "You can't get lumber like that any more, maybe never will again." He gestures upward with his hand. "I reinforced the loft and put on a new roof when Virgil was thirteen or fourteen years old. It was about the first man's work he ever did. I sent him over here with Ernest and they did it together. It would worry me to death trying to get any work out of him then, but he'd work for Ernest. I saw how that was and remembered how it was with me. Mighty hard to get a boy to come to it right under his daddy's hand. I don't know why."

There are cows and calves scattered over the lot in front of the barn, others lying down around the door and inside the driveway. These get up and move slowly out of the way as Mat and Hannah step up to the doorway and into it.

"Well," Mat says, "I *do* know why. By the time a boy gets big enough to work, his daddy's already been his boss for a long time, and not always an easy one. They've already pretty well tested each other, and know each other's weaknesses and flaws. There are a lot of old irritations all ready-made. And then a man teaching his own boy gets misled by pride. What he does wrong looks like *your* failure as much as it is his, and so you don't correct or punish for his sake, but yours. The way around it—or the way my daddy took with me and I took with Virgil—is to let him work with somebody older than he is, like Ernest, that you know he admires."

"Was he bad?" Hannah asks, "When he was a boy, I mean."

"Fairly," Mat says, and grins. "Though it's hard for me to tell how to judge a boy's behavior. He wasn't any worse than I was, I'll put it that way. Nor any better, I reckon. He did a good many things he ought to have got a whipping for. And did, and got a few he didn't deserve, which"—he opens his hands and folds them slowly, one in the other, behind his back—"I wish he hadn't."

"He told me several times that you were a good father."

"Did he? I'm glad he said that. I'm glad you told me."

They are standing inside the barn now, looking out through the doorway. Mat makes a vague abrupt movement with his forearm and hand, whether to dismiss the foregoing part of their conversation or to begin the next, she cannot tell.

"When he came home from college after his last year, I asked him, 'What are you planning to do?' Lord knows, I'd wanted to know a long time before that, and he'd mentioned wanting to farm before, but the time to ask and be told never had come until then. And I was worried a good deal, because I wanted him to come home here and take this up—or wanted him to want to—and was afraid he wouldn't. And was afraid, too, that he'd see what I had on my mind. But I held right steady, watching him, and he said, 'I want to stay here and farm with you.'"

There is a pause now, while Mat seems to steady and gather himself.

"I'll never forget it. I'd have liked to just stop everything right there and celebrate. But I knew we'd only come to the beginning, and you don't celebrate at the beginning—even at the risk of never celebrating at all.

"I said, 'All right. I'm going to lend you a thousand dollars. You take that, and the old cattle barn over yonder, and those two fields between it and the road—and let's see what you can do. When you're not working for yourself, you can work by the day for me.' There were hard times then, and it nearly emptied me to get him the thousand dollars. But I did it. It was enough money to put pressure on him, which I aimed to do—and then, of course, stand pretty close behind him, to see that he didn't get *too* badly into trouble.

"Well, he made it do. He never let me in on it at all. He saw my game, and was proud. And I waited, sort of keeping to the other end of the place, to see what he would do—scared again, of course, that he'd make some bad mistake. And then one morning he said to me, 'Come look at my cattle.' And I came over here with him, and we stood out there in the lot and looked them over. He'd bought six or seven cows and calves and a pretty good bull, and they were all right. He hadn't broke any records, in judging or buying either, but they were all right. It was a fair start. There are forty-five head of these cows now, and the quality of them has improved right along."

He raises his arm and points.

"Look. There's one you ought to recognize. That's the newest one. She's the one you and Virgil brought from Indiana that night in the truck, not long after you were married. Don't you remember?"

"Yes," Hannah says. "I do."

Mat turns and goes on back into the barn, Hannah following. He opens the door to an empty stall. "I'll put some feed in now. You stand inside there, honey, where you can watch and won't get tramped on."

He empties several buckets of ground corn into the troughs and calls the cattle, and then goes up a ladder into the loft and begins filling the mangers with hay. She can hear him walking back and forth in the loft, the forked hay sliding over the floorboards and dropping down into the mangers. The cattle crowd to the troughs, latecomers throwing their heads up and wedging their way in. The calves, forgotten, play or stand or lie in the open spaces. For the time being, the old cows are held at the trough by pure violence of appetite. Hannah can hear them breathing, their rough tongues sweeping the bottoms of the troughs.

She feels a strange, threatened happiness. They have talked easily about Virgil for the first time in a month. Mat has told her things about Virgil that she never knew. She feels herself surrounded closely now by this place of his life, his love for the placid hungry lives of cattle.

Mat comes down, goes into the feed room, and comes out with two big buckets. Turning them upside down against the front of the stall, he helps her to sit down on one of them, and he sits on the other.

"You oughtn't to be standing up so much," he says. "I should have thought of it before."

"I wasn't tired. I'm having a good time."

"Good. Well, you tell me what you need. Don't wait for me to think of it." He leans forward, putting his elbows on his knees and lacing his fingers.

"I remember the first crop of his own that Virgil ever tried to raise.

He broke about two acres out back there on the ridge, and fenced it and laid the rows off to suit him. I'd told him as much as I knew about it, and let him go. Well, you know this is difficult land to farm. So much of it steep. Hard to keep it from washing. I expect I've seen half the topsoil go off of some farms around here in my time. More, maybe. We've been slow to have enough sense to farm this kind of land, and lack plenty yet. My daddy hurt some of these hillsides badly in his time. Made some bad mistakes. I tried to learn from his, and went right on and made some bad ones of my own. Anyhow, Virgil broke his ground farther over the brow of the hill than he should have. Like a boy, you know. Didn't stop in time. But he got his rows laid off about right, and got his crop out—and I didn't say anything, hoping he'd have luck and get that mistake free. Thought I'd show him later what he'd done wrong, soon as I could do it without hurting his feelings.

"But there was an awful rain one night after his crop had been out, I guess, two weeks. I heard it begin and lay awake listening to it, knowing what was bound to be happening. And the next morning I said, 'Let's go look at your crop.' So we went, and walked all the way around it. It was hurt. Bound to have been. There's no way to plow sideling ground so it'll hold in a rain like that. 'Virgil,' I said, 'this is your fault. This is one of your contributions to the world.' That was hard for me to say. And he took it hard. I saw he was about to cry. And bad as I hated to do it, I let it work in him while we stood there and looked. I knew he was hating the day he ever thought of raising a crop, ready to give up. Finally I put my arm around him and I said, 'Be sorry, but don't quit. What's asked of you now is to see what you've done, and learn better.' And I told him that a man's life is always dealing with permanence—that the most dangerous kind of irresponsibility is to think of your doings as temporary. That, anyhow, is what I've tried to keep before myself. What you do on the earth, the earth makes permanent."

He laughs, and looks at Hannah. "Every time I make a mistake, that gets more painful to believe."

He shifts his position on the bucket, letting his eyes go back to the feeding cattle.

"I think of the pain I've given to my children. Especially to Virgil—now. You hope for a realization in them, finally, that the pain is given out of love, inept and blundering and blind and wrong as it can sometimes be. I don't worry so much about Bess. She's had a family of her own long enough to know the terrified love you can sometimes have for your children. But Virgil I feel like I owe an accounting to. There's maybe only weakness in it. You want your good intentions recognized, even the failed ones. You want it known by the ones nearest you that your good intentions are a real part of your life, and your love for them."

His eyes move over the ranked backs of the cattle, attentively, though Hannah cannot tell whether he is thinking about them or not. She studies his face, seeing in it something she has never seen there before, an old man's sorrow for the imperfection of his life and of his fatherhood. She understands suddenly how a young man might be borne up, might justify everything, by the hope of perfection—and, growing old, must realize that he has done nothing perfect. She knows that Mat has allowed her to see, as Virgil never was allowed to, the pained underside of his severity. And she feels, as Mat must, the tragedy in the possibility that Virgil will never see it. She would like to be able to say something comforting, but realizes that she cannot. She cannot comfort even herself.

Still watching the cattle, as though nothing else has been said, Mat says, "Whenever I can, I take a Sunday afternoon and do what we're doing now—go to each barn and feed, and then sit down and watch the stock eat. It's a way to take time enough to see what I'm doing, and get a little pleasure out of it."

"You haven't been getting much pleasure out of it lately, have you?"

"No. For the last two or three weeks I've been here and seen them and fed them and gone before they could hardly get to the troughs. There's no satisfaction in that. And I tell you, if a man doesn't farm for his own satisfaction, he'll have a hard time finding another good reason to do it."

"But you *do* like it?"

"There's *not* any other life for me. That's why I wanted Virgil to have it, I reckon—I knew if he wanted it, it would be a good life for him. I'm not saying it's not hard. But I can tell you that all my life, in spite of the worst, I've been inspired by this place, and by what I foresaw or hoped I could do in it. I've lived my life the way a hungry man eats."

Mat stands up.

"I'm about to forget the main thing."

He grins at the curiosity that comes into her face, but does not tell her what the main thing is. The resemblance between him and Virgil is suddenly strong. She watches him go into the feed room with his bucket and come back. He helps her up and opens the door to the next stall.

"Here's a family I thought you'd like to see."

Inside there is one of the cows, gaunt from giving birth, the afterbirth still hanging. And in the corner, on the clean straw, her calf is lying asleep, curled tightly, making a nest of itself.

"Oh," Hannah says, and lets herself clumsily down beside the calf. "Look how little," she says. She lays her hand gently on the red and white hide. The cow comes over and smells her.

Mat puts feed into the cow's trough, and brings fresh water, and then he squats down beside Hannah.

"Is it a boy or a girl?"

"A boy. A bull."

"He's so clean."

"He was pretty messy at first, but she licked him clean."

Mat strokes the calf's back briskly, roughing the hair. The calf wakes up, lifts its white head and looks at them, and then puts it down again. The white-lashed eyes stay open.

"And gentle. He's not afraid of us at all."

"Well, his mammy's not, which helps. But that's the wonder of anything newborn. He's clean and unworried and not afraid. And dinner's ready all the time. Here. Feel his hoofs. See. They're already hard. When he was born, they were soft, like gelatin."

"I never thought of that, but I see how necessary it is."

"It's all pretty well worked out. I'm always a little surprised every time I see it happen. He's a nice calf. See how well marked he is?"

"He's very nice. It's a nice idea."

"Which idea?"

"The idea of something newborn." She smiles.

"One of the best."

He helps her up and then picks up the calf and stands it on its feet. "Stand up there, old chap. Let's see how you are."

The calf balances shakily for a moment, its legs looking too weak, its head too heavy. Mat turns him loose. Unsure whether its legs are for propping or walking, the calf starts toward the cow. It reaches her finally, tries to nurse between her forelegs, nudges, blunders, staggers, collapses into a mess of legs, straightens itself, gets up, finds the tit at last. They hear its mouth smacking as the milk starts to come. Hannah laughs with pleasure and relief.

"If he can find his way back there a few more times," Mat says, "maybe he'll learn the way."

He picks up his bucket and opens the door. "Well, let's go. We've got the rest of the rounds still to make." At the door he stops and turns around, looking back once more at the cattle. "When he went, you know, he wanted me to sell them—not trouble myself with them. I wouldn't do it, and I'm glad I didn't. They're here."

It is still clearing. When they come out of the dark barn the whole ridge is in sunlight. The green ridgetops before them are sprinkled heavily with dandelions, the woods along the draws and bluffs beaded with leaf buds. In thickets scattered over the slopes of the river valley are the clean white and pink of wild plum and redbud. The shores of the river have turned pale green with the new leaves of the willows. The shadows of clouds slide rapidly over the face of the country, dimming it, leaving it somehow brighter than it was.

Farther back there is another barn, a tobacco barn, where Mat has wintered a little bunch of steers. Leaving the truck where it is, he and Hannah walk toward this second barn. Mat is pointing out various houses and farms in the valley, and saying who used to live there, and who lives there now. Two or three times, as their perspective on the valley changes, they stop and look.

"When I was a boy," Mat says, "the showboats used to come up the river in the summertime. You'd hear the calliope commence playing, and then you could hear the people holler for miles on both sides. And that night, when the show time came, they'd all be there, as many of them as could rake up the ticket money. We'd talk about it afterwards for a month."

When they come to the barn Hannah stays outside, and Mat goes in alone. She walks on out along the top of the ridge, the sun on her, miles of sunlit country blooming around her. She is comforted by all that Mat has said to her, and by the country filling with spring.

She turns to the side, going through a gate and down the slope above the bluff into a small patch of woods in a shallow draw. Here over the dead leaves of the last year, the sunlight is webbed with the shadows of branches. On the far side of the little woods there is a white thicket of wild plum, and there are several redbuds at the woods' edge, brilliant against the dark trunks of the taller trees. And blooming out of the dead leaves there are bloodroot, trillium, trout lilies, Dutchman's-breeches, twinleaf, yellow and purple violets. Everywhere the fern leaves are uncurling. The May apples are coming up, the two leaves creased and bronze, bent and furled downward from the round flower-bud like a young animal folded to be born. The buds overhead stain the light. Through a rocky trough in the center of the draw runs a clear stream, dropping from one mossy ledge to another, the sound of it filling the grove. On the ridge above her, she can hear Mat calling the cattle. She wanders slowly over the dry leaves, picking violets.

And then it is not long before she hears him calling her. She answers him, and shortly sees him coming in among the trees, the netting of their shadows falling over him.

"Well, haven't you found a nice place!"

"Isn't it? Look at all the flowers."

"Yes. And a pretty bouquet."

The little branch keeps up its steady chattering over the rocks. They stand without talking.

Finally Mat says, "It's a mighty nice place to have to leave. But I guess we'd better do it. Are you rested? You feel all right?"

She nods. They begin the climb back up over the ridge. Mat takes her arm. They step a little formally now, he supporting her, she holding her bouquet.

"I'm a great one for places. This farm's just full of places I've picked out to spend a day sitting in, if I ever get time to do it. Cool places or quiet ones, with water running or an overlook. I've thought of some of them nearly all my life. And looks like I've never had time to sit down and be still for very long in a one."

"Whoo," she says.

She stops to rest and Mat stops beside her.

"Getting steeper all the time, ain't it?"

She laughs. "Much steeper than it was coming down." But she feels too heavy. She looks up at the rest of the climb with dread. She has got herself into a pretty foolish predicament for a woman eight months gone.

"You just rest all you need to," he says. "Take your time. You'll make it all right."

"Of course," she says. She looks straight into his eyes now and laughs. "I'm not worried. Think of all the calves and lambs and things that you've helped get born."

"Oh, Lord," Mat says, "that's different."

They both laugh.

"I can go on now," she says.

"All right. Let's angle around and over the point. That'll be longer, but not so steep."

He goes beside her, giving her his arm to lean on. They go slowly, taking a gradual upward slant along the face of the slope. High up, clear of the trees, the valley lying open again below them, they stop again to rest, standing facing the valley.

"Oh, I've been here before," Hannah says. "Virgil brought me here once to show me where he'd like to build a house." She stops, confused, having said that.

They turn a little away from each other, cautious.

"Well, ain't it a nice place for one," Mat says.

Around her she can see the stones Virgil laid down that night to mark the corners, scattered out of alignment now, but still there. The fear of great loss comes over her, the great wanting of what may be lost. She turns around and starts up on the slope. Mat catches up and takes her arm. They go on, without talking and without stopping, to the truck. Mat helps her in and gets in himself.

"How you making it?" he asks her.

"Better now. Much better."

They look at each other now and smile, having made it so, for one time at least.

Something in the World to Do

Old Jack opened the door of the woodshed for the first time on a warm afternoon two weeks ago. And since then he has made it his place. When he first looked into it, it was full of cast-off furniture, scrap lumber, old fruit jars, tin cans, rusty tools, an old mattress, the smell of mildew.

He spent odd hours of three or four days cleaning it out, burned all that was burnable, stacked the rest neatly in a corner, swept the floor boards and walls, left it open in the warm afternoons to air. The results of his work, he admits, are not very impressive. The old shed is far gone. A man could take a broom handle and knock it down. Still, he finds the neatness he has made in it satisfactory. As in his room in the hotel, there is nothing here to show that he has appropriated it. He has put nothing in it except a little order. Between him and the ramshackle building there is only the pleasure of sitting in it on warm days, looking out at the big pasture behind the town. Sometimes he sleeps there, the sun shining in on him. Mrs. Hendrick has seen him going back there, has even made a little habit of watching his comings and goings from the kitchen window, but he always uses the back door of the woodshed, and so she has no certain idea what he is doing. She will, she supposes, sooner or later go out and see, but she tells herself she will have to wait and do it sometime when he will not see her—not that it would make a whit of difference to him, even she knows that, but she has a secret little flair for detective work, also plenty of curiosity that she could not satisfy so well in Old Jack's presence as she can in his absence. She did get alarmed at the smoke he made, but so far she has—wisely, she thinks, and virtuously—held her peace.

Now Old Jack picks up a rusty scythe and, chipping and pecking with the end of the file, begins flaking the rust off the blade. What he is going to get around to today is the weeds. Already in the lot behind the hotel, growing up green among the last summer's dead stalks, the weeds have begun to come. He whets the edge of the blade with the file, leaving the metal bright.

It has been a long time since he went to work early in the morning. Though he did not think he had, he has forgot the delicate flavors of the satisfaction he used to get out of that. The best of it, it turns out, is unrecallable. The realization fills him with a sense of loss that would be hard to bear if he did not have the scythe in his hand. He tests the cutting edge with his thumb, and is satisfied. The sun is just getting up into the branches of the old locusts around the woodshed and along the back fence.

He starts a narrow swath along the crumbling foundation of the hotel, cutting the creeper stems off at the ground as he goes, leaving the weeds, the green and the dead together, lying down behind him.

He gets tired quicker than he thought he would—though he has not been working at what you would call an old man's pace. He goes back and pulls the creepers loose from the weatherboarding. By the time he does that he is short of breath, a little staggery. He goes back to the woodshed and sits down.

His weakness saddens him. He can remember when a little job like this would just be something to do after supper some night. But he might as well admit it: it is not anymore. And he will have to mend his licks. He will have to get back in that old man's gait, and stay in it, if he aims to get anything done at all. "Where's the fire at, old man?" he asks himself.

He whets his scythe and goes back. He is startled by the change he has made. He has done more than he thought. He can change the look of the world still. A kind of inspiration comes into him, the familiar lifting of the thought of what can be done here by a man. He finishes his first swath, and starts a new one. But now he is working more slowly—a pace he thinks maybe he can stand for an hour or two.

He is in the middle of this third swath when the kitchen window opens with a clatter and Mrs. Hendrick puts her head out.

"*Mis*-ter Beechum! You've got no business to cut them weeds! If I want them weeds cut, I'll cut them my*self!*"

Old Jack accepts the challenge. He stops, and looks at her as if she is farther away than she is.

"Me and weeds never have lived in the same place together, old woman."

He goes back to work, same pace. She goes straight to the telephone and calls Wheeler Catlett. And while Old Jack goes on slowly and happily at his work in the back lot, Wheeler is pleading his case with Mrs. Hendrick in the hotel dining room.

"Could you see that he was doing any harm, Mrs. Hendrick, by cutting those weeds?"

"Yessir! He's doing harm, my opinion, cutting them weeds. Them's *my* weeds."

"Well, Mrs. Hendrick, it's good for the old fellow to have something to do. And I'd think it would be to your profit to have those weeds cut."

Mrs. Hendrick's voice becomes tremulous. "He never even *asked,* is what I mean, Mr. Catlett. That's what's so insulting to me. Just went out there and sharpened my scythe and went to cutting them weeds just like he owned the place. Just a cutting and a cutting, and a calling me 'old woman.'" She wipes her eyes with her apron. "Sometimes a widow woman, seems like, just don't have no place to turn. If he'd *asked* me, Mr. Catlett, *I'd* have let him do it."

"Well, Mrs. Hendrick, now that he has begun, won't you be so kind as to let him go on? Don't you think that would be best?"

"I *reckon* so. I just hope there won't no more trouble come of it, Mr. Catlett."

When Wheeler comes around the hotel, Old Jack's back is turned to him. "Good morning, Uncle Jack."

Something's up, Jack knows right away. Whenever Wheeler comes in the morning, something is up. "Why hello, Wheeler. How are you, honey? I was just cutting a few of these weeds. The damnedest mess of them ever I saw. Just look a here," he says, gesturing around him, "what that old woman has let grow up right in her door."

"Shhh!" Wheeler says. Old Jack always refers to Mrs. Hendrick as "that old woman," though she is at least twenty years younger than he is. "Uncle Jack," he says, "*don't* call her an old woman—at least not to her face."

Old Jack smiles and lays his hand on Wheeler's arm. "Don't you worry about that, honey. Me and her get along."

By the evening of the next day—working a while and sitting a while—Old Jack has finished the weeds on Mrs. Hendrick's lot, and has made a good beginning on the weeds behind the store. It looks fairly good, he thinks, a big improvement.

In the next couple of days the frontier is pushed across Jasper Lathrop's back lot, and on down behind the doctor's office and the drugstore.

A great litter of old cans and bottles is picked up and piled in an out-of-the-way corner. The burnable trash and the cut weeds are piled on top of the old crates behind Jasper's store and burnt in a smoky fire that draws all the boys in Port William and a considerable number of the men.

Saturday morning after breakfast Old Jack goes out into his clearing and stands and looks. Childish as he suspects it may be, he cannot help feeling a little elated at what he has done. But along with the satisfaction there is growing an uneasiness, a sadness. It is finished, and what will he do now? Having escaped it a little while, he has again knocked square against the realization that there is mighty little left in this world for him to do. And this morning what he has done seems threatened by the possibility that it was done for nothing. What can he do now but sit and look at it? And know that the weeds will come back, and he will go.

As if in answer to a prayer that he has not even thought of praying, he sees Floyd Mahew's boy driving a team of mules and sled along the fence, as he has morning and noon and evening all week, only today there is a breaking plow lying on the sled.

Something to be *growing* in it: the idea is born full grown into Old Jack's head. He waves his cane.

"Oh, son! Whoo! Hello, boy!"

But the mules are coming at a brisk trot and the boy cannot hear over the rattling of the harness.

"Deaf and dumb!" Jack says. He waits until the team comes up even with him and calls: "Whoa!"

The mules stop. The boy falls forward, catching himself against the fore-standard of the sled, and looks around in some confusion until he sees Old Jack coming.

"Boy," Old Jack says, "can you run that plow?"

"Yessir," the boy says, grinning and nodding. It's a Mahew grin, a Mahew face. The Mahews have always reminded Jack just a little bit of catfish. He gives the boy a good looking-over, not sure he is telling the truth. He is not a very big boy. "Well," he says finally, "go on up yonder to the gate and come in here. I've got a little piece of work here I want you to help me with."

The boy looks doubtful. "Uh, I better go on to work like my daddy told me to."

"You're Floyd Mahew's boy, ain't you?"

"Yessir." Again the nod and grin.

"Well, I ain't worried about him. You just drive up to that gate and I'll help you get it open."

The old gate into the alley along the upper side of the hotel has not been opened in maybe fifteen years. The slats are rotten, some of them broken. The whole thing has been bound together in place with baling wire.

They do finally get it open. The boy drives the sled into the alley. They unload the plow and hitch to it.

"I'll drive, son, and you handle the plow. Can you plow a straight furrow?"

"Yessir. I'll try."

"What in the hell does that mean? 'Yessir. I'll try.' Well, I'll drive straight. You just keep your plow running level."

"Yessir," the boy says. "Uh. How long do you think this'll take?"

"Ne' mind! Don't you worry about your daddy. *Gee, boys!* Take hold of your plow, honey."

The boy takes hold, and they go across and back the long way of Mrs. Hendrick's lot, leaving a straight, neatly turned backfurrow through the middle. The black earth bursts at the touch of the share and crumbles. Hard telling when it ever was broken, if it ever was. If it is not virgin ground it might as well be. It has been a long time since Old Jack has seen any dirt like it. He is delighted by the look and the smell of it, and by the feel of it when he stops and picks it up and crumbles it in his hands.

"Lord Amighty!" Old Jack says. "Look what dirt you're plowing," he says to the boy. "Did you ever plow any dirt like that before?"

"Yessir."

"*Nosir.*"

"Nosir."

"That's what new ground looks like. You've never seen any of it on that place of your daddy's."

"Oh."

"I've broke a fair amount of it in my time. You'll not break but mighty little in yours."

"Yessir."

"Do you know why?"

"Nosir."

"Because all of it, you might as well say, has been broke, and a lot of it used up. From my day to yours is a long time, and a lot more is used up, and not much to the improvement of the world, far as I can see."

"Yessir."

"Yessir, what? Yessir, Hell! Do you know what I'm talking about?"

"Yessir."

Old Jack looks down at the boy, studying him, and then snorts. "Until you get enough sense to worry about it, I reckon I'll have to. Well, look at that ground you're turning and remember it."

They've come to the end of a furrow, and they look at each other, each a little perplexed by the other.

"It's something you ought to remember. Not many in your generation will ever see it."

"Yessir."

They begin the next furrow.

"Did you ever imagine what an improvement it would be to the world if everybody cut his own weeds?"

"Nosir."

"Well, you won't come to that with a boy's head. But I'll tell it to you. It'd be a hell of a big improvement."

"Yessir."

"What's the biggest fish you ever caught?"

"About the size of that mule's ear," the boy says. "But I ain't fished much."

There's a slam behind them, and when they look Mrs. Hendrick is standing on the stoop at the kitchen door, a wet dishrag dripping in her hand. She is red in the face, bent forward as if about to dive off the stoop.

"Just keep ahold of your plow, honey."

"*Stop!* You all just stop them old mules *right there!*"

Jack addresses the mules quietly and gently: "Whoa, boys." He turns slowly to face her.

"Mr. Beechum! What're you plowing up my back yard for?"

"For the good of the world!"

Whack! she shuts the screen door. Wham! she shuts the kitchen door.

"Come up, mules! Gee! Come up!"

When Wheeler comes this time it is a good while before he can get in a word. Mrs. Hendrick tattles on Old Jack, describes the look on his face, quotes him a number of times so as to make obvious the outrageousness of his tone. She speaks of her own decent life, of her great sympathy for a lonely old man such as Mr. Beechum, and of the hardships and travails of widow women in this world. And Wheeler has to allow her some sympathy. She *is* having a rough time of it. She *oughtn't* to have to put up with insults from Old Jack.

"Well," Wheeler says. "I'll certainly talk to him about the language he uses, Mrs. Hendrick, and I'll ask him to show you more respect. But I'll also have to tell you again what I told you the other day. I can't see why you object to what he's doing. I can't see that it won't be to your advantage to have a garden back there."

"A *garden?*" she snaps. "How'd *I* know it was going to be a garden? Well, I just hope there won't no more trouble come out of it, is all I hope."

When Wheeler goes out back, the ground-breaking is finished. Floyd Mahew's boy is gone, and the old gate has been shut and wired up. Old Jack is standing and looking.

"Hello, Wheeler boy!"

"What're you going to plant here, Uncle Jack?"

"A little bit of a garden. Maybe raise that old woman something she can cook."

"That's fine," Wheeler says. He had not known any better than Mrs. Hendrick that a garden was what Old Jack intended to raise.

"These here shirt-tail lawyers looking after my business, I'm liable to have to go back to working for a living, so I reckon I'd better keep my hand in."

They laugh.

"Wheeler, did that old woman call you down here to complain about me?"

"That's right."

"The damned old thing hasn't got any sense, Wheeler."

"Not much. But you haven't been giving much consideration to that."

"You're right, son. I haven't been giving her a thought. And it's causing you trouble, ain't it? You reckon I'd better hunt another place to go?" He looks over his garden patch—not altogether liking that thought. "Or"—he grins—"we could buy this place and throw her out. Get us a couple of old women about eighteen years old to come in and keep house."

Wheeler laughs. "No, Uncle Jack. I think the best thing to do now is let things be as they are. I just ask you, for my sake, don't insult her, and try to show some respect for her rights in her own property."

Old Jack sees that the crisis is over, and he turns away, wanting to change the subject. Good company is going to waste.

"I want you to look at that ground," he says.

They pick up handfuls of the black moist dirt, letting it crumble through their fingers.

"It won't take but mighty little working to get that ground ready to plant."

They stand there a few more minutes, talking about the newness and richness of that neglected place.

And then Wheeler starts toward the street. Old Jack watches him go. He is going to have to begin making some kind of peace. He has been mighty unwilling to have that woman on his mind. But now he will let her be there—for the sake of peace, and for Wheeler's sake, and his own.

He looks at his watch. It is three-quarters of an hour until dinnertime. The sun has begun to dry the surface of the turned ground. He paces the length and width of the plot, and then goes into the woodshed. He sits in his chair and takes out his notebook and pencil and figures how much seed he will have to buy.

A lot, it proves. They will have plenty to eat fresh, and plenty to can, and some to give away. He goes out to the street, his list fluttering in his hand, the ground waiting.

A Pleasant Place to Sit

April 22, 1945

Dear Nathan,

Here I've let a month go by without writing, in spite of getting two letters from you. We've been working mighty hard since I wrote last—daylight to dark, and seven days a week. Last week we worked right through Sunday, and didn't know we'd passed it until Tuesday.

Well, *this* Sunday morning I decided I couldn't put off writing any longer, so I slipped out early and walked to town. Thought I'd get where Jarrat can't find me and I can't hear him holler, and get this letter written. When it's done I guess I'll have to go back and let myself be found. I'm sitting here on the sidewalk in front of Jayber's door. It's a quiet fair morning, and a pleasant place to sit. Jayber was just finishing his breakfast when I got here. He came down and hung around and talked until I thought I might as well give up and go home. But he finally went back upstairs.

What Jayber was wanting to talk about was Old Jack Beechum's doings up at the hotel. The old man has cleaned the weeds and trash off of all the back lots from the post office clean to the pool room. Then yesterday morning he got one of Floyd Mahew's boys to break up a big garden patch behind the hotel. I didn't know anything about it until yesterday evening. I'd finished cutting some ground at Mat's and had loaded the harrow onto the sled and was starting home. It was, I imagine, an hour or so before sundown. I shut the gate and pulled out into the road, and here come Old Jack, waving his cane and hollering, "Whoo! Oh, Burley! Whoa there!" I pulled on up even with him and stopped. He wanted me to come out back and work that garden patch for him so he could plant it.

I went and did it. It didn't take long. That ground worked like new ground, which I imagine it is—fine and black and loose as ashes. When I got it worked good, Old Jack brought out a sack full of garden seed and we laid off some rows and started planting, him dropping the seeds and me a covering. It was right remarkable to see that old man all buttoned up in a winter coat—for he tells me he never gets quite warm—going along dropping seeds in the ground. While we were planting the garden Jayber came by. He'd closed his shop for supper and come to hunt up Old Jack, since he hadn't seen him for three or four days and had got to wondering if maybe he was sick. Well, he soon found out all he wanted to know about the old man's health, and got put to work pretty suddenly too.

Nothing at all has been heard of Virgil Feltner beyond what I already told you. It'll soon be two months now that he has been missing. I know that for Mat and them it has been a long wait and a long hope, and they've maybe only begun. Once in a while when you're talking to Mat you'll realize all of a sudden that he has quit listening, ain't there, is way off somewhere in his trouble, and then you can see the pain in his face.

That *missing* doesn't give him much to take a hold of. These last seven weeks have aged Mat right sharply too. He nearly always seems steady, reined pretty tight. But it's no trouble to look at him now and see that it has been a long time since he has been at rest in himself.

Nobody has seen hide nor hair of Gideon Crop either. Several of us are working down there, turn about, to help Ida keep things going.

You asked me to tell you what things look like now, and I'll try it the best I can. It's full spring now. The trees are leafed out. The big ones here in town reach over the road so that from where I'm looking the town seems sort of roofed with leaves. The yards are green and flowers are blooming in some of them. Now and then when I look up into town I see one or another of Minnie Lathrop's old hens chasing a bug across the road. Uncle Stan has got his old Jersey tied to a stake in the empty lot next to the church. The grass is coming good everywhere and people will be putting their stock on pasture before long. Out home your Grandma's old lilac is in full bloom and various ones of her flowers is blooming, or has bloomed. As fine a spring as you'd ever want to see.

Telling you about it makes me wish mightily that you could see it. Which, if the predictors are right, you may before too long. I think a mighty lot of you, old boy. Let me hear a little something when you get the time.

Your uncle,
Burley

11

Green Pasture

For the last time until next winter Mat has fed the herd of cows. Now, while they eat, he walks out across the barn lot and the small pasture in which the cows and calves have been kept all winter. It's a bright clear morning, the first of May. From the ridgetop where he walks, he can see the white mist in the valley just beginning to rise into the sunlight and dissolve. Beyond the trampled close-eaten winter pasture the grass is heavy and green along the ridge and on the slopes above the woods. He opens the gate.

The winter, which has kept him going the rounds of the barns twice a day and more, is all behind him now, and Mat feels his life changing. As though this finishing has cleared the way, he can foresee the long hot days of the summer, when the stock will no longer be so dependent on him but the crops will. And from somewhere still far off in those long weeks, he feels the approach of suffering for him and his house.

Virgil has been missing now for nearly two months, and in all that time he and Margaret and Hannah have never spoken of the probability, growing stronger every day, that Virgil is dead, or worse, that they may never know. And along with everything else, Mat feels lonesome for Margaret and for their old life.

Lately he has returned many times to the thought of Gideon Crop's vigil over the floodwater. It has become a kind of waking nightmare in which he wanders, imagining all that a man might be moved to by hopelessness and hope at the edge of a dark flood in which his best is lost. Often in the midst of these visions he will hear himself curse or groan.

Out of his understanding of that horror that speaks so to his own, he manages to find time every day or so to see Ida Crop, taking Margaret with him sometimes, other times going by himself. He has become dependent on her, as if her survival of her loss is a lesson to him that he will have somehow to learn.

Once, after she had made some mention of Annie, he asked her: "How do you stand it, Ida?"

And she said, "You're thinking about your boy, ain't you, Mr. Feltner?" She was looking away toward the creek. "I don't know," she said. "Sometimes I just have to sit down and bawl." She gave him another one of her studying looks. "What I wish, I wish she was buried somewheres close in a little grave."

He nodded. He realized that this was familiar to him.

"I tell myself that when Gideon gets back it'll be better."

She amazes Mat, and encourages him, though he comes on the pretense of encouraging her. Beyond her pain and endurance and will, it seems to him that there's a hopefulness in her that is almost calm. It comes, he thinks, from the knowledge, not just that she is young enough yet to have more children, but that other women will get with child, other children will be born, it will go on. It seems to Mat that this must be one of the powers of women. He does not have it in him.

The cattle have cleaned up the feed he put in for them and are drifting out again into the sunlight. The cows have shed their winter hair and their close summer coats shine in the light. Mat goes into the barn and drives out the stragglers. Beyond the doors, working back and forth, he gathers the herd and starts it toward the gate. The cows are fat, their calves vigorous and in good flesh. Looking at them, he feels the satisfaction of success. The winter has been met and dealt with; ahead of them now is the grass.

Coming closer, the cows see that the gate is open and they go toward it at a trot, no longer needing to be driven. They enter the pasture and begin to graze. Mat closes the gate and leans on it, watching. The only sound now is that of the grass tearing.

Caught

Before Ernest finished taking down the lower part of the old barn, seeds had already begun to sprout out of the dirt floor that the roof and walls had kept dark for years. Since he took off the roof, the work has gone slowly, involving much moving of ladders, a lot of temporary propping and shoring up as he worked around the weakened corners, days of great painstaking and difficulty in freeing and letting down the heavy timbers of the framing. And there have been rainy days when he could not work at all. But at last the whole lower half of the barn has been torn down, and Ernest has begun siding up the open end of the half still standing. Around the carefully sorted and stacked piles of old lumber and roofing, the weeds have begun to grow tall.

As soon as he finishes the barn, he will paint it. After that there will be the other jobs of repair and maintenance that Mat has asked him to do. On Mat's visits to the little farm the two of them have gone the rounds of all the buildings, looking them over, deciding what ought to be done for the preservation of each one.

Every morning Ida brings him water in the half-gallon vinegar jug, and sees to it that he carries it back with him, freshly filled, in the afternoons. And every day at noon he goes up to the house and washes and sits by himself at the table while she brings the food to him as she did the first day—though in the mornings he still shows up at Dolph Courtney's at opening time and buys his customary packet of sandwiches. He cannot bring himself to give up either Ida's company, such as it is, or her hospitality. And because he is a man deeply in the habit of secrecy about himself, he cannot bring himself to give up his deceptions. When he knows that she will be feeding the Coulters or Mat or any of the others who are helping with the work of the place in Gideon's absence, he finds it easy enough to go back to town at noon on the pretense of needing materials or tools.

He has misgivings at the thought that she feeds him by her own troubling and providing even though the work he is doing there is not necessarily for her. Aware of the delicacy of the question, and made awkward by it, he has asked several times if there is not some way that he can repay her for her kindness to him. And each time she has scoffed at the idea.

"I've got plenty of canned stuff in the cellar," she told him once, "and meat in the smokehouse. Somebody just as well be eating it."

Now and then when he sees she needs it, he will buy some staple such as salt or coffee or flour and bring it to her, and always she will take it with simple thanks and the observation that she was needing it, as if the whole business is perfectly natural and even ordinary. It would delight him to bring more, to buy and bring by the armload, but he knows that to buy more where there is already plenty would seem ridiculous to her.

Nothing has passed between them except her hospitality, the same as she would offer to anybody who might come there to work—not just her hospitality, as she offers it, but Gideon's as well. Or you could say that it is not her hospitality that she offers at all, but only Gideon's, her offering of it being necessarily more meticulous because he is not there to offer it himself.

But during the weeks that Ernest has been at work there, eating in her kitchen, studying her ways and looks and movements, she has come into his mind. In spite of her careless old dresses, her apparent unconcern about her looks, there is a certain beauty that she has, and a certain dignity and strength that draw him toward her. Wherever she moves at her work, in or out of his sight, he is aware of her. A kind of imagining sight and touch carries his mind to her against his will. He imagines himself living there with her, doing such farming as his lameness might allow. In this dream of his, his shop is lifted intact out of Port William and set down in place of Gideon's old toolshed under the oak tree. Except for this holding on to the idea of the shop, one of the emotions of his dream is surprise at the ease with which his old life can be given up.

That her mind is not on him at all—that except for what she would think of as a decent and necessary kindness toward him, her attention is turned away from him, as though she is always listening for the approach of somebody else—this makes him all the freer to cultivate his dream.

There are times when he realizes vaguely that he is trapped, endangered, like an animal that has crept through a narrow opening and fed until it has grown too large to escape. The orderly interior of his shop is remote from him now, of little use to him. In these moments of understanding, he knows that something behind him in his life is being destroyed. Even if he could escape and make his way back to it, it would no longer serve.

Daylight

Old Jack never did have any trouble waking up. Now out of the light sleep of his old age he wakes more easily than he ever did. And he is hardly awake before he is up, cap already on, standing in the middle of the floor, scratching his stomach and getting his bearings. Unhooking his cane from the bed, he goes to the window and looks out. Above the pale whitening of dawn in the east the morning stars are bright. It will be a clear day.

Beyond the window the town is quiet. There is not a light burning anywhere. As usual he is the first one up, and he likes the feeling of that, has liked it all his life. Most of his days have begun in that silence, and it is still one of his needs. He slept with the window half-open and he opens it wide now and, turning back into the room, puts on his clothes. He makes his bed in the dark, and instead of sitting at the window to wait for daylight to come as he usually does, he goes out the door and starts down the hall.

Wheeler has promised to come by for him early this morning and take him out to spend the day at his farm. He has been planning this with Wheeler for a couple of weeks, but for various reasons it has had to be put off until now. Wheeler has a case to try in Frankfort today, so he will not have to go much out of his way. Jack could just as easily have asked Mat to take him, but Wheeler is his lawyer, not Mat, and he sees Mat every day anyhow.

At the top of the steps he can hear Mrs. Hendrick snoring in her room. He rakes his cane along the balusters lightly, and hears her stop and groan and turn over.

He decides not to bother with waking her. Let all the day be good.

He goes on down the stairs and back along the hall and through the kitchen and out the back door. Going out near the fence, he urinates, making of the necessity an opportunity to look at his garden, which is growing well. He cleaned it of weeds yesterday, and that cleanness and the dewy freshness of the morning seem to him to go together. In the grey light the young plants in their rows show dark against the ground.

He goes back into the kitchen and turns on the light. Pawing around in the old refrigerator, he finds bacon and eggs and, lighting the coal-oil stove, makes himself a breakfast, cooking plenty and helping himself to a bowl of cold biscuits that he finds in the dish cabinet. The bacon is not well done and the eggs are too greasy, but he eats heartily, offsetting the grease with half a dozen biscuits and a lot of water.

Last night he had Dolph Courtney make him some baloney sandwiches for his lunch today. He gets the packet out of the refrigerator now, turns off the kitchen light, and goes to wait on the front porch. The daylight is getting strong, though it will still be half an hour or so until sunup. Things have begun to stir at Mat's, and up and down the street other houses have begun to show signs of life. Old Jack goes over to the edge of the porch and looks out the road toward Hargrave. He imagines that Wheeler is on his way. He lets his mind leave Wheeler's house down at Hargrave and come up the road toward Port William at what he thinks is about thirty-five miles an hour, careful to observe all the landmarks as they go by. By the time his mind comes up out of the river valley and starts across the ridge to Port William it is making at least sixty, though if he knew it he would never let it go that fast. He lets it drive in over at Mat's to take some message from Wheeler's wife, and then back out and pull down in front of the hotel and park itself under the shade trees. But Wheeler still has not come in sight. Old Jack looks and listens out the road, but does not hear a thing. The east has begun to redden ahead of the rising sun, and he knows she will be right on up. He takes out his watch and—considering that it is late, and that *how* late does not matter—puts it back without looking at it. He has not spent a full day at home since he moved to Port William last fall, and now that the day has finally come he grieves for every lost minute of it. Standing there, watching the sky redden, thinking of how much daylight is already behind him, he is overcome by a kind of sad panic. He decides he had better call Wheeler's house to see if he has left.

On the wallpaper over the telephone he has written in strokes an inch high:

WHEELER CATLETT
OFFICE 7–2854
HOUSE 7–3672

He dials the house number and waits, hopeful. He can just hear Wheeler's wife answer the phone and say, "Yes, Uncle Jack. Wheeler left a good while ago. He ought to be getting up there about now." It rings and rings. It does not take Old Jack long to guess what that means. Wheeler is not up. It is a fact that Wheeler sometimes sleeps as late as seven o'clock. That is the only bad fault Old Jack has ever found in Wheeler. He must have told him a thousand times, by various subtleties and hints, that a man cannot hope to get anywhere lying in the bed so late of a morning with the sun shining in his face.

"My Lord Amighty!" Old Jack says in disgust, as ashamed and humiliated and angry as if Wheeler was his own boy.

He lets her ring.

Finally the receiver clicks up on the other end.

"Hello!" Old Jack does not have much faith in the instrument, and he talks loudly.

Somebody speaks into the other end.

"Hello!"

"Hello." The sound still seems to come from too far away.

"Who is that a talking?"

"It's Wheeler, Uncle Jack. What's the matter?"

"Wheeler, I'm ready, honey. It's daylight. Are you coming?"

"I told you I'd be there, didn't I? And I didn't say when. I said pretty early."

"Well?"

"Well," Wheeler says, "the *sun's* not even up!"

Old Jack was not aiming to let on what he thinks, but he cannot help it. "Damn it to hell, don't tell *me* what the sun does in the morning! I know and you don't!"

They're both good and mad now.

"Well," Wheeler says.

"Well *what?*"

"Never mind!"

"Well, are you aiming to come or not? I got business I want to take care of."

"I'll be there, Uncle Jack," Wheeler says. "Just hold on. It'll be about thirty minutes. Be ready."

"Ready, hell!" Jack says. "I *been* ready!" And he hangs up.

He goes out and, seeing that Dolph Courtney has opened up and Ernest Finley has come for his sandwiches, starts down to the drugstore.

Old Jack going in, Ernest coming out, they meet in the door.

"Good morning, boy."

"Morning, Uncle Jack."

"Well, are you on your way to work?"

"Going to try it another day."

"You're all right, son, You're a good 'un."

Old Jack likes to see a man start his day's work when the day starts. But instead of comforting him, the sight of a man getting up the way he ought to only makes him more bitter toward Wheeler—and everybody else in the country who is still lying in bed. He cannot get used to this new fashion of sleeping until the sun is three or four hours high. He cannot imagine how a man could ever do anything worthwhile in a day he had already slept the best part of.

"Morning!" Dolph calls from the back of the store where he is cooking his breakfast.

But Old Jack does not hear him. He has turned around to watch through the door glass while Ernest gets into the truck and starts to his work. All his life—when he was on his place, *in* his place—he and the ones who worked with him got up before the sun.

"If they stay with me they've got to get up!" he thinks, repeating in his mind words he has said many times aloud. He feels the emptiness of that boast now. Now the truth is that there is not a soul living—Wheeler included, damn him—who cares whether Old Jack gets up at daylight or not. And everybody knows that after he does get up there is not much he can do. But *he* demands that he get up. And once he is up, because his life has taught him, he can see what needs to be done. A man who has learned to see cannot help seeing.

"Ay, Lord!"

"What's that, Uncle?"

Dolph's gold tooth is shining in the middle of a grin.

"Too damn many people sleeping in the daytime," Old Jack says.

He pauses, the necessity of speaking to Dolph making him realize that he is making the wrong point.

"And better *off* asleep, some of 'em."

Old Jack's anger has carried his indictment far beyond the point where it might apply to any fault of Wheeler's. He is well aware of that and is comforted by it. Now, watching Dolph eat his breakfast—thinking how Dolph's wife will come flopping up to Burgess's store in her bedroom slippers about nine o'clock, eyes still half shut, hair full of curlers—Old Jack feels all of his anger go out of him, leaving only sadness that what he has said is true.

"Surely," he says, "a man can get up and be ready when the time comes."

He looks at Dolph and shakes his head. He might just as well be hollering down a groundhog hole. But he will say what he means.

"Look at Mat Feltner up there. His boy's gone, he's getting old, he's troubled in his mind—and you'll never see him hit a half-assed swat at a fly."

Toot! Toot-toot!

Old Jack is on his way out, Dolph Courtney forgotten, before the horn stops blowing.

Outside he sees that it is not Wheeler at all, but somebody in a truck, already going out of sight up the road.

But before he has time to be disappointed Wheeler *is* there, his car coming up over the rise beyond Mat's house, slowing up and stopping in front of the hotel. Old Jack waves his cane.

"Oh, Wheeler! Whoo! Hold on!"

Wheeler lets the car roll on down the street to where Old Jack is hurrying to meet him, and stops and opens the door. Old Jack gets in, puts his packet of sandwiches on the seat between them, puts the point of his cane between his feet, slams the door, laces his fingers over the crook of the cane.

"How're you, Wheeler?"

"All right, Uncle Jack. How're you?"

"Tol'bly well."

"It's a fine morning."

"It is that."

They are both over their anger and glad to see each other. Old Jack suddenly feels a lot better than tolerable. He is on his way home, his day begun. He glances over at Wheeler, who is looking mighty fine in his suit and clean white shirt, and feels a tremor of pride that he knows that fine man.

"Wheeler," he says, "you'll see that you'll be in good shape today on account of getting up early. It gives you time to think over what you've got to say, don't it?"

He could not help saying that, though now that he has said it he reckons maybe he should not have.

"Right!" Wheeler says, laughing. "I'll be two times better than I usually am—if I can just stay awake until I get there, and find some breakfast."

Laughing too, Old Jack says, "A real lawyer would have finished breakfast two hours ago."

Well, he is glad he brought it up. There is no doubt now that their quarrel is over.

Wheeler, from his side of the car, has been watching Old Jack with amusement and growing sympathy. The old man is sitting there in his whopsided old cap and big coat and puttees, blood dried on his face from last night's shaving, leaning toward the windshield, taking in everything, and it comes to Wheeler what this day means to him.

They drive out past the edge of town and turn right onto the Bird's Branch road. The gravel road stays up high along the backs of the ridges, and as they go along they can see miles of the country, the points and ridges marked by long shadows in the red light of the sun still not far above the horizon. They go slowly into the turns and slants of the road, talking about the weather and the prospects of the year. Finally Wheeler asks:

"Have you seen Mr. Feltner lately?"

"I see him every day."

"How do you think he looks?"

"Ay, Lord! He looks like a man that's hurt."

Wheeler, as if considering that, says nothing for a minute, looking down the road. And then he says: "Bess is worried about him, and so am I. He's taking this mighty hard."

"It's hard on all of them."

"Yes, but Mrs. Feltner and Hannah have the baby to think about and get ready for. That seems to be some help to them. But Mr. Feltner doesn't—or won't—have anything but his work. And he's doing too much of that. I've never seen him tireder."

"Ah! And everything he does is bound to remind him of what he hoped for his boy."

"Yes."

Old Jack touches Wheeler's leg with the end of his cane to make Wheeler look at him.

"Do you think his boy's alive?"

Wheeler doesn't answer for what seems a long time, as though he is wishing Jack had not asked. "Not likely," he says finally, "though we may not know for certain for a long time. And may never."

Seeing that the old man is saddened by what he said, Wheeler says kindly: "Nothing anybody can do, Uncle Jack."

But surely Wheeler knows better than to think *that* is any consolation. It is just the truth. And a man who is depending on the truth to console him is sometimes in a hell of a fix. To Old Jack, the sorrowful thing *exactly* is that there is nothing anybody can do.

"Not a thing in the world. And he's as fine a one as ever set foot on the ground."

They come to Old Jack's place—a big white house set back from the road in a yard full of trees, clean well-fenced pastures and fields sloping away from it, barns and outbuildings all painted white too and in good repair. It is plain from the look of it that a man's competent love for it has dwelt in it. Old Jack has neglected nothing, let nothing go.

Wheeler stops in front of the barn and names a time late in the day when he will be back. Old Jack gets out and stands watching and then listening while Wheeler drives out to the road and disappears and then the sound of his engine goes out of hearing over the next hill. Much as he likes to be with Wheeler, he is glad he has gone.

The sun has risen above its first redness now, and is slanting down clear and bright. The dew is still on. The pastures are in excellent shape, the grass thick and deep. In the fresh sunshine, amidst the green of the trees and the grass, the buildings are white and clean. Old Jack stands and looks, gathering it all in. The place itself comes back into his mind. They come together like the two halves of the same thing. There is smoke rising from the kitchen chimney, and he hears from somewhere out back of the barn the sound of harrow disks striking rock, which tells him that his new tenant is at work. That is a relief. He purposely gave no warning of his visit, the better to get an idea of this man's way of doing, but he came half afraid of the pain it would cause him if this one too proved incompetent or lazy.

During his declining years Old Jack has had a number of tenants who contracted to raise the tobacco on the shares and to work by the day when he needed them and they could spare the time. Most of these were men living on neighboring farms who wanted to take on the extra work, and except for one, who was called to the Army after staying only a year, all of them have proved unsatisfactory in one way or another. Most of them, in fact, nearly worried Old Jack to death with their poor ways of doing—messing at their work or neglecting it, losing his tools or leaving them in the rain, forgetting to fasten gates, mistreating the stock. Sooner or later he would always get disgusted with them and make them go, or they would become sulky under the demands he made on them and quit. It was a bad situation, Jack knew, but nothing else seemed possible. And in spite of everything, because he was still living there, and was constantly watchful and busy, the farm stayed in good shape.

But when he had made up his mind to move to town, he and Wheeler decided that a more stable arrangement would have to be made. Old Jack left everything to Wheeler. A young man—the tenant for the past year on a neighboring farm—was recommended, was interested, and a contract was signed in January in Wheeler's office. Since then, on his trips with Wheeler to the farm, and on chance meetings in town, Old Jack has seen his tenant maybe a dozen times, but only briefly, without having a chance to form a judgment of him. Until recently he has just trusted Wheeler's continuing good opinion, knowing he would find out for himself sooner or later.

He has always liked the young man, but has wondered about him too. And he has wondered what will happen to his place now that he no longer lives on it. The question has troubled him. He would have come out two weeks ago if Wheeler had not stalled him, waiting for better weather.

Standing in front of the barn, he has already begun his exploration of the young man's ways, looking into the fence corners and into the open sheds and at the back porch of the house. All that he can see is orderly. The tools that are not in use have been put into the sheds out of the weather. The gates and doors are all closed and latched. Rows of young vegetables are growing in the garden. A flock of hens is scratching around the henhouse in the sun. In one of the front fields he can see three milk cows grazing, and there are a couple of sows and pigs in one of the small pens below the barn. All that is as it should be. These people are not the kind who will be running to the grocery store to buy all they eat. That means a great deal, to Old Jack's way of thinking.

The young man's wife is carrying water from the well into the kitchen, and Old Jack imagines that she is heating water to wash clothes. The first time she came out she waved to him and called, "Good morning!" And he waved to her. Since then she has gone on with her work, paying no attention to him. It pleases him that she has started her work so early in the morning, and that she goes about it without stopping to talk. Though he has seen her only a few times, and then at a distance, he can tell that she recognized him, and that pleases him too. For a long time he can remember exactly the cheerfulness of her voice. He makes up his mind about her on the spot. She is a good woman.

Turning and going into the feed barn, he puts his packet of sandwiches up on a shelf inside the doors, and goes back through the clean-swept driveway, opening the stalls and looking in. All the stalls have been freshly bedded. The barn looks the way it ought to. He goes to the other barns and buildings. Everywhere there is the same orderliness. Everywhere he can see the signs of the presence of a good man, a good manager, a good head—a kind of intelligence that he recognizes and feels akin to.

He goes through the lot gate and, following a pair of wheel tracks worn in the grass, walks out along the broad back of the ridge. The tracks turn after a couple of hundred yards, cross a shallow swag, go through a grove of big white oaks, and come to a second gate, which opens into the broken field where he expects to find his tenant.

When he first comes into the field there is no one in sight. He sits down on a sled up the fence a few rods from the gate, and rests and waits. Before him lies the long, evenly worked strip of crop ground, sloping gently toward the woods on the lower side. Looking up and down the length of it, he sees nothing at first except a few black birds walking over the newly stirred earth. And then over the rise to his left a team of three horses, two blacks and a bay, comes into sight, stepping at a brisk pace, their heads nodding, a brown plume of dust rising behind the harrow as they draw it along. As they come nearer down the long field, Old Jack can hear the harness creaking, the rattling of the trace chains and the metal tripletrees. Now and then the disks of the harrow grate on a stone. The horses stride powerfully over the loose ground.

Knowing a good team when he sees one, Old Jack comes wide awake. He sits, leaning a little forward now, on the edge of the sled. He grins and shakes his head.

"Ay, Lord!" he says.

You can see that there is no deadhead sitting behind that team of horses. The man is driving, not riding. And though Jack has not heard him utter a word, the horses move in a way that shows they know exactly who they have behind them and what he expects.

With a great rattling and creaking and loud breathing the big team draws down toward Old Jack, and then even with him.

"Whoa! Whoa, boys!"

The tone of the young man's voice is full of praise. He speaks as he might speak to three other men well known to him. The horses stop and stand. The young man turns to Old Jack, grins, raises his hand.

"Good morning, sir!"

He loops the reins over a lever and steps off the harrow, hurrying toward the sled. Old Jack, seeing how he hastens at his work, gets up and goes out across the harrowed ground to meet him—in a kind of panic trying to remember what his name is.

"How are you, Mr. Beechum?"

For the life of him, Old Jack cannot think of the young man's name. Usually it does not matter to him what somebody's name is. But he has begun to think a lot of this young fellow, and he would like to call him by name.

"I'm all right, son. You're working a good team of horses."

"They do pretty well," the young man says.

But Old Jack can see that he knows they do better than pretty well, and that he recognizes the value of the compliment and appreciates it. Old Jack was a fine horseman and teamster in his day, and it is clear that the young man knows that.

They talk briefly about the weather and about the prospects for the crops. Old Jack asks a question or two, and the young man answers. He is a lean, hard-muscled fellow, clean-cut, with the curious ability to look neat in dirty work clothes. Respectfully and good-humoredly he fulfills what he considers to be his duty to his landlord, explaining what he has done and how he has done it and what he plans to do and what his thoughts are about the work of the farm. And beneath the pleasantness with which he does this explaining can be felt his confidence in his own work and his own judgment. A good head. Old Jack gets the impression that his opinions and approval are not being asked for, and instead of being angered by the young man's independence as he would have expected, he finds that he is delighted. It is a meeting of two of the same kind. While he was taking the measure of the younger man, his own measure has been taken. That tickles him. When his last question has been answered, he raises his hand.

"You go right ahead. Satisfy yourself, and you'll satisfy me."

Old Jack never said that to anybody before. He looks at the young man, wondering if he understands, and sees that he does.

The young man nods. "I thank you."

Starting back toward the harrow, he says, "Well, will you be around a while, Mr. Beechum?"

"About all day, son," Old Jack says, waving. "I'll be talking to you."

He watches the young man swing up onto the harrow seat and take the reins in his hands.

"Come up, Prince! Dan!"

The horses step at once into the pace they were going in when they stopped. The young man does not look back. As though no interruption has taken place, the great hooves lift and fall, the harrow disks slice through the ground, the plume of dust rises into the sky.

Old Jack stands and watches until the man and team reach the end of the field and make the turn and start back, and then he goes to the sled again and sits down. The terms of an unexpected happiness have begun to work themselves out in his mind, the possibility of an orderliness in his history that he has not dared to hope for, a clean transition from his life to the life of another man. It is as though he has come to a window looking out onto a lighted country where before was only darkness. While the young man makes the long rounds of the field, the old one continues to sit there on the sled and watch.

After a while he sees the wife come through the gate carrying a water jug. Seeing him, she comes on up the fence and offers him a drink, which he accepts and thanks her. She smiles.

"He went out this morning and forgot to bring it," she explains. "I thought he might be thirsty."

"It's a fact, honey," Old Jack says. "He might."

He cannot remember her name either.

When he has drunk and thanked her again, she takes the jug and goes out across the worked ground to meet her husband, who stops the team and takes a long drink. Putting the top back on the jug, he says something to her. Old Jack is too far away to hear what he says, but he can see his white teeth as he smiles. The wife does not come back to where Old Jack is, but goes directly to the gate. As she looks at him and waves, going out, he raises his hat to her and bows.

After she goes, the sun growing warm against his back, he drops off to sleep, leaning forward a little over his hands, which are folded on the crook of the cane.

When he opens his eyes he is looking at the ground between his feet. And then, as often when he wakes up after sleeping in the daytime, he feels go through him the ache of panic, afraid he has slept through something he should have been awake for. He raises his head. The field and the sky dazzle and sway in the brilliant light. A crow is calling loudly in the woods. He cannot at first realize where he is, and when he does his reasons for being there appear strange to him. He feels as though he is falling from a place where he has kept himself dangerously balanced.

And then he sees the team coming toward him a long way up the field, sits forward, and watches attentively, studying the motion of the horses and the harrow, the steady rising and spreading of the dust cloud behind them. And gradually the familiarity of these things comes back to him. The field steadies and grows quiet under the daylight. He begins to hear the small sounds made by the harrow. The band of freshly worked ground along the edges of the field has grown wider.

He is suddenly ashamed of himself for sleeping while right before his eyes a good man is at work. He does not want to be sitting there when that young man comes by, does not want the young man to see that he has waked up and wave to him, cannot stand the thought of himself waving back as though he does not mind being useless. He gets up and with a show of purposeful haste, which he does not feel and which disgusts him by its falseness, goes to the gate and lets himself through.

He finds himself now in the predicament of hurrying off toward the barns without the slightest notion of what he will do when he gets there. He supposes there were several more things he planned to see to, but it is annoying to have to think of them now only to save face, and his annoyance keeps him from being able to think.

But before he has gone much farther, his mind has completely changed its subject. He has left the wheel tracks and begun to wander, though he keeps the same general direction. He goes out through the grove of oaks, down across the small wet-weather stream at the bottom of the swag, and up the opposite slope to the high point of the ridge. Now and again he stops and stands a long time, looking. He is studying his land, the shape of it, the condition of the growth on it, with the interest in it that he has had all his life.

When he gets back to the barn lot he takes another look around, measuring the work there against his new estimate of the workman. There is little that needs doing. Such small evidences of neglect as he can find are attributable to the hurry of the spring work. He finds a loose board in the granary door, and nails it tight. He does a little straightening up in the harness room, though it is not really necessary. He finds a couple of hoes and an axe and a scythe that need sharpening, and he sharpens them. He cuts a few weeds that have begun to grow up along the lot fence. Hearing the ringing of loose trace chains, he looks up and sees the young man coming in with the horses. He looks at his watch and then at the sun. It is dinnertime.

He hurries to put his hoe away, and to open the lot gate ahead of the team. He gets it open just in time and the horses come through without having to stop. The young man is riding the lead horse, the bay one, and leading the others. As he rides by Old Jack he smiles and raises his hand.

"Thank you, sir!"

"That's all right, son."

Taking the horses on around to the well in front of the barn, the young man jumps to the ground and begins pumping water into the trough. Old Jack stands in the barn door and watches. Seeing the good team of horses drink after their hard morning's work makes him happy. They drink a long time, pausing now and then to raise their heads and stand with a far-off gaze in their eyes, mouthing the cool water. When they are finished the young man leads them into the barn and puts them in their stalls.

"Give them plenty of corn," Old Jack says, not to be bossing, but as a tribute to the horses.

When the young man comes out of the barn, Old Jack is making himself comfortable on an upturned bucket beside the well, his lunch packet on his lap, a can of fresh water on the ground at his feet. He is about to untie the string on the packet when the young man stops him.

"Mr. Beechum, come on to the house, now, and have a bite with us."

"Naw. I thank you, son. I can make out fine on what I brought."

"Well, we wouldn't want you to do that. We were sort of looking for you to eat with us, and I expect there's plenty fixed."

Old Jack figures that is not entirely true, but he accepts, glad to escape the baloney. He gets up and puts the packet back on the shelf in the barn.

They go together across the lot and through the yard, where the morning's wash is drying on the line, and up onto the back porch. The young man opens the screen door, and Old Jack goes ahead of him into the kitchen.

"Hello! Come in! How are you?" the young wife says to him.

"Fine. Fine, thank you," Old Jack says to her, again bowing and smiling. "And how're you?" Because she is young and pretty and is kind to him, he speaks to her with the indulgent tenderness with which he would speak to a little girl.

He looks at the table and sees that it is, sure enough, set for three. As he washes and dries his hands, he takes a look around the kitchen, finding it a good deal changed from the way he remembers it—though he has to admit that it looks nice the way it is, better certainly than it did during the years after his wife's death when he did his own cooking in it, letting the windows and the paint grow dingy and the finish wear off the linoleum. Again, as in the morning—while he stands there pretending to look out the window, and the young man washes—he feels a mixture of pleasure and pain, only this time the pain is different and more intense. Around the barns and in the fields all has been scrupulously kept as it was when he left it, because it had been left in good shape and because he has licensed no changes. But here, clearly, where an old life deteriorated and came to an end, a new strong one has begun. Though he doubts that he will ever have occasion to see for himself, and knows that he does not want to, he imagines this change to have taken place in all the rooms of the house. The thought saddens him and freshens in his mind all his old feelings toward his wife and his daughter. There in the old kitchen in which he has eaten nearly all the meals of his life, he feels the loss of what has gone by and he wishes he had not come.

But now the cheerful voice of the young wife is asking if he wouldn't like to sit down. The meal is ready.

He and the young man go to the table. The wife finishes bringing the food and sits down with them. They pass the dishes to Old Jack, urging him to take as much as he wants of everything. They are doing all they can to put him at ease, trying to relieve the awkwardness they feel in their understanding that this house is his home, though he has come back to it as its guest. Young as they seem to him, they *do* put him at ease. Their manner toward him is respectful, but without any of that self-effacing humility which as landlord he has learned to expect, and to distrust.

The meal is ample and well prepared, and Old Jack eats with the keen pleasure that good company and the work of a good cook always give him. He compliments the wife on her cooking, and compliments the husband on his wife, calling the young couple "son" and "honey." He has racked his brains but he cannot remember their names.

While they eat the young man asks how long it has been since a crop was raised in the field he has been working in during the morning. Telling him, Old Jack is reminded of the last crop grown there—a good one—and he tells about that. Prompted by the young man's questions and his interest, Old Jack remembers and tells more about his younger days than he has thought of in a long time, in the course of the conversation twice filling and emptying his plate.

During the meal he has not ceased to study both the young man and the wife, and he is more than satisfied with what he sees. Everything about the young man speaks of his decent pride. Though he works for another man, he has the ways of a man who intends one day to work for himself. He has resigned himself to nothing inferior. And the husband's character, it seems to Old Jack, is answered in the character of the wife.

His vision of the morning returns to him. He can see this place passing out of his own good keeping into that of the younger man—can see him at work and alive here long after he himself will be dead. He turns to the young man, intending to tell him that he can depend on his goodwill and can trust him—that he will help him to have what he wants. But he cannot speak. He looks out the window, getting hold of himself, and then he says: "Son, you're a fine boy. And you've married a fine girl. I'm going to stick to you."

After he has eaten, the young man gets up from the table and goes to the barn, leaving Old Jack to eat a second piece of pie. After a little they hear him going out the lot gate with the team.

Old Jack finishes his pie, scraping the last traces of filling off his saucer. Getting up, he thanks the wife, complimenting her again at some length. She tells him she is glad he came, and that he must feel welcome to come any time. Seeing that she is already busy clearing the table, he does not detain her with more talk, but tells her good-bye and starts to the barn. As he crosses the back porch he sees, lying on a shelf beside the milk buckets, the morning's mail: a newspaper, an advertising circular of some sort, a post card. The post card is addressed to Elton and Mary Penn. As soon as he gets to the barn he takes out his notebook and writes their names in it. He moves the bucket from the well over against the front wall of the barn, then sits down on it, and goes to sleep.

When he wakes up this time he is not confused, but rested. He can see from the lengthening of the barn's shadow out into the lot that he has slept a long nap. The middle of the afternoon has come.

He gets up and walks to the back of the place to look at his steers that have lately been put out on grass. He finds them and spends an hour watching them graze. They are doing well. There is plenty of grass and plenty of water. It is the kind of sight a man can look at for pleasure. But feeling the day going on, he starts back. He cannot remember now what time Wheeler said he would pick him up, and he does not want to be late.

On the way back he stops on the top of a rise and from that distance watches the young man and the team go the length of the field—a man who needs no boss in order to work well, but will require more of himself than another man will be likely to require of him. By the excellence of the young man they are made free of each other, though that freedom is a bond between them.

It seems to him now that the day is finished, and turning, putting it behind him, he hastens on to the barn. Not finding Wheeler there, he does not stop, but goes on through the lot, past the house, down the long yard to the road, and turns toward town. He is filled with a sense of loss that now gives no pain. The young man at work behind him, his bed at the hotel ahead of him, it seems to him that he knows better than he ever has from how high he is going down.

When Wheeler meets him half an hour or so later he has walked considerably more than a mile.

"Why didn't you wait?" Wheeler asks, leaning across the seat to open the door for him.

"Why didn't you come on when you was supposed to?" Old Jack says, guessing from the tone of Wheeler's voice that he must be late.

Wheeler laughs, but says nothing.

Old Jack gets in and arranges himself and slams the door. The car moves off.

"Aw, Wheeler, I was taking a look at the country. Thought I might see some old woman about eighteen years old smiling at me as I went by."

They come to a driveway and turn around.

"But none did."

"Well," Wheeler says, "what do you think of Elton Penn?"

"I think he's a good one."

"Uh-huh," Wheeler says.

He has held a high opinion of Elton a long time, but Old Jack would not take his word.

They go along in silence for a minute, and then Old Jack says, speaking of his daughter and son-in-law: "Wheeler, as soon as I die they'll sell that farm."

Taken by surprise, Wheeler only nods. He thinks so too.

"And when they sell it, I want you to see that that boy gets a chance to buy it, if he wants it. I want you to help him get hold of the money, and stand behind him. Will you do that?"

"I'll do it," Wheeler says.

"Maybe I'll last long enough to help him a little myself."

A Birth

Mat spent the morning at odd jobs and errands, the endless little tasks of management that keep him going back and forth between his own land and Roger Merchant's as the season and the work advance. After dinner he harnessed a team and spent the second half of the day helping Burley Coulter work the tobacco ground. The Coulters, in spite of long days and seven-day weeks, have fallen behind in their work, and Mat has been giving them odd half days whenever he can. Today, driving the slow rounds of the field, he was glad to have been needed.

When they quit at dusk, because he will be coming to work there again tomorrow, Burley stabled his team at Mat's. And as often lately when they have been together during the afternoon, Mat asked Burley to supper.

Supper has been over a long time now, and the two of them are sitting in the wicker chairs on the back porch, each smoking one of Mat's cigars. The dishes washed and put away, the kitchen is dark. The evening is quiet. Only now and then Mat and Burley can hear down in town a shout or an outburst of laughter. They are tired, no longer talking. The only communication between them is the alternate slow glowing and dimming of the cigar ends, the release into the darkness of invisible fragrant smoke. The sky is clear, filled with brilliant stars; against it can be made out the massive, faintly stirring tops of the maples and, nearer, the shape of a hanging flowerpot and the drooping foliage of a begonia. As often after a day's work, Mat's left shoulder is hurting; he shifts restlessly in his chair, trying to find a comfortable way to prop his arm. All day he has carried the thought of loss. His body has grown heavy with the desire to sleep, but he dreads going to bed, afraid that once there he will lie awake, afraid of the thoughts that will come then. His discipline now is to think of nothing, to look at the darkness, pleased to be sitting there smoking with Burley.

Footsteps come back through the house; the screen door opens and closes quietly.

"Mat?" Margaret says.

"Here we are," Mat says.

Burley gets up. "Here's a chair, Mrs. Feltner."

"No, thank you Burley. Mat," she says, "Hannah's pains have started."

"Have!" Mat gets up. "Well, call the doctor."

"I did. He said to take her on down to the hospital. He'll come as soon as he can."

"Is she all right?"

"Yes, she's fine. Get the car."

"All right," Mat says. It seems to him there is something else he ought to ask, but he hears the door open and shut, and Margaret's steps go back through the hall. He starts off the porch toward the shed where he keeps the car, Burley following a step or two behind.

Burley has begun to wish he was on his way home. There may have been a time when he could gracefully have taken his leave, but he does not know when it was. And so he tags along, a friendly stranger, at what he hopes is an obviously respectful distance. If Mat would say something—or, better, give him something to do—that would ease him. But Mat does not say anything, his footsteps hurrying on into the darkness, and Burley subtracts himself by another couple of steps. Keeping distance between them like a stretcher, they cross the barn lot.

Mat throws open the doors of the shed, and feels his way in between the wall and the side of the car. The car is an old black coupe, bearing the marks of use that has been long and casual and hard—not much better fitted to the occasion, he thinks, than the truck. Turning on the lights, he hastily sweeps out the dirt, gathering up odds and ends of paper and clothing and flinging it all into a corner. It seems to him that lately all he has done is make the rounds from one mess to another, always a little late. A sort of guilt creeps into him that he has done so little to prepare for this arrival. But he sees the uselessness of that.

He backs out, turns, and drives out to the road. It is not until he stops in front of the house that he remembers what it seems he never really saw: Burley standing in the beam of the headlights, holding the gate open for him, his hand raised in what might have been blessing or farewell.

The women are waiting. He picks up Hannah's suitcase and takes her arm. Behind them, Margaret shuts the door.

As they leave the lights of the town behind them, beginning the descent into the river valley, the two women begin to talk. To Mat, though he does not trust himself to guess what they are feeling, their voices sound unsure. Glancing down into the light of the dashboard, he sees that they are holding hands, and his heart labors suddenly with love for them both.

Coming into Hargrave, they go slowly through the quiet streets, in and out of the pooled light of the streetlamps, and the sound of the car's engine, resonant in the silence, reaches ahead into the echoes of itself.

At the hospital Mat lets the two women out near the front door and goes on to park the car. When he comes into the lobby Margaret is standing alone beside the admissions desk.

"Where's Hannah?"

"They've already taken her to the labor room."

That they have hurried her away before he could even tell her goodbye strikes Mat as outrageous. Because he is tired and afraid—or so, later, he will explain it—he is suddenly beside himself with sadness and anger.

"God *damn* it!" he says. "They run this place like a jail."

"Mat?" Margaret says, and he stops, sorry.

Margaret smiles and says, "For Heaven's sake!"

The old nurse sitting there pushes some cards toward him. Her face wears a look of complacent disgust; her worst suspicions have been confirmed many times, and she is used to it.

"There's a waiting room near the delivery room on the second floor," she says as if to the general public. "You may like to wait there."

Except for them the room is empty. Margaret sits down and turns on the shaded lamp beside her chair. "Mat, you're worn out. Why don't you go on home now? I'll be fine. As soon as anything happens I'll call you."

"No ma'am," he says. "I'm in this for the duration. What would I do off by myself? I couldn't sleep."

Margaret takes her embroidery out of her purse, puts on her glasses, and sets to work. "Well, sit down then, and make yourself at home."

"Shouldn't we call Bess and Wheeler?"

"I don't think so, Mat. Not tonight."

He figured so. She is too practical to call for unnecessary help. All they have to do is wait, and they can do that by themselves.

"Well. All right."

But he does not make himself at home. It is not in him to yield to this impersonal place. He shifts about the room, looking at the pictures on the walls, looking out the windows, rattling the change in his pocket. He still has his hat on. Because it is, to him, so insistently a waiting room, a timeless space wedged into time, far from any place where he would be at home, it seems to exclude some thought that he needs to think. Whatever might be done cannot be done here. He thinks of Hannah suffering in this alien place, kept apart from them, with such defiant love as makes him an enemy to all the world but her.

From a door saying DO NOT ENTER a nurse comes into the waiting room. As Mat turns to question her, she goes through the swinging door on the opposite side. He wonders if the doctor has come. Surely, he thinks, if he was here they would have seen him come in. Coming aware that he is cursing under his breath, realizing what a doubtful hold he has kept on his feelings, he makes himself sit down. Though he has wished to be dependable and useful, he has failed even to be quiet. The thought shames him, reminding him of other times when he has failed of that steadiness that he most required and expected of himself, and would most have prided himself in had he been capable of it. The only sounds now in the silence that has come over them are the cries of nighthawks flying above the hospital and the town.

Suddenly, without the sound of the approach of footsteps from the other side, the forbidden door is flung open and Dr. Markman comes in, looking the same as he always does—hair in his eyes, tie loosened, rumpled suit looking as though the pockets might be filled with wrenches or fish or garden seed.

"Well," he says, "how the old folks bearing up?"

"Tolerably well," Mat says.

"How're you, Margaret?"

"I'm fine. How's Hannah?"

"She's all right. And *going* to be all right, too. There is no need to worry." He looks at his watch. "Well, I'm going to try to nap for a couple of hours. This is probably going to take a while."

"When do you think it'll be, Doc?"

"Oh, about morning. Hard to say."

He goes back through the door he came out of, and it is quiet again. Now that the doctor has gone, Mat can think of half a dozen questions he should have asked. He wishes he had asked to have word sent from time to time. But that chance is gone now. It could be a long time before they will hear anything more. He tries to read, but only stares at the blurring print, not seeing it, his mind filled with anxiety in which the cries of the nighthawks circle and approach and recede like thoughts. Finally he gives up, and folds his hands. His shoulder is aching again. He is both painfully tired and wide awake. They are in the midst of what they must go through.

Margaret's head is again bent over her work, and he watches her now, for several minutes as intent on the movement of her hands as she is. Finally, leaning forward, he says: "I wish somebody would come out and tell us something."

"I'm sure they will, if there's a reason to."

He looks at his watch. It is only two o'clock. He gets up again and stands at one of the windows.

Years ago Anvil Brant's old father, having come in his last years to the troublesome habit of waking up hours before daylight, sat in Burgess's store listening to a conversation about spring weather and the lengthening of the days. "Days and nights *both* getting longer," he said. "*I* can tell it." Mat remembers that now and laughs and tells it to Margaret. "I know what he meant," he says.

"Morning will come," Margaret says, "It always does. And the baby will be born."

"It won't be as long as it has been, anyhow," he says, but that doesn't comfort him. "Well," he says, "I believe I'll go see if I can find some coffee somewhere."

"Do you think you'll find a place open?"

"Oh, I expect so," he says, doubting it, but determined to go. "Do you want some coffee?"

"I suppose not. Maybe I'll go to sleep."

What he is hoping is that while he is gone the baby will be born, and that he will come back to find all well and the waiting finished. Once down the stairs and out the door, he walks rapidly through the sleeping streets of the town, the silence broken only by the cries of the invisible nighthawks still circling in the air over the trees and the roofs and by the echoing beat of his own footsteps.

He comes to the main street and turns along it. The lights are brighter here and more frequent. From time to time, a car or a truck passes. Mat walks nearly the whole length of the street, finding no place open. He is nearly ready to turn around and start back when, just before the approach to the bridge, he sees a lighted sign: MORT'S DINER.

Going in, he sees at the end of the counter a waitress in a soiled white dress, sitting on a high stool, head propped on her right hand, sound asleep. He is still standing in the door, holding the screen open. So as not to embarrass her he lets it slam behind him. Looking at the signs on the walls, pretending not to have seen her, he notices that she wakes and, hurriedly picking up a wet rag, begins mopping the top of the counter. He goes over and sits on one of the stools opposite her.

"Good evening," she says. "What for you?" She looks and sounds like she must have been asleep a long time.

"Hello." He smiles. "Long nights, aren't they, to have to work by yourself?"

She studies him a moment, and then says: "Well, he ought to be here before long. He usually comes right about this time."

Irritated at first to have been cast so automatically in *that* role, Mat sees that the girl's assumption implies a compliment to herself that she must need—she is remarkably homely, and sleepiness does not improve her. Careful this time not to smile at her, he says: "I'll have a cup of coffee."

She fills a cup for him, slides it across the counter, and pushes sugar and cream toward him. She sits down again, propping her head up as before with her hand, though now her eyes stay open. On a shelf behind her a small radio is playing dance music, turned low.

The coffee is both stale and strong, the taste of it a shock.

"Pew!" Mat says to himself, setting the cup down. But to the girl he says: "Now there's something to wake a man up. You'd have trouble sleeping through a drink of that."

She merely looks at him, her face long, bony, blank. Whether the look is meant to express indifference or suspicion, or is just empty, he cannot tell.

The music fades off the radio. The clipped neutral voice of an announcer comes on with a news report. Though Mat listens, especially to the war news, when it is over he cannot remember anything that was said.

He realizes how tired he must be. His mind, though almost unbearably wakeful and restless, is failing to connect one time to another. That he is there in the diner, staring down into his half-emptied cup, seems strange to him, hardly believable. His own two hands seem to have reached into the circle of his vision out of a dream.

Deliberately, he forces his mind back to Hannah and the baby about to be born, maybe already born. And he goes back to the hospital, hastened by imaginings of what may have happened during his absence.

When he steps into the waiting room, Margaret is sitting with her eyes shut, her head leaned against the chairback. At first he supposes that she is asleep, and he walks quietly. But she sits up and opens her eyes.

"Were you asleep?"

"No. Resting."

"Has anything happened?"

"No."

"Have you heard anything?"

"Not yet."

He looks at his watch. It is a quarter after three.

He sits down, the quiet of the room grows round him again, and it is as though he never left. He only feels tireder, more exposed to what is happening and will happen. For the first time all night he admits into his mind the awareness of the pain surrounding him in the rooms of the hospital. He submits to the fact of it, nerves bared to it, knowing that it surrounds him in ever-widening circles that finally take in the world. Over the roof the nighthawks circle and cry, their voices like small stones striking together under water.

Without expecting to, he falls asleep. The familiar ache sits on his shoulder now like a red bird, not moving.

He dreams he is at work, harrowing a broken field. He can see nothing. He can see a cloud of bright dust rising thickly from the disks of the harrow. He can smell and taste the dust. His eyes are gritty with it. And then the dust seems to draw in and around him until he can no longer see it. He becomes aware of the compactness of his body. He can see his hands holding the reins as he drives the long, slowly shortening rounds of the field. He can see all the surface of the worked earth. He is aware of a point like an eye in the center of the field that his circling will finally bring him to, and where it will end. The dust rises around him again, blotting his sight, to become what next he does not know.

It grows dark. He is aware of water near him, and trees around him, the sound and feel of a cold rain falling steadily, though he can see nothing. For a long time he has been walking in this dark place, stopping to listen, and going on. Unable to see, never knowing exactly where he is in the double strangeness of a familiar place made strange, he must cover all the great dark breadth of the water with his listening, though he expects to hear nothing. He is without hope. He may never have had hope. But he is torn by such grief and love for the child lost or dead that he *does* hope.

Now in the darkness the sound of the laboring of a powerful engine seems to approach him and grow louder. Now he feels beneath his body the lurching and swaying of a heavy machine. For some time he cannot bring himself to realize who he is or what he is doing. And then there comes a little more light and he *does* see. With the blade of a bulldozer he is trying to scrape up enough dirt from a frozen, rocky slope to fill a grave. The grave is as big as a field. Young men, soldiers, lie in rows in it, awaiting the covering earth. They lie on their backs, unspeakably submissive to the approach of the great machine. He has a hurt in his shoulder, but whether it is a wound or the claws of a red bird perched there, he cannot tell. He knows with sorrow who he is. He knows that there is a face among all those of the dead that he cannot bear to see. The engine pulses steadily on.

"Mat."

He knows that the voice calling him is outside the dream.

"Mat."

It is Margaret's voice, near, but outside. Now her hand has taken hold of his arm.

"Mat! Mat, wake up!"

He thrusts himself forward, opening his eyes, breaking through, and out, into the room. Margaret is leaning over him, her hand still on his arm.

"Mat?" she says.

"Hm?"

"Are you awake now?"

"Yes. I believe so."

Elbows on knees, he rubs his hands over his face.

"What in the world were you dreaming?"

"I declare, I can't remember," he says, lying. "I can just remember it was a bad one."

Out on the river, half a mile or more away, he can hear the engine of a towboat laboring up against the current. Though he is awake, he still feels the dream near him, and the sound of the engine still carries its fear.

It slowly fades into the distance, and he sees that the dawn light has begun to grow, drifting through the windows into the heights and corners of the room, dimming the lamp. He grows aware that the birds are singing. The trees, the streets, the air over the town are filled with their voices. They seem to spend themselves recklessly in singing, as though willing to die of it. He gets up, goes to the window, and stands looking out. He can see two rows of houses set back to back, their yards and gardens fenced in neat rectangles, big shade trees growing in them so that not far off he can no longer see the ground but only the billowing green treetops, broken into here and there by the slants and angles of roofs. In the nearest garden there are flowers blooming, irises and peonies, purple and pink and white. The people in the houses seem not to have wakened yet. As far as he can see up and down the street there is no one in sight. Thin shelves and strands of mist stretch over the back lots and among the roofs and the still tops of the trees. As he watches, the mist slowly takes the stain of the rising sunlight.

And then, into the forgotten room behind him, he hears a door swing open.

"Oh!" Margaret says.

He turns, blinking to accustom his eyes to the dimness, and sees, lying half upright in the doctor's gloved hands, naked and red, still wet from the womb, a newborn child.

"Look, Mat," Margaret says. "It's Hannah's baby. A little girl."

Mat is looking, afraid to open his mouth, not knowing whether he would laugh or cry. The baby works legs and arms helplessly in the air, twists its body, manages a weak yell, and keeps yelling. The joy he heard in Margaret's voice swells in Mat now, leaving hardly room for breath.

Dr. Markman, hair in his eyes, a day and night's growth of whiskers on his face, stands there holding the baby, grinning like a fisherman.

Part Four

12

Going Down

"It's Hannah's baby," Margaret said.

Nor did Mat call it or think it Virgil's. Tenderness for Hannah cried out in him too at that moment, and he thought of her.

But from those words, it seems to him, though joy crowded upon him for a while, he began a second descent into sorrow that carried him down more steeply than the first.

Though in his joy he spoke of Virgil to himself, he did not speak of him to Margaret or to Hannah. He does not dare to risk the possibility that Virgil is alive, because he does not dare admit the possibility that he is dead. There is a shame in that, and it has killed his joy.

Going to Hargrave with Margaret to bring Hannah and the baby home, Mat feels a growing premonition of dread. He can foresee the coming days as clearly as if they had already happened. The life of the house will change, accommodate itself to the needs of the new life, and then in a few days the new will be learned, what once was unexpected will become a habit—and they will go on as before. Mat dreads that leveling-off. He has begun to look forward without hope.

On the drive home he keeps mostly silent. Margaret and Hannah are in good spirits, happy in the thoughts and plans that surround the child. Mat is aware that his silence must be noticeable to them, must seem unkind. But fated to go down into the intelligence of death—already going down—he feels himself beyond the reach of all that might lift him back. All the force of his life seems to have withdrawn into his own body, to survive or perish there beyond the help of anyone but himself. Beside him, lying in the crook of Margaret's arm he can see the baby's head, covered with bright down. Aware as he is of the potency of hopelessness and death in himself, the sight of that head is almost more than he can bear.

Once they are home, the women and the baby safely inside, he leaves without a word.

Dangerous Ground

In the guest room the new order is quickly established. Hannah is helped into bed, the baby given to her to nurse and then put down in the cradle to sleep. Tiptoeing and whispering, Margaret and Nettie put things away and straighten the room.

They have hardly finished and slipped out, closing the door quietly behind them, hoping Hannah will sleep too while the baby is asleep, when there comes a knocking on the kitchen door so loud it seems to rattle every loose thing in the house.

"Oh, Lord!" Margaret says to Nettie, "Now who's *that?*" She hurries off in the direction of the racket, hoping whoever it is has not come to visit.

It is Old Jack, making a great show of wiping his feet on the doormat, though they are not muddy.

"Good morning, Uncle Jack," Margaret says. "How are you? Come in."

"I'm all right," Old Jack says. But he stands there, leaning his hand against the wall, slowly scrubbing his left shoe against the mat, as if he has come just to wipe his feet. The trouble is that he is making a formal social call, and he does not know quite how to manage it. But now he hastens to mend his manners.

"How're *you,* honey?"

"Just fine, Uncle Jack."

"Honey," he says, "I come to see the baby. Where's he at?"

"It's not a boy, Uncle Jack, it's a little girl."

"I knew it," he says. "Excuse me, honey."

At the door of the room Margaret tells him, "Be quiet now, Uncle Jack. The baby's asleep." She looks in, whispers to Hannah that company has come, and then goes in, beckoning Old Jack to follow.

He does go in quietly, following Margaret to the cradle, where he stands a long time, leaning over, looking down at the baby. Then, making a vague gesture toward it with his right hand, as if starting to touch it and remembering not to, he goes around the bed to the side where Hannah is lying. Smiling up at him, she gives him her hand, and he takes it, pulling off his cap and bowing as he speaks.

"What do you think of the baby?" she asks him.

"I think he looks mighty nice. Mighty nice."

Hannah makes the sort of bright conversation with him now that she usually does, asking him questions, talking of pleasant, inconsequential things. He stands beside her, nodding, answering, smiling, admiring. Now that he is no longer cramped by any obligation to speak of it, the tenderness he feels toward her and toward the baby becomes plain. This place of mothering and renewal, though he cannot approach it in words, draws him to *be* in it, to lighten and warm himself in the idea of it.

The conversation pauses. Old Jack turns away, and Margaret starts to the door to accompany him out. But then, coming to a chair near the foot of the bed, to the surprise of both women Old Jack sits down, turning the chair sideways to the bed, back to Margaret, facing the front window. He comes to rest, hands folded on the crook of the cane.

"Uncle Jack," Margaret says, allowing the hint to become broad in the tone of her voice, "I expect Hannah may want to rest now. She has just had a long drive, you know."

Ignoring her, Old Jack turns to Hannah.

"Honey, you go right on to sleep if you want to. It won't bother me atall."

"Well," Margaret says, trying again, "I expect she'd like to have it quiet."

Old Jack nods. "I won't make a sound."

Though she would like just now to be left to herself, Hannah smiles and nods to Margaret: Let him stay. And Margaret goes out, shutting the door.

Having understood that Hannah needs to sleep, Old Jack is careful not to look at her or make a sound. It was not, anyhow, to make conversation that he came. He has come in Hannah's honor. But also, since Mat came to tell him that the baby was born, he has thought of the absence of Virgil. And he stays now because of that, sitting in that vacancy, though he knows that he cannot fit or fill it.

He sits still for a long time, gazing out the window. Glancing up finally toward the head of the bed, he sees that Hannah is still awake. She smiles, and so does he, but still without looking directly at her. Digging in the pocket of his coat, he pulls out a sack of candy. It is a variety he particularly favors: coconut inside hard frosting, mixed pastel shades of green and pink and yellow, a penny apiece. When he bought the dime's worth from Milton Burgess this morning, he had a sort of vision of himself giving the sack to Hannah.

"I brought you this little bunch of candy, honey," he would say. "It's mighty good."

And she would say to him: "Why, thank you, Uncle Jack. That's mighty sweet. They *are* mighty good."

Holding the twisted neck of the sack, he sets it flat on the palm of his extended left hand, and then looking at it—the neck of it twisted and crooked over, the brown paper wrinkled and mussed from being carried an hour in his pocket—realizes that it is not right. It is damned exactly wrong. Cursing himself and Milton Burgess for their lack of a pretty box, he fails to be able to offer it to her.

It is a bad moment. He would give a hundred dollars to have that sack back in his pocket, but the expedient of simply putting it there somehow seems the least plausible of all possibilities. She would surely think that was strange—that he would pull a sack of something out of his pocket, and sit there with it stuck out in his hand, and then put it back in his pocket. Though he may have to settle for being thought an old fool, he would rather she would not think he is crazy. Meanwhile the sack sits like some kind of bad-smelling pet on the flat of his hand. Looking out the window, he is pretending for the time being that he does not know it is there. But realizing that she is watching him, he reaches out with his right hand, untwists the neck of the sack, takes out one of the candies, and sticks it into his mouth. Only slightly modifying the cramped posture of offering, his eyes fastened on the window as if there is something of absorbing interest going on out there, he eats all ten pieces one after another.

Hannah watches him helplessly. If she had understood quickly enough, she could have asked to have a piece of the candy, and so made it all right. But as soon as she realized that candy was what it was, he had already begun eating it. Pretending to pay no attention, she watches him.

Now, as from the extremity of his embarrassment, she grows aware of his caring for her. She understands, with shame at her misapprehension, that he is not there because he is flattered by her small attentions; he has come to offer himself. In all her life she has known nothing like it. She sees how free he leaves her. His love for her requires nothing of her, not even that she find it useful. He has simply made himself present, turning away, as he has now, to allow her to sleep if she wants to. She feels enclosed by this generosity as by a room, ample and light. Turning on her side, she does sleep.

When Margaret tiptoes to the door half an hour or so later, opens it softly, and looks in, Hannah is still sleeping, and Old Jack is sitting at the foot of the bed, gazing out the window, his hands folded on the cane as before. In the cradle the baby too lies quiet, still asleep, her breathing slightly moving the blanket, one of her hands opened in the air like a leaf, at rest. Margaret stands for several minutes, looking in, moved by the sight of them, they are so quiet.

By and by, not long after they have begun expecting him, Mat comes in. He goes into the hall, hangs his hat up, and comes on into the kitchen, where he begins running water into the wash pan.

Margaret watches him, aware of the change in him. She knows that since the morning of the baby's birth, when like lovers they seemed to meet and gather in the same joy, something has been breaking between them. This morning she felt it in his silence.

And Mat is aware of it too. He knows that he is in retreat from her. He knows how lonely that must make her, and he pities her—but as if from a great distance, helplessly. It seems to him simply that their lives have gone out of control, and he is grieved and resigned.

Leaving the house in the morning, he plunged into his work, abandoning himself to it and to his expenditure of himself in it. And once it was set forward again he began to sense powerfully the movement of it, its using up of time, and he became grimly exultant in it. Nothing that happens can touch him now. He is out of reach, set apart by the certainty of death. The solitude of his knowledge rings in his mind, hard and insistent as a bell.

Looking at his back bent over the sink, Margaret feels something inside her spring up in pursuit of him. And at the same time she feels herself turning in opposition against him.

"Your Uncle Jack is here for dinner," she says.

He finishes drying his face and turns to her. She meets his eyes, and is defeated by them, her pain revealed to him. He stands there grinning at her, a brittle light in his eyes, daring her to tell him one thing that will be worth telling.

She is angry, and hurt, near to crying. Mat sees it, and is sorry, but still he exults, as if he would ride his loneliness over her very body.

Past bearing it, she turns away. Taking hold of herself, making her voice matter-of-fact and easy, she says, "You can go tell him dinner's ready. Hannah and the baby may still be asleep, so be quiet."

He walks through the house, his body feeling lightened and quickened. He feels charged with his own life, compact and resistant, his hands awake at his sides. The strength of his refusal presses out around him against the walls of the house.

Coming into Hannah's room, he sees that she has waked up. He nods, smiles, asks how she feels, leans over to look at the baby. And Hannah, too, notices the change in him, and it troubles her.

Going up behind Old Jack's chair, Mat touches him on the shoulder and tells him that dinner is ready. When Old Jack looks around, smiling, glad to see him, Mat has already turned his back.

As they eat, Margaret and Old Jack defend themselves with silence against Mat's silence, turned watchful against him, wondering at him.

When the meal is finished, Mat goes out.

"Making tracks, *ain't* he?" Nettie says.

And getting no reply from Margaret, she too understands that they are on dangerous ground. She thought so.

He's Dead

On Sunday afternoon Mat is sitting in the living room, reading the paper. Hannah not long ago finished nursing the baby and carried her in. Now Margaret holds her in the rocking chair, rocking slowly and humming some quiet song almost as tuneless as the back-and-forth creaking of the rockers. Hannah sits on the couch, watching, a faint unconscious smile on her lips. It is restful and peaceful, and it goes on that way a long time, the quiet seemingly deepened by the small sounds that occur in it—the creaking of the rockers, Margaret's breathless humming, the rustling of the paper as Mat turns the pages.

Finally, suspecting that the baby is still awake, Margaret whispers, "Is she asleep, Hannah?"

"No," Hannah says, "her eyes are still wide open."

Margaret shifts the baby down onto her lap. She lies there quietly, wide-eyed.

"Won't Virgil be proud of her when he comes back!" Margaret says, her voice resonant with the thought.

And an anger begins in Mat that he seems to have been waiting for, and that he welcomes. "Don't, Margaret."

He speaks quietly, making an effort to do so, but his voice tightens and hardens with his anger. "Don't talk like that anymore. That's not doing us any good."

The two women look at him.

It is not until then that he fully realizes what it is he has to say. A kind of panic hits him, a kind of sickness. But his words are empowered by anger as they never could have been by grief.

"Virgil is dead. He's not going to come back. He's dead, Margaret. Hannah, he's dead. Say so."

He gets up, and without looking at them again goes out the back door.

"So be it," he tells himself. "It had to be."

He knows that remorse over what he has done is held off only by anger, that he will suffer from it. But he also knows that his anger is clearer than his sympathy. And he is glad it is done, relieved that they have come to the worst at last. It is upon them now. They have begun to bear it at last. So be it.

Feeling his anger begin to leave him, he walks faster, going back through the chicken yard. He feels himself going down into sorrow, his body filling with the pain of it, anger yielding to love—for Margaret, for Hannah, for Virgil dead and lost.

"So be it. It had to be."

He goes into an old wagon shed at the back of the yard, closing the door behind him. In the dimness streaked with dusty slats of sunlight he sits on the ground against the wall and rests his head on his knees.

When he leaves the shed, done with his weeping and quieted, he feels that he reenters his life at a new place, farther on. He will not live again in Virgil's life.

It is getting late, the light weakening and reddening, the shadows beginning to run together. He opens the corncrib and shells corn for the hens, scattering the grains. The hens gather around him, their feathers white in the glow.

13

Hard at It

June 7, 1945

Dear Nathan,

I'm ashamed to hand you the same poor old excuse *every* time, but it's the truth that I haven't had a chance to write. It's raining this morning, and in spite of the rush we're in I have to admit I'm just a little bit grateful for a chance to rest my old bones.

We've been hard at it, trying to get the tobacco set. We've got out only about an acre of our crops here at home. And at Mat's we're not but a little better than half done. So we've got a long pull still ahead of us.

Also, sort of between times and when we can, we work some down at Gideon's and Ida's. Gideon is still unheard from, but we're keeping the place going. And Ida keeps the slack taken up when we're not there. When we are there she works right along with us.

There's a lot of talk in Port William just now about her and Ernest Finley. Ernest has been working down there all spring, carpentering and painting on those old buildings of Roger Merchant's—working there a good deal of the time without another man in a mile of him. So you can see what a fine chance that is for them rattle-mouths there in town. And I don't reckon you need me to make a list of what is being said. It don't cost them anything to see the visions they see.

They don't know Ida, for one thing. And for another, they don't know Ernest. You don't have to be around Ida long to know that she's as mindful of Gideon as she ever was. If I ever seen a woman whose ways gave the signs of belonging to one man, it's her. And I'm just about certain that Ernest don't even know how to make the sort of proposition the talkers are accusing him of.

Which don't mean that everything is right. There's some things I believe I do know that haven't turned up yet in the talk. I do pretty surely know that Ida cooks dinner for Ernest on the days he works down there, just like she cooks for us when we're there. And I know for certain that he never eats there when we do—always fixes it so he won't *be* there at dinnertime on those days. Which means, as near as I can figure, that Ernest has Ida on his mind in a way he don't want us to see. I know Ida's a woman who can take up a lot of space in a man's mind, like a big bed in a little room. And all this worries me. There seems a possibility of pain in it.

I wrote you, I think, that Hannah Feltner's baby was born down in the hospital at Hargrave three weeks ago. I've stopped by to see them three or four times, and Hannah and the baby are doing fine. It's a girl. They've named her Margaret. A couple of times when I've been there Mrs. Feltner and Hannah have started wondering who she looks like. They never decide. You can see they want her to look like Virgil, but are afraid to say either she does or she doesn't. So both times I just out and said, "Well, it looks like to me she favors her daddy a good deal." I figure I wasn't really lying. The baby *is* Virgil's, and looks like she's bound to get so she favors him some sooner or later.

Well, old Nathan, be careful. I'm always thinking about you. And thinking the world of you. Don't forget it, whatever you do.

Your uncle,
Burley

P.S. I meant to tell you—the other day we went out to salt the cattle, and we salted them and stood there watching them. And your daddy turned and stood looking out over our ridges towards the river. And directly he said, "Well, I reckon it must be night now over yonder where Nathan is, and he must be asleep." He don't speak of you often, but I wanted to tell you how plain it was to me, the way he said it, that he keeps you in his mind.

It's night now. I'll have to end sure enough this time.

A Widow Alone

Hannah's pregnancy was like a long lovemaking, a long continuance of Virgil's body in her own. And then, with the birth, they were divided. Now she feels her body going to waste. Her mourning over Virgil is also a mourning over herself—is the same. She feels his absence *within* herself, a vacancy, as though some vital part of her own body was removed in her sleep.

On the Sunday afternoon two weeks after Mat forced on them the fatal words "Virgil is dead," finding herself alone in the house, Hannah puts the baby to sleep, and climbs the stairs and goes into the room that was hers and Virgil's. It is the first time she has been there since the birth of the baby. As she comes into it, the room is familiar, but it is a familiarity from which she is now estranged. She stops just inside the door, the quietness of the house grown big around her.

Like a swimmer, filling herself with breath and determination, she goes into the room and moves in it, resting her hands from time to time on the furnishings, the dresser, the chairs, the table, the bed. She walks with her arms folded tightly across her breasts, reaching down sometimes to touch one or another of the furnishings. She stops before one of the windows, and stands looking out northward over the tops of the ridges, the opening of the river valley, the ridges going on to the horizon on the far side. The country is in the full green of summer. For several minutes she watches it attentively as if listening to it. In the windless clear sunlight of Sunday afternoon it lies before her, shining. But the room is waiting, and finally she withdraws her mind into it, and turns and watches her steps go back across the rug.

She goes to the closet and opens the door. Hanging there are clothes that now belong to the past—her winter dresses from the time before she needed maternity clothes, Virgil's civilian suits and overcoat and, folded on the shelf overhead, several suits of his work clothes. She kept their clothes there together after Virgil's departure, one of the rituals of her hope.

But now she begins slowly to take the suits off their hangers and fold them, making a neat pile of them on the bed, finality in every move she makes. It is not possible to stop or go back. She seems not even to work by her own will. Beyond any power of hers, Virgil's death claims all that is his. Handling his clothes, as though her fingers touch through the fabrics their own palpable remembrance of his body, her body becomes vibrant with loss as a struck bell.

She goes and finds two empty boxes and some string, packs in the suits and the work clothes and all the clothes of his left in the dresser drawers, closes the boxes and knots the string around them, carries them one at a time up into the attic, and sets them down in the musty darkness under the slope of the roof.

She comes back down, turning off the light at the foot of the attic stairs, and returns to the room. It is only then that it occurs to her that she has nothing more to do. The room is filled with brightness, dazzling after the darkness of the attic. She stands, looking around. And then her widowed dresses hanging alone in the closet declare her misery to her, and she sits down on the bed and cries. After some time, hearing the baby wake, she gets up and wipes her eyes and shuts the closet door and goes down.

She takes the baby up, changes her diaper, and then wraps a blanket around her and goes out by the back door. Once outside, she feels better. Lately the house has seemed to her the very embodiment of her plight and her grief, filled with innumerable marks and signs declaring Virgil's absence, her loss, the life she will never have. But now, lying around her in the sunlight, the country seems purified of all deaths, past and to come. No griefs cling to it.

She goes through the yard and the chicken yard and starts up the rise of the ground behind the barn. She goes at a slow wandering pace that does not take her directly up the slope, but here and there over the face of it, looking around her as she goes, feeling sudden pleasurable intimacies with the sunlight, the curving hill, the clover and grass at her feet.

She does not free herself of the thought of Virgil. Intimations of him are still all around her. But out here the remindings of his life remain peculiarly intact, as though only stopped, not changed, by the thought of his death. Something of him seems still to be present in the life of the place. She senses him almost palpably, just outside her reach.

She remembers walking up this way, carrying a water jug, one hot July afternoon in the summer before the war. They were shocking hay on top of the ridge, Virgil and the others. After helping wash and dry the dinner dishes, she picked up the jug and went out. Stopping by the cistern at the barn to pump the jug full, she carried it to the field to them, climbing slowly, oppressed by the heavy brilliance of the heat. She came to Virgil first, and handed the jug to him, and he tilted it and drank. She stood watching him—his shirt and the waistband of his pants dark with sweat, his face and throat and bare arms glistening with it, the green haychaff sticking to his skin and his clothes. He finished and handed the jug to the next man. Smiling at her, he made some casual remark to her that she cannot remember, and went back to work. What came to her then—and comes to her now—was the sense of the abundance of strength in him that accepted the heat and the tiredness of that day with a kind of joy.

Like an answer or echo to the life that so filled and moved him then, she feels grow and quiver in herself the pain of the subsiding of his body, of stillness coming over him. But also, as she climbs steadily upward, bringing more and more into sight that country so charged with her memory of him, there is a strengthening in her of the sense that what he was still is. And with a kind of yielding, she receives him into herself, not to be lost again.

She walks along the ends of the tobacco rows, in which the young white-stemmed plants have begun to grow again after the transplanting. The field has just been plowed, and the earth between the rows is dark and fresh. The small plants are erect and green. Looking at them, she feels the world going on, her life continuing with all that is alive.

The baby becomes restless, and she walks more swiftly now, climbing straight on to the top of the ridge. At the highest point she sits on a pile of posts in the shade of a walnut tree. She lays the baby on her lap, and leans over and smiles down at her. The baby lies still, appearing to look up through the airy mass of the leaves.

"Look up at the sky," she says. "See the sky?" But the baby's face crumples and she begins to fret and then to wail. "I'm sorry. Don't cry. Don't cry. Hush now." She opens her blouse and lifts the small reddened face to her breast. Once the milk begins to come, the baby relaxes against her, beginning a tiny breathless singsong.

Settling herself, Hannah lets her head rest against the tree, looking up through the yellow-green of the leaves at the sky. She becomes conscious now of the stirring and murmuring of the life of the place—the voices and comings and goings in the town below her, the humming of insects among the blooms of the fields, now and again the far-off bleating of Mat's sheep somewhere back of the hill. The light has begun to cool. On the slope below her the swallows are curving over the still face of the pond.

The baby finishes nursing and sleeps. Having buttoned her blouse and made the baby comfortable on her shoulder, she resumes her stillness.

A small yellow-striped fly, known around Port William as a steady-bee, comes and stands still in the air in front of her. It moves several times back and forth sideways, from one standing-still place to another, remaining at each one several seconds before moving abruptly and exactly to the other. And then it comes down and lights on the back of her hand, its clear wings outspread. Its pointed curved abdomen pulses up and down, tapping at her skin. She waves it off, and it goes two or three feet away and stops in the air again as though watching her.

Again she leans her head back and looks up into the tree. The black branches fork, taper, diminish, supporting the luminous, airy globe of leaves. The sky shows raggedly through, and now and then the winged black speck of a bird appears in one of the openings, wavering and turning in the high blue an instant. For a long time Hannah sits there, not thinking of herself, or of the child slackened against her in sleep, but filled with awareness of the tree, its green and gold hung in the light above her.

Finally, as though waking, she lifts her head and looks around. The steady-bee is not there anymore, and the air is cooler. Before her the town is a silhouette against the low sun. The half-dark of the evening has begun. The weedy dampness of nightfall is beginning to rise out of the hollows. The silence has altered, deepened, but the sounds that take place in it now are more distinct and clear: a voice calling cattle, a dog barking, a voice shouting "Hush!"—and the silence returning deeper than before.

The melancholy of it comes over her, and she shudders. The place, in its submission to the night, now seems to withdraw from her and to leave her alone.

She hears Mat's old truck come into the lot, and she gets up. Gathering the baby firmly against her, she hurries down the long slope to the barn.

Haunted

In the depth of Mat's grief there are stretches of days in which he loses track of time. He seems to work through these days almost without consciousness, coming aware of himself at odd moments with a kind of shock, a fearful sense of the strangeness of everything—held to the place and his work only by old habit. These are times of heavy dreamless sleep, from which he can hardly force himself awake.

There are other times of almost unbearable clarity and activity of mind, when he can hardly sleep for thinking, when he wakes knowing he has been thinking in his sleep.

At these times his thoughts more and more take the form of talk between himself and Virgil—Virgil having become obsessively the other person of his thoughts. He is haunted by Virgil as though he summons him from the dead in order to explain himself. Becoming aware of his thoughts in the midst of his work, or lying awake at night, he will find himself already explaining—telling how he felt when Virgil did this or did that, telling what his plans were, telling some clarifying fragment of their history. And Virgil listens, smiling in sympathy and understanding. "That's all right," he says. "Yes. I know." Mat can rarely visualize more than his face. Now and then a hand appears—a muscular hand, strongly veined—and touches his cheek or temple, or scratches thoughtfully in his hair.

14

A Famous Escapade

On the Thursday of the second week of July, Andy and Henry Catlett come to the Feltner house for a visit. Their usual early arrival having been delayed this summer by first one adult circumstance and then another, they carry their bundled clothes into the house with an impatience born of the certainty of missed excitements.

"Well," Henry says, dropping his bundle at the foot of the stairs, "where's Uncle Ernest?"

"At work," Margaret tells him. "Way down there on the creek."

"Where's Grandad?"

"At work too. I don't even know where."

"Take those clothes upstairs and put them away," Bess says.

They do as she says, and then come back down and kill time listening to the women's conversation in the living room. But that is tame and disappointing compared to what they *hoped* to be doing by now. They sit there, settling deeper and deeper into the bitter sense of having come too late.

Finally, as their mother is getting ready to leave, they hear the rumbling of a wagon out toward the barn. Margaret glances at them and smiles, giving permission, and they head for the back door.

When they come to the barn, Joe Banion has just driven his team and wagon into the lot, and stopped to go back and shut the gate. The boys call to him, and he grins and raises his hand.

"Hello, buddies."

He shuts the gate. They run up to him.

"Let us go with you. Where you going?"

"Just over yonder to the wagon shed to put away the wagon." He laughs at the disappointment in their faces, and says, "But I reckon you can ride with me that far."

"What you going to do after that?" Henry asks.

"Going to unhitch the mules."

He climbs slowly up onto the wagon and helps them up after him.

"Let me drive," Henry says.

"Ain't going far. Just over to the shed."

"Well, let me drive just that far."

Joe hands him the lines. "Now you let them go slow and do what I tell you."

Henry clucks to the team. "Come up."

They don't move.

"Come *up!* What's the matter with them, Joe?"

"They ain't used to you, buddy. I expect they don't believe what you say."

Henry shakes out one of the lines and swats the off mule hard across the rump.

"COME UP, you son of a bitches!"

In a second or two a good many things happen. The mules throw their heads up and plunge forward. Andy falls backwards, rolling, onto the bed of the wagon. Joe lurches back two or three steps, and then stumbles forward, grabbing the lines with one hand and Henry's arm with the other.

"Whoa, Jack! Whoa now! Sit down, Henry!"

The mules run the length of the lot, the wagon bouncing and pounding and rattling behind them. Joe manages to get control of them as they come near the fence, and he brings them around, making a long turn, settling them down to a trot, and then to a walk, and finally bringing them to a stop about where they started.

"Whoa now."

He turns and looks down at Henry, who is sitting pop-eyed on the boards behind him.

"Now, buddy, that don't do. And you know better. We all like to got killed. The mule ain't going to stand to be insulted that way—specially not by a stranger."

"I ain't any stranger," Henry says. "He's my grandaddy's mule."

"That Jack mule don't care who your ancestors is, boy. He ain't no respecter of persons. President of the United States whap him for no reason, he'd better have his ass close to the wagon, 'cause he's going to travel."

"You said ass," Henry says.

"Well, what was that you called them mules?"

Joe drives across the lot and backs the wagon into the shed and gets down to unhitch, the boys crowding up beside him.

"Ge' back! Ge' back!" Joe says, cross sure enough now.

"We ain't doing anything but watching."

"And you liable to see something, too. She show you the bottom of her foot. Now you all behave or I'll have to tell Mr. Mat."

He knows that Mat's displeasure is more fearful to them than the possibility of being kicked, and so he knows he will not have to tell on them.

They get back, and stay out of the way while Joe does up the lines and leads the mules to the barn and waters them and takes their harness off and puts them in their stalls.

At quitting time Burley Coulter comes down from the tobacco patch, bringing his team to the barn, riding one mule and leading the other. He comes through the gate and around the barn to the cistern. The mules walk up to the water trough and lower their heads, and Burley drops to the ground. He looks at Andy and Henry, and grins.

"Hello, boys."

They tell him hello, grinning back, expecting him to say something funny. There is something fine, Andy thinks, in the way he stands there, one hand still holding the mule's hame, and takes off his old felt hat and scratches his head with the same hand and puts the hat back on—good-humored and at ease, done for the day.

The mule standing next to Burley has raised his head, and stands gazing out across the lot, his muzzle dripping. Burley gives him a little nudge with his elbow. "Drink!" The mule wearily lowers his head again and drinks. "He knows when his daddy's talking to him."

The boys giggle. "You ain't his daddy," Henry says.

"Well, I am. But he got most of his looks from his mother." He looks at Joe. "I seen you all was having a race down here," he says. "Who won?"

Joe shrugs and shakes his head. "That Henry there can tell you. Don't ask me."

"That Henry," Burley says, "he's a driver."

"I'd really have got them going," Henry says, "if Joe hadn't took away the lines."

"You'd have got them going, all right," Joe says crossly. "You'd have got us killed, and hard telling what else."

Duty-bound to keep Henry reminded of the seriousness of his offense, Joe makes a final attempt to frown. But watching the face of the little boy, which since the mules ran off has been big-eyed with startlement and impudence, he begins to struggle to keep his mouth straight. His eyes begin to fill at the corners with a little glistening. And suddenly he seems to wilt, bending over and slapping his knee, and then rearing back. They watch him, Burley with amusement and the boys with relief, knowing that his laughter implicates him and he won't be likely to tell on them now—if he ever meant to, which they doubt.

And now they all laugh, allowing it to be as funny as it was. Joe tells what Henry said, and how he swatted the mule, and how the team started, and how scared he was, and how he got them turned and then stopped, and how Henry looked. And Burley tells how it looked to him from up on the hill, and describes the motions each one made. The boys stand there, laughing, looking from one of the men to the other, proud to have been in such a famous escapade, and knowing better than to show it. If they were to seem too cocky about it, they know, the laughter would stop, and Burley or Joe would have to say in a dutifully sober tone: "Well, it's damn lucky nobody got killed. You boys ought to be careful."

In the midst of the laughter, Joe throws up his hand and says: "Shhh! Mercy sakes alive, here comes the boss!"

Not wanting Mat to learn what has been going on, though not wanting either to admit that to the boys, Joe and Burley get busy in a hurry—

with a burlesque of caution that makes Andy and Henry laugh again. Joe starts out to the gate to call the milk cows. Burley leads his team back into the driveway and begins taking their harness off. The boys go down across the lot and open the gate for Mat, who looks up the hill and sees them and waves.

He has unhitched the mules and is walking behind them, the slack of the lines looped in his hands. Shifting both lines into one hand and stopping the mules as the boys run to him, he hugs first Andy and then Henry.

"Hello, Andy! How're you, hon? Hello, Henry boy!"

"We've come to stay, Grandad," Henry says.

"Well, good! I'm glad you have."

Burley is putting his mules into their stalls. Mat does up the lines and waters his team, and for a few minutes there is a steady hustle of activity as Burley helps to unharness Mat's mules and put them away. Joe drives the cows in and Burley and Mat put in hay and corn for the teams.

And then they are finished. In the silence they can hear the mules eating their corn, the ears rattling in the troughs.

"Well, Mat," Burley says, "looks like you got about all the help you need now."

And Mat smiles and says, in what seems to the boys a very loving and proud way: "Yessir. It looks like I have."

The four of them stand in the driveway, looking out at the red sunset, Mat holding the boys' hands. And then Burley slips his hat off and scratches his head in that way Andy admires, and settles his hat back on, and lights a smoke. "Well, Mat, I'll see you tomorrow. Take it easy, boys."

The Presence of Grief

After Virgil went to the war, Andy, as soon as he learned to write, wrote him letters, and Virgil replied—letters full of the familiar old foolishness, and promises of fine things they would do when the world got straightened out. And he sent him a soldier's hat, a knife, and other odds and ends picked up with a fine sense of what would be of interest.

Andy got into the habit of thinking, whenever he was displeased or lonely, and whenever he wanted to do something he was not big enough to do by himself, that if Virgil were there it would be different. Virgil, in his absence, became the hero of the boy's daydreams—the embodiment, in perfection, of whatever power he lacked at the moment. In all the conflicts Andy got into with his teachers and playmates and parents—and there were quite a few, for he has always been a moody, headstrong sort of boy—he imagined Virgil as his defender, the dealer of whatever justices and vengeances his injuries required.

But the letters stopped, and he was told that his uncle was missing in action—which meant, his mother said, that they were all worried about him, but maybe everything would turn out all right. Andy took that to mean that there was not much to worry about. It had been his experience that most grownups' worries were without consequence. He adopted a certain caution in speaking of his uncle to his playmates, and he developed a new curiosity in observing the grownups of his family—which revealed nothing to him except that they were all filled with an anxiety that they tried to keep hidden from each other and from him.

And then, not long ago, after he had made some idle remark about his uncle, Bess took him aside and told him that they believed now that Virgil was dead. They had no reason to hope that he might be alive. She ended by saying that he should not tell Henry. He was old enough, and should know, but Henry might not understand.

But Andy does not understand either. He is in the bewilderment, the bad luck special to children, of experiencing the effect without any of the clarification or relief that might come with some understanding of the cause. For weeks he has felt himself surrounded by the grief of the family, but he has not yet felt any grief of his own. He has continued, in a sort of guilty secrecy, to believe that Virgil is somewhere and somehow still alive. And he has kept on praying for his safe return.

Lying in bed in the dark, he is aware of the presence of the grief of the household, and aware of the difference between that and the pleasantness of it, so familiar and comforting to him, and kept there, he knows, partly for his own sake. His consciousness widens slowly out of the bounds of the room and the house into the night overlying the world. And he feels himself to be present, placelessly, in all the far and wide of that darkness, filled with a vague troubling over all he feels but does not know.

At last tiredness seems to place and shape him there in the bed in the room. The sweet familiarity of the house presses around him again, and he falls asleep.

A Ramble

"Come in," Aunt Fanny says. She is sitting in a rocking chair behind the cold drum stove, rubbing an ointment of some kind on her fingers. She looks up inquiringly at them, squinting hard through her round brass-rimmed glasses, blinded by the brightness of the doorway until they shut the door, and then she raises her hands and opens her mouth in a broad show of pleasure and surprise.

"Awww, well I declare *to* goodness, if it ain't Miss Bess's little boys! How's your mother, honeys?"

"Fine," Andy says.

"And your daddy's fine, I reckon, too? Well, ain't that nice. Sit down, children, and talk to me. Let me look at you. My, ain't you growed! I'm so glad to see you. Yes indeed! Just a while back I say to Joe, 'Well, now it's summer and I expect little Andy and Henry'll be to see me, if I live and nothing happen and all go well with the world!' She gives a long cackle of laughter and says, "Yes indeedy."

The boys sit down together on a wicker settee placed between the door facing and the side of an iron bed, both of them a little abashed and awed having come into a different kind of life, though it is familiar to them from many other visits.

Aunt Fanny is Joe Banion's mother, older than anybody knows. She sits a little wearily in her chair as old women often sit, her short, squat, ample body bunched into the angle of seat and back like a heap of cushions, her bowed knees set wide apart. Her hair has been gathered and braided into perhaps a dozen short erect grey pigtails. Her mouth contains only a few widely spaced amber-stained teeth. Her lower lip bulges slightly with the snuff packed inside it. A coffee can, her "spit-can," is set at the end of one of the chair rockers at her feet. Her shoes—work shoes, probably a cast-off pair of Joe's—have been so ventilated for the easing of corns and bunions as to have the look of sandals. Her long dress reaches to the tops of her shoes, and over it she wears a starched white apron.

She is a woman of much pride. Her manners, though peculiarly her own, are impeccable. She is an accomplished seamstress, and the room is filled with her work: quilts, crocheted doilies, a linen wall-hanging with the Lord's Prayer embroidered on it in threads of many colors. In the house she is nearly always occupied with her needle, always complaining of her dim eyesight and arthritic hands. Her dark hands, though painfully crooked and drawn by the disease, are still somehow dexterous and capable. She is always anointing them with salves and ointments of her own making. The fingers wear rings made of copper wire, which she believes to have the power of prevention and healing. She is an excellent gardener. The garden beside the house is her work. She makes of its small space an amplitude unlike anything else in the town: rows of vegetables and flowers—and herbs, for which she knows the recipes and the uses.

That is the daylight aspect of Aunt Fanny. But there is a night aspect too. And to Andy the garden, the quilts on the bed, or the quilting frame always seem threatened, like earthquake country, by an ominous nearness of darkness in the character of their maker. Aunt Fanny has seen the Devil, not once but often, especially in her youth, and she calls him familiarly by his name: Red Sam. Her obsessions are Hell and Africa, and she has the darkest, most fire-lit notions of both. Her idea of Africa is a hair-raising blend of lore and hearsay and imagination. She thinks of it with nostalgia and longing—a kind of earthly Other Shore, Eden, or Heaven—and yet she fears it because of its presumed darkness, its endless jungles, its stock of malevolent serpents and man-eating beasts. And by the thought of Hell she is held as endlessly fascinated as if her dearest ambition is to go there. She can talk at any length about it, cataloguing its tortures and labyrinths in almost loving detail. Her belief in Heaven is just as firm, but she simply depends on that and lets it go. It is Hell that draws her mind to its tightest focus, and entices her into the depths and rhapsodies of prophetic vision. Next to Hell, she is drawn by visions of the End of the World and the Judgment Day. And what most frightens the two boys in her talk of these things is not so much the horrors themselves as the old woman's delight in them, as though in telling of them she affirms, beyond any power of small boys to doubt, that these truly are the foundation of the world. She seems to give a respectful credence to the statement that God is love, only to hurry on to explore with *real* interest the possibility that God is wrath. She can read from the Book of Revelation with a ringing of conviction in her voice that can make the Creation seem only a stage-setting for the triumphant thunderation of the End. Stooped in the light of a coal-oil lamp at night, following her finger down some threatening page of the Bible, her glasses opaquely reflecting the yellow of the lamp, her pigtails sticking out like compass points around her head, she looks like a black Witch of Endor.

She possesses a nearly inexhaustible lore of snakes and deaths, bottomless caves and pools, mysteries and ghosts and wonders. One of her stories can populate a month of nightmares. There have been nights when, after listening to her, Andy and Henry have been unable to go the dark way home by themselves, and Joe has had to hold their hands and lead them up the hill toward the happy lights of their grandad's house. But though they are frightened by her ominous knowledge, they are as fascinated as she is by the dark spaces between days and stars that she opens toward them and fills with the designs and impendings of dire purpose.

But her daylight aspect is as bright as the other is dark. Now, as she sits there in the chair among the substances of her life, anointing her hands, the world seems firm enough around her. Her dark company of visions and devils and spirits seems to have withdrawn from her and from the daylight like so many bats and owls.

"How's your rheumatism, Aunt Fanny?" Andy asks.

"Aw, honey, it's bad." She laughs, as though to affirm that hers is a faithful pain and can be depended on. "Oh yes, it don't get no better. This ointment just keep it from getting worse."

"Well, I'm glad it's not worse."

"Oh yes, just bad, not worse. I rub my hands and put heat on them, set with them in the sun, and they stay so I can use them. I say to Joe a while back, 'Well, if I live and nothing happen and all go well, I believe they'll last me.' That's what I say, and I believe they will. Eyes too. Old eyes and old hands. Old feet too, and old knees. Old everything. But I believe they'll all last me, long as I'll need them. I pray so, and trust the Lord. All you can do, honeys."

She laughs again, and screws the top back on the jar of ointment, and gets heavily up.

"What're you going to do this morning?" Andy asks. He is suddenly anxious. Sometimes she is too crippled to do anything, and it is always disappointing to have the good possibilities held back by old hands or old feet or old knees. But this morning the prospects are better than he hoped.

"I been thinking I'd go on a ramble."

"Can we come?" Henry asks.

"You mind and *be*have, you can come."

"We will."

"No squibbling and squabbling, I mean. And you walk behind me so you won't be trampling up everything before I can get to it."

"All right."

They follow her into the kitchen, where she ties on a faded blue sunbonnet and hunts up a basket and a sharp paring knife.

"I'll carry those for you," Henry says.

"Or I will," Andy says.

"*I'll* carry it, I expect," Aunt Fanny says. "You all just keep busy watching yourself."

She loops the handle of the basket over her arm, and they set out, pulling the back door shut behind them and going through the still long shadow of the house into the open daylight.

Aunt Fanny moves at a slow, hobbling, off-balance gait which seems unlikely to carry her as far as the yard fence. But it does, and is, if not fast, indomitably steady.

She goes along a cow path down the steep side of the hollow behind the house, and across the rocks of the streambed, and up the other side, giving a great shaking to the saplings she catches hold of to help herself along. The boys follow her uneasily, expecting her to give up what seems the enormous effort of the going and turn back.

But she advances steadily, leaving one yard and then another of the steep path behind her. And by the time they have come out of the trees into the sun again on the far side, and turned and followed the edge of the woods some distance around the point of the next ridge, the boys have begun as usual to accept, as she does, that her old feet and old knees will last. By now their shoes and the hem of the old woman's dress are wet with dew.

They walk a little behind her, respectfully staying out of her way. She leads them in long slow zigzags between the fringe of the woods and the open pasture on the ridge, now and then stooping and cutting and dropping into the basket some herb or mushroom or flower. She makes no attempt to cover the ground thoroughly: when she zigs she apparently gives no thought to the possibility that it might be better to zag.

"Why do you want to skip so much?" Andy asks her. "Why don't we go down there?"

"That ain't how you ramble," she says. "You got to be getting and going both at once. You ain't supposed to get everything, but just only enough. Take some and leave some."

"Aunt Fanny," Henry says, "I thought those old toadstools were poison."

"Some is, some ain't. Them bad ones you want to stay away from. I heard about a man ate one of them once. They say he just died *pain*ful. Whooee! Say he died screaming the Devil was coming after him. *Seen* him!"

For a moment the story seems to cast a shadow over them, as though a dark tree has suddenly grown up beside them. But she hushes and moves on. They leave the shadow then, and when Andy looks back he sees only the sunlight shining there. Ahead of him, the sun bright on her bonnet, Aunt Fanny walks, studying the ground.

She seems to see everything. Invariably she sees what she is looking for before the boys can see it, in spite of their efforts to be of use. It is as though over a spot of the ground where nothing is she bends, and miraculously there *is* something—a white round mushroom, and she cuts it off and drops it into the basket, cackling gaily at the boys' amazement.

Watching her, Andy is again aware that hers is a kind of life different from any other that he knows. He is made happy by her pleased easy taking of the good things that the world provides without effort, that nobody else wants, that most do not even see. Aunt Fanny's basket, as it slowly fills with the clutter of her discoveries, comes to have for him the excitement of a chest of treasure found in a cave. That these things have grown out of the ground into their secret places apart from anybody's intention, and that she takes them familiarly and freely without attempting to take them all, that they are the harvest of a ramble and not a search or a labor, all this bespeaks a peaceableness between her and the world.

In their zigzagging between pasture and woods they gradually turn the curves of the long S of their ramble, going around the point of the first ridge and up along the wooded hollow on the far side, and then crossing the hollow and going down around the point of the next ridge. They scare up two or three rabbits. Once, ahead of them, they hear a squirrel barking, and hear the rushing in the treetops as it retreats deeper into the woods. In the open pasture on one side of them the meadowlarks are singing, and on the other the patches of underbrush along the edge of the woods are stirring and rustling with the movements of redbirds and towhees and sparrows. Aunt Fanny walks steadily on, here and there stooping and cutting and naming and dropping into the basket a sprig of this, a few leaves or a bloom of that.

At last they turn straight up the side of a ridge and go through a gate and past the cattle barn on the far place and through another gate, and down the next slope. They can see the river valley below them now.

Above the woods on the bluff there are two tall stone chimneys and the heaped foundation stones of a house. This was the first house that Mat's people built and lived in after they came to Kentucky. The last member of the family to live there was Mat's Great-Aunt Milly, who, crippled by some childhood disease, died there, an old maid, when Mat was about fifteen. After that, until it was torn down a generation later, it was lived in by one or another of the Negro families who worked on the place. Aunt Fanny was born and raised in a cabin that used to stand behind the house, and later lived for a while in the house itself.

"Here we are where you used to live," Andy says to her, hoping for a story.

But she only says, "That was long gone years ago," and laughs as if to convey her familiarity with the darkness that has swallowed all that time.

They continue their rambling down through the ragged, half-dead locusts of what used to be the yard, and make a sort of loop on the hillside below the house site, skirting the upper edge of the woods. The basket filled at last, they sit down to rest on the hearthstones of the eastward chimney, leaning back into the cool, stony-smelling shadow.

"A mighty fine place to rest yourself," Aunt Fanny says. "So pretty and nice."

"Tell about you all sitting on the porch," Andy says.

"Old porch," she says, gesturing with the paring knife, "used to go all the way across the back of the house. And a mighty fine setting place too. After the hot days we'd go out there and set till bedtime. Be a breeze. And we'd talk, and now and then see the lights of a steamboat on the river and hear it whistle. Mighty fine to do. Oh yes, I remember them old gone times. I can see them clear."

She subsides, and pokes with satisfaction into the contents of the basket.

"Tell about Aunt Milly's ghost."

She glances up and is silent for a moment, as if examining her memory for a good starting place.

"Well, not long after Miss Milly died, the house we was living in begun to leak and get in bad shape. And Mr. Mat's daddy Mr. Ben says, 'Ain't got money to fix it now. Move in the big house.' So we moved in. And wasn't long after that till we begun to hear things at night. Hear them crutches walk. Be laying in the bed at night, and all quiet, and here they'd come, down out the old attic, step at a time down the stairs, and on down the next stairs, just like they used to sound when she was alive and walking on them. And then they'd just wander, in and out the rooms, out on the porch, and up and down. We nailed the attic door shut, and here they come again same as ever: *thunk*-a-tunk. And sometimes it'd sing:

> Whooooo is that all dressed in red?
> Must be the children that Fee Fo fed.
>
> Whooooo is that all dressed in green?
> Must be the children that Fee Fo seen.

"And it'd go on that-a-way, singing in all the colors there was, whooing like a hoot owl:

> Whooooo is that all dressed in blue?
> Must be the children that Fee Fo slew.
>
> Whooooo is that all dressed in black?
> Must be the children in Fee Fo's sack."

To Andy, again, there seems to have grown up beside them a dark tree, veiling the sun. And within that darkness he seems to see as with an owl's vision the hobbling wraith of his great-great-great-aunt in its mournful wandering in the old house—and to sense beyond the house, in a windy, ever-deepening darkness, the tireless walking of Fee Fo.

When Aunt Fanny intones the mournful drawn-out singing of the ghost, Henry shudders.

"Didn't that scare you?" he asks.

"Didn't that scare me! Lord, honey, you wake up in the middle of the night, and you hear that thunk-a-tunk and that singing, it'll make the hair stand up offen your head! It sho will!" She laughs, and the little boy shudders again. "When you shiver like that," she says, "somebody's walking on your grave."

"I haven't even *got* any grave." Henry says. "*I* ain't dead."

"Well, maybe you ain't got one yet that you *in*, honey, but you got one that you going to *be* in."

The darkness of the old woman's knowing hangs over them, and they fall silent, the boys wanting to know more, yet dreading the answers too much to ask the questions. Andy wants to ask her about his Uncle Virgil—is he dead? Was whatever grave he may have come to appointed to him in his childhood, or when he was born, or at the beginning of the world? But he knows that her answer will be one he will have to struggle with. And he does not ask.

Aunt Fanny gets up presently, and they start home. Again they seem to Andy to move out of a dark place back into the sunlight.

The ramble over now, they go by the straightest way. Aunt Fanny puts the paring knife in the basket, and sets the basket on her head. The dew has dried long ago. The waverings of heat have begun to stand over the fields.

When they come back into the dimness and wood-smoke smell of the kitchen, Aunt Fanny hangs up her bonnet, and they sit down at the table. The boys watch as the old woman brings the cluttered gatherings of their ramble finally to an orderly harvest. Piece by piece she sorts out the contents of the basket. When she gets done she has lying on the newspapers spread out before her a bouquet of flowers, two or three small piles of herbs, a small clutch of mushrooms like a nest of eggs. She sits there looking a moment, and then gets up and puts the flowers into water, and goes into the next room and sits down with snuff and spit-can to rest.

The boys remain with her, sitting again on the wicker settee, hoping to prolong the pleasure of the morning. But she seems to them to accept the end of the ramble too complacently, talking now of sleeping a few winks after dinner, and of the cool of the afternoon when she will go out to work in her garden. And gradually the excitement leaves them, and they begin to wish to go, only kept there by politeness. They stay until the ringing of the dinner bell calls them up the hill to eat.

As they walk up through the blossoming pasture toward the barn, the look of things seems changed. As always, the old woman's talk has alerted them to the presence somewhere of their graves, to the welling up of death and night into the world. The coloring of the day seems to stand tremulously on the surface of a darkness from which neither it nor they will ever go free.

A Result

Late Monday morning, August sixth, the president announces that on the day, before an atomic bomb was dropped on Hiroshima. Mat, who was at work in the garden, happened to come to the house with a bucket of tomatoes just as the news came on the radio. And so with Margaret and Hannah and Nettie he hears most of the story, the correct voice of the newsman reciting what there is to tell, standing the event nakedly among them in the room, leaving it there without explanation or comment. Or at least, in the silence after the radio is snapped off, such explanation as was given seems overwhelmed by the event itself.

After he finishes his work in the garden, he hitches his team to the mowing machine and goes until sundown in the unending rounds, cutting the weeds and tree-sprouts that rise against him year after year in the opened fields.

Better than any other work he loves the mowing. He goes through the long afternoon, watching with a kind of ardor the tall growth in its flowing backward fall over the chattering teeth of the cutter bar, the slow uncovering of the shape of the long ridge. It is, as always, one of the heights of his intimacy with the place, and he does not flag in his attentiveness. When the sun has reddened and cooled and come down, throwing deep shadows into the hollows, he turns the team toward the edge of the field, and speaks, stopping them. He throws the machine out of gear and, getting stiffly down, raises the cutter bar and bolts it upright. He takes up the reins again, lifts himself back onto the seat, speaks to the team, and the iron wheels begin to turn in the direction of the barn, soundlessly for the first time in hours, over the cushion of mowed grass.

And through all that time he has been followed by the unfinished knowledge of the bomb and the destroyed city. He has felt his mind borne, like a man in a little boat, on the crest of history, in a violence of pure effect, as though the event of the war, having long ago outdistanced its cause, now escapes comprehension, and speeds on. It has seemed to him that the years of violence have at last arrived at what, without his knowing it, they had been headed for, not by any human reason or motive or wish but by the logic of violence itself. And all the events of the war are at once altered by their result—though he cannot yet tell how or how much.

The Sense of Time Passing

The next afternoon Mat and Joe take the two boys and walk back on the ridge to help Jarrat and Burley clean up the barn there in preparation for housing the tobacco crop. They scrape and rake and then sweep the dirt floor, making the place safe for the coke fires that will be used to cure the tobacco—in the process moving and rearranging the tools that have been stored there in the course of the summer's work, and the troughs and gates and pens that will be used when the sheep are fed and sheltered there during the winter. They work steadily but—since the crops have long been laid by—without hurry. With a sort of conscientiousness they allow the boys to play at the work, knowing that earlier or later in the year such indulgence is not possible. When one of the boys gets in the way, they get him out of it with a patient kindness that becomes one of the pleasures of the afternoon: "Better work over yonder on that side now, old chap." "Let me get a hold there, honey boy. That's still a little above your breakfast."

After one heavy lift Burley sings:

How many biscuits can you eat?
Forty-nine and a ham of meat
This morning.

And does a dusty double shuffle down the driveway that gets the boys so tickled that even Jarrat laughs. And then, as if reluctant to give up the free high spirits of that laughter, Joe shuffles and stomps around his broom handle, singing:

Mamma, Mamma, what a pain I got.
Take me to the pothagate shop.
Get me something, don't matter what,
So you ease this pain I got.

The afternoon is hot, and they go out now and again to rest at the shady end of the barn and breathe the clean breeze there. They talk and smoke, easing themselves, feeling ahead of them the hurry and strain of the harvest.

"Not many days until we'll be into it," Jarrat says at one point. "Be here before we know it."

And that is the theme of their talk. The sense of time passing. The sense of the future as a reality they will not quite accept until it is upon them.

What Is Left

Tired after the hot day, they have been sitting quietly on the front porch since supper, Margaret and Hannah in the swing, Henry in Mat's lap, Andy on the floor with his back against one of the posts. The katydids have begun their annual life, and in the twilight the sugar maples in the yard are filled with their singing, a harsh foliage.

"What are they saying, Grandad?" Henry asks. He knows, but being a questioner he likes the question.

"Some say Katy did," Mat says. "Some say Katy didn't."

"Why?"

"Some are katydids, and some are katydidnts."

"What do they care if she did or not?" Andy asks.

"It's one of the eternal questions. You're liable to ask it yourself one of these days."

"I don't know what you mean," Henry says.

"I do," Andy says.

"You do not."

"Andy," Mat says, "if you go up to one of those trees and lay your hand against it just lightly they'll hush."

"Why?"

"I don't know. They will."

"Is that true?" Hannah asks.

"Try it."

And so Hannah and the boys leave the porch and go across the yard to one of the larger maples. Andy lays his hand against the trunk, and in the throbbing canopy of the singing there opens a globe of quiet the size of the tree. Andy steps back and stands with Hannah and Henry, looking up. Mat and Margaret sit watching them. For some time, while the katydids in the tree start singing and again Andy lays his hand on the trunk and stops them, nobody speaks. And then Margaret asks:

"What are you thinking about, Mat?"

The question startles him, for he gathers from the tone of her voice that she *knows* what he is thinking, and asks with daring and with fear.

"Loss," he says.

Hannah stands with the two little boys, looking up into the darkening tree, holding the boys' hands in hers, her back to the porch. Maybe because she stands so with the two boys, who wait only for the katydids to sing again, Mat is deeply touched now by the look of her. It seems to him that loss is in the way she stands.

He looks at Margaret, meeting her eyes.

"Loss. It singles us out."

She is smiling at him, shaking her head. And he realizes that the singleness he is talking about never has belonged to her. She has been without even the comfort of that—not single and whole, but broken. He grows ashamed of his bitterness. He too is broken, as he has been, and has known, all along—that singleness of his an attempt, typical of him, to prescribe terms to the world. The loser prescribes no terms.

"Mat, when we've lost it all, we've *had* what we've lost."

"But to *lose* it. Isn't there anything in you that rebels against that?"

She looks steadily at him, considering that—whether unsure of her answer or unwilling to answer too readily, he cannot tell. He is aware that Margaret is trying him, drawing deliberately at the bindings between them, as he has tried her with his singleness.

"No," she says.

"None at all?"

"Virgil," she says, as if to remind or acknowledge what they are talking about. "From the day he was born I knew he would die. That was how I loved him, partly. I'd brought him into the world that would give him things to love, and take them away. You too, Mat. You knew it. I knew so well that he would die that, when he did disappear from us the way he did, I was familiar with the pain. I'd had it in me all his life."

A tone of weeping has come into her voice, though not openly, and Mat does not yet move toward her. The weeping seems only the circumstance of what she is saying, not the result—an old weeping, well known, bearable by an endurance both inborn and long practiced. The dusk is thickening so that their eyes no longer clearly meet, though they still look toward each other.

"But I don't believe that when his death is subtracted from his life it leaves nothing. Do you, Mat?"

"No," he says. "I don't."

"What it leaves is his life. How could I turn away from it now any more than I could when he was a little child, and not love it and be glad of it, just because death is in it?"

Her words fall on him like water and like light. Suffering and clarified, he feels himself made fit for her by what she asks of him. He shakes his head.

She is clearly asking him now, and he gets up and goes and sits down beside her. He puts his arm around her.

"And, Mat," she says, "we belong to each other. After all these years. Doesn't that mean something?"

It is a long time before he answers. The night has nearly come. He can see only the drifting white blur of Hannah's blouse under the dark hovering of the tree.

"I don't know what it means," he says finally. "I know what it's worth."

15

That's Fine

Early Monday morning, the thirteenth of August, Ernest is driving up the creek road to work for perhaps the hundredth time. The valley is deep in fog. Since he plunged down into it out of the sunlight on the upland, he has been able to see only a few feet of the road, and he has driven slowly, now and then turning on the wipers to clear the windshield.

The metal bed of the truck is filled with loose tools, odd scraps and remnants, a dozen and a half empty paint buckets. As the truck works its way slowly over the rough road, it is accompanied by a clattering and jarring and rattling absurdly disproportionate to its speed.

Riding in the littered cab in the midst of that commotion, Ernest becomes conscious at a certain point that Ida will have heard him coming by now. And at the thought of her time seems to establish its continuity again from the moment the evening before when as usual he let her out of the truck at the mailbox, and watched her in the mirror until she was out of sight. He imagines Ida hearing the sound of the truck and turning her head toward it a moment, confirming her recognition of it, before going on with her work as before. That is not what he wishes she would do—he wishes that, hearing that sound, she would smile; he wishes that she would put down her work and come out to meet him—but it is what, with a desperate realism, he imagines her doing. The sight and nearness of her still raise in him an insurgence of heat and want. And the most passing thought of her still wakes the dream of household and farm, in which she moves as troubling and elusive as an unborn spirit. But desire and dream are hounded through his mind now by awareness of their futility. The whole structure has begun to be undermined by his understanding that it is licensed only by Ida's innocence of it and by his failure to bring it to the test of any reality.

But the sense of futility has grown in his mind to the sort of restrained terror that he would feel working without a rope on the incline of a high steep roof. It is the middle of August already, the downward slope of the summer. He has come in sight of the end of his work on the valley farm. And the return to winter work in the enclosure of his shop, which once so strongly appealed to him and which he would look forward to with such a deep presentiment of pleasure, has become unimaginable. He feels himself set loose and at large in the world, freed of all the limits of habit or duty or pleasure that might have held him back, pursuing through the boundlessness of his own fantasy his fleeting, hopeless obsession, pursued by a disaster to which he is blind. Like one of the damned, who with an indomitable loyalty even in Hell suffers only the thought of his irrecoverable sin, Ernest goes back each morning, always one day nearer the last, to his burning.

He drives up onto the bench where the house sits and stops in the yard. After he has turned off the engine, he sits still, listening. At first there seems to be no sound at all. And then he becomes conscious of the trees dripping. That is the only sound. Ida is nowhere in sight. He does not know whether she is at the barn or in the house. He cannot see to the barn. The house looks shut and quiet like a house at night. Now his own silence has begun to hold him. He waits for a sound.

But hearing none, he reaches over and unfastens the glove compartment, takes out a package of cigarettes, and flips the door shut. He lights a cigarette and gets out and goes around to the back of the house. There is an old shed there where he keeps paint and brushes and the few tools he still has a use for.

He is in no hurry. He cannot begin painting until the sun burns through and dries things off. He stands in the door, looking into the shed at the clutter of his stuff, finishing his smoke.

When he is done with it he steps inside. He spends a few minutes rearranging things, collecting his tools where they are scattered on the floor, gathering up the empty buckets and piling them in with the others in the bed of the truck. He carries out a new bucket of paint and sits down in the doorway and opens it. He stirs it carefully, taking his time, watching the pigment rise and blend and smooth out, and then sets the top back on the bucket. He takes his brushes out of the can where they have been soaking overnight and works the turpentine out of them.

He carries his ladder around to the side of the house where the sun will strike first, and sets it up. Taking a putty knife and a wire brush, he climbs the ladder and begins scrubbing away the old paint that has cracked and loosened around an upstairs window. For a good many minutes he works with concentration. As he works down from the top of the window, his eyes come below the level of the half-drawn shade. He leans sideways and looks in.

It is a child's room—Annie's room—and the sight of it is a revelation to him. He braces his right hand on the sill and looks closely. The room is neat, the bed prettily made with a patchwork quilt spread over the counterpane. But he can tell, without quite knowing how, that it has not been entered in some time. The door opposite him, that must go into the hall, is shut. The shades of the other two windows are tightly drawn. Only this one is partly raised. He understands, as if by an instinct born of his long preoccupation with her, that though Ida wanted the room closed, needed to have it closed, she could not bear to leave it dark.

What is revealed to him, what dawns on him with a kind of shock as he stands there looking into the room, is Ida's life, the complexity of it, the uncountable details of its making and being. There are secrecies and intimacies of it that are as forbidden to him, as far beyond his reach, as if he had never known her. The drive of his feelings has so oversimplified her that he has forgot, if he ever allowed himself to know, that there was bound to be such a room, and that it was bound to be closed to him. The recognition seems depthless, and it fills him with a nameless heavy fear. And yet he stands there, cramped and unmoving, looking into the room, caught by the mystery of it.

There is an almost sexual intimacy about looking into that room. And yet his strangeness to it is so strongly proclaimed by everything in it that it is not an intimacy at all but an invasion. And his sense of himself as a stranger is immediately joined to a sense of Gideon's belonging there. Gideon would know, and his knowing, though he might suffer it like death, would make him free in that room, and in Ida's life. In that knowing he would be carried toward Ida, toward such a giving and having as Ernest will never know.

He becomes aware that he has heard the yard gate open and shut. Seized by shame and the dread of being caught, he begins scrubbing at the loose paint again, not changing his position at all, bluffing through the pretense that he only leaned over that way in order to do his work. He does not look around. And then he can hear footsteps come up near the foot of the ladder and stop. He can feel the nearness of her.

"Don't fall," she says.

He does not stop work, and he does not look down at her. "I won't."

"Well, you might, leaning over that way."

"That's part of it too," he says. "It takes some stretching and some bending over."

"I guess it must. I don't know much about it."

As he straightens and begins working in a different place, he glances down at her. She is standing within three or four feet of the ladder, a bucket of milk on the ground at her feet. She is wearing a pair of four-buckle overshoes that must belong to Gideon. She is no longer looking up at him, but has turned, and is standing with her back to him, gazing absently out into the fog, which is thinning a little. He can see the yard fence now, rusty wires and spider webs beaded with clear drops. He knows that she has stopped because she gets lonesome and wants somebody to talk to, but he also knows that she will not say anything to him that she would not say to Mat or the Coulters or anybody else who might come to work.

"I like to never found them old cows," she says.

"Huh!"

"They'd laid down in that fog and I couldn't see them—of course—but I couldn't hear them either. Not a sound of a bell."

"I thought they usually come in by themselves. Didn't think you had to hunt them."

"They do. They wasn't a hundred feet from the barn this morning. I just couldn't see them or hear them. If that old spotted one hadn't got up and started her bell to ringing I'd be looking yet."

"Well. I swan."

She's silent a moment, and then he can hear the bail of the bucket rattle. "I reckon I'd better get on."

She goes around to the back porch. He hears her set the bucket down and, after a pause to take the overshoes off, go into the kitchen. Very shortly she comes out again and strains the milk and carries the filled crocks to the cellar. Though he goes ahead swiftly with his work, he is almost wholly attentive to the sounds she makes, translating them into visions of her as she moves among her tasks.

He scrubs out all the nooks and seams and edges on that end of the house, and moves his ladder again to the starting place. Going back to the shed, he tosses knife and brush into the pile of tools. The fog has begun to thin, and the pale disk of the sun to show through, but it will be some time yet before the wall will be dry. He sits down in the shed door and lights a smoke.

Ida comes out, carrying a water bucket. "A bad morning to paint."

"Yes. Too wet."

She goes to the well and pumps the bucket full and lifts it off the spout, turning toward him again. "This old fog. It makes you feel a thousand miles away."

She goes back inside, leaning a little against the weight of the bucket, her free arm raised for balance, but stepping quickly up onto the porch and across it and into the kitchen.

Her footsteps go rapidly across the linoleum two or three times, and then he hears her washing dishes. She washes her breakfast dishes, the skillet and coffee pot, the milk buckets and strainer. She comes out and empties the dishwater over the yard fence and goes back. This time, preoccupied, she does not look in his direction, and he feels a secrecy in his presence there, a flickering of shame. But he listens again as she begins preparing their dinner.

He hears her footsteps recede toward the front rooms. Now she will straighten the house, sweep, make her bed, and go out to work in the field until time to finish up dinner. There is an almost unbearable sweetness in his knowledge of all this. He has come to follow her through her days with the pleasing anticipations and recognitions with which one reads a familiar and much loved passage, but with anxiety, too, as though the passage is but a fragment, leading to the verge of a revelation that is not told, or lost.

Suddenly, somewhere deep inside the house, he hears her begin to sing. He has never heard her sing before. The sound—muted, wordless, whole phrases inaudible—comes to him with the same sort of shock he felt when he looked into the child's room. Any suggestion of change in her, or in his idea of her, is fearful to him—mainly perhaps for the reason that he has no way to respond to it. No matter how either of them may change, nothing changes *between* them. No matter what may happen, he is doomed to go on as always, obeying the void appearances of his old self and his old ways.

She quits singing. Presently he hears her footsteps return toward the back of the house.

His attention has been so fixed on Ida that he is alarmed to see that he is sitting in the full light of the sun. He does not know how long it has been shining on him, but he should already have been at work. The day seems to have slipped a little beneath him. What is he doing?

Shame gathers him up and with clear force turns him toward his work, and he submits to it with the relief of a man who has arrived at a critical solution, righted himself. Standing high on the ladder, for the better part of half an hour he concentrates with deliberative self-mastery on spreading white paint over the weathered cornice.

But as he reaches and turns at his work and turns back and leans to dip his brush, he can glimpse the wheel tracks of the road going down from the house to the barn. And his mind, as though it has gone wild and will not be brought to confinement again by the bait of a simple regularity, begins to stray out into the place.

His work, since spring, has followed the incline of that road upward from the barn to the house, repairing and painting the buildings along the way. He has made a difference in the time he has been there. But beyond the vestige of workmanly satisfaction it gives him to look back at it, there is a sense of irrevocable loss. Each one of those buildings represents one of the little periods of his life. Around each one in its turn his life formed a pattern. He has had an intimate knowledge of each one—has been attentive to the condition of every board and nail. And each has stood in its place in the transforming light of his dream.

But it was an intimacy purely professional, purely temporary. There is not one that he has had reason to go back to. And he has not been back. He will not go back. That is the condition of his trade. He has scarcely ever worked in a place that he did not come in some way to like. But then the liking was dependent on the work, and ended when the work did. Here the use of his skill, which always before has transcended and carried him past his jobs, has failed him. He is not able to relinquish this place as he passes through it. He cannot think of work beyond this work, a place beyond this place.

He has lost track of Ida's whereabouts when he hears her speak to him.

"Mr. Finley."

She stands at the foot of the ladder, ready to go to the field, holding a large white envelope. He can see the address written on it, heavily, in pencil. An ache of premonition swells in the pit of his stomach. He lays his brush across the mouth of the bucket, and takes a step down.

"I wanted to show you this. I got it yesterday. I'm sorry to make you get down."

"That's all right. I had to anyway."

He sets the bucket on the ground and props his crutches under his arms. She hands him the envelope.

It is one of those stamped envelopes that you buy at a post office. There is no return address, and he cannot read the postmark. The handwriting of the address is awkward, blunt, black, deeply impressed in the paper. Looking down at it, Ernest stands as though shadowless, in an inescapable brilliance. He has begun to sweat.

"You want me to read this?"

"Sure. Go ahead."

She is smiling, facing him with her hands clasped behind her. He would not be surprised to see her suddenly dance up and down. She reminds him just now of a young girl and that again makes her strange to him. Again he is aware how far his knowledge falls short of her.

He removes from the envelope a large sheet of lined paper and unfolds it. Again there is no address, there is no date. As on the envelope the black angular script is sunk into the paper as if by the weight of it: "Dear Ida, I am straightened up. I am coming home."

Had that been all, the meaning might have revealed itself slowly, and might have been bearable. But Gideon had trouble spelling *straightened.* He spelled it twice—first "stratened" and then "straytened"—before he got it right. And somehow the record of that struggle—there are no erasures: the words are simply crossed out with a single deep stroke of the pencil—gives Ernest as immediate a sense of Gideon's presence, wherever he is, as he has of Ida's, who is standing within his reach. It seems to him that if it were not for the crutches, if he were not propped there like a tripod, he might fall. But he keeps staring down at the letter, the writing having disappeared into the bright whiteness of the page. He feels Ida becoming impatient for his response.

"That's fine," he says.

"Ain't that fine?"

"Yes indeed. That's good."

Not a foot and a half from his hand he can see her, wearing the bonnet and the man's shirt she has put on, as she usually does, to work in the field. That close, it seems to him that he can feel in the hair roots along the back of his hand the swelling and rounding of her breasts, soft under the faded blue cloth of that shirt that he knows to be Gideon's.

"You're surprised, I reckon, to be hearing."

"No. I knew he'd be back. I didn't know when."

"You don't know for sure yet. He didn't say."

"Well, it'll be pretty soon. Soon as he can get here."

She reaches and takes the letter out of his hand.

"I just wanted to show somebody."

"Why sure," he says. "I'm glad you're going to be happy now."

That is as far as he can go. He stands there on the high stalk of his pain.

She folds the envelope twice and buttons it in one of the shirt pockets.

"Yes," she says. "Maybe I sort of will now."

He seems to get through the rest of the day by holding on to the handle of the paint brush. He dangles from it, the place vanished around him as if sunk into the blinding whiteness of Gideon's letter. He holds to the handle of the brush, spreading whiteness, as one would hold to the last hand's-breadth of a swinging rope.

Another Result

Mat has washed his hands and come out to sit on the back porch to wait for supper. He quit work early, as he has for the past several days, and has been sitting there already for more than half an hour. Margaret is waiting for Ernest to come now before setting the food on the table.

On the arms of the rocker Mat's hands have gone into a kind of sleep. The sun, ready to set, casts a last flush of reddish light against the westward end of the barn. He has been watching that light rise toward the peak of the gable. And the light does rise and crest and depart, reaching out over the rising edge of the night. He can hear Andy and Henry playing in the front yard. And now he hears Margaret cross the kitchen and stop in the door.

"Where do you suppose Ernest is? He's never this late."

"I don't know. I reckon he'll be along in a minute."

"Do you suppose that old truck could have broken down somewhere?"

"Could have done it." The more Mat thinks about that possibility, the more likely it seems.

"Well, maybe I'd better drive down that way." He gets up regretfully, fishing in his pocket for his switch key. As he steps off the porch, he hears Margaret come out of the kitchen and sit down to wait in the chair he left.

He starts down through town toward the little farm in the creek valley. But as he gains speed he catches sight of Ernest's truck parked in the alley between the post office and Jasper Lathrop's store. He stops and backs up and pulls his truck in behind Ernest's.

The presence of Ernest's truck cancels the only probable explanation of his lateness. As Mat walks the few steps back out to the street, it occurs to him that, so far as he can remember, this is the first time in twenty-five years that he has not known within a reasonable guess where Ernest is and what he is doing. Mat feels an uneasiness in that thought that he did not expect. But he puts it aside and goes out to the street. He will look in the drugstore.

As usual this time of the evening, the drugstore is deserted. Dolph Courtney is sitting at one of the tables in the thickening twilight of the place—until a customer comes in he will not turn on a light—picking his teeth and watching the street. Mat opens the screen door and looks in.

"You seen Ernest, Dolph?"

"Not since this morning. Why? You looking for him?"

Mat turns away at once and lets the door spring shut behind him. He starts to cross over and ask at Burgess's. And then he sees Jayber Crow and Burley Coulter coming up the street from the barbershop. Maybe Ernest went to get a haircut, he thinks, and got held up there. The logic of that makes him quickly happy, and just as quickly evaporates; Ernest would not be in the barbershop with Jayber gone.

"Jayber," he asks, as the two men come up in front of the drugstore, "have you seen Ernest?"

A little to Mat's surprise, both men's faces immediately show the concern that he has begun to feel himself.

"Not for two or three days," Jayber says.

Feeling their eyes on him as he goes, Mat walks up the street and back through the alley to Ernest's shop. The door is shut, and he knocks.

"Ernest?"

There is no answer.

He works the latch and gives an experimental push to the door. It is not locked. He shoves it open and steps inside.

The big westward window over the workbench has filled the shop with a pinkish backwash of light from the sunset. And whether because that makes the lower three or four feet of the room proportionately darker, or because he is already warned by some glimpse, for a good many seconds after he steps through the door Mat does not see Ernest. But the room is filled with an intimation of what he will see. And a part of his mind is saying to him as if in a whisper: "You should not have come."

"Ernest?"

And he sees then.

Against the far wall, a little out from the end of the workbench,

Ernest is sitting on the floor, his head bent forward. His arms hang down wearily at his sides, the left hand and part of the forearm hidden in a freshly cut hole in the floor. The crutches, one resting on top of the other, lie beside him.

Mat crosses the room and, kneeling, picks up Ernest's right hand and feels for the pulse. There is none. For maybe a full minute he kneels there, the dead wrist in his hands seeming to infuse its quiet into him and into the room. His mind, as if in a fit of avoidance having leaped clean over the fact of Ernest's death, begins to grope at the problem of how to tell Margaret. The simplicity of it seems its difficulty—that he will have to go, without qualification or offer of hope, and tell Margaret: "Ernest is dead. He killed himself."

His mind flinches again and turns back. "Why didn't I know?" He leans and draws Ernest's left hand up out of the hole in the floor. The wrist is cut deeply open, as Mat knew it would be. There are no more surprises.

He looks around for the auger and keyhole saw that Ernest used to cut the hole in the floor and sees them hanging in their places. And he sees on the right leg of Ernest's pants the two dark narrow stains where he wiped the blade of his knife before returning it to his pocket. On the floor, a foot or so to the right of him, there is a neat pile of ashes and the extinguished butt of a cigarette.

Mat gently lays Ernest's right hand back on the floor and bends his left arm so that the bloodied hand will rest in his lap. He lifts him, gathered in his arms as one would lift a child, touched beyond tears by the vulnerability and innocence of the abandoned body still pliant and warm, carries him to the workbench, and lays him down.

16

Six Feet

"*Dang* tootin!" Uncle Stanley says. "Man just up and put a end to hisself that way! *Crazy. Bound* to been!"

He is sitting on the lower lip of Ernest Finley's grave, his feet dangling in the hole. To his right the top of Jayber Crow's bald head can be seen at intervals as he straightens to throw out a spadeful of dirt. The grave is nearly as deep as it needs to be; they have been at work—or Jayber has—since early in the morning. On the headstone of Ernest's mother's grave, the nearest neighbor to the one he is digging, Jayber has put his hat and shirt, giving it the rather startling appearance of a man rising out of the ground.

It is a sweltering day and the ground is hard. The shade of a tall cedar a little to the west of the grave is still turned tantalizingly in the wrong direction. Jayber's earth-stained undershirt is soaked with sweat. He hasn't grown used to the work of gravedigging, and maybe he never will. Nothing in his experience as scholar and barber could have prepared him for the agony involved in loosening and spading out that much dirt.

"Six feet is a lot deeper than I thought it was," he confessed to Uncle Stan from the bottom of the first one he dug.

"By grab," Uncle Stanley said, "things look different from down there, don't they, son?"

And that is the truth. There is a suggestiveness about the whole business that, though it seems not to affect Uncle Stanley, Jayber has never become immune to. Each time, as he digs his way down and grows tireder, he grows bluer. And today the mood is intensified by a particular sorrow, for as well as anybody did, Jayber knew Ernest and liked him.

He is tired now and hot and full of the misery of mortality, and about one time in three as he heaves the loaded shovel upward from the floor of the grave he makes an utterance which much against his will sounds like a groan.

At the foot of the grave Burley Coulter is standing in his best clothes, his face set in disinterested amusement at the argument that has been going on, to his knowledge, for at least half an hour. He cleaned up and walked in to town in the middle of the morning with the intention of going to Mat's house. But when he came by there the house was quiet, nobody in sight; he grew doubtful after all that the family would want to be bothered with outsiders at that time of day. And so he walked on past and out the road to the graveyard, where he knew he would find Jayber.

"*Bound* to be crazy," Uncle Stanley says, "feller do that to hisself. It's a dad-burned insult to humanity."

"Oh," Jayber says, "if you haven't got the most unpardonable old mouth!"

"Says which?"

"I said, are you sure about that?"

"Durn right!"

Burley would really like to go on back to town. He is never very comfortable in Sunday clothes anyway, especially not in the hot sun watching somebody else work. His plan was to come out and talk a few minutes with Jayber, finding out—if Jayber knew—how Mat and his people were, and then go back to town and eat a sandwich at Dolph Courtney's, and then go to Mat's.

But since he came up and said good morning, he has not said another word. He was prepared neither for Jayber's low spirits nor for the antagonism between Jayber and Uncle Stanley—two good reasons to be sorry he came and to wish to be gone. But he has stayed. Coat slung over his shoulder, hat pushed back, the sleeves of his white shirt rolled above his elbows, his tie loosened, his collar slowly wilting, he has stood there in a sort of fascination at the goings on, with a perishing hope that things will take a turn for the better. At one point he intended to stay until the job was finished, so he and Jayber could go to Mat's together. But now he has about decided not to wait.

"*He* said," Uncle Stanley says, with a downward backhanded wave in Jayber's direction, "*he* said he thought we'd just as well quit after the sun got hot, and finish up early tomorrow morning in the cool. But *I* told him, dad whack it, that ain't no way to do. In this work you're dealing with the *Powers,* by grab, and you can't diddle around with them. Why, what if somebody else dies tonight? And somebody's *liable* to."

"It could be you," Jayber says. "And what about that?"

"Maybe *two* of them will. And then look at the digging piling up on you. Says which?"

"I said, Well, if *you* aren't going to kill yourself, that's *one* we don't have to worry about."

"You *dad*-blamed tootin," Uncle Stanley says. "I ain't."

This quarrel has been in progress a good deal longer than the half an hour that Burley has been listening to it. It began, in fact, at the moment Jayber made the first cut into the sod. The old man sat down with his back against a headstone.

"I been studying about it," he said, "and be durn if I can see why that young feller wanted to kill hisself."

"Is that a fact?" Jayber said, thinking that would make an end to it.

But in the course of his studying about it, Uncle Stanley had evidently discovered in himself a righteous argument against suicide, and he wouldn't let it drop.

"Be durn if I think he had any *right* to do it."

"Well, it was his life, wasn't it?"

And that started it.

"It weren't his to put any such of an end to."

"How do you know that? And what right do you have to say that he didn't have that right?"

"Because I *believe* it. It may be Scripture, I reckon. If it ain't, it ought to be."

"Well, maybe *he* believed another way."

And so it has gone. Ignoring the obvious futility of it, Jayber accepted the challenge. And untouched by all the shrewd and telling logic of Jayber's questions, Uncle Stan has insulted both Ernest's life and Jayber's intelligence with as much passion as if suicides were threatening to overthrow the government. And Jayber has continued to ask the questions, at first with an exasperated patience, and then, as he dug deeper and grew tireder and sadder, with anger.

"If you're so hot on suicide," Uncle Stanley says, "why don't you just take that there rock and knock your blame *self* in the head? I'd have to say you had a point then. Go on! Bust your durn head!"

Jayber straightens up in the hole and points his finger at him.

"One thing, old man. Just remember one thing. You can only speak for yourself. You never know what the other man has to go through."

"Well," Burley says—he has had all he can stand, he is leaving now—"we've all got to go through enough to kill us."

It's Over!

Much of the Feltners' house has been rearranged to make space for the coffin and flowers and undertaker's furnishings in the living room. A large part of the furniture belonging to that room has been carried out and crowded into other rooms or stored in outbuildings. This was accomplished before midnight last night, Burley and Jayber and Frank Lathrop helping Mat with the work. And toward noon today the coffin was brought in, flowers were placed around it, and a number of folding chairs set up. The effect of all this, because it seems to substantiate the greater and subtler change, is as persistently disturbing as if it had been the result of some natural calamity.

Against custom—against the ill-concealed wishes of the undertaker, who was proud of his work—the coffin has remained closed. "It seems best that way," Margaret said. And that was all she said.

Early in the afternoon, as the day grew hotter and the house more crowded, Mat invited the men to come out on the porch, where there was a breeze. And they have sat there until now, smoking and carrying on the allusive conversation of men who know much in common. Now there are only five of them—Mat and Old Jack and Burley and Jayber and Wheeler Catlett—the rest having gone home to eat or do their chores.

The stillness of suppertime is beginning to settle over the town. The five men on the porch, all friends and comfortable with each other, have ceased to talk, each occupied in that wide quiet with his own thoughts. Through the openings among the treetops they can now and again catch sight of hurrying swifts.

Across the street Frank Lathrop's door suddenly is flung open, and Frank appears, doing a sort of dance across his porch. He seems headed for the street, but as he reaches the edge of the porch, coming aware of those watching him, he stops and, looking sheepish and confused, turns and walks back into the house.

All five of the men on Mat's porch have watched him with the same sense of improbability. Now that he has gone back into the house, none of them says a word, mystified and embarrassed at the impropriety of such a display then and in that place. The sight of Frank dancing for joy, oblivious to the mourning he danced in the face of, will stay in Mat's mind a long time.

But Frank's behavior does not go long without an explanation. Less than a minute later a door slams somewhere down in town, and they hear a young strident voice crying:

"It's over! It's over!"

And that voice is quickly joined by others. Doors are thrown open, footsteps run in the street. From the lifting of that first voice, the commotion in the town builds toward a crest it will not reach for hours.

Nobody has to ask what it is all about. Even those who failed to hear the bulletin on the radio recognize it at once, as though they have waited for it familiarly for four years.

Within fifteen minutes after the first shout, crowded automobiles have begun to come in from the countryside. In front of the stores the street has begun to fill with erratically parked cars and trucks and milling people. And the bells have begun to ring—dinner bells, the church bell, cow bells—their sounds finally meshing into one sound beating and quaking in the air. Frank Lathrop comes out of his house again, and without looking across at Mat's house turns down the street, soon disappearing into the crowd. The makings of a bonfire have begun to pile up in the street in front of Jayber's barbershop.

Against that tumult Mat's house holds its quietness. Like everybody else the men on the porch are grateful that the end has come, but they do not speak of what they feel. Perhaps Ernest's silence makes too heavy a claim upon them. Or perhaps if Mat should openly welcome the event they would speak gladly of it, would quietly celebrate it there among themselves. But Mat is thinking, with maybe more bitterness than he could disguise in speaking, of what this would mean to him if he could now expect Virgil to come home.

The noise of the crowd seems to rise into the air over their heads and remain there and accumulate like smoke. But except for its racket, the crowd is orderly and peaceable, perfectly contained by the one aim of making as big a to-do as possible. As nightfall approaches there begin to be cries of "Light her up! Let's have a light!"

Jayber gets up. "Mat, I hate to go, but I reckon if they're going to light that fire I'd better."

"That's all right, Jayber." Mat walks with Jayber out to the steps. The fire has been lighted. The flames are already high, casting a flickering globe of light over the crowd. "I expect you'd better, too."

Burley's starting to get up now. "I'd just as well be going myself. It's getting late."

"Stay, Burley, if you will," Mat says. "We'll have some supper in a little while, and there's plenty for you."

So Burley sits down again, and in a few minutes Bess comes to the door and calls them to supper. As they get up and start into the house, they can hear somebody beginning to tune a fiddle.

And long before their quiet meal is finished they hear through the open kitchen door two guitars spring into a wildly pacing beat, and then the curving and looping figures of the fiddle. Presently a cracked breathless old voice begins calling a dance.

"That's Bill Mixter and his boys and Uncle Stanley," Burley says.

At the head of the table Old Jack eats without looking up and without joining the talk. Though he has been at Mat's since morning, he has hardly spoken three sentences, and much that has been said to him he has not heard. He has been preoccupied, despondent, as if, added to all the other deaths he has known, Ernest's makes too many.

His silence makes them aware of him. Margaret, who is sitting on his right, lays her hand on his arm.

"Uncle Jack used to be quite a dancer," she says. "He used to never miss a dance."

That makes a claim on his attention and he smiles and shakes his head.

"Ay, Lord! I could work all day and dance all night. I had a good bay mare then that I used to drive to a buggy—a steady sensible thing, and you could trust her. I've woke up many a Sunday morning, sitting in the buggy with the reins in my hand, and that mare standing at the barn door."

They laugh. As though following a change of meaning in what he has told, he shakes his head again, and goes on. "I had a lot of music in me then. I couldn't stay still where it was. Couldn't stay still if I knew there was some somewhere I could get to." He pauses. "But that was a long time ago."

But then as if hurrying to qualify the sorrow of that, unwilling to imply to them that that ought to stand as his judgment on his life, he looks at Hannah and smiles.

"And the pretty girls," he says. "I've always had a great admiration for pretty girls."

When the meal is over the men go back to the porch. Now they can see the dancers around the fire—figures in silhouette, or lighted by the wavering light of the flames, and against the faces of the buildings their enormous wildly leaping and prancing shadows. When the women are finished with the dishes they come out too, to be in the breeze there. Nobody pretends to ignore the celebration, simply because it cannot be ignored, it has so filled and claimed the town. But watching that bright scene, lifted and moved and contained by the hurrying beat of the music, they are conscious of their separateness from it.

Smoking one of Mat's cigars in the quiet, Burley is beginning to have trouble keeping still. In spite of his loyalty to Mat and his persistent good intentions, Ernest's death has moved far out of the center of his attention. What he is thinking about is Nathan: If he has lived until today he will be coming home. He will be here. As Burley has sat and thought about Nathan coming back, an exultation has grown in him. The music has begun to get into his head, and his mind is wandering. Where he wants to be is down there where they are dancing, where he can find somebody to talk and laugh with. Half a dozen times already he has caught himself grinning and patting his foot. In a sort of dutiful shame at the vagrancy and disloyalty of his mind, he has so far made himself stay on. But he is beginning, by the same involuntary running of his thoughts, to supply himself with good reasons for going.

He has been here since noon, and that surely is long enough. Mat and his people probably would be glad if he did go. The house has been full of company all day, and Mat and them surely will be glad to see the last one go. Also he is tired, and he really ought to go on home and get some rest—after mixing around just a minute or two down there in the crowd. Also he is making himself a living insult to the dead just by sitting there and wanting so badly to leave.

At last he picks up his hat from the floor beneath the chair, and stands up.

"Well . . ." he says.

"Don't go, Burley," Mat says, and Wheeler says, "Burley, don't be in a hurry."

"Well," he says, lying desperately, "I got a thing or two needs seeing about out home."

He is staring intently down at the hat, which he can hardly see in the darkness, fussing at the shape of it with his hands.

Understanding his need to escape, or just sensing his discomfort, Margaret comes to his rescue: "We understand about that, Burley. I appreciate your coming. All of us do."

"That's all right, Mrs. Feltner." He goes to the steps and starts down. "I'll see you folks."

Redounding and Sublime

He walks off down the dark street toward the dancers and the fire. As he goes farther away from Mat's house and his mind comes free of the embarrassment of his escape, he walks faster, free to do what he cannot resist.

On either side of the fire the road is choked with the dark bodies of automobiles that have simply been driven as far toward the dancing as possible and stopped. There is something exciting about the massive disorder of the cars jammed in the road, the light of the flames glancing off fenders and hoods. The crowd claps and shouts and talks and laughs, massing in toward a circle surrounding the dancers who surround the fire. From that tightly pressed and vividly lighted circle the crowd frays outward into the dark, smaller groups and couples scattered along the walks under the trees and in the spaces between automobiles.

As Burley passes voices begin to call to him—"Hey, Burley!" "Come over here, Burley"—offering a drink maybe, or a good place to sit and watch, or some bit of talk. But he only raises his hand to these without stopping, not bothering even to make sure who is talking. He is impelled toward the very center, toward the music and the fire. He cannot rest until he gets there.

Now he can see the musicians standing on the bed of a truck turned at a right angle off the road in front of Jayber's shop, making a high platform just at the edge of the circle of bystanders. Bill Mixter and his two boys and Uncle Stanley are on the truck bed under the shadowy and greenly flickering foliage of the sugar maples. The three musicians stand in a close triangle, their heads inclined inward. Bill Mixter bends a little forward over his fiddle, his eyes hidden under the visor of his striped cloth cap. The two sons, slats of oiled hair loose over their ears, stare fixedly ahead at the same invisible point over the crest of the fire. They have been playing almost without letup for an hour or more. They are sweating, beating their rhythms with their feet on the worn boards, listening to themselves, paying no attention whatever to the dancers or to the crowd. Uncle Stanley is four or five feet in front of them, as near the edge of the truck bed as he feels safe, beating his hands, patting his feet, uttering the calls and songs at the top of his voice. He is as much aware of the crowd as the musicians are oblivious to it. He is in a state approaching transport—in his element. Now and then he does a shuffling turn, his feet flying in a way that threatens to snap his spindly old legs, and the crowd laughs and cheers. He sings:

> "Old Dan Tucker was a fine old man,
> He washed his face in the frying pan . . .

And got it all greasy."

The crowd whoops.

"Yes!"

"Sing it, Uncle!"

"Swing your partner and promenade!" he says, and steps back with a wide sweeping gesture of his right arm as though turning the dancers around the fire.

"Haw! Look a *thar* now!"

After watching the labor on the truck bed for a few minutes Burley pushes on to the very edge of the crowd around the fire, and only then is able to stop with the sense of arrival. He is restrained from hunting a partner and going on into the dancing by a doubtfulness of the propriety of that so soon after leaving a place of mourning, but he is also aware of being fifty years old. He has not danced for a long time. And so he just stands, as near to the dancing as he can get without being in it, feeling the impulse of the music sway in the crowd around him. It comes into him too, and he begins clapping his hands and patting his feet. He has loosened his tie, and now he takes off his coat and hangs it over his left shoulder. His hat, as usual when he is resting or enjoying himself, is pushed back off his forehead. He is grinning, forgetful of everything. The music has departed from its occasion. Simply present and sufficient, it has freed itself of beginning; it involves no premonition of an end. It only continues, in profound union with the dancers—pulsing and urging, turning, whirling, tramping, and circling—the ground, the air, the dark leaves of the trees, the glancing firelight brought to a tranced obedience to it.

With a few sharply declarative strokes of Bill Mixter's fiddle, seeming to tie a swift bowknot in the air, it stops. The silence hangs in the air and then descends slowly over the crowd. While it lasts they hear Bill Mixter laugh quietly and, turning to look, see him and his boys putting their instruments down. Bill Mixter walks over to the edge of the truck bed to take a cup that somebody is holding up to him over the heads of the bystanders. The crowd begins to murmur, loosening and dividing within itself.

Let down from the music, the scene becomes ordinary. As he looks around him, it seems to Burley that he is in a place altogether different from where he thought he was. The crowd is made up mostly of women and girls and boys, and men his age and older. The young men, who ought to be the force and grace of it, are not there. Among the dancers, who still stand resting where the music left them, are a number of pairs of girls and young women who have been dancing with each other. It looks to him more aimless than he thought. Some that are not here never will be. And what does it mean? Has what they are celebrating happened yet? Or will it ever?

There has come to be a fierceness in his thoughts, and no happiness. No, this is not where he was headed, or where he thought he was headed. He turns, and finds he has been standing in the midst of a group of school-age girls, who have been much amused by the involvement of such a grey head as his in such regardless exuberance. Thinking of it, he finds it amusing himself. He grins.

"Hello there, girls. You all look mighty pretty tonight."

They giggle, backing out of the way to let him pass.

He wanders through the crowd, watching for Jayber, making two slowly widening turns around the fire. The music soon starts again, but it is as though it plays now in a more distant place, and he is headed away from it, outside the crowd that forms and tightens again around the circling dancers. Coming by the truck where the musicians are playing, he pauses and studies the bunch of men gathered in front of Jayber's shop. About every third one there, he estimates, has had more than enough to drink, and the rest have had plenty.

"Uh-*huh!*" he thinks.

Grover Gibbs wheels out into Burley's path and gives him a prolonged vacant grin, as though trying to hold his attention until he can think of a greeting suitable to the occasion. Finally he gives up and executes a knowing wink.

"Howdy do, Grover."

"Mighty fine, old friend. Mighty good. Glad to see you, Burley, old friend."

He lands a great clap of affection on Burley's left shoulder blade. Burley steps around him and starts on. "I'd say you're feeling friendly, Grover."

"*I* do," Grover says. "*Yes* sir! Yes *sir!*"

Burley goes around the corner of the barbershop, and there finds Whacker Spradlin with his wagon and cream can. Whacker stands, in his usual perfection of drunkenness, between his wagon and the wall of the shop, swaying to the music.

"Uh-*huh!*" Burley thinks, not now in the tone of making a discovery, but of finding that things add up as expected.

He goes on past the stairway that climbs the outside of the building to Jayber's living quarters, beginning to be certain now that he is close on the track. But certain as he is, it still scares him when a hand reaches out from behind the building and takes hold of his arm.

He feels a bottle pushed against his breastbone, and Jayber's voice says: "Take a shot of *that*, pistol. It'll do you a certain amount of good."

A piercing giggle follows that statement out of the shadow, and Burley recognizes the silhouette of Big Ellis against the white of the wall. He is glad to be with them. Comfort comes over him. He holds the bottle up against the sky.

"Why, hello, Mammy," he says, and drinks.

"We were looking for you," Jayber says.

"Well, I thought you'd never find me."

Big Ellis giggles.

"How're you, Big Ellis?"

"Fine. Better. Glad to see you, Burley."

Burley corks the bottle and hands it back. "Thanks."

"Well, just hold on to it," Jayber says. "When we want it, we'll ring."

Big Ellis laughs. "Jayber says this is penthouse style. When we want anything, we ring."

"Well, kind of keep your eye on me," Burley says. "I ain't used to this high society."

He leans against the wall, holding the bottle by the neck until whoever wants it next will ring for it. It was a large drink that he took, and he feels the heat of it spreading through him. The celebration is far behind him now. Where they are it is quiet. They have ahead of them the dark slant of the pasture, and above them in the blackness the tremendous blooming of the stars. As Burley looks up, one suddenly loosens itself somewhere in the depths of the black, and falls. It makes a brief streak on the sky, so quick, so short, so arbitrarily placed that he immediately forgets where he saw it. For a moment that seems to matter a great deal. And then, as he recovers the sense of himself there where he is, it quits mattering.

The next one who wants a drink turns out to be him. He rings.

"By all means," Jayber says.

Burley drinks, and again feels the warmth sink into him and spread, opening slowly, a lethargic summer blossom.

After a protracted silence Jayber begins to talk.

"As I was saying," he says—and Burley will never know whether he was saying it earlier or just thinking it—"drinking is not ordinarily accomplished in circumstances most conducive to its highest development and enjoyment because of the preponderations of conglomerations of commotions commingling with assorted distractions indigenous to those places in which it customarily takes place—which is to say: bars, roadhouses, bootlegging establishments, et cetera, et cetera, all of which encourage the forgathering together of sundry rowdies, roughnecks, spongers, fiddlers, weepers, know-it-alls and big talkers, who create a concoction of meaningless distractions enough to give a sober man the headache, which if he is sober he'll perceive immediately, forthwith, and at once, not to say suddenly, that this is not a satisfactory place even to get drunk in—you got, that is to say, to be drunk to stay in such a place, even though it's no kind of a place to be drunk in, which you'll perhaps understand better if I explain . . ."

Big Ellis rings, and Burley passes the bottle.

"Believe I'll just have to greet her as she comes by," Jayber says, hardly interrupting himself.

And he greets her and passes her on, and goes on talking.

Burley tries dutifully to listen, though it seems to him that he must have begun listening too late and has not caught up yet. He seems to have been delayed by astonishment at such a stream of talk beginning to flow so fully and without warning right there next to him. He does not see that it makes any sense. He thinks it may, if he could just catch up.

He rings. The bottle is passed. Jayber greets her going by, and continues:

". . . book I've been projecting for some considerable time to be titled *The Esthetics of Sin,* by which (the sin of the title) I mean not the larger ones invented and propounded and promulgated by Moses, brought down from some mountain whose name I, at the moment, forget—a sign, I suppose, that I'm aging—but those small ones, made sins perhaps only by being so insistently so called by the clergy, so called perhaps only by virtue of the fact that they are so pleasant, or at least so lively, as to threaten distraction from the Protestant thought of Heaven—the aforementioned Heaven being, as is well known, inhabited only by dead people, or perhaps a few missionaries and their wives, a great conjugal conflagration occurring there nightly, I assure you—the sins presently under consideration being, to wit: loving, drinking, thinking, playing or singing or dancing for no pay and only pleasure, being idle when not sick, loving the world both as it is and as it might be—et cetera, et cetera—these having been, though certainly not neglected among us here, certainly not much refined, I intend to include in my book a chapter on each, defining, praising, prescribing, and elaborating upon the whys, whens, whethers, wheres, hows, and who-withs—for have I not seen with mine eyes the half-baked marriage feasts—for is not the abuse of the mortal the abuse as well of the immortal, and the abuse of life the abuse of life everlasting, and the abuse of the earth the abuse of Heaven?—for is it not upon this dust that the word and the law tread and leave their tracks?—and is it not upon this little that the great shall be lifted up?—Sinai—Sinai was that mountain's name . . ."

He goes on, almost without inflection or pause. There comes a time when this sentence untangles itself out of Burley's mind and goes on, leaving him quiet where he is. He experiences a moment of amazement at it—at the abundance and rapidity and strange force of it. The little sense he has been able to catch from it has seemed to him true and eloquent. But he hears it depart with relief. Listening to it has been a great strain on him. If it had stayed tangled up in his brains much longer it was going to give him the headache.

He stands propped against the back of the shop in blissful immobility, seemingly without the effort of standing, as though hung by his collar from a hook in the wall. He looks up at the stars. It seems to him there are more now than there were. And into his deep quietness come moments when he parts from the feeling that they are "up there," and he feels himself and the shop and the town to be up there too, the world one of them, among them. Now and then he sees one fall. Now and then he or Big Ellis will ring and the bottle will be passed, and Jayber greets her as she goes by. Sometimes the bottle comes to Burley when he does not remember ringing at all.

At some point in Jayber's sentence the bottle gets metamorphosed into the maid of the penthouse where they are staying. And every time she passes in the hall Jayber pleads with her to lay down that pile of dirty sheets and come away to a better land. But she will only give him a little kiss on the mouth and go on wherever she was going. And once in his talk Jayber sings, his voice very sweet and quavery as though he is not thinking of the maid at all, but another girl far away:

When your baby starts to stepping,
Lord, you nearly lose your mind.

Later Burley comes aware that Jayber has fallen quiet, not finished with that sentence surely, but just for the time being washed ashore by it. Later still, seemingly without having intended to, or making any effort at all, they are all three standing in a row at the front corner of the shop, looking out into the street. The crowd is smaller now, but the fire is still burning, the dancers are still dancing, and the musicians play on as before. Uncle Stanley is singing in the same strident voice:

Going up Cripple Creek, going in a run,
Going up Cripple Creek to have a little fun,

The girls up Cripple Creek are just about half—
Always a bulling, but they never have a calf.

Standing in the shadow against the wall of the building, Whacker is still swaying ponderously to the music as though the whole festivity is run by a pendulum hidden secretly among its works, and he is it.

The better part of the remaining crowd having by now come under the influence of Whacker's merchandise, there is a great deal of loud laughter, all conversations are being conducted in shouts, everything moves by plunges and jolts. Dancers, swinging, launch their partners out into the crowd, never to find them again, and continue dancing, alone or with some bystander snatched out of the crowd at random.

"Gentlemen," Jayber says, "we cannot pursue our high aims amid this tumult."

And the three of them turn and trot around to their place at the back of the building, feeling they go high at each step, floating and gliding like balloons between kicks at the ground. They ring and drink to celebrate their return, and stand in their old places and watch the stars, and watch the stars fall.

"You can't remember where they fall from," Burley says.

"It don't matter," Big Ellis says. "You don't have to put 'em back."

"Well, it just looks to me like a fellow ought to keep track of something like that. Kind of sad that he don't. He can't, I reckon. But it's sad. A whole star fall spang out of the blooming sky, and not a word in the paper, not a monument, not a plaque, not any kind of a notice at all."

"Don't matter. Plenty of them up there. Keep track of one that's still hanging."

"Most of those stars," Jayber says, "are many light-years away—I forget just how many, and a light-year is how far light can travel in a year, and I think that's about a trillion or so miles or so, and . . ."

"Light don't travel," Burley says. "It just shines wherever it's at."

"It *does* travel. You just can't see fast enough to see it."

"If it ever *moved* I'd see it."

"Well, where does it go when it goes out?"

"Hah!" Burley says. "*Where?* Where does a fire go when it goes out?"

"That's what I mean! Where does the beam of a flashlight, for instance, go when you turn it off?"

"That's what I mean! Where does music go when it stops playing?"

Big Ellis is finally getting uneasy about the tone of the conversation.

"Jayber sure is a mighty smart fellow," he says, "ain't he, Burley?"

"That's right," Burley says. "All right. I agree. No question about it, light travels. What do you do about it?"

"Nothing," Jayber says. "Nothing you can do. You just know it because you have to, because you know it travels and you know it goes, and you know it flies about a trillion miles a year through all that blackness on its way from there to Port William, that is to say right here, where we're at, to wit, and the light of some maybe never has got here *yet,* and we're looking at the light of some maybe that burnt clean out and black a hundred years ago. And them that we see falling perhaps fell and went out a long time before we saw the light of them falling, for it's farther up there than your eyes will believe . . ."

"Hush, Jayber," Burley says. "Don't talk like that. It's too sad. Don't say no more. Let's just be right here where we are."

"Right, colleague," Jayber says.

And then a thought comes to Burley that seems to have been approaching him, and that he seems to have been waiting for, ever since he came. Now that it has come it seems to clarify a great deal, and is a relief to him.

"What we're celebrating is celebration," he says. That started out to be clear, but did not wind up clear. Somewhere before the end his statement came apart like a flimsy basket and let most of his meaning spill out. "We're not celebrating any happening or anything," he says, "but just celebrating.

"We're not shellerbrating any *thing,*" he says, "because of how things have of being what they are. They ain't over apt to stay celebrate-able. Because they ain't."

"Which is to say," Jayber says, "as aforesaid. And *to* wit."

"*Because,*" Burley says, "to cellerbreak *things* ain't hardly barrelable because they won't always stay cellerellable."

"And the celebration of celebration," Jayber says, "will make celebrities of us all. You really had the cerebral horsepower behind that one, old chap."

"I thank you," Burley says. "I 'preciate it."

They fall silent again, and except when one of them rings and the bottle is passed they stay still for a long time.

And then Jayber, raising his hand toward the stars pontifically as to bless the universe, intones:

"Et ceterah. Et ceterah."

And they are quiet for a long time after that.

After a while they turn up again at the edge of the street. The town is deserted, quiet, and, except for the embers of the fire, dark.

"I declare," Burley says. "I believe the dance is over."

"And nobody told *us,*" Jayber says.

"I be durn," Big Ellis says, saddened and amazed.

Detached from thought or motive so that they learn what they are doing with surprise, Burley and Jayber are out in the street doing an Indian dance around the fire. They dance silently, staggering, but with great solemnity and pomp. They hear a whoop from Big Ellis, and hurry back over to the shop.

"Look at this little fellow I found here," Big Ellis says.

In the dark against the side of the building they make out the hulk of Whacker Spradlin, sitting flat on the ground.

"*Passed* out," Burley says. "Passed *clean* out. Such as never seen before."

Jayber nudges Whacker with the toe of his shoe. No response. He shoves the big straw-hatted head and it falls forward. He lifts one arm and then the other and lets them fall; they lie where they drop. He kneels on Whacker's stomach and lifts the brim of the straw hat and looks into his face. He draws Whacker's two heavy hands together and laces his fingers over the bib of his overalls, and pushes his head back against the wall and covers his face with the hat.

Straightening up, swaying forward and back, Jayber peers down at his work, and turns gravely to his associates.

"He's dead, gentlemen."

Though Whacker quite audibly and visibly breathes, the longer they look at him the clearer it seems to them that he is dead. There is something about the way he sits with his straw hat stuck over his face, loudly breathing, yet clearly and indisputably dead, that is surely one of the funniest things ever seen in Port William. For several minutes they weave and stagger and laugh, slapping their knees and each other's backs. Jayber then strikes a tragic pose and beckons them to hush. Accompanied by giggles that leak out of Big Ellis as if under high pressure, he declaims:

> Death doth sit upon him like a fly
> Upon the carrion flower, fairest of the field.
> To how sad metamorphosis are we come
> When such a weighty beggar shall be brought low
> To stop the bunghole of the world.
> Flights of buzzards wing him to his rest!

A great spluttering giggle bursts out of Big Ellis; as if propelled by the recoil of it he falls backwards and lands sitting up, facing Whacker, still giggling. "He'll stink! Big as he is, he'll stink till New Year's."

"He's stinking already," Burley says. "You don't have to be no undertaker to tell that."

Jayber at once stands himself erect at Whacker's shoulder, and pounds on the wall. "Meeting come to order!" And as Big Ellis quiets down he proceeds: "Fellow members of the Port William Sanitation Commission. It has been duly noted, I believe—I believe I speak for you gentlemen as well as myself—*et* ceterah!—that by the cooperation of the winds of fate and the tide of victory there has been washed upon the shores of our fair city the mortal remains of this erstwhile creature, the nature of which in its previous state remains somewhat—uh—questionable, not to say *dubious,* if not doubtful. However, gentlemen, having been entrusted by our fellow townsmen with the removal of any and all vagrant corpses as shall occur within the jurisdiction—that is to say, to wit, the say-so—of the aforesaid Port William, I move we go forward with the business. For let us be mindful of our mighty motto, for mightier there is none: Keep—Our—City—Clean. Is there a second to the motion?"

"Second the motion," Burley says.

"Noted. And you, honorable sir," Jayber says, addressing himself to Big Ellis, "I assume you vote with the majority."

But Big Ellis is lying on his back, laughing.

"He does," Burley says solemnly.

"Then it is unanimous. And, sir, have you not a suitable conveyance close by?"

"Big Ellis," Burley says, "you know where you left your car?"

"If it ain't gone, I do," Big Ellis says.

"The commissioner attests," Jayber says, "that if his conveyance has not strayed, wandered, decamped, fled, flew or absconded from the place he left it, he knows where it is. Let us then adjourn until said commissioner shall seek out, and return with, said conveyance."

He gavels mightily on the wall, and then helps Burley help Big Ellis get up. As soon as he is up, Big Ellis's feet try to walk away and leave the rest of him hanging there between Burley and Jayber, and they all fall in a heap. They lie as they fell for a considerable time, as though asleep, or resting, or waiting to see what they will do next.

After a while Burley says, "If I knew which way is up, I'd get up."

"You see any stars?" Jayber says.

"No."

"Well, turn over."

"Ah!" Burley says. "That's them."

He gets up, and Jayber gets up, and again they help Big Ellis to his feet.

"The idea is to keep your feet on the bottom," Burley says, "and your head on top. Watch this." He gives a walking demonstration, first one way, then the other.

"That's *good,* Burley," Big Ellis says. *"Really good!"*

"You think you got the hang of it now?"

"Yes-sir-*ree!"* Big Ellis says. "*Turn* me a-loose! I'm a tomcat! I'm a ring-tailed twister!"

"You know where you going?"

"Yes I do! To my car."

"You know where you are?" Jayber says.

"Yep. Right here."

"Jayber's shop," Burley says. "Don't get lost."

"Never was lost in Port William but once in my life," Big Ellis says. "And that was three or four years ago."

He goes off into the dark; his footsteps fade into the silence.

Burley and Jayber stand and wait. They lean against the building and wait. They sit down and wait.

"Well, he's either lost, or gone to sleep, or parked his car clean outside town," Burley says, "—or something."

The roaring of an engine rises in the darkness not thirty yards up the street. There is a long scream of gears, the engine roars again, and they hear the tires beginning to move over the gravel.

"Turn on the lights!" Burley shouts.

As if he was only waiting to be told, Big Ellis turns them on—to reveal that he is backing rather rapidly away from them, heading—as nearly as they can tell—straight for Milton Burgess's store.

"Whoa!" Burley shouts.

Again, as if grateful for the advice, Big Ellis obeys. The tires slide a little and dust rises into the beams of the headlights.

"Put her in forward!"

Big Ellis puts her into something different—high maybe—and brings her back down the street at a canter.

"Whoa!" Burley says. "Now cut the wheels over this way, and back her easy."

With the help of much loud instruction and a good deal of trial and error, Big Ellis succeeds finally in backing the car up onto the sidewalk. They open the trunk, and then gather around the still inert and snoring corpse of Whacker.

"And now, gentlemen," Jayber says, "with deep respect, with reverence, with kind and loving thoughts of the dear departed, let us bear the body to the grave."

All three of them tugging at Whacker's shoulders and arms, with great heaving and grunting, they manage to turn him away from the wall and drag him perhaps a foot before they have to stop to rest. Letting him lie full length on the ground, they stand swaying over him, getting their breath. He lies in massive repose, like a hill, his belly cresting higher than their knees. They no sooner begin to rest than they begin to anticipate and dread the weight of him, but after many struggles and stops to rest they manage to lift and drag and push him over to the car, and cram him into the trunk.

"What we going to do with his feet?" Burley asks.

"The wagon," Jayber says. "Where's his wagon?"

They find the wagon and unload it and tie it to the bumper and put Whacker's feet in it.

"And that's a meaningful and moving and beautiful example of the funeral director's art," Jayber says, "if ever I saw one—and I have saw a few.

"Driver!" he says.

Big Ellis, giggling, goes around and gets into the driver's seat. And then for many seconds nothing happens at all.

"What's matter?" Burley says.

"You all coming?" Big Ellis says. "Get in."

"No!" Jayber says. "We got to carry this out with due propriety, and a due sense of what is fitting, and with due solemnity, and with dignity. He must have a procession, a cortege. You drive ahead, Big Ellis, at a slow, a stately, an elegiac, and a dirgeful pace. And we will walk behind."

Big Ellis starts the engine. He guns it fiercely to test its mettle and discipline it thoroughly beforehand. He throws it into gear. The car makes three hunching lunges and dies with a cough in the middle of the road.

"Low, sweetheart," Burley says. "Put her in low."

Big Ellis gets her in the right one this time, and the procession moves off, Big Ellis driving at an elegiac and a dirgeful pace, followed by the red wagon carrying Whacker's feet, followed by Burley and Jayber, each with an arm around the other for consolation and for help in walking, their hats dangling in lamentation from their free hands.

"A famous cortege, if ever I saw one," Jayber says. "Drum!" he says.

And Big Ellis begins to beat with his fist against the car door the ponking concussions of a funeral march.

"Oh, a redounding and a sublime cortege," Jayber says. "Nothing is so redounding and resounding in the history of a town as a good calamity or a classy funeral or an event of that stripe. God knows they happen seldom enough."

Inspired by the thought of mending the history of Port William with a funeral of unimpeachable class, he lines out the chorus of a dirge:

> We are hauling,
> We are hauling
> His aaaaass
> To the graveyard.

And they sing it a second time together. Jayber chants:

> We'll haul him to the graveyard,
> And there lay him down.

And they all sing:

> We are hauling,
> We are hauling
> His aaaaass
> To the graveyard.
>
> We'll bury this peckerwood
> In six foot of ground.
>
> We are hauling,
> We are hauling,
> His aaaaass
> To the graveyard.

They have raised around them by now a great barking and howling of dogs. Citizens' voices are shouting out of the darkness. House lights are snapping on. People are coming out onto lighted porches in their night clothes. But nobody follows except four or five dogs who, though they make a loud boast of barking and growling, keep a respectful distance.

Through it all the members of the cortege maintain an invincible solemnity and dignity. They sing their chorus many times over with the strength and loudness of deep conviction. In the pauses Jayber makes hieratic and indecipherable gestures in the air with both hands, intoning: "Et-t-ceterah. Et-t-ceterah. Et-t-ceterah."

As they bear down on the outskirts, he becomes inspired again, and sings some new verses, holding his right hand in benediction in the air each time Burley and Big Ellis come in on the chorus:

The forementioned peckerwood
Was a mountainous bootlegger.

And if the grave don't fit him
We will have to dig it bigger.

Do not scoff, my townsmen.
We all need a grave to fit us.

They sing the chorus, Big Ellis pounding the car door, the dogs barking, Whacker's feet keeping their perfect repose in the wagon.

Yes, that old dark and silent
Ground is finally going to get us.

Jayber is shaken and a little sobered by the turn his song has taken. "A true grave digger's tune," he tells himself. And he tells himself, "Once a preacher, always a preacher." But now that he has sung his way into it, he reckons there is nothing to do but dig in and sing his way out of it.

If you think that stops the story
And puts an end to the matter

Burley and Big Ellis bawl the chorus.

Maybe so. But maybe there's a glory
Where you'd rather we'd all gather.

There is something incorrigible about his mind. He has always known it. No matter how near home he sets his mind to work, it always beelines for the final questions. His thoughts return to the verge of this life, the place of their defeat, with fascination and with strange delight. Is it noble faith or cowardice that, though he cannot *see* that all loves do not end in the dark, he cannot believe they do?

> It can't be seen with the naked eye,
> And the grave's not a telescope

They sing the chorus. The end in sight, Jayber begins to be conscious of the darkened country lying quiet beyond their singing and the commotion of the dogs.

> To see a land beyond the sky.
> But, brothers, we will hope.

That movement of his mind completed, he feels himself returning, fully and gladly present again with the others. As he listens to his companions singing the chorus, the sense of the rarity and extravagance of the occasion comes back to him, the sense of the rarity of their comradeship, and he laughs aloud and sings with them. They are approaching the graveyard now, and the dogs, as if having pursued to the limit of their jurisdiction, have quit following.

Their turning off the road at the graveyard gate seems to Jayber to mark a culmination of large significance, and he calls to Big Ellis to stop.

"A few appropriate words will be appropriate at this time," he says.

"Gentlemen," he says, "that was a procession, I dare say, without equal, and will not be forgotten, I dare say, in the lifetimes of those now living—it being in any case an accomplishment—a glorious achievement in the pride of which we may all rejoice—a triumph—a gilded pinnacle in the history of this noble city, this alabaster village, this fairest flower, this *yaller rose* of the valley of the green Kentuck. Can you say amen?"

"AMEN!"

"Forward!"

In solemn triumph they advance between the stone pillars of the gate and up the hill, Big Ellis's headlights picking out the white of the headstones under the cedars. They have hushed their singing.

At the top of the rise they follow the road as it turns to the left and goes among the graves along the ridge.

"Right here," Jayber says. "Whoa!"

Big Ellis gets out, and in the red glow of the taillights, as quietly as they can, they begin the job of getting Whacker out of the trunk. Getting him out is for some reason harder than getting him in. At each straining heave they move him only inches. As they tug and haul on his great arms and legs, they are intimidated by the size of him.

"What a tub of guts!" Jayber says. "He must weigh five hundred pounds."

"He don't miss it far," Burley says.

They laugh.

"Shhhhh!"

"We look just like devils in this red light," Big Ellis whispers.

They are all stopped a moment by the thought of that.

Burley whispers: "We'd look like the devil if it was daylight." And straightening from their labor, they laugh. They are wavering helplessly now between hilarity and a strict silence that they feel to be demanded of them by the silence around them—not so much the heard silence pierced by the voices of insects as the imagined perfect silence of the dead. And though in their silences they are beginning to be troubled by what seems to them their disturbance of the dead, that seems to make what is funny even funnier.

They finally get Whacker out and lay him on his back on the wagon, his head dangling over one end and his legs over the other.

"Now . . ." Jayber whispers.

But he does not finish, for they become aware that Big Ellis's old car, relieved of its burden, has begun to roll. It has eased off slowly, rocking a little over the bumps, following the road down the gentle slant of the ridge.

"Oh, Lordy!" Big Ellis says. "It's got a *hant* in it!"

They stand transfixed, chilled to the bone by what, in that place under those circumstances, seems a certainty.

Finally Jayber says, making a blind leap in the direction of rationality: "You didn't put on the *brake,* Big Ellis."

And Burley says: "Oh *mercy!* All that crockery!"

And all three of them begin to run after the car, which has a good head start and is rolling faster.

As they run they whisper violently to each other: "Run!" "Hurry!" "Watch out!" "Oh, Lordy!" And running in the dark, their feet pounding the uneven gravel, they stagger and lurch, bumping into each other, ricocheting both ways out of the road. And somehow they gain on the car, which keeps its even pace straight ahead in the wheel-ruts. Then where the road makes a right angle turn to the left, the car keeps going straight, climbs over the low embankment, which checks its speed, and comes to a stop against a large granite tombstone whose markings show with sudden clarity in the beam of the headlights. And then the three pursuers fetch up against the tombstone too. Leaning down between the stone and the car, Burley inspects for damage.

"Not a dent, not a scratch."

And then they all sit down to get their breath. They sit facing the car whose headlights peer steadily at the tombstone, almost touching it, for all the world like a nearsighted person trying to make out the inscription.

As soon as they have rested, they get up and walk back to where they left Whacker. Following Jayber's whispered orders, Burley and Big Ellis each pick up one of Whacker's legs, and Jayber taking the tongue of the wagon, they start slowly down among the stones toward the newly dug grave of Ernest Finley. All the way there they labor in conscientious quiet, keeping the wagon uneasily balanced as with great effort they lug it over the mounds.

They halt it at the end of the grave and begin the difficult and perilous business of lowering Whacker down. Gravity is too much in their favor now, and they accompany their work with much grunting and whispered cautioning as they roll Whacker over on his belly and start him in feet first and backwards.

"Oh, me!" Big Ellis whispers. "I believe the grave will be the end of us all."

And leaving Whacker bent like a hinge over the lip of the grave, they let go and laugh, rolling on the ground until, intimidated by their noise, they fall silent again.

Now, Jayber getting down into the grave to pull and the other two lifting at Whacker's shoulders, they work him carefully backward and downward. But it is not until Whacker's balancing-point slides over the edge that they realize that instead of leading they are being led. For Whacker is going on his own now, and they lack the strength to pull him out—or to hold him, either, for very long. Down in the grave Jayber fights off the impulse to turn loose and run, knowing there is no place to go; he takes his stand where he is, shoving at Whacker's great buttocks for dear life, his voice rising up quick and small from under his burden.

"Hold him, boys, hold him! Take hold and rear back!"

Burley and Big Ellis do take hold and rear back, with the strength of desperation, but there is nothing to do, seeing that Whacker is bound to go, except slow him down. But the farther he slips into the grave, the faster he goes. His arms are too large even at the wrists to take much of a grip on, and Burley and Big Ellis finally hold him only by his fingers. Below them in the grave they can hear Jayber grunting, yielding ground inch by inch as the big man comes irresistibly down.

But they do at last get him laid down in the bottom of the grave without letting him fall. The big head comes to rest between Jayber's feet. They pitch in his hat and Jayber places it over his face and folds his hands, and steps up onto the mound of his stomach and is hauled out.

And now the difficulty and danger of their labor only serve to increase their sense of accomplishment. They feel that they have achieved a rare distinction. Up on the hill they can see Big Ellis's car lights growing dim, the battery nearly played out, but that seems not to matter now.

"Well, it did fit him," Big Ellis says.

Burley laughs. "It's not exactly what you'd call roomy, is it, Jayber?"

"No," Jayber says, "'tis not so deep as a well nor so wide as a church door, but 'tis enough, 'twill serve."

"Durn if that ain't fine, Jayber. Say some more."

"Say some more, buddy."

Jayber straightens himself at the head of the grave and raises his hand. And as though seized by meanings he cannot resist, he speaks slowly and with feeling:

> Water into water, earth into earth,
> Breath into breath, light into light,

Singing into singing, birth into birth,
Thought into thought, sight into sight,
Let this man's makings be unmade,
Let stillness be, let peace come
To this place that was a man.

Stooping, he lifts in his cupped hands some dirt from the mound at the grave's edge and lets it sift slowly in.

Overtaken and sobered by Jayber's words—Jayber as much as the others—they stand with their heads bowed after he has finished. Apart from anything any of them could have intended or expected, Jayber's words have transcended drunkenness and farce. The meaning of the time has been lifted far above the snores that come with astonishing power out of the grave. Jayber's words have returned them to the occasion they started with—the end of the war, the dying, the deaths—the graves of the millions that, beyond knowing, peace has come to.

A Passing Dirge

Mat wakes up in one of the folding chairs in the dim light of the lamp left burning at the head of the coffin. He wakes to resume the heaviness of Ernest's death, cramped from sitting asleep in the hard chair, the old pain lying deep and keen in his shoulder. He knows he cannot have slept long.

Slowly, so as to make no noise, he straightens himself in the chair, feeling with that movement how tired he is. This is the second night in a row that he has passed with little sleep—and, he might as well say, no rest. Seeing from the slight paling of the windows that dawn has begun, anxious for the night to be over, he reaches up and turns off the lamp, letting the grey of the sky seep into the room. It is not as light as he thought it might be.

His awareness of the room fades. All his attention is caught now by the pain in his shoulder. The pain is like a four-inch sliver of hot light burrowing in under his shoulder blade. Or like a bullet; the pain of a wound would be the same as other pain. It could be borne. A man gets used to pain, he thinks. He learns it. It gets to be familiar to him, a part of what his life is and feels like. And what good does it do him? It teaches him to make light of the pains that are less, and to respect those that are greater. It teaches him what he can stand. And what good does that do him? He needs to know what he can stand because the chances are he will have to stand as much as he is able. That is what is ahead of him—to suffer and to stand it. And so is there virtue in standing it? Maybe. Surely. But there are limits too, and suffering kills. Ernest stood a great deal, and kept quiet, until there came a greatness of it that he could not stand. And that—what it takes to kill a man, what his limit is—is his mystery. The mystery of his death that becomes the mystery of his life. In the flow of his strange half-dream, Mat becomes conscious of his own mortality upon him. And he does not care.

He rouses. The light has grown stronger. The outlines of the room have begun to emerge out of the shadows. Changed to accommodate Ernest's coffin and the ceremonies of his death, the room has an austerity that seems to Mat not only to stand for the sadness of all else, but to be in itself a cause for sadness. He longs for it to be the way it was.

In the paling gloom he can make out the figure of Old Jack slumped in another of the uncompromising chairs, still asleep, his hands resting on his knees, the cane propped against the seat between his legs.

They sat out on the porch until after midnight, listening to the music and the noises of the crowd. After Wheeler had started back to Hargrave, it was decided that the three women would go to bed, leaving Mat and Old Jack to sit through the rest of the night beside the coffin. Old Jack had insisted on staying, over the protests of Bess and Hannah, who thought he ought to rest.

"All I do is rest, honey," he said to Hannah.

He and Mat sat in the living room and talked, Mat sitting at the head of the coffin with his back to it, and Old Jack facing him, as they still sit. Mat, as though to lead his own mind as far from that room and that night as possible, turned the conversation toward the past. The old man spoke of the names and landmarks and happenings of a time before Mat's birth, and Mat listened, his mind drawn back before its own beginning, held and quieted by the vision of another time, and by the sense of the continuance of the land, the place, through all that has happened on it and to it—its history of little cherishing and much abuse. For as always it was finally the land that they spoke of, fascinated as they have been all their lives by what has happened to it, their own ties to it, the wife of their race, more lovely and bountiful and kind than they have usually deserved, more demanding than they have often been able to bear.

After the house grew quiet, Old Jack's interest in the talk began to flag, and soon he quit talking altogether. He yawned and rubbed his eyes, and then nodded, and his head dropped forward. With a kind of anger he shook himself, and roused. Looking up at the lamp by Ernest's coffin, he scratched his head, and in the midst of scratching dozed off; his hand came slowly down and found a resting place on his thigh. His face, tilted forward, was shadowed, but the lamplight gleamed in his white hair.

Mat remained wakeful a long time. In the silence then he seemed to have reached the end not just of talk but of thought as well. He felt the pressing in of it—the silence of Ernest's death, the ever-waiting silence that surrounds all speech.

He was still sitting there in that suspension when he heard the approaching clamor of Whacker's funeral procession. At first it seemed only a fitful last resurgence of the festivity, an indecipherable mingling of shouts and laughter, but as it drew nearer he made out the measured heavy beat of a dead march and, above it, the strained wailing of a dirge.

Mat's first impulse was to take the irreverence of it as an affront. And for that reason, though it seemed to him he recognized the voices, he did not get up as the clamor drew near to try to see who was making it. But as the procession drew even with the house, he felt himself irresistibly drawn into the spirit of it. That following the giddy jubilance of its victory celebration the peaceful sleep of the town should be broken, not by any song of victory or thanksgiving, but by voices singing a dirge—that seemed to him to be fitting. For in his mind, at least, and the minds of the others who had sat in silence on the porch, hadn't the night been burdened with the knowledge that the dead have lost and are absent from victory?

But that they went by singing, voices raised in the rhythm of loss and grief with unabashed glee, seemed to Mat to change the night, to start it toward something else—though he was not able to say what.

He shifts in his chair, needing to be up and stirring now that he is awake. There is no longer a comfortable way to sit. But he does not want to disturb the sleepers, and the silence still presses on him as with a weight.

He thinks of the women and the baby, still asleep. And then there comes to him not only the thought of Margaret but the sense of her, lying asleep, alone in their bed in the dim room. He longs to go in and lie down beside her and take her in his arms.

Though he does not go to her now, the longing to do so makes a small cell of happiness in his mind. It has been a long time since his thought has gone so freely toward her.

Among the Dead

Lying on his back among the headstones and mounds of the graveyard, Burley wakens, changed by his sleep, his head filled with a throbbing dull ache. He lies still for some time before he opens his eyes.

He can hear the roosters crowing, close and far, and birds singing. He has got to get up. They have got to get out of there before the whole town is awake and watching. A kind of panic seizes him and he uncrooks his arm from over his face and begins to blink and squint, trying to accustom his eyes to the light. At every blink the light floods into his head, glinting and scratching.

Finally he becomes able to hold his eyes open, and with a summoning of will pushes himself up. He sits there unsteadily, the ground for a moment threatening to dump him over onto his face. He props himself, and again risks opening his eyes.

Somehow, as if in a dream, the possibility that the runaway automobile might have done great damage among the brittle slabs overpowered the knowledge that it did none, and now he looks around him in surprise and relief to see that the dead still lie undisturbed. The place is flooded with the weak first sunlight of the morning, and the dead are absent from it.

As gently as he can he lies down again, easing his head back into the crumpled crown of his Sunday hat. He will be sorry about the hat, he knows, when he gets around to thinking about it. He has the wakened dreamer's sense of escape from something he might well have done. That eases a little of his anxiety, but not all. He will not escape so easily from what he did do. For now he thinks of the betrayals involved in his participation in the profane clamors of Whacker's funeral. He feels an urgent need to get up and get the others up and clear out, and at the same time an overpowering wish to lie there with his eyes shut, and never move. He is thirsty. The only good thought in reach is the thought of water. His head throbs.

"Oh me," he says.

"Are you awake, Burley?" Jayber asks.

"Sort of."

"I'm afraid I am too."

"Jayber, we've got to get up and get out of here."

"I know it. We don't want to get caught here, or be seen leaving either, if we can help it."

"Yeah."

But neither of them moves, and they say nothing else for some time.

And then Big Ellis sits up. He shakes his head and says, *"Shoo!"* Looking around him he grins. "Resurrection morning, ain't it?"

As though to confirm the unsuspected truth of that, Burley points down the slope. "Look!"

Over the mound of loose dirt they see the broken crown of Whacker's straw hat slowly rising. His shoulders appear over the mound, and he stands up. And then, as though to sleep in a grave is no more remarkable than to sleep in a bed, he picks up the tongue of his wagon and moves off down the slope toward the gate.

They watch him go, hardly believing that without help he could have drawn his bulk up the sheer six-foot walls of that hole. There is something apocalyptic about it, both ludicrous and sobering. Jayber says:

Unfazed by the grave,
He doth awake and walk.

"He'll never get a better funeral," Big Ellis says, "if he lives to be a hundred."

And then, with all the force of a crucial realization that comes too late, it dawns on Burley that the possibilities have been out of control from the beginning. Suppose Whacker *hadn't* been able to get out by himself. *They* certainly had no idea how to get him out. Suppose he had got sick down there, or died. Suppose they had forgot him and left him there—as it surely did look like they were going to—and they had come bringing Ernest.

He plunges to his feet.

"Let's go! Let's get out of here!"

They get up and follow him among the stones to where the car sits, doors and trunk still open, and in the daylight still appearing to labor myopically at the granite inscription. They set the wheels and, heaving mightily at the cost of much pain to their heads, push it back over the embankment into the road.

"Well," Big Ellis says, "looks like there's no place to go now but home."

"Get in the middle, Burley," Jayber says. "You'll be getting out last."

But Burley feels a sudden reluctance to go with them. He wants to part from them now. Wants the night's doings to be finished now, and done with. Here is a day started, it seems to him, that is going to ask a lot of him, and he wants to get himself set for it.

"You all go on," he says. "I'm going to walk. I think it'll do me good."

Jayber gets in, but as the car starts to roll he says: "Wait! Listen!" The car stops and he opens the door and leans out. "Listen," he says. "I don't think anybody actually *saw* who it was making all the racket last night. So if we make it out of here without getting caught, it was all done by Unknown Citizens. You see?"

They see.

"Big Ellis," Burley says, "when you come around to where the drive forks, if you'd back out to the road from there it might look like you'd just pulled in to turn around."

Big Ellis nods. The car rolls forward, picking up speed, lurches as Big Ellis throws it into gear, and, as the engine starts, grumbles off toward the gate.

Burley stands there, watching them go. He should be going himself, but he does not move. As soon as he has seen them back out and turn and go out of sight toward town, the weight of his guilt comes down on him, too heavy to bear away. At the time when Mat may have needed him, and when he should have been sorrowful himself for the death of Ernest, and when he should have been attentive in some decent way to

Tom's memory and the hope of Nathan's return—at that time of all times, that one and only and now past and unchangeable time, where was he?

Drunk. Bawling and singing and laughing at the funeral of a live drunkard. In the graveyard, insulting the peace of the dead.

And he lay down and slept among them. Among the dead in their graves he lay down and slept. And what awful quiet came on him then?

He stands there, his suit and shirt wrinkled and dusty, his good hat battered into early old age, the knot of his tie slipped down to the third button of his shirt and jerked tight, his head full of pain and regret and difficult thoughts. He looks at his long shadow pointing down the gravel track ahead of him, and he knows for certain that he will die. He foreknows the stillness that, whichever way he walks, he is coming to. A tremor shakes him from head to foot.

Even as he starts toward the gate he is strongly tempted to go the other way, to go home across the fences and through the fields. But he rejects that. The day summons him into the clear and that is where he is going to go.

"No," he says to himself, "I may have to brazen, but I ain't going to sneak."

He sees his shadow move its long leg, sees its foot separate from his foot, light flowing between. There will be a time when he will come here and not leave, but this is not the time.

Part Five

17

Straightening Up

Home again, Burley hangs his desecrated coat and hat on the yard fence and goes straight to the barn. He attends to the few chores that need doing there, and then, having put it off as long as he can, he goes outside to the pump. He cups his hand under the spout and pumps and drinks. And having filled himself, his thirst far exceeding his capacity, he douses his face and pumps water over his head. He keeps pumping, breathing in great spluttering gasps. Pumping on his head, the water flowing through his hair, around his ears, down the sides of his face, streaming off his eyebrows and nose and lips and chin, splattering and darkening the dry boards of the well top—that seems to him the finest quenching of his life. Bent, dizzy under the spout, hanging on to the pump with one hand to keep from falling, pumping with the other, he glimpses his brother approaching around the corner of the barn.

He does not want to talk to Jarrat this morning and so he keeps pumping, hoping that Jarrat is just on his way someplace and will go on. But Jarrat does not. He stops and leans against the barn wall and watches.

"That looks like a hell of a hard way to drown."

Burley straightens up, shuddering as the cold water runs down the collar of his shirt. Blinded by vertigo, he quickly sits down on the edge of the stock trough and props himself with both hands.

"Huh?" he says. Though it does not matter, he feels caught, feels guilty and most uncertain of himself and of Jarrat. For the thousandth time, surely, he is the wayward younger brother, confronted by the righteousness of the older. Or is that how it is going to be this time? He risks a quick glance at Jarrat's face, and discovers to his surprise and relief that Jarrat is grinning at him.

"I said there ought to be some easier way to drown."

"There ought," Burley says, and he laughs. He looks directly at Jarrat now. "Did you know the war's over?"

"I heard the commotion start up out there at town and figured that was what it was. And I came over here then and heard the news on your radio. I didn't reckon you would mind."

"I didn't."

"I listened a right smart while, sort of waiting for you to come back."

Burley feels a pang of disappointment—of loss. That was the first time in years, maybe since the death of their mother, that Jarrat had come to the house just to visit—and him not there. There could have been nothing finer, nothing be would have liked any more, he realizes with grief, than to sit in the old living room with Jarrat late into the night, listening to that good news come in on the radio.

"Well, I stayed pretty late at Mat's and then me and Jayber and Big Ellis spent the night with some folks there in town. Just to keep from having to come home so late."

He can see—with relief, actually—that Jarrat does not believe a word of it. But he appears to be amused. He watches Burley with a skeptical, critical gaze that Burley knows will not neglect or misinterpret anything. But there is amusement in it too. Some change has come over him. Is it, Burley wonders, the war ending? Or *what* is it?

"It was hard to sleep, I reckon, in all that racket."

"Well," Burley says, "the folks we spent the night with, they was quiet."

He wishes Jarrat would go on home now. Or go somewhere.

"What time is Ernest's funeral?" Jarrat asks.

"Two-thirty, I think. Are you going?"

"I thought I'd go a little beforehand, and speak to Mat and them."

"Mat'll appreciate that."

"Well, I'll be seeing you," Jarrat says. He shoves himself away from the wall with a little thrust of his shoulder and starts home.

"Be seeing you," Burley says. And then he says, "Come again! We'll listen to the radio!"

As soon as Jarrat is out of sight Burley eases himself to his feet and, after a careful start, walks to the house.

He builds a fire in the kitchen, puts on the coffee pot and a kettle of water, and sits down at the table to wait. His encounter with Jarrat has left him with a trying consciousness of his misery. To save trouble he just admits that he is totally corrupt and unsalvageable, and yields to the misery of that too. "Oh, me!" he says.

The smell of the coffee rouses him. He sits watching the spout steam until it has boiled long enough, and pours himself a cup.

It seems to him that from the minute he sits back down at the table and leans over the fragrant steam of that cup, he begins—surely, this time—to mend. He drinks it hot, sitting by the raised window, watching the wind in the grass down the hillside. The grass is green in the sun, and the wind combs it, laying it down, rippling it like water flowing over it.

"Eat! Put something in your stomach!"

Those are his mother's words, and they return to him in her voice, the weary, determined inflections of her old Sunday-morning efforts to sober him up and set him straight, revealing the strain between her persistent faith that this would be the last time and her suspicion that it would not. They come back familiarly and painfully, his inheritance from her.

To silence them he gets up and obeys. He poaches two eggs, and toasts some light bread, and pours another cup of coffee. That puts some strength into him. That he will make it through until bedtime begins to seem likely. He begins to welcome the duty of going to Mat's and being there to do what he can. What there will be for him to do he does not know. Maybe nothing. For a few minutes he wishes, like a boy, that there might be some task of great difficulty that Mat will ask him to do—something to redeem all the failures, past and to come, of his best intentions.

He washes his dishes and makes things neat. And then, stripping off his clothes, he bathes and shaves and combs his hair. Everything he does now makes him feel better. This is the starting place. From here a lot can be imagined and hoped for.

Standing naked in the breeze from the window, combed and shaved and thoroughly scrubbed, feeling better already than he expected to feel before tomorrow, he applies himself to the question of what to do about his suit. He picks up first the pants and then the coat, turns them this way and then that, and hangs them back on the chair post. He shakes his head. "Looks like they been slept in on the ground, boy."

His hat turns out to be more or less salvageable. He whacks the dust out of it, and scrubs it lightly with a damp rag, and molds it into shape, and puts it on. His shoes, after being rubbed a little with a rag, look very well too.

Carrying a shoe in each hand he goes through the house and up the stairs to his bedroom. Opening a bureau drawer, he finds a pair of socks quickly enough, and puts them on. Digging into another drawer, he finds at the very bottom an extra white shirt, put away hard to tell how long before his mother died. It has begun to turn a little yellow, but he shakes it out and holds it up. It will do, and he puts it on. He gets out his newest work pants and puts them on. He will have to go without a coat, but surely, he thinks, the weather is hot enough to justify that. He puts on his shoes. Rummaging in the closet, he finds his other necktie and stretches it out on the bed and studies it critically. It is a broad, bright red silky one with a large yellow flower on it. Too pretty for a funeral, he thinks, but he has no choice. Standing close and then far back, he examines himself in the mirror, and is reasonably satisfied. He is not what you would call finely dressed, but he has contrived an appearance of discomfort that ought at least to vouch for his proper sense of the occasion.

Ready at last, he leaves the house with the sense of having perfected a narrow escape. He is still pretty shaky, and his head still hurts; he can surely remember mornings when he left home in better health. But he has begun to have a decent feeling in his mind.

At the same time he keeps mindful of where he is going: to Mat's house, to Ernest's grave, sorrow and darkness. He is going, faithfully and uselessly, to be a comforter where there can be no comfort, and a friend where friendship is powerless—a duty a man cannot do gladly for another except for the love of him. And he goes bearing the thought of the death of Tom, which now begins its long outlasting of its cause. The words of Jayber's elegy still stand in his mind, seeming to open and contain the depth of his grief.

But he goes into the light too. The sun is getting high and hot. He has already sweated through his shirt, and unconsciously has unbuttoned and turned back the cuffs. Several times he has caught his hand ready to loosen his collar and necktie, but so far he has resisted that. From the graveled track of the lane high on the ridge, he can sometimes see the river valley lying below him, and across the upland the town's gables and rooftops among the trees. All the country is astir with the wind, and he can feel it flowing steadily against him as he walks. Overhead big white clouds fly rapidly from the southwest; their hundred-acre shadows slide invincibly over the ups and downs of the land. Along the river the water maples, leaves blown underside-up, are silver and brilliant.

It seems to him that time has now begun to shorten toward Nathan's return. Though still from far off, he feels approaching him a good day, the best of all. And then, in that deep wheel track on the ridge, he stops and deliberately savors the air. It is the first morning of another time.

A Homecoming

As soon as he has thanked the driver and the car door has slammed behind him, Gideon resumes the stride in which he has crossed the intervals between rides. He turns into one of the pounded wheel tracks of the creek road, and is soon out of sight of the blacktop.

When he left in the early spring, the valley was still leafless and open to the eye as in winter. Now the road burrows through the foliage. And though the morning shade is still deep, the air is already close and hot, and he begins to sweat. The foliage along the roadsides bespeaks the length of his absence. And he walks faster, filled with the anxiety of one who is late.

He comes out into the open bottom. There is a field of corn now to the left of the road. As he reaches the end of that he can see the house. A thread of smoke rises straight up from the kitchen chimney. Though the fields of the bottom are in full sun, the shadow of the hill still lies over the house. Ida comes around the house from somewhere in the back, carrying a bucket. Seeing him, she stops and looks while he walks perhaps fifteen steps, before she sets the bucket down, and runs down the slope of the yard and down the lane and along the path across the bottom. When he comes to the footbridge she is standing at the other end, waiting for him, smiling at him as he crosses the springing planks.

"Gideon, I seen you coming. I looked, and there you were coming up the road."

He comes to the end of the bridge and steps down.

Ida looks away, and back at him. She asks: "You been gone a long way?"

"Yeah. I have, Ida."

"I imagine you're hungry, ain't you?"

"I ain't eat yet this morning."

"Well, come on to the house."

He puts his face down into his hands. She comes to him then, reaching out to him.

"Well. Don't, Gideon. Come on to the house."

For some time after he is quiet he continues to stand there the same way, his face covered. Finally, at her urging, he allows her to take his hand and lead him toward the house, although still he does not look at her.

"Did you come riding or walking?"

"First one then the other. Sometimes folks give me rides. Sometimes I had to walk."

"Hard as you look, it's a wonder you ever got to ride at all. You look worn out, Gideon. I bet you haven't taken any care of yourself at all."

"I can't tell you, Ida. It ain't to be talked about."

"Can you remember the last time you shaved?"

They cross the bottom and climb the slope to the house and go around to the back and into the kitchen. Ida pulls a chair away from the table and places it near the stove as though Gideon might be cold.

"Sit down in that," she says.

And he does, obediently, watching her as she begins stirring around him. She makes the old room jolt and clatter as if all its uses have been roused in it at once. She shakes the ashes out of the stove, and pokes the fire, and puts in fresh wood. She scoots the teakettle over the fire, and fills another kettle and puts it on, and fills the coffee pot and puts it on. She goes out and brings in a fresh bucket of water. She sets him a place at the table. She fills a large wash pan with hot water and sets it steaming on the floor at his feet.

"Wash," she says. She puts the soap down by the wash pan, brings him a wash rag, hangs a clean towel on the back of his chair. "Get them filthy clothes off. And them old shoes." She gathers up his shoes and his shirt as he takes them off. As she stands there watching him, waiting, he hesitates. His hands seem to grow clumsy at the buckle of his belt, and then stop altogether. He looks out the window, and down at his feet, and at last, with great effort, at her.

"Ida," he says, "I ain't bothered any women while I been gone."

For the first time since they met at the bridge, she smiles at him.

"Well, ain't *you* something! I reckon you must be feeling pretty botherish by now."

"I reckon I am."

"That don't surprise me."

For many seconds they look at each other.

He takes off the rest of his clothes. She gathers them up with the rest and flings them through the door onto the back porch. She brings back clean clothes for him, and lays them on the edge of the table within his reach. She brings shoes for him. And then she busies herself at the stove.

When he has washed and put on pants and shoes, she says to him: "Shave. Get them whiskers off."

He does, and puts on the clean shirt, and combs his wet hair. He comes to the table as she is taking his breakfast from the stove. She looks at him.

"Well, well, it *is* you. Sit down. Eat."

Into the Woods

As seems bound to happen now and again, in spite of Mat's watchfulness against it, one of his young cows got with calf late. Uncertain of the breeding time, he has been watching her for a week. This morning when he went to count the cattle she was not in the bunch. He knew what that meant, but other obligations were pressing him, and after walking the length of the high backbone of the pasture he gave up the hunt until later.

It is not until the afternoon that he can come back. He leaves his truck at the pasture gate, and this time, instead of walking the high ground as he did in the morning, he turns along the fence and follows it down toward the woods. It is a brilliant day, the air warm and still. In spite of his worry about her, the job of searching for the cow is suited to his mood and to the weather, and he is happy in having it to do.

The leaves on the branches, and falling, and on the ground, are so golden that going in under the trees is to enter not the shade but a doubled sunlight. Though there is no wind, the leaves fall steadily, flashing in the air, with a constant pattering against trunks and branches and the ground.

Mat considers his course, and goes down to where the bluff steepens, and turns again, following the contour of the slope. He might, he knows, be wrong by ten feet or a hundred. If he is, he will have to come back at a different level—and go again at yet another, if he is wrong again. He feels too stiff in the knees to zigzag up and down the bluff, and so there is nothing to do but choose a line and follow it. He takes his time, picking his way with care, keeping close watch on the woods above and below.

And it happens that within half an hour he comes upon the cow grazing among the thicket growth over a little patch of ground that not too many years ago was cleared and cropped. He quickly sees that she *has* calved, and he approaches cautiously, not wanting to scare her off for fear he will not then be able to find the calf. But he does not go many feet before he is seen, and he stops. He can tell by the set of her head that she is alarmed, preparing to run.

"Sook," he says quietly. "Sook, cow."

At that she does run, head and tail up, crashing into the undergrowth at the edge of the clearing and out into the woods.

"*You* crazy bitch!"

She is out there in the woods, walking away from him now, bawling. Mat goes on into the clearing and, again more quickly than he expected, finds the calf curled up in some long grass in a patch of sumac. It lies perfectly still, obeying like its mother an instinct still wild in it. For the moment it *is* wild, and Mat is aware of that wildness, and aware of himself there, about to be the first man it will see, about to cross yet another time the gap between his kind and its.

"Here you are," he says to it, to be saying something before he touches it. "Your old lying mammy said you weren't, but I knew."

He has come up beside it and leaned over it. And now he slips his hands under its belly and raises it to its feet. It stands up, pretty wobbly, but all right—a bull calf, well marked, big enough. "Well," he says.

Leaving it spraddled on its weak legs, he goes back into the woods. As soon as he is gone the cow, having circled around, comes anxiously back into the clearing, and goes straight to the calf. Mat sits down with his back against a tree, and watches, pleased with them and with himself.

After nuzzling the calf briefly as she came up to it, the cow has paid him no more attention. She stands over it, head and ears up, watching Mat. Her whole aspect has changed from when he saw her a day ago. Instead of the complacency of a domestic animal, she now has the alertness of a deer. After standing shakily for some time on its spraddled legs, the calf more or less collapses into the grass, but though her whole body is tense with awareness of it she never looks at it. She has not moved at all. And Mat himself has not moved. Into the tensely quieted space between them the yellow leaves fall.

Finally Mat gets up and turns away. But instead of starting back the way he came, now that he has done what he came to do, he goes on into the woods. He has got ahead of his plans. There is nothing else that he intended to do today. He is going on now for the pleasure of the going. Since leaving the cow and the calf, he has continued to make an effort to be quiet. He picks his way with care, walking slowly along the flatter ground above the bluff. Now and then to his left there is an opening among the treetops and he can see down out of the woods to the river and the fields in the bottoms, and those openings keep him aware of being on a height and on a verge.

The age of the woods varies with the lay of the ground. On some of the gentler slopes the trees are young, and in these places there are neat piles of rock, showing that once, where trees are now, there were crops, and the rocks were picked up out of the furrows and carried to the edges of the field and put down. Those steep fields did not last long. Mat believes or imagines he worked in these places as a boy. He knows he is bound to have worked in some of them, but it is hard now to be exact about which ones. The character they took from human use is gone from them. The trees have wholly claimed them. The piled rocks, covered with lichens and moss, have grown natural again.

He comes to where a stream has cut its way into the hill. The ground tilts sharply as the bluffs turn in to the crease of the ravine, and here the woods is old. In the face of the bluff on the far side of the ravine there is a sort of amphitheater, its floor, relatively flat, affording a gathering place for a stand of great beeches, whose silver trunks branch into the gold masses of their leaves. Their brilliance, as Mat comes around the hill's shoulder, stops him for a moment before he crosses over and goes in under them.

He sits at the foot of one of the big trees at the edge of the grove, leaning back against the trunk. He faces the way the stream falls, the stream passing below him and to his left, the grove of beeches extending back into its enclosure to his right. In front of him there is an opening through which he can see a part of a bend in the river—within the bend of the water the bend of the trees along the bank, within the bend of the trees straight rows of corn shocks in a field. Around him the woods is free of undergrowth, and the tree trunks rise cleanly up into the foliage. There is a little water running in the stream, so that here, in addition to the sound of the leaves falling, there is the steady trickling and splashing that the water makes coming down over the rocks. Mat sits with his back against the tree, his hat on the ground beside him, sorting out and examining one by one all the aspects and attractions of the place. It is one of those places that, many times in his life, he has thought would be a good place to rest, and now to be resting there makes him happy.

Below, across the stream, there is a place where the slope gentles. And as he looks down there, Mat begins to see, scattered among the big trees, the familiar cairns of rocks. They mean that that place too was once cleared and broken and planted in crops. The trees on it are much older than he is. The work that was done there was done long before his time, and no doubt before his father's—the axe-work and the burning, and the jumper plows breaking for the first time the black leaf-mold. And before that the big trees standing without age or history, whose silence and whose shaking in the wind Mat imagines now, shivering as he does.

And afterwards, now, the trees rise on the slope again. And the dead who made that clearing are as forgotten as the forest they destroyed. As he sits looking at the heaped rocks, guessing the little he is able to guess about them, there comes to Mat the sense of a lost and dead past, a past perfect, without even the force of a memory. And though he resisted the thought, fearing it would sadden him, it does not sadden him. There in the presence of the woods, in the sounds of the water and the leaves falling, he does not feel the loss of what is past.

He feels the great restfulness of that place, its casual perfect order. It is the restfulness of a place where the merest or the most improbable accident is made a necessity and a part of a design, where death can only give into life. And Mat feels the difference between that restful order and his own constant struggle to maintain and regulate his clearings. Although the meanings of those clearings and his devotion to them remain firm in his mind, he knows without sorrow that they will end, the order he has made and kept in them will be overthrown, the effortless order of wilderness will return.

The leaves brightly falling around him, Mat comes into the presence of the place. It lies clearly and simply before him, radiant as though a light in the ground has become visible. He has come into a wakefulness as quiet as a sleep.